ARCANA

PAUL KANE

PRAISE FOR THE AUTHOR

"Paul Kane's lean, stripped-back prose is a tool that's very much fit for purpose. He knows how to make you want to avoid the shadows and the cracks in the pavement."

—Mike Carey, Bestselling author of the Felix Castor series of novels and *The Girl with All the Gifts*, *Fellside* and *The Boy on the Bridge* as M.R. Carey

"Kane finds the everyday horrors buried within us, rips them out and serves them up in these deliciously dark tales."

—Kelley Armstrong, Bestselling author of *Bitten*, *Haunted*, *Broken*, *Waking the Witch*, *Spell Bound* and *Thirteen*

"I'm impressed by the range of Paul Kane's imagination. It seems there is no risk, no high-stakes gamble, he fears to take … Kane's foot never gets even close to the brake pedal."

—Peter Straub, Bestselling author of *Ghost Story*, *Mr. X*, *Lost Boy Lost Girl*, and *In the Night Room*

"Paul Kane is a name to watch. His work is disturbing and very creepy."

—Tim Lebbon, New York Times bestselling author of *The Cabin in the Woods*, *The Silence* and *Relics*

"His stories not only, at his best, put him neck and neck with Ramsey Campbell and Clive Barker, but also in the company of greats like Machen and MR James. You don't rest easily after reading a Paul Kane story, but strangely your eyes have been somewhat opened."

—Stephen Volk—BAFTA winning screenwriter of *Gothic*, *Ghostwatch*, *Afterlife*, *The Awakening* and *Midwinter of the Spirit*; author of *Whitstable*, *Leytonstone* and *The Parts We Play*

"He stands out as one of the better writers I've read."
—*Eternal Night*

"Wonderfully dark and satisfying."

—*Dark Side Magazine*

"Kane is best when taking risks with his bizarre flights of imagination."

—*SFX Magazine*

"Kane is a highly regarded author whose influence can be felt across the genre, with a large and notable body of work behind him."

—*Starburst Magazine*

WordFire Press
wordfirepress.com

Ebook ISBN: 978-1-61475-945-4
Trade Paper ISBN: 978-1-61475-944-7
Hardcover ISBN: 978-1-61475-908-5

Cover design by Janet McDonald
Cover artwork images by Paul Kane, and Adobe Stock
Kevin J. Anderson, Art Director

Kevin J. Anderson & Rebecca Moesta, Publishers

Published by
WordFire Press, an imprint of
WordFire, LLC
PO Box 1840
Monument, CO 80132

WordFire Press eBook Edition 2019
WordFire Press Trade Paperback Edition 2019
WordFire Press Hardcover Edition 2019
Printed in the USA

DEDICATION

For my family, who put the real magic in my life.

PROLOGUE

"Thou shalt not suffer a witch to live."
Exodus 22:18.

They were all going to die.

But it was for the cause, and they were not only glad to do it—they felt *compelled* to do it. Their sacrifice would not be in vain, of that he was sure. The man looked up and back towards the rear of the packed bus, past the heads of the other passengers to where his companions were sitting. One, dark-haired with even darker eyes, glanced back, but didn't make it too obvious. The other, bearded and slightly more gaunt, didn't take his eyes off the view passing by: that of the road and the street and the people going about their everyday lives. He didn't know his allies' names, didn't need to: it was easier if you didn't. If you formed any attachments or friendships, they were bound to be short-lived.

He faced forward, gripping his haversack tightly. If the other passengers only knew what was inside. These people who were oblivious to what was going on right under their noses; the war that was being waged. Oh, they knew what they saw on TV and in newspapers, or at least what they were *allowed* to watch and read. But most of them had no clue about the scale of it. Nor the stakes that were being played for.

Only those involved knew that.

The bus hit a bump in the road and he looked nervously to the bag. A couple sitting diagonally opposite—mid-late twenties, holding hands—had spotted him. More importantly, they'd noted his reaction. He threw them a smile that came out all wrong. They didn't smile back. *Do they suspect?* he wondered. They couldn't know for certain what was in the bag, but they could certainly mess this whole operation up. One call, one word to someone in a position of authority, and it would all be over. He relaxed when they started kissing, knew only each other, forgetting about him. Good: all was not lost.

Like his comrade, he too looked out of the window now, as their target drew into sight. He saw the three turquoise domes, the expanse of orange-red walls: the architectural equivalent of a building made from children's toy bricks. No one would miss it. In the distance he could see that the car park was full, the different coloured vehicles adding to the illusion that this was just a child's scale model. Would that help to ease his conscience, to think of this as a game? That if you knocked all these wooden people down—knocked this building down—a large pair of hands could simply pick them up and put everything back together again as if nothing had happened?

But this was no game: that had been drilled into him time and time again. This was life and death, and once these people were knocked down there was no way on earth they were getting back up.

The bus finally pulled into the terminal with a hiss, shaking him from his thoughts. The driver turned and said to the passengers, "We're here folks, *All Seasons*."

The passengers got up out of their blue leather seats and made their way along the aisle towards the front. He let one or two go before standing, picking up his bag, and carrying it out with him. He blended into the crowd and knew that behind him, the other two men were doing the same.

The people leaving the bus met up with more of their kind, and the crowd suddenly swelled, surging forward like a force of nature, taking him along with it. That was all to the good. He was just a single face here in a sea of other faces: black, white, olive-skinned, it didn't make any difference. He risked a quick look over his shoulder but couldn't see his companions. They would be splitting up anyway once they made it to the main entrance.

The crowd took him over a bridge with clear glass sides. The inane chattering almost drove him mad: the weather; what the latest fashions were; which celebrity was sleeping with a toyboy or an older woman. It did little to feed what guilt he might be feeling. If anything it made him happy that he was going to rid the world of at least some of these morons. It would be a better place.

But that wasn't the reason he was here, was it. He should focus, had to get this right or they'd lose their one chance to make a statement.

They were approaching the main gate. Above it was a big sign that read: "Welcome to *All Seasons*. We hope you enjoy your visit." *Not today they won't*, he thought. *Nobody will enjoy their visit today* … It was such an insipid greeting anyway; if a person came here to indulge in whatever pleasures awaited them inside then they deserved everything they got.

He was conscious of the closed-circuit television cameras at the gate, swivelling on their armatures like cyclopean sentinels. He tried to keep his head down as he made his way inside; eager to at least appear part of the group.

There were security men stationed just inside the doors, their white and black uniforms immaculate. All must have passed a height test, because he couldn't see any that were under six foot five. Batons hung by their sides, radios on belts. From beneath peaked caps they surveyed the scene in front of them, eyes slowly gliding from left to right.

He slipped past, doing his best to hide the bag on his back. If any of them saw him, they'd almost certainly ask about it, so he tried to blend in. There was less chance of being caught when he was actually inside the inner sanctum, although he should keep an eye out for anyone who could be an undercover guard.

There were two levels to this place, this one and another below. As he walked in and looked around, the whole building opened up to him. What struck him first was the brightness. Though the turquoise bubbles above let in light from outside, there were row upon row of artificial strip-lights, too. There wasn't a corner the light didn't reach.

Next he saw the shop-fronts advertising their wares: music and DVD/Blu-ray stores with the latest albums and films proudly displayed in their windows; clothes shops with expensive designer suits and dresses modelled by anorexic mannequins with no faces; book stores promoting the most recent autobiography by some footballer or actress that had so obviously been ghost-written; furniture shops with leather sofas in the window and "distressed look" ornaments on coffee tables. The one thing you would not find here in this overblown advert for the consumer society was homeopathic or herbal shops selling pills or homemade soaps guaranteed to make your skin smoother and fresher. No, the chemists had a clear run in this shopping centre: manufactured drugs the only kind you'd find on sale today.

Dotted here and there were plants meant to give the illusion of a natural environment, but he couldn't think of anywhere more false. He would indeed be doing the world a massive favour by obliterating it and those who flocked here.

Innocent men, women and children …

He shook his head. *None* of them were innocent. And he'd do only what had to be done. The plan was a good one and they would succeed. When the time was right they would strike their blow.

Turning left he made for the west wing of the upper floor, passing the escalators taking people up and down. He almost collided with one of the plants, the leaves making his nose itch as he wafted them away, but he regained his composure quickly. He had to get into position.

He looked at his watch, then at the big round clock which hung above the shoppers as if to signal how much time they had left to live. At precisely one o'clock, he and his friends would detonate the devices they had in their rucksacks, crippling this mall—the biggest in the country—and bringing traffic along the motorway that ran alongside it to a standstill. There was no way anyone would be able to ignore what they'd done here today. He followed the ticking of that clock, the massive second hand making its arc around the face. 12:54, it told him. Right now, his comrades would be taking up their posts, at just the right places: one under a supporting pillar that would bring down a section of the second floor; the other in the packed restaurant section of *All Seasons* where punters were stuffing their faces with burgers, fries, pizza and hot dogs, washing them all down with fizzy drinks that were rotting their insides. He, on the other hand, would take out the wall facing the motorway itself, ensuring maximum damage and impact. Not long to wait now, not long.

He had the strangest feeling he was being watched.

Looking across, he saw a man in a sports jacket on the other side of the divide, pressing his finger to his ear and talking. The man then glanced up at him and nodded, talking again. Must be a hidden transmitter and receiver. Damn and blast, had he been spotted? A bead of sweat trickled down his forehead, running over his cheek and dripping from his chin to the white, polished floor. He licked his dry lips, aware of how much more suspicious it made him look, but not able to do a thing about this natural human reaction.

Another man joined the first, then a third. The man in the sports jacket was pointing across and nodding. He'd definitely been made. What confirmed it was when he looked down the length of the precinct and saw the uniformed guards from the door approaching.

The clock read 12:56.

Not yet ... please, not yet! He began to back up and saw the plain-clothes men stiffen. They looked ready to rush him at any moment. But would they be able to reach him in time? That was the question.

12:57.

The jacketed men began running towards him, the other two following closely behind the first. At the same time, the uniformed men sprang forwards, shoving aside shoppers.

12:58.

He couldn't let them stop him. Not now, not when he was so close. He made a break for it, darting towards the escalators. It would throw off the plan to move away from that west wall, but he was left with little choice—if he didn't shift he'd be trapped. At least this way he'd have the space to set off his device, maybe on the escalators themselves.

"Stop!" shouted one of the plain clothes security guards. Needless to say, he didn't listen.

12:59.

Scrambling past the crowds that had hidden him and secured his entry into the mall, he jumped onto the escalator, looking up at the clock. He had to get ready, the rest of his team would be taking action any second now.

"We have the other two," his pursuer shouted. "We've been on to you since you came in. You might as well give up."

No, it wasn't possible! How could they? He waited for the seconds hand to tick round and hit the twelve.

1:00—nothing happened.

He frowned. The man was telling the truth. His brothers had been captured before they'd had a chance to fulfil their destinies. They would not be a part of history now. But while he still had his bag—which he was shrugging off his back—there was time for him to act out his part. He felt a hand on his shoulder and spun round. One of the uniformed security men was behind him, baton drawn. Instinctively, he pushed the security guard backwards. The man's feet caught the edge of one of the escalator steps and he fell over the rail, plunging to the ground below.

There were more guards waiting at the bottom of the escalator. Shoppers, aware now that something was happening, were fleeing from the area like frightened wildebeest. Those people on the moving staircase on either side were giving him space. The guards below were beginning to climb the escalator. Soon they'd stop him, grab the bag and wrestle him to the ground. He couldn't let that happen.

He opened the bag and reached inside. There was a faint glow from its interior.

One of the guards climbed over a cowering shopper in an effort to reach his target. They were too late. He took out the pulsating globe, mesmerised for a moment by its blue-greenness. The bag slid out of his grasp. There were crackles of energy inside the ball, like tiny lightning strikes against clouds. He looked straight at the guards and said: "For Arcana. For freedom!"

Then he crushed the sphere with his bare hands, the resultant blast spraying over him like molten lava.

And *All Seasons* shone even more brightly for a few seconds.

Illuminated by the glow of the single gas-lamp, the gnarled hand reached out for the deck of cards.

These were stacked neatly to his left. The old man picked them up with some difficulty, but when they were actually in his hands they seemed to have a life of their own. When the man—his eyes as white as his thin, wispy hair—smiled, he showed the stumps of his yellowed teeth. He began to shuffle the deck, the painted surfaces on both sides flashing momentarily, showing a glimpse of the pictures, of the decorative pattern on the backs. But only a glimpse.

His first step was to pick out a significator. He did this now, spreading the deck on the table face up and running his fingers across each card until he found the one he wanted. He didn't look at the deck when he did this; didn't need to. It was as though his fingertips were doing the seeing for him. He picked up the card in question: it depicted a figure in a suit of armour charging across the landscape on horseback. In spite of the way the card looked, he knew the figure's mission wasn't warlike. In one hand the young man carried a piece of wood with a handful of leaves still attached. It became clear what the stick was when he "looked" down at the name of the card: The Knight of Wands.

Gathering the rest of the deck, he placed the card he'd picked face up in the middle of the table. The young man in the picture stared at him, and if he'd been able to the old man would have stared back. But his eyes were long past seeing, at least in the conventional sense of the word.

He shuffled and cut the pack three times, keeping the cards face down. The old man remained silent, as if pondering some great question. Then he overturned the first card and laid it on top of the

Knight, covering it completely. A third card was produced, which he placed lengthways over these. He then lay cards to the north, south, east and west of the original trio, before placing four cards like a tower alongside, from top to bottom, in what was commonly known as a Celtic spread.

Returning to the first cards chosen, he studied them closely. The one he'd covered the significator with, he knew, represented the general atmosphere around the person he was focussing on. It showed a hand emerging from a cloud and cupping a pentagram, which was itself encircled. The old man nodded sagely. *The Ace of Pentacles. A time for the realisation of goals.*

The second card signified the obstacle to these: a picture this time of a small child on horseback at the bottom, with the smiling face of the sun at the top. *A time of change, of new beginnings.*

Next he went to the northern card in the spread, to discover that which had not yet happened but surely would. He found a picture of a young woman, blinded (not like himself, but instead with a blindfold) standing bound at the shore's edge with a row of swords behind her. Eight swords to be precise. It was upside down. *A time of disquiet, treachery, difficulty … even hopelessness*, the old man silently mused.

At the south he found the root of this problem: The King of Swords himself. Again, the card was upside down, the King sitting on his throne holding his sword downwards instead of aloft. Its nature was cruelty, barbarity and evil intent.

The eastern card now, and that was meant to illustrate what was happening right that minute. This one showed a sculptor engraving pentacles on stone circles with a chisel. Working away intently, reflecting the fact that whoever this person was, he was focussing on laying the foundations of future success. Or thought he was.

To the west, the old man "saw" a card he knew all too well. It showed a man with a figure of eight symbol on its side, hovering above his head. He was holding up a candle with the other symbols of the deck in front of him on the table: the pentagram, the cup, the sword and wand … all within his grasp. This was the future, the old man realised. And the name of the card: The Magician.

It made him pause, that one—the possibilities of it not wasted on the old man. The ramifications so great they practically made him shudder. So much power, but how would it be wielded? For good, or for evil?

He moved on to the four cards in the tower on his right. The bottom one again related to the person in question's current state. The picture was of a hand emerging from a cloud again, this time holding the same kind of stick the Knight had, complete with leaves. The Ace of Wands meant there was a focus on achieving potential, yet still a chance to be open to new possibilities. The blind man nodded again; that was a positive sign.

Above this was The Devil: a horned creature with wings and hairy legs, holding court over chained demons; one in the form of a man, the other a woman. This card normally related to the influences at work on the querent—signifying they were involved in a negative situation, and their ability to remove themselves was being prevented by clouded judgement. Whether they would be able to in the future was unclear at this time. But the picture was also symbolic in another way. These were the three characters who would be at the heart of this story. The key to it all revolving around a figure who might well lay claim to the title of Satan himself.

On to the next one: hopes and fears. Again he paused, knowing this card intimately as well. It brought back memories of someone's face, someone he'd lost so long ago. The card depicted two figures, male and female: both naked, to show their innocence and youth. A comparison could be made with Adam and Eve, and indeed it had been in the past when considering The Lovers. A focus on matters of the heart, to help in times of great difficulty. Attraction, beauty, romance … it meant all of these things, yes. But, as the saying went, the course of true love never did run smooth. Nor would it this time. The old man also sensed this would be tied in to a choice of some kind.

The final card was the one that struck terror into the hearts of the uninitiated, a skeletal figure on horseback. One of the apocalyptic visions, Death rode across a landscape of ragged rock. Falling beneath Death's horse, the old man saw a king, a maiden and a child. Nearby, a man of the church was praying. In the far distance, a beacon of hope: the sun of immortality shining between two towers. The seer knew the Death card did not necessarily mean what some thought. Chiefly, it denoted endings and beginnings, a stage in one's life drawing to a close, making way for another.

It was then that his meditations were interrupted by the sound of footsteps close by. A teenage boy bringing news, skidding to a stop at the doorway, completely out of breath.

The old man smiled and waved him in. "There is word, Gavin?" he asked.

"There is, Master. It's all over the news, the stations are running reports. They didn't manage to destroy the building, two were captured before they could act. But one—"

"One evaded them long enough to discharge his mission. Yes, I know."

"How did—" Gavin began, then remembered who he was talking to.

The old man steepled his fingers and pressed them to his lips. "There were many injured, many killed."

Gavin nodded. He knew that although the old man's milky eyes no longer functioned, they still saw everything. Saw him, even though he was standing some way behind.

The old man picked up the last card. Perhaps there was more to its meaning this time than simply the symbolic. There had been a great many deaths, with yet more to come.

"Tell the others," said the old man.

"Master?"

The seer turned to face him, and that cold vision made Gavin shiver. "Tell them it is time."

Gavin still looked puzzled so the old man added theatrically: "Tell them it has begun." Then, as Gavin watched, he covered the card with his other hand, and it promptly vanished.

As surely as if it had never been there at all.

CHAPTER ONE

First days were always difficult.

He'd woken that morning at five, after no more than three hours' sleep. It had taken a few cups of coffee to stop him from falling headfirst into his breakfast, and even now, as he stood with one foot up on the bench—tying his shiny boot—he felt an overwhelming urge to let out the biggest yawn ever known to man. He shook his head, finished doing up his laces, and rubbed his face. Still it persisted, and he couldn't help letting out a tiny one when he thought no one else was looking.

"Are we keeping you up, McGuire?" asked a voice beside him.

His head snapped sharply around and he took in a uniformed man of around fifty, with the kind of paunch normally only seen on women who are eight months pregnant. With triplets. Superintendent Wallis had done his best with his hair, combing over what few strands Mother Nature had left him, but essentially he was bald—the attempted subterfuge only making matters worse.

"Ah … no, sir. Never, sir," replied the younger, fair-haired man. He kept his face perfectly straight, his posture too. Though this wasn't the army, it had a similar feel to it. He'd heard from others that Wallis ran a tight ship and discipline was the order of the day; he didn't want to give the man any excuse to start on him from day one.

"Good, good," said Wallis, examining him with one eye closed. McGuire couldn't help noticing that the other officers in that changing room—who had barely said a word to him since he'd walked in—had now disappeared. All of a sudden there was just him and Wallis, face to face. "Well, finish dressing, man. Don't let me stop you."

McGuire nodded and continued putting on the rest of his uniform: white shirt and dark tie, blue padded vest with radio clipped to the shoulder, belt—complete with cuffs and utility pockets—and last, but not least, his cap. Wallis watched with a level of scrutiny that made McGuire feel uncomfortable. It was almost as though he was checking to make sure he did it correctly. McGuire wasn't at all sure what to make of his new commanding officer. He struck him as efficient, had done since that first encounter in his superior's office: all the paperwork neatly arranged on his desk, filing cabinets on either side behind him (if McGuire could have looked inside, no doubt he would have found records and files completely in order, dated to the day, if not the hour and minute). There was a crease along the front of the man's dark trousers, so sharp you could have sliced your hand open on it, plus his boots put even McGuire's to shame … and he'd been polishing them for hours the previous day.

But there was something about that veneer, something beneath the pristine and perfect façade that didn't sit right with McGuire. He had a sense for these things; a sense about people. It was one of the reasons he'd made such a good officer back home, and how he'd landed this job in the first place. Special transfers to these kinds of divisions didn't come along very often, and he knew there were those who resented him for getting it at his age, especially when he was up against such stiff competition. It meant more money, better hours and an opportunity to do work that really made a difference. All right, so he'd already been doing that when he arrested thieves and pimps, when he was on riot patrol or helping out the Criminal Intent Unit on certain cases—like the time they'd swooped on the drug den back in Camden. But this promised to be something else entirely.

He pushed aside the niggling thoughts about Wallis. *Sometimes what you see is exactly what you get*, he told himself. *The guy's just a stickler.* And McGuire wasn't about to balls up his prospects by getting on the wrong side of the guy.

When he'd reported for duty that morning, he'd been told by the desk sergeant to go get himself a locker, and that someone would give him his orders in due course. McGuire hadn't expected this "someone" to be Wallis himself, the very person who'd interviewed him. Yet here he was, telling McGuire to come with him.

He followed Wallis out, and though he couldn't help it McGuire's eyes were drawn to that slight limp. He'd noticed it before, of course, but then there wasn't much room to walk around in that office. Now it was much more prominent. Out in the corridor there were three uniformed officers chatting. "Gibson," called the Superintendent. One of the men turned and the others immediately dispersed. Gibson, who looked to be somewhere between McGuire and Wallis in age, had a plain face, the only distinguishing feature being a dimple in his chin.

"Sir?" he said on approach.

"Gibson, I'm teaming you up with our newest recruit—Officer McGuire. He's joining us from London."

"London, eh?" said Gibson, his manner friendly enough. "So you thought you'd see what it was like on the frontline for a change rather than the sticks of old Londinium? What's your background, McGuire?"

Before he could say anything, Wallis told Gibson, "Almost ten years on the streets; firearms trained. Worked in five different divisions. Impressive list of arrests, haven't you, McGuire?"

He felt distinctly embarrassed by this run-down of his career so far, but nodded nonetheless.

"Fair enough, so long as you're not *totally* green," Gibson offered with a smirk.

"Well," said Wallis, shaking McGuire's hand, "I'll leave you to show him the ropes then, Gibson."

It was the older officer's turn to nod. "He'll be in safe hands with me."

Wallis pointed a finger. "And don't go getting him into any bad habits."

Gibson touched his chest. "Me? As if I would." The exchange was a playful one and McGuire got the impression that these two men had known each other a long time. Wallis gave a grunt to indicate the introduction was over, then left the two of them alone, limping up the corridor and back towards his office.

"He seems …" McGuire didn't finish the sentence.

"Wallis can be a complete bastard when he wants to be," Gibson said. "But he's good at his job. See that limp?"

McGuire gave a vague nod.

"He got that taking down three sparkies. The fuckers led him down a blind alley, into a trap. Old Wally put up one hell of a fight, but ended up in hospital for almost a year. He's been deskbound ever since."

"Jesus," whispered McGuire.

Gibson started walking and the younger officer set off alongside him, trying to keep up. "I 'spect you think you've seen everything on the streets?"

McGuire shook his head. "Not everything. But I've seen enough."

"Muggers, rapists, killers."

McGuire shrugged.

"You ain't seen anything, my young friend. So what's your name, then? I can't keep calling you Officer McGuire."

"Callum. It's Callum McGuire."

"All right, Callum. I'm Tully. Now come on, your training begins right now."

After buzzing themselves out, Gibson took McGuire across to their squad car: a white Sierra with yellow and blue chequered sides and the symbol of their profession on the door. The older officer went round to the driver's side, and McGuire let him. He was still a little unfamiliar with these roads and, after all, Gibson was meant to be showing him the ropes. But he got the feeling that even after a few years of this job, if he was still partnered with Gibson by then (which he sincerely doubted, partners come and always go), that man would still insist on being behind the wheel.

They set off through the gates of the station and turned left up the street, into traffic on the busy main road.

"So, you see the news last night?"

Callum shook his head. He'd been too busy getting ready for today. Besides which, he didn't have a TV in his place yet.

"You're joking?"

"No … why?"

Gibson spluttered, apparently unable to grasp this. "'Why?' he says. They've been at it again, that's why."

Callum knew he was probably going to look incredibly thick, but he didn't know what Gibson was talking about.

"Those bloody Arcana lunatics. Blew up part of a shopping precinct this time, didn't they. *All Seasons*, off the main motorway. Knew exactly where to strike, snarled the traffic up for hours."

"God," whispered Callum.

"Fucking fanatics, they're not bothered about who they hurt. Would have been a lot more killed if the security guards hadn't caught two of them."

"I had no idea."

"You're going to have to keep track of things a bit more if you want to work around here," Gibson warned him.

There was quiet between them for a short while, then Callum asked, "How long have you been working for this division?"

"Started off on the beat, like you. Then when this came up … Let's just say I fancied a change. I've been here about fifteen years."

"That's a long time," said Callum, stating the obvious.

"Tell me about it."

"So …" Callum began, "you've seen a lot of action, then?"

Gibson didn't answer him immediately, but then suddenly blurted out, "My fair share."

They drove for about an hour, Gibson giving his rookie partner a chance to see some of the sights. But one city was pretty much like any other, even a metropolis as big as this. They travelled down side streets, under bridges, down dual carriageways. Finally, Callum asked, "What's on the agenda for today?"

"Itching to get started, are we? Begin racking up the numbers again?"

"Kind of," admitted Callum with a slight smile.

"Okay, hotshot. Well, we're on our way to visit somebody our snoop squad's had their eye on for a few weeks. They think we don't know about them ..." Gibson winked. "But not much gets past us."

Gibson steered the car into what looked like the centre of a business area, all high-rises made from glass and steel. It looked like an affluent part of town, not the kind of place Callum would expect them to be making a call.

The squad car pulled up on double yellow lines outside one of the bigger structures and Gibson climbed out. Callum followed him round as he opened up the trunk. In there were a variety of weapons, from gasses and stun grenades to automatic pistols and shotguns. "Now we're just going to be asking a few questions, but you never know." Gibson looked like he was about to reach for one of the pistols, then picked up a canister of clear liquid instead. He slotted it into a plastic receptacle with a nozzle on one end, then tested it by squirting some of the liquid onto the road. "Perfect."

This wasn't the kind of place Callum imagined you'd need to incapacitate anyone, but took the spray when he was offered it. Gibson shut the trunk and made his way to the glass doors of the building.

Callum's mouth hung open when they walked into the reception. It was huge, with a marble floor and pillars that led up towards a gigantic circular desk, where four people in green jackets were answering phones. Gibson nodded over at a huge board telling them which businesses occupied which floors. "That's who we want: Temple, of Temple, Hill and Lynch. On the twentieth."

"Solicitors?" queried Callum, who still couldn't quite grasp what they were doing here. But Gibson was already at the reception desk, talking to a woman with curly brown hair.

She picked up a phone at his request, and by the time Callum joined them was saying, "I'm sorry, officer, Mr. Temple's in meetings with clients all day. If you'd like to make an appointment ..."

Gibson nodded, as though he understood. "No, that won't be necessary. Thanks."

He took Callum by the arm and dragged him from the reception desk. Gibson walked away with the younger officer as though they were heading back to the main doors, then veered off towards the lift at the side. He pressed the button for attention.

"What are you doing? She said Temple wasn't available to talk to us."

"I know," said Gibson. "Wonder why."

Callum was desperate to ask a whole string of questions, but he knew that the best way to learn was to observe. So he'd go along with Gibson, even though he didn't understand what this was all about, and he'd watch.

The lift doors opened. A group of men in suits and women in charcoal two-pieces stepped out. When they were clear, Gibson stepped in.

"Come on, then," he said when Callum hesitated. "What're you waiting for?"

Looking around him, Callum walked cautiously inside as Gibson pressed the button marked "20."

The lift took its time getting to the twentieth floor, stopping to pick up a variety of people on the way—some going up, some waiting to go down.

"You okay?" asked Gibson, when he saw him fidgeting.

"I don't like these things," Callum told him by way of an explanation.

"We could have taken the stairs." Gibson grinned at his own joke.

"It's fine," Callum lied. "Just don't like to be closed in, that's all."

The lift finally arrived with a jolt, and Callum stepped gratefully out. Gibson gave a small laugh and shook his head. "Come on." He led the way through yet another reception area, this one only moderately smaller, with mock wooden walls.

Callum looked around at the paintings that hung there. He didn't know much about art, but bet they were worth a tidy sum. One showed a ship in a storm being battered about on the waves. Another had a knight in armour on a white charger fighting a red dragon that was breathing fire.

"Cute," said Gibson when he saw it.

"So, what exactly *are* we doing here?" Callum asked as they approached another receptionist.

"All in good time," was the only answer he'd give. Gibson stepped up to the desk to talk to a woman who could have been a clone of the one downstairs, except for her blonde hair. "Mr. Temple, please."

The secretary looked at him, puzzled. "He's in a meeting … with a client." It was exactly what they'd been told before.

"Oh, okay," said Gibson, then made his way past into the foyer. The receptionist got up to stop him, but the policeman brushed her aside, reading the names on the doors to see which one belonged to Temple. He opened it and burst inside.

A tall man with pinched features wearing an immaculately cut suit rose from his desk, while the woman—middle-aged, wearing a black dress and hat with a veil—turned around in her leather seat. Surrounding them, on almost every wall of the room, were rows and rows of books.

"What's the meaning of this?" shouted the man, who had to be Temple.

"Sir, I tried to stop them," offered the receptionist.

"That's right, she did," Gibson confirmed. "But we kinda insisted."

"It's all right, Gloria," Temple told her. "Go back to your desk."

Gloria did as she was told, casting both Gibson and Callum a dirty look as she went.

"Now then," Temple said, "I demand an explanation for this!"

Gibson walked further into the room. "What was the lure, Mr Temple? Was it boredom? Is that how you got into it?"

Temple frowned.

"Someone with your kind of money, drugs and drink not cutting it for you anymore?"

Temple's distressed client looked up at him, seeking some sort of explanation.

"I … I don't know what you're talking about, Officer. What I do know is that I can have you pulled up on charges at the drop of a hat. Let's see, intimidation for a start, breaking and entering, abuse … Who's your superior?"

"Does the name Zola Bates mean anything to you?" Gibson demanded, eyes narrowing. That certainly wasn't his boss.

Temple appeared to think about this for a moment, then shook his head.

"Oh, come on—let's cut the bullshit, shall we? We pulled Zola in a couple of weeks ago. She gave up all of *her* clients."

"I'm afraid I still don't—"

"We've been on to you ever since. You've been consorting with the wrong kind of people, Temple. You think nobody knows about your visits to the back room of that wine bar on Avon Street. But we have the rest of your lot, mate. And I'm here to take you in."

"You have no right to—"

"Your fancy lawyer talk won't save you this time. We have all the evidence we need."

"This is absolutely preposterous," announced Temple, rounding the desk, hands balled into fists. "What's going on here, some kind of witch hunt?"

Gibson smiled. "Yes, that's right. That's exactly what this is." The smile broadened. "I'm here under Section 27 of the James I of England Act, Temple."

Then he pulled the canister from his belt and sprayed Temple with the liquid. Gibson aimed for the eyes first, and Temple howled, rubbing them with his knuckles. Then Gibson sprayed lower: into Temple's mouth, covering his suit with the liquid. The smell was strong, even across the room.

Gibson then took a box of matches from his pocket and struck one.

Temple opened his eyes. "Oh sweet Heaven no! *Please* …" His hands were clasped together.

"No good praying, I doubt whether *He'll* help you now," Gibson spat. Then he tossed the match. The little wooden stick seemed to spin over and over in slow motion. Callum watched it turn, the yellow, blue and white flame flickering as it did so. When it collided with Temple's chest there was a fraction of a second's pause. The next moment the lawyer himself was engulfed in flames. They spread all over the area Gibson had sprayed, down across his trousers, up into his face. The female client put her hands to her mouth, but that didn't stifle her scream; though it was nothing compared to Temple's cries while his flesh bubbled and seared. As Callum watched, shielding his face from the heat, the material of Temple's suit stuck to its owner. Temple staggered around a little, then fell over. The plush carpet beneath caught fire too.

Callum looked around and saw an extinguisher by the door. He grabbed it and was about to move forward, when Gibson stopped him.

He shook his head. "Not yet. He's still alive."

Temple's client was up out of the chair now, and seconds later out of the door. Callum couldn't say that he blamed her. The sight of Temple's eyeballs melting in his skull wasn't exactly appealing. When the lawyer's head dropped back and his arms—which had been reaching out even as he writhed on the floor—finally went slack, Gibson finally nodded for Callum to put out the fire. Wincing, the young officer sprayed the man, and the flames died down as suddenly as they'd sprung up.

Callum stood back from the blackened mess that had been a human being just a few minutes ago. Only the white of Temple's teeth shone out, as what was left of his lips were pulled back over over them.

"Best way for sparkies to go," said Gibson from behind him. "Old-fashioned, but effective."

Callum turned to face his partner, who was still smiling. He could think of nothing to say.

"You see, we're the real knights on the chargers. They're the dragons." His smile faded. "And we fight fire with fire."

CHAPTER TWO

"Witchcraft and magic," the teacher said, her voice echoing off the walls in that large room, "has been the thorn in humankind's side for centuries ... if not longer."

The boys sat in pairs at their desks, arranged in neat and precise rows. Their hair was shorn in a uniform way; they all wore white shirts and blue-grey jackets and shorts, with knee-length white socks. As the teacher—a severe-looking woman, her hair held back by a headband—lectured them, she walked up and down on her raised stage in front of the blackboard, a desk between her and the children. Every now and then she would tap her cane against the palm of her hand. Now she stopped and looked out over the faces gaping up.

"Who can tell me what the turning point in history was? When the tide turned against the pagan scum?" she asked in a serious tone.

No one moved.

"Someone ..." She swished the cane in the air like a sword, finally bringing it down by the side of the table. "*Someone* answer my question!"

A quivering hand rose in the air, forced up by a neighbouring lad: a ploy to save the rest of their skins.

"Ah, Mullins," she said with a tight grin. "Enlighten us."

He looked terrified, eyes wide open, teeth virtually chattering. It clearly crossed his mind to tell her he'd been bullied into this situation by his classmate, but thought better of it. "The … er … The Inquisition, Miss."

She nodded and he gave a sigh of relief, already planning what he'd do to the boy who'd got him into this. "Very good, Mullins. Of course it was. I would have been very disappointed if you'd got that one wrong. But what century are we talking about?"

Mullins, who'd assumed he was safe, now looked twice as scared as before. His mouth opened and closed, but nothing came out.

"I'm waiting," said the teacher. She gave him a few more seconds of respite, then came around the desk and descended to his level, grey dress flapping, cane still in her hand. Another hand went up about halfway down the second aisle, drawing her attention, and she walked towards the new volunteer—leaving Mullins to let out another breath and slump forward onto the desk.

"All right, Jacobs, what century?"

"Ah … I think it was the thirteenth."

She slammed the cane down on his desk, missing his hands by centimetres. "There is no 'think,' Jacobs, you either know or you don't."

"T-Thirteenth century, Miss Havelock," he said, as confidently as he could.

"That's better." She turned her back on Jacobs and strolled off up the aisle again. "Yes, the Roman Catholic Church's inspired campaign to stamp out heresy did begin in the thirteenth century, children. Until then those who secretly practised the blackest of all arts thought themselves to be safe, due largely to a document called the *Canon Episcopi*—incorporated into a canon of law a century beforehand. It stated that *anyone* who even believed in witchcraft was to be considered an infidel, and all magical activity was but a delusion. Would that it were, children, would that it were. It was surely the Devil's work to persuade people that such heathens didn't exist at all." She reached the head of the class again and swivelled to face them, cane behind her back. "We have the views and teachings of one man to thank for showing us the way. And his name was …" She stared at a boy to her right, who'd had his head down while she'd been speaking. "Glover? Care to tell me who we have to thank for removing the scales from our eyes?"

Glover looked up, biting his lip. "Er …"

She closed in on her new target. "Don't you know, Glover?"

"I … er …"

Gritting her teeth, Miss Havelock hefted the cane and whacked him on the back of the neck with it. She nodded with satisfaction at his yelp, then leant in. "See me after class," she whispered in his ear. "I think some time in the cupboard might be in order."

The rest of the group sat back in their chairs, hoping they wouldn't be the next to be picked on. Luckily she answered the question herself, with nothing but admiration in her voice.

"I was, of course, referring to the Dominican theologian, Thomas Aquinas. Dates …" she snapped, bending to address a boy on her left.

He swallowed hard. "12 … 1224 to 1276."

She narrowed her eyes. "Close, Flynn. You just got the last numbers the wrong way around. Aquinas was born in 1226 and died in 1274." Flynn brought up his hands, expecting a strike from the cane, but it never came. Miss Havelock had already cut through the rows, cane jammed under her arm, ending up almost in the centre of the classroom. "He revealed to the civilised world much about *their* practises: the fact that some can fly, some can change shape, some raise storms … Gifts given to them by Satan in exchange for their very souls."

All heads at the front turned to see where Havelock was going next as she continued the lesson. "He did much to change the church's view about this matter, and it wasn't too long before the *Canon Episcopi* was discredited and dismissed, making way for much more sensible and necessary laws. Thus, as the Inquisition rose, so did their ability to be able to hunt down and try those who were involved in magical activities. A glorious age reigned, not just in Spain where the Inquisition was at its most effective, but throughout Europe. The Inquisition itself was aided greatly by the powers invested in them by Pope Innocent VII's papal bill from … what year, Sykes?"

The ginger-haired youth she'd stopped behind closed his eyes.

Miss Havelock placed her hands on his shoulders, the cane waving about in front of him, forcing Sykes to open his eyes again. Sykes took a chance. "14 …"

"Good. Go on."

Encouraged by the fact that at least he had the right century, Sykes went for broke. "1450." It was midway; all he could think of under pressure. A sudden flick of the cane at his ear told him he was way out. "Ow," he cried, but sniffed back the tears when Miss Havelock glowered at him. They were ten years of age, on their way to manhood—she'd tolerate no crying in her class.

"This," she continued when Sykes had shut up, making her way to the rear of the room, "paved the way for one of the most influential books ever written on the subject, by two German members of the Inquisition in 1486. Which was … and if you get this wrong, God help your immortal souls …" Havelock extended her cane and tapped a boy on the shoulder. "McGuire."

The fair-haired child looked up at her with blue-grey eyes that almost matched the uniform of this place, and said nervously: "The … *The M-Malleus Maleficarum*, Miss. *The Hammer of Witches*."

She nodded and smiled, removing the cane. "Good." Then Miss Havelock strode back up to the front of the classroom, returning to her desk. She picked up a slipcased book. "And here it is. Jacob Sprenger and Heinrich Kramer's masterwork." She patted the front lovingly. "In it they explained all about the sick and twisted rituals of witches and warlocks. The most shockingly terrifying being the black masses or Sabbats, where the Devil himself would appear to them in the form of a horned goat and seal their pacts by demanding they kiss his … ahem … anus."

The children screwed up their faces and she nodded. "That's right. Though there have been attempts to discredit much of what they wrote, especially in the later parts of the nineteenth and early parts of the twentieth centuries, the vast majority of true believers still swear by its words. Pointers on what distinguishing marks to look for, as well as how to deal with those accused of witchcraft, are all in here."

Havelock placed the book down. "There are copies like this one in all the major libraries in the world, and of course here in the orphanage's own central library. But what of the history of witchcraft in our own country, would that not seem more relevant? I hear you ask. Well, we were a little slower on the uptake, children—although you can rest assured we have made up for it in the meantime. *The Malleus Maleficarum* wasn't translated into English until a hundred years later in 1584, but that's not to say we were oblivious to the threat."

She was on the move again and it had the same effect as before, the boys pressing themselves back against their seats in fear. "Henry VIII had already passed an act to allow those caught practising witchcraft to be tried and punished by the state. What year might that have been in, Cochran?"

All the colour drained out of her latest prey's face, but in spite of this he answered correctly. "1542, Miss."

Their teacher folded her arms, cane sticking out behind her now. "Very good. Yes, it *was* 1542. And in spite of the fact it was foolishly repealed in 1547, Queen Elizabeth passed another in 1563 which was much more stable. Though not as thorough as the laws passed by its European counterparts, this did at least allow the death penalty for those found guilty of murder by witchcraft or sorcery. Elizabeth wisely listened to some of her bishops who had witnessed the trials and burnings in Europe. It was a good job she did, too, because this prepared us to combat the evil lurking in our midst, so prevalent at that time."

Havelock swept down the aisles again. "In order to do this, a new breed of men was needed. Those who would root out the scum that used magic in all its forms: from influencing others to causing harm or even death in some instances. They called these men the Witchfinders, as I'm sure you're aware. And the greatest of these was …" Time for the next victim, leaning in, virtually breathing in the little boy's freckled face. "Williams?"

"Ma … Ma … Ma …" he stuttered like a stuck record. A clip around the top of his head shifted the needle. "Matthew Hopkins, Miss."

"That's correct! Many of the techniques still used today are based on his work. He and his fellow witchfinders operated in the East Anglia area, which was at that time fragmented into smaller villages and towns, like Chelmsford, scene of one of the most famous trials of that era. Now, of course, the region has been amalgamated into one of the largest cities in the world, even giving New York a run for its money. That's in the USA, children—location of another famous historical trial, which was where exactly … anyone?"

Not surprisingly, no one rushed to provide the information. So she picked on one poor kid called Jameson, not too far away. "S-Salem."

"See, wasn't too difficult, was it? That's correct. However, today our methods are the envy even of the United States, who regularly send over foreign exchange officers to observe our procedures."

"How …" The voice came from a child behind the teacher. She spun, cane at the ready; Havelock wasn't used to an open classroom. She spoke and the children listened. Unless *she* decided to pounce on them with a question, naturally.

"What? *How* was what?"

A hand was up at the back, too late, but at least it showed some courtesy. It was the boy who'd answered before: McGuire. "Please Miss, how do you become one?"

"Excuse me?" she said, a little taken aback.

"How do you become a 'finder'?" asked McGuire, his voice quivering slightly but showing much more strength than the others.

Miss Havelock stormed down to where he was sitting, pulling up sharp by his desk. "We do not call them 'finders' anymore, McGuire, as you should know!" He shied away from her fierce expression. "That name went into disuse when they were absorbed into the police force in the late 1800s, before going on to become their own autonomous division within it. From that moment on they were known as Magick Law Enforcement Officers—MLEOs—or simply M-forcers."

McGuire looked at her and opened his mouth, about to say something else. The little boy at the side of him yanked on his sleeve in an effort to shut him up. At this rate he'd put her in a bad mood for the rest of the lesson. Nobody would be safe then, not that they were at the moment. McGuire ignored him, though, determined to get an answer to his original question. "Yes, Miss. But how …"

"*How!*" she virtually screamed. "How? By listening in class, McGuire. By doing as you're told, by watching and taking things in. By studying and following the rules. And by strength of character," she added finally. "Now hold out your hands."

McGuire stared at her, and the rest of the class stared at him.

"Do it!" she shouted.

The boy did as she said, arms shaking. Miss Havelock told him to turn them over so they were facing palm upwards. She fixed him with an evil glare, bringing the cane back, holding it high. McGuire didn't cringe, he held his arms and hands as still as he could. Miss Havelock was savouring the moment, keeping the cane up and looking for any signs of weakness. Then she suddenly brought it down. The thing made a whipping noise, and McGuire braced himself for the pain that would inevitably come.

But it didn't. For whatever reason, Miss Havelock's cane halted millimetres from his hands. She continued to stare at him, then moved the cane back and away from his hands. "Good. You can put them down now," she told him.

McGuire's furrowed brow asked the question for him. He'd been expecting a beating but she'd changed her mind right at the last moment.

"Strength of character," she reminded him. "You must always know who you are and never waver. But, most importantly, be prepared to suffer. Be prepared to sacrifice everything for what you believe in. Then, and only then, will you be ready to join their ranks."

McGuire nodded, understanding the lesson. She nodded back at him. In spite of everything, he still couldn't help himself. He had one more question to ask. "Miss?"

She raised an eyebrow. Somehow his bravery—or stupidity, she hadn't decided which yet—had earned him the right to this one last query. Miss Havelock gave a curt nod for him to continue.

"Have you ever met one?"

"You mean a finde … a MLEO?"

McGuire shook his head. "A witch."

Miss Havelock opened her mouth, then closed it again, then opened it a final time. She gave a snide laugh, turning her back on McGuire. The teacher started to walk towards the front of the classroom again. "Take your text books out of your desks, children," she told them. "Turn to page 83. Historical methods of dealing with witches. The most popular of which, once a confession had been obtained, was burning at the stake."

CHAPTER THREE

The city glistened at night-time.

Over every ridge there were dancing orange and yellow lights. From a distance they looked like fireflies, except for the fact they were stationary. Instead, he was the one moving: staring out of the monorail's window as it took him to the south sector of this zone. It really was huge, this metropolis—this *megalopolis*—seemingly never-ending, with no borders he could discern. The capital of Anglia was so different to London, where he'd been raised. His hometown was a fraction of its size. There was little wonder Gibson referred to it as a backwater. As far as people here were concerned, it was.

He'd certainly never witnessed anything quite like the events of that morning when he'd been in "Old Londinium." As Callum turned them over again in his mind, he saw Temple in flames, then a blackened confusion of a thing on the floor with only its teeth shining out to mark it as a man. "Fairly standard procedure for anyone above a Level Two rating," Gibson had informed him, "who might be about to use magick on you."

As they'd called for the clean-up crew, his new partner had continued: "You wait for them to pull something and it's bye-bye time. You could be a puddle of liquid on the floor, or blasted into a million pieces. I've seen it happen. Once these sparkies get a head on to start that invoking, no amount of armour or protection will help you. Not even that mugwort woven into your uniform."

When Callum thought back to what had happened, he could almost convince himself Gibson was right. Temple had been coming around the desk in an aggressive manner—forget the fact they'd just barged into his office while he was with a client—and his fists *had* been balled. If they'd given him a chance to get off an incantation, who knows what might have occurred.

And it was true that when they'd made a thorough search of the office, they'd found casting books amongst the legal ones, some dating back a hundred years. "Must have paid a pretty penny for these," Gibson had said, whistling.

Because they weren't sure how far his influence had spread, or whether he'd been using mind control on anyone in the offices, all the staff—even the widow he'd been talking to that day about her husband's will—had been taken back to the station for interrogation. The other partners, Hill and Lynch, quoted the law at officers on the scene, but it hadn't made any difference. In fact, once they knew that Section 27 had been employed, they practically gave up. Their kind of law held no sway here.

"What will happen to them back at the station?" asked Callum.

"First they'll look for any distinguishing marks—which they'll prick to see if it causes pain. Then they'll be seen by experienced interrogators, all trained in psychology. They'll weed out anyone who might have been *tainted* by Temple." It was an interesting word, that, thought Callum. "Believe me, they'll sort it."

"And if they find someone who *is* tainted?"

"Then they extract a confession. Come on, you know the score. You're not telling me you transferred here without brushing up on at least some of our procedures."

Callum knew them all right, he'd been studying as much about their practices as he could for years. But it was one thing to read about that stuff, quite another to be around when it was actually in progress.

"It's thrown you a bit, hasn't it?" said Gibson, clapping a hand on his shoulder. "Bound to. I can remember my first day in this division; we raided a coven on the west side. One of the women came at me and I just froze. Luckily I was with an experienced officer, too, that day. Lincoln, his name was—passed away a few years back, sadly. But he noosed that bitch, then kicked her over some banisters into a stairwell. Hung her good and proper. I'll always be grateful to him for that, though at the time I was about ready to throw my guts up all over the carpet. It was Lincoln who taught me that the old ways are mostly the best."

"I'm not about to throw up," Callum assured him.

"Good … good. So how about we grab a cup of coffee, then?" Gibson smiled again. "Lincoln taught me that, too. Keep yourself wired. Who needs sleep, eh?"

They'd got the coffee for free from a stall Gibson knew. He chatted with the vendor for a few minutes before returning to the car, and passed Callum the cup through his open window.

"See, always spend a bit of time with people, talking. You never know what you might pick up. I mean, sure, they have snoops for that, going in undercover, finding things out. But there's nothing wrong with keeping your eyes and ears open."

Callum sipped the coffee. "I once had a teacher who said exactly the same thing."

Gibson nodded. "There you go. Sparkies can be anywhere, Callum. They hide in plain sight. Could be him," Gibson waved his cup across at a man walking down the opposite side of the street. "Could be her." He indicated a teenage girl wearing a bright red jacket and an incredibly short skirt. "Could most definitely be *her*." This time he waved across at an old woman stooping, walking with a stick. She was dressed in black with a lace shawl, her grey hair up in a bun. "Bit of a stereotype, I'll grant you, but like I said: plain sight."

Callum shook his head. "I just can't help thinking what we did back there—"

"It was necessary. Trust me." Gibson took a gulp of his coffee, then a bite of a doughnut from a white paper bag (Gibson could hardly talk about the old lady, thought Callum, in some ways the guy was a stereotypical policeman himself). "They're dangerous, now more so than ever. You only have to look at Arcana to see that. We exist to stamp out their kind, Callum. Now I know you won't be used to on the spot executions, but this is different territory. You've got to develop a thicker skin or you won't last five minutes."

"Okay, I get it," Callum told him.

"So, you think you can handle it?"

"*Of course* I can handle it," said the young officer, flashing his eyes at Gibson. Then, more quietly: "I can handle it." He didn't know who he was trying to convince, Gibson or himself.

A complete contrast to the start of the day, the rest had been quite mundane. They'd followed up another lead about a street performer who'd allegedly been using magick as part of his act: an anonymous tip-off from a member of the public. When the man, dealing out cards on a portable desk with a green top, had seen them approach, he'd knocked over his table—the cards scattering everywhere—and made a run for it. But Gibson had already worked out a plan of action with Callum before their approach. While he went one way, Callum cut the man off from another. He tackled the guy to the ground, placing the cuffs on him while he waited for Gibson to catch up.

"I ain't done nothing," argued the man.

"We'll be the judge of that," Callum said.

"Your first score, eh?" Gibson said, standing over the pair. "Good collar."

"Thanks."

They ran him back to the station, but as Gibson had said after examining the ordinary playing cards the man had dropped, he'd only be done for petty crime. "He's a con man, using sleight of hand to rip people off. Find the lady, that kind of thing. Wrong kind of magick," muttered Callum's partner. "But we'll let the boys back at HQ have a bit of fun with him first. You never know, it might turn out that he can levitate or turn himself into a rat. Though somehow I doubt it."

This prompted a final question from Callum back at their base. "Have you ever got it wrong, Gibson?"

"What do you mean?"

"You know, fried someone who was … normal. Or just a sleight of hand con artist?"

"No," said Gibson with complete conviction. "Never."

"You sound very certain."

"Look, let me give you one last piece of advice on your first day. You start to question yourself in this job, you make mistakes. Those mistakes get you and everyone around you killed. See what I'm saying?"

Callum nodded.

"Good boy."

It was at that point, virtually the end of their shift, that Wallis spotted them in the corridor. He limped over as best he could. "So, how did he do?" asked the Superintendent.

"He did fine," Gibson said. "I think he's going to make a good addition to the team."

Though he didn't smile, the corners of Wallis's mouth raised slightly. "That's what I like to hear!" Then he continued on his way.

"Just like a proud father," said Gibson, smirking. "Speaking of which, I bet your folks were pretty happy to hear about your transfer?"

Callum shook his head. "No … no, not really."

Gibson frowned. "Why's that? Haven't you told them?"

He looked his partner in the eye. "They're dead."

"Oh … oh Christ, I'm really sorry. Look, ignore me and my stupid mouth," said Gibson.

"It's okay," Callum told him, though his expression said otherwise. "Look, I never knew them. My dad died before I was born, my mum got cancer when I was about two."

"I see." He didn't probe any further; in fact they both got changed back into their civvies in silence. Gibson didn't say anything more until they got outside the station. "You fancy a belt? I could definitely use one."

Callum declined the offer with thanks, he had too much to do at home. He'd only moved up here over the weekend and there were boxes still to unpack, a flat to get straight.

"Right, so I'll catch you tomorrow. Bright and early … partner."

Callum watched Gibson walk off to his car. He was usually so good at reading people, but this man he was having difficulty with. Ostensibly, he liked him. The guy had been nothing but friendly today, when he could have acted like a complete dick. Sure, there was the occasional comment because Callum was green, but he was also offering him some sort of mentorship—and seemed glad to do so, probably because of Lincoln. Like Callum, Gibson was passionate about his work. But Callum couldn't forget the glee he'd caught in the man's eyes as he set Temple on fire; as dangerous as the magick user might have turned out. It might well have been standard procedure—and who knows, after a few close calls Callum might also get to the stage where he didn't bat an eyelid at on the spot executions either—but the difference was Gibson seemed to enjoy it far too much.

These and other thoughts were occupying his attention as the monorail rattled along. In fact he almost missed his stop, the lights of the city hypnotising him, the remembrances of the day haunting him. He alighted along with a handful of other people, the last remnants of the rush hour commuters, and walked down the street carrying his holdall. It was only the second time he'd had to find his way back to his apartment block at night and the streets took on a different pattern to the one he'd followed that morning. Consequently, it took a few wrong turns before he got the right street: turning a corner to see his complex ahead of him. Like the city itself, this building glowed; here and there lights dotted up the side of the facing wall to show that some of the residents were home. In one window he saw a man walk past with a plate, heading for the kitchen. In another a little boy, couldn't have been more than six or seven, was gazing up at the stars—which were almost a mirror for the city itself. In yet another there was the silhouette of a couple kissing against the blind, holding each other close. This caught his attention more than the others and he watched until the figures moved away, the lights going out in their apartment.

Callum walked over to the main door of the block, opening it with his key card. Making his way across the lobby, which was decidedly smaller and infinitely less stylish than the one he'd been in that morning, he thought about using the lift again. He dismissed the notion almost immediately. Even when he'd moved into the rented flat last Saturday (thankfully furnished—though, it had to be said, sparsely), he'd dragged his belongings up the stairs rather than take them in that tiny metal box. It wasn't that he was claustrophobic as such. Rooms full of people were fine, caves like the ones up north he'd once visited on a day trip with the orphanage: not a problem. It was more the thought of being sealed inside that thing which really made his flesh crawl. He'd endured it for the sake of appearances with Gibson, though the man had noticed his discomfort. He hadn't wanted to show any weakness if he could help it, but all the way up and down he would cheerfully have bitten his way through the steel if it meant he would be back out in the open.

Though he was only on the seventh floor (much better than the twentieth) he felt the same way about this contraption. Besides, the stairs were good exercise.

When he reached his floor he was barely out of breath, but was sweating a little. He mopped his brow with his jacket sleeve before emerging on the landing area. The corridor stretched out in front of him like a zoom shot in a film. He hadn't really had much of a chance to speak to any of the residents of the block yet, though he did know the family that lived opposite. The mother, father and small child had returned home while he was busy moving boxes and the dad even helped him into the flat with the last of them.

"Dan Hodgson," the guy had said, extending his hand after they'd done.

"Pleased to meet you," Callum replied, after telling him his name.

"That's my wife Tina. And in the buggy, that's Sam."

Callum had crouched down and the boy, who couldn't have been more than a year old, had started crying. "I have that effect on everyone," Callum said, laughing. "So, what's this place like, Dan?"

He shrugged. "Same as any other, really, people tend to keep themselves to themselves mostly … which can be good, and it can be bad. Where is it you come from?"

"London. I moved here for work."

"Right. And what …" Dan had begun, then left the question

hanging in the air. "Look at me, sticking my nose in. It's none of my business what you do."

Callum paused before speaking again. It could only go one of two ways when you said you were an M-forcer: and neither were particularly favourable. First there was the immediate back out and run. Or perhaps it would be the ventriloquist's dummy reaction, where the person suddenly turns to wood and can only speak by moving the bottom lip. They were waiting, however, so he told them the truth.

"I'm a cop." It was as much as Dan and his family needed to know.

He thought the man had gone for the ventriloquist look at first, so much so that Callum expected him to try and pronounce "gockle of geer." But this blank phase only lasted a second or so. To his surprise, Dan appeared quite overjoyed by the fact. He even shook Callum's hand again. "It's nice to know we can all sleep soundly in our beds at night," was his parting comment when they said goodbye.

There was no sign of the Hodgsons tonight, however; all was quiet. It wasn't until he was slotting in his keycard to open his door that another one opened at the same time at the far end of the corridor. Out stepped a woman of about his age, with long black hair tied in a ponytail. She was wearing a navy cardigan, but the rest of her dress was light blue: a uniform. The girl was a nurse, on her way out to work. One shift ending for him, one just beginning for her. Callum was aware that he was staring, and looked away before she'd finished locking up. But he found himself glancing up again as she walked towards him on the way to the lift. This was the first time he'd seen her around. Maybe she'd been working most of the weekend, wherever it was she worked. A surgery, a hospital? Whatever the case, she looked up and caught his eye at the very last moment.

Callum found himself smiling, a reflex thing. The girl offered a faint smile back—giving nothing away with it. As she passed by, his eyes trailed her.

Any minute now, she's going to look over her shoulder, look at you, Callum told himself. But she didn't. At least not until she reached the lift and it opened. Then, standing inside, she glanced over. Their eyes locked again momentarily, then the doors closed and she was descending to the ground level.

Callum shrugged and opened his front door.

Flicking on the light, then locking the door, he surveyed the disaster area that was his living room. Cardboard boxes stacked in precarious piles had turned it into an assault course, and he had to clamber over them to find any hint of a couch. He looked around vainly for somewhere to put his holdall, then placed it on top of another box, making it wobble even more. He'd promised himself he would unpack in the evenings this week after work, but now he'd actually finished a shift that was the last thing he wanted to do. They'd keep until the weekend. As long as he could reach the kitchen, the bedroom, and the loo, he'd be okay.

Callum slumped down on the sofa, rubbing his face with his hands. The day hadn't exactly gone how he thought it would when he transferred. But then what in life ever did? This was something he'd dreamed about since he was old enough to *have* dreams. He was actually here, in Anglia, doing the job he was born to do. So what if it wasn't what he'd imagined.

Tomorrow was surely another day.

CHAPTER FOUR

For Callum that day started early.

He hadn't intended it to. After fixing himself something to eat from the "overwhelming" choice he had in his fridge and cupboards—basically what he'd brought with him from London, which amounted to a chicken spread sandwich—he'd barely been able to keep his eyes open. It was hardly surprising; a sleepless night followed by a long day … Not even all the coffee he'd drunk was going to keep his eyelids open.

Callum barely made it to the bed, tumbling out of his sneakers and jeans and welcoming the mattress like a long-lost friend. If he'd dreamed of anything that night, he didn't remember it.

Then the noise woke him from his slumber.

It wasn't quite a scream, it was more like a prolonged series of cries: tearful and gurgling. He wasn't sure, but he might have even dismissed them at first in his desire to stay asleep—in the same way people often block out an alarm clock in the mornings. Yet this was more persistent than any alarm, and it played on his conscience that someone might be in trouble. Asleep or awake, he was always on duty.

He hadn't unpacked his bedside lamp, so it hardly mattered whether he had his eyes open or shut to make it to the bedroom door.

Callum staggered out into the living room, promptly knocking over a tower of boxes on his left, which luckily—or not, if the sound of broken crockery was anything to go by—fell away from rather than on top of him.

"Shit!" he said, doubling back and belatedly putting on the bedroom light. The bulb came alive and he felt like he was going blind, turning to shield his eyes from the glare. Though its influence only stretched so far into the living room, it was enough for him to pick out the other box sculptures he'd made in this makeshift gallery. Enough for him to find his way to the front door, following the source of the cries.

As he navigated his way through the living room, still alien territory for him, the sound grew clearer—and he could tell that the lungs expelling those cries were not very old. Callum fumbled with the lock, keeping him inside more than it was keeping anyone out right now.

He finally cracked it and cast open the door, only to be hit by another wave of light from the corridor, which was perpetually illuminated, day and night. Because his eyes had had time to adjust a little, he recovered more quickly. Squinting, he looked up and down the hallway. A couple of heads were sticking out from behind chained doors, but nobody was out here apart from him.

Callum looked at his watch, the hands and figures gradually making some kind of sense. It was almost four in the morning. He cocked an ear to try and work out where the wailing was coming from. It was the flat opposite his.

"Isn't it dreadful," Callum heard someone say. This was from one of the doors open a crack. He thought it was a woman's voice at first, then realised it was an old man's. "It's been going on for ages."

Callum was shocked at that; he must have been in a really deep sleep for it not to have reached his ears until now. Until it was reaching fever pitch.

"Someone should call the police," said another neighbour, communicating with the first man through a similar gap.

Approaching the door, he put his ear against the wood. The screams were definitely coming from inside Dan and Tina's place. He banged on the door, calling their names. There was no answer to begin with, and Callum was about to knock again when the locks were undone from the other side and Dan's face appeared. It was the epitome of worry. Not only had the lack of sleep done its worst—his hair dishevelled, bags under his eyes—but the furrows on his brow looked like they'd been ploughed by a corn farmer.

"Callum … Callum, come in, quickly." Dan virtually pulled him inside their flat where he saw Tina on the couch with little Sam. The boy was laid down, but he was crying out in agony, his face red, tears streaming down his cheeks. But as he drew nearer Callum saw that it wasn't just his face that was crimson: the child's arms were blotchy as well.

Tina looked up at Callum, her face an exact duplicate of Dan's. "We thought he was just teething at first. Nothing to worry about. But he's burning up, and look at his skin!"

Callum *was* looking. It wasn't simply mottled, there were lesions there too. "He must have had an allergic reaction to something," Dan added.

"You need to ring for an ambulance," Callum said without hesitation. "Right now!" He couldn't actually believe they'd waited this long.

"We can't," said Dan. "Our Med-fee card is almost exhausted. There were complications during the birth, you see. We just don't have any more credit."

Callum let out a big sigh. Med-fee. Since the Health Service had been privatised and a new "pay as you go" system put in place, the amount of medical attention you received depended on who you were and, more importantly, how much you were able to afford. He didn't tend to think about such things himself because it was all covered as part of his job, but when something like this happened it brought home how unfair the damned thing was. "Look, we can put him on my card. I've barely had to use it this year," he told them.

Dan started to shake his hand again. "Oh thank you, Callum! Thank you!"

It was then that Sam's cries died down. His breathing was coming now in short gasps. "I don't think there's time to get him to hospital!" shouted Tina. "What are we going to do?"

Callum had a basic knowledge of first aid, but somehow knew that wouldn't cut it. Sam needed expert help, and fast. "Wait a second …"

He ran back out into the corridor, sprinting up it. The people with the cracks in the doors shut them briefly as he passed. Callum had lost count on his way up here—far enough that the cries wouldn't have reached this part of the landing—and he prayed this was the right door. He banged on it with his fist.

Please be back, pretty lady. Please be back from your shift. Come on, come on.

He banged again, then heard noises. There was definitely someone inside. Callum thumped again, just to make sure they'd heard him.

"Who is this?" said the woman. "If you don't go away I'm calling the police."

"This *is* the police!" he told her. "I need your help. Open up!"

There was a gap when he figured she must have been looking through the peephole at him. Then, just as he'd done at Dan's place, he heard locks being removed. The chain was still on when the door opened up, though. There she was, the woman he'd watched walking to the lift, as beautiful as she'd been then. More so in fact, because she'd taken off what little make-up she'd been wearing and the natural look definitely suited her.

"You?" she said, her voice slightly strange.

"Yes … I need you to come with me. Quickly!"

"What is it, what's wrong?"

"Someone's sick, a little boy."

"What?"

"We don't have time for all this. Please, you have to come with me. *Now!*" Perhaps it was the edge to his plea that made her take off the chain, or maybe she could see he was genuinely in distress. But she opened the door fully, the room in shadows behind her. The uniform she'd worn earlier had been replaced by cotton pyjamas. Either she'd been in bed or getting ready to go to sleep after finishing work. Her hair had been let down, and now flowed freely over her shoulders.

Lucky ... very, very lucky, thought Callum. He took her by the hand which—to his surprise—she didn't resist, and ran with her back down the corridor to the Hodgsons' flat. Inside, Tina was frantic.

"I think he's stopped breathing!" she shrieked.

The newcomer didn't have to ask anymore; she went straight to the couch to examine Sam. Politely, she asked Tina to move and Dan came over to put his arm around his wife, who was in floods of tears.

"It's okay," said Callum, "she's a nurse."

The dark-haired woman knitted her hands together and started to press on Sam's chest; even compressions, interspersed by the kiss of life. Callum watched as she placed her mouth over the boy's, breathing for him. After a minute or so, it became clear that this wasn't working. Tina's cries were growing more high-pitched. Now the nurse finally did look over her shoulder at Callum, and he would have given anything for her not to have done. She gave a slight, almost imperceptible, shake of the head.

"Take them outside," she told him.

This elicited another piercing cry from Tina, but Callum placed his hands on both her and Dan's shoulders, ushering them out of the apartment. "Let her do her job," he said. "Give her space to work."

A few people had ventured out of their flats, curiosity and Tina's screaming too much for them to resist. Now he wished they'd stayed in their little self-contained units, looking out through cracks in the doors. A crowd was the last thing Tina and Dan needed. Callum pushed them further out into the corridor, then cast a quick look over his shoulder.

The nurse still had her hands on Sam's chest, pumping on it. Then they moved up to his throat and she seemed to be talking to herself. Obviously going over some sort of procedure as she did it, he thought—or mulling over what to do next. His guess was tracheotomy, cut open the windpipe. But if the child wasn't breathing *at all* ... Then he saw it, or thought he did: a faint glow coming from beneath her hands. Callum blinked, his eyes still very sore from tiredness, and then it was gone.

"I need to get back in there," Tina wailed, trying to evade Callum's grip. He turned around to prevent her, holding the woman at arm's length. When he looked back again, the nurse had finished what she was doing and there was a small cough from Sam. Then another, louder cough, the kind of noises you'd hear from a man who'd been saved from drowning, only dry and rasping instead of watery.

The nurse was rising, standing back from the boy. Callum's mouth was hanging open and he let Tina through again, followed closely by Dan. "Sit with him," she told his mother, "I'm going to fetch my kit. I have some cream that should help with the redness."

She walked towards the door, motioning for Callum to move out of the way, which he did. The nurse returned a couple of minutes later with a small bag. This time he stopped her before she could go in.

"What did you do in there?" he asked.

She looked at him with eyes that were as dark as her hair. "He couldn't breathe, his tongue was swelling up. Massaging his throat relieved the swelling, now if you'd excuse me …"

Callum let the woman through again, but watched her closely. *Trick of … trick of the light*, he told himself. *An effect of being half-asleep. She'd been massaging his throat, just like she said. You didn't see anything else.*

But he hadn't been breathing at all, he argued with himself. *You saw that; how would simply relieving the swelling have done that? That's assuming you actually* can *relieve it by massage.*

The nurse took out a pot of cream from her bag and applied it to the rash on Sam's skin. He'd gone back to crying, but it wasn't as loud as before and nowhere near as distressing. By the time she'd covered his arms, legs, chest and belly with the cream, he'd stopped altogether and was gazing up at her.

Tina was looking from the nurse to Dan, then to Callum in the doorway. There was a strong smell wafting across from the pot, which the nurse screwed the lid back on when Callum approached. "He should be okay now," she said to the three of them.

"I don't know how to thank you," said Dan. "We thought …"

Tina was still crying, but they were tears of joy now. She gave the nurse a hug, rubbing her back as she did so. "God bless you," she said. "God bless you."

The woman left them alone with their son, and wandered over to Callum.

"What was in the cream?" was the first thing he said to her.

"It's an antihistamine. Should stop his body producing toxins."

He nodded.

She leaned in and whispered her next sentence. "Are you really … you know?"

Callum knew what she was asking him: was he with the police? "Yes."

The woman pulled a face. "Listen, I could lose my license for this. Practising medicine without a registered Med-fee doctor present."

"I know."

"So, you going to arrest me?"

Callum didn't answer her at first, then he said, "You saved his life."

"Yes." She nodded. "Yes, I did. But that wouldn't stop me going to jail."

"I fetched you," Callum reminded her. "I'd be in just as much trouble."

She let out a relieved sigh. "Thanks. Right, well I think that's more than enough excitement, especially for this time of night. I'd better be heading back to—"

Callum caught her by the arm. "Wait."

Turning to face him, she said sharply, "Changed your mind?"

"No … I … I just wanted to know what your name was."

It wasn't at all what she'd expected him to say, and she laughed. "It's Ferne. Ferne Andrews. Officer …"

"Callum," he said, releasing her arm. "My name's Callum."

"So I'm free to go?"

Callum nodded. "Sorry about the banging before. I didn't mean to disturb you and … ah, anyone else."

"Did you *see* anyone else back there?"

"Not really," he said, but then he'd only been offered a glimpse into her flat, and it was dark at that.

"That's because I live alone."

"Oh."

"Well," she said again, "it's much too late to be standing in hallways." Ferne started to walk back up the corridor with her bag.

Callum watched her for a few moments, before turning his attention to the other residents who were gathering to see what all the fuss had been about. "All right, all right, go back inside, folks. There's nothing to see here, nothing to see."

Ferne turned around, walking backwards and pointing. "Oh, I wouldn't say that." He followed her eyes and finger downwards, realising for the first time that he was still only wearing his boxer shorts. He felt the blood rushing to his cheeks as she gave another small laugh, then disappeared inside her apartment.

"Goodnight, Ferne," he whispered under his breath. "And thank you."

CHAPTER FIVE

Once inside, Ferne shut the door and leaned against it, head back against the wood. The smile had faded from her face.

What the hell had she been thinking, to even answer the door let alone go out there and get involved in something so public—and with a policeman, too? What if he'd seen something? Those questions he'd been asking her, about what she'd done. Had he bought her answers? Yes, she thought so.

Thought? Thought? There's no room for doubts, no margin for errors. That kind of thinking only leads to trouble.

He seemed nice enough, though. *Very* nice, in fact. Besides, what else was she supposed to do, leave the poor boy to die? She'd tried to bring him around by normal methods, but he'd given up the fight long before Ferne had even got there. She tossed her bag over to the nearest chair, rubbing her forehead nervously.

"Just what was I supposed to do?" she asked out loud.

"I think you know the answer to that," replied a male voice from the corner of the room.

"It'll be okay," Ferne said, walking further into the gloom.

"I don't think so."

"It will, really—"

"You put yourself … put *all* of us in danger." There was anger in that voice.

"I had to do it. I'd do it again," she snapped back.

"I wonder …" said the voice. She could just about see the shape of him, leaning forward in a chair. "I wonder: if you could see into the future, would you say the same?"

"But I can't. And neither can you."

"You are quite sure of that?"

"Second-hand, perhaps, over Unwin's shoulder. Look, I did what I had to," she repeated. On this she would broach no argument.

"Then I hope you are ready to pay the price."

"Price? What price?"

The man sitting in the darkness gave a hollow laugh. "There's always a price Ferne. *Always*. The universe demands it, you should know that. An eye for an eye, a tooth for a tooth. A life …" He left a deliberate pause. "For a life."

Then he spoke no more and she knew he was gone. Ferne sat down on the sofa, brought her knees up to her chest, and hugged herself.

Suddenly and uncontrollably, she began to cry.

CHAPTER SIX

It had been the site of some of their most famous historical victories.

Chelmsford, as it had formerly been known, was the Essex town where their originator had taken on his most deadly opponents. It was here that Elizabeth Clarke—whose own mother had been accused of the craft, found guilty and then hanged—had also finally come to accept her fate. Though torture was banned at that time in Britain, they'd found a way to extract the all-important confession: depriving her of sleep, making the old crone sit cross-legged on a stool or walking her up and down for hours until she was ready to collapse from exhaustion.

The resultant trials saw seventeen of their kind strung up, although even more were subsequently brought to justice. Thirty-eight in total. It decimated their numbers, hitting them where it hurt the most. That was an attitude adhered to even today—*especially* today. Little wonder then that this location should serve as their nerve centre, though anyone who'd known it as Chelmsford in those days would barely recognise it now. Part of the East Anglican City, while it was not literally at its heart, Chelmsford definitely represented that organ. Nothing happened in the rest of the sprawling metropolis without this sector knowing about it, on every level. Everything was monitored from here: every single police station in every region, all the news stations, CCTV cameras dotted on street corners around Anglia … and beyond.

Communication with Central European M-forcement Divisions went through this sector, as did any liaison with their US counterparts. It required a level of staffing that was almost unbelievable. Yet even with one eye on the "big picture," there was still a thorough scrutiny of the smaller details. From the arrest of an underage offender practising the dark arts alone in his bedroom for "fun," to the larger scale crimes such as the one that had happened recently at the *All Seasons* shopping centre, no stone was left unturned, no lead ignored.

But what of the actual physical headquarters? It was a building like no other, unparalleled in the history of architecture. Made from the finest stone in Britain (no metal that could rust, no glass that could crack), constructed in the 1920s, it had been built to last. And last it had, serving the needs of the Magick Law Enforcement Division for almost a hundred years. Standing in front of this marvel of design was Sherman Pryce. He'd climbed out of the black car that had delivered him here for his weekly-meeting—that was fast turning into a thrice-weekly ritual—and was admiring the view.

The two men assigned to protect him, day and night, clambered out of the vehicle as well, and the driver was told to amuse himself for at least an hour. Sherman's own offices were impressive, but this was beyond words. Once he'd finished craning his neck, something he did habitually whenever he visited, the trio walked up to the main entrance—itself flanked and patrolled by guards carrying MP5 rifles—and Sherman demanded admittance. Once inside he knew he could leave the two gorillas behind, for there was no greater state of the art security system than the one in operation here. Not even a fly would be able to get in through an open window without clearance and a security check … and papers in triplicate. Now Sherman had to undergo both a retina and saliva test to gain admittance. Not the most pleasant of experiences, but he understood.

There were many enemies that had to be kept at arm's length; not even the King of England had this much security and he was the one

—supposedly—signing the orders. Of course Sherman knew differently. The King was merely a puppet, it was the man he was on his way to see who wielded the real power in this country; some might say even the world. Sherman had seen foreign ambassadors kneeling in his presence, diplomats shit in their pants rather than offend him, military leaders cower because of one wrong word.

None of this put him off. He had been Nero Stark's second-in-command for too many years. Sherman Pryce passed the tests they gave him at the door, including the good old-fashioned metal detector (he'd handed in his two P226 SIG Sauer automatic pistols before submitting to this), and a search through the briefcase he was carrying. At last he was allowed access to the deeper chambers of the building. The levels above were merely a distraction: the architect wisely concluding that if anyone attacked this fortress, insane as they must be, the upper levels would be the primary target. In other words, fuck being close to God, being alive was more important.

But there were further tests to come once the lift he was in reached the right floor. As he emerged, he was stopped by two cloaked men. It was a little known fact—and if it did get out it would probably signal the end of the current regime—that Nero Stark had in his employ two of the most powerful masters of the Mental Arts known to mankind. He called them The Cerebrals. Though nobody knew for sure where they had come from, many rumours surrounded these men. Maybe they'd been captured and subjected to mind control experiments to get them to switch sides, though this didn't seem very likely. Who would have the ability to tame them? Another rumour was that they'd been genetically engineered, utilising the very best scientists the Med-fee Corporation had to spare (Med-fee was in Nero's pocket anyway). This would seem the most plausible explanation, though it would mean the men had been "grown" almost thirty years ago; all attempts at speeding up the cloning process having ended in complete disaster.

The only other theory involved members of their own elite corps having intimate knowledge of the craft themselves. It was possible, but went against everything the M-forcers stood for. That would tar Nero with the same brush as those out there who used magick. The so-called Sparkies, as the street cops labelled them. In any event, one never questioned the logic of their employ, neither out loud nor to oneself. The latter because their greatest power was the ability to read minds.

Nero might argue that in order to properly protect himself against such an evil, it was necessary to employ guards with the same skills, however unpalatable that might be. Though Nero would never dirty his own hands, he would quite happily let someone else have free rein if it meant stopping some fanatical Arcana rebel from breaking in and causing havoc.

It was why Sherman had to submit himself to their attentions now, so they could verify his identity with one final check. It was why he had to let them go where nobody could hide their true selves, no matter how good they might be at masking their features with a glamour. You could create the illusion of being Sherman Pryce, but only the genuine article had his thoughts and memories.

The largest of the two cloaked figures stepped forward, slamming down his staff and pulling off his hood. His head was completely shaved and his eyes were an icy blue. His companion followed suit, standing on the other side of Sherman. As one, they each placed a hand on his head, fingers digging into the scalp through his salt and pepper hair. He grimaced; this was the part he hated most.

It felt like someone sticking red-hot needles into his brain, which wasn't far from the truth. The men sifted through his consciousness like prospectors panning for gold. When they found something interesting, however, they suddenly became archaeologists, brushing away earth or sand to uncover an ancient artefact hidden from human eyes for so long.

They went through it all, starting with his younger years: the only child of well-to-do parents who spoilt him rotten but gave him the finest education money could buy, and if nothing else, taught him the value of knowledge. On into his teens, where he couldn't even hide his furtive sessions in his bedroom, pleasuring himself with magazines spread open on the bed. Women with made up names and staples through their bellybuttons gazed back at him, lustily licking their lips as he worked his length harder and harder. Though it was the ones dressed in leather that really got him going, holding whips or chained to walls.

On through his twenties where money had also bought him a place in the higher echelons of the force. Then a sideways transfer into its most elite division, where he was able to satisfy those adolescent urges for real during interrogation sessions. One particular memory they dredged up was him asking questions of a thirty-five-year-old woman. While not exactly chained up, she was held down by leather straps while he undressed her, ripping off her blouse and kneading one large breast in his fist, while he frantically licked her neck and came in his trousers before he could do anything more. She'd suffered for his excited state, and he'd handed her over to the execution squads that very afternoon along with a falsified confession: attempted malicious harm through spell casting, resulting in the deaths of two people. The fact that the Med-fee examiner had told him they'd both died of natural causes, only to be expected when sitting too close to a gas fire with a blocked flume, was irrelevant. All the "evidence" pointed to foul play—and nobody questioned the fact it was Sherman doing the pointing. Nobody dared. He hadn't been the first and wouldn't be the last.

It was actually that case which gained him a promotion, bringing him to the attention of Stark. And when his little deceit had been discovered, Nero had praised Sherman's ingenuity rather than punishing him. "Who's to say she didn't cast a spell to block the flume?" was his boss's philosophy. "We cannot afford to be cautious in our fight against the dark arts. Everyone is a suspect, all of them potentials."

Had Nero seen something of himself in Sherman's behaviour? *No, don't think such thoughts, not while they're probing your psyche …* More likely, he saw someone just as dedicated to the cause as he was. Someone who'd rise in the ranks and would make a perfect right-hand man. His title changed from Officer, to Inspector, then to Chief Inspector. He now held the coveted position of Commander in Chief, responsible for the day to day running of all the special MLE divisions across the country. The only person above him was Nero.

Sherman was aware of the fingers pressing even harder into his scalp, so hard it felt like they were burrowing through the skull and into his grey matter. The robed men had their eyes closed, images flashing across their retinas of those first meetings with Nero, the initiation ceremony to prove his loyalty.

Sherman flinched when they came to these memories. He'd been brought in to the regional sector house to find Nero waiting for him, with a very special surprise. The door to the interrogation room was opened and inside had been Sherman's own uncle, on his mother's side.

"What? I don't—"

"He has been under suspicion for some time," Nero told Sherman, "but we thought you should do the honours."

Sherman hesitated only a fraction of a second before setting to work. Any more would have indicated collusion and meant sharing the same fate. He'd pushed aside memories of those visits from Uncle Charlie when he was little, bringing gifts from his business trips abroad, playing cricket out in the garden. The man had been like a second father to him, yet Sherman could show absolutely no mercy. Nero had insisted on the very basest of interrogation techniques, modelled on their forebears in the Inquisition. Modern though the implements they used were, they still had the same effect: a rack made not from wood, but gleaming steel; laser burns replacing red hot pokers; and where digits or limbs had to be removed, they could keep the wound open for hours, if not days, without infection setting in. Although, as Nero was so fond of telling him, some of the old methods really couldn't be improved upon. There was nothing quite like simply pummelling the prisoner with your fist from time to time, maybe cracking a few ribs or loosening teeth. His uncle had watched him do all this with tears in his eyes, the seal around his mouth preventing him from speaking until they wanted him to, until he was ready to confess. Which, inevitably, unfortunately, he did.

Nero then encouraged Sherman to put the man out of his misery. Leading him, battered and only vaguely aware of what was happening, to an incineration chamber.

"If we are to purge society of the menace that faces us—that has faced us for generations, Pryce—then we must begin by ensuring our own are cleansed." Those had been Nero's final words before instructing Sherman to press the button. Just as he'd held back the emotion and tears during the interrogation, Sherman did the same when he watched his uncle heat up, his body glowing red, then finally reduced to a pile of ash on the cubicle floor that would receive a decent scattering on consecrated ground.

He'd passed the test, his loyalty ensured. And Sherman truly believed that if Nero said his uncle was involved somehow in black magicks, then it was the truth. If he didn't believe this, it meant he'd just murdered a man he loved for nothing. Nobody's mind could cope with that.

Therefore when the Cerebrals scanning his thoughts came across this memory, all they saw was that Sherman knew he'd done the right thing. For King and country.

For Nero.

The rest was a mish-mash of remembrances since that day, of countless meetings and interrogations, relationships with women he paid and which was glossed over because of his status. The increasingly macabre activities he got up to behind closed doors that made the incident with the woman look like a first date in the park. More and more of this, then still more: flesh, blood, nails raking skin, masks with zips and the eyes cut out. It went on until Sherman could take no more of his past and actually tore his head away from their hands, breathing heavily.

"That's enough, you bastards," he told them.

They showed even less emotion than he'd been forced to when judging his uncle. They merely turned to face each other and nodded. "You *are* Sherman Pryce," said the one on the left.

"Thank fuck for that. Now are you going to let me in?"

They parted, allowing him access to the entranceway. Like the building itself, it always left him in awe: Nero's private chambers, books lining the curved walls with ladders attached, pillars stretching up to a ceiling covered in painted classical figures. His footsteps echoed on the floor as he moved further inside, searching for his superior.

"I apologise for their enthusiasm," said a voice from behind, making him jump and almost drop his briefcase. Sherman twisted round, seeing Nero standing in the space he'd just occupied. "They have to be sure. *I* have to be sure." The man was not that much taller than him, but the way he carried himself added a good foot or so. He was broad at the shoulder, but his pseudo-military jacket was cut just right so as not to strain the material. His dark moustache was neatly cropped, sideburns running up to meet slicked back hair, which formed a semi-circle on the crown of his head. Equally dark bushy eyebrows sheltered the pupils below, which consequently remained in shadow most of the time. It was said that Nero Stark had the blood of Matthew Hopkins himself flowing through his veins, that he was an ancestor, a distant relation of some kind, and Pryce could well believe it. One gloved hand held a baton wedged under his arm; the other was in the pocket of his jacket and he removed a handkerchief, then handed it to Sherman, before walking on ahead of him. The clacking of his boots was even louder than his second-in-command's footfalls.

Sherman stared down at the handkerchief, wondering why Nero had given it him. Then the first spot of blood dripped from his nose onto the white cloth. "Jesus," he said, bringing the handkerchief up to stem the flow. He had a headache now, too; delayed reaction to the scan. "They get worse every time."

"But completely necessary, my old friend," said Nero, walking away from him into the hall.

Sherman followed, dabbing at his nose. "Are they? Is it really necessary to delve quite so … deep, Nero?"

His superior stopped, looked back over his shoulder at Sherman, and gave a crooked smile. "Scared of what they might find?"

"You know all my secrets," came the reply.

"That's right. I do." Nero strode on ahead again. The place really was gigantic, home to one of the world's most comprehensive archives on witchcraft, magick and the many ways to put a stop to both. As Sherman ventured further inside, the books were replaced by banks of monitors, all linked to one keyboard. The database was not just on paper, but electronically organised as well. At Nero's fingertips was a resource banned to all but him and his kind: the internet. An invention which had been denied to the public because it couldn't be monitored or sufficiently controlled. And at the back of the room, a strange museum of weirdness, souvenirs and artefacts in glass cases, perfectly preserved: from stone runes to broomsticks; from an African witch-doctor's rattle stick to a Native American shaman's headdress. But pride of place in Nero's collection was a battered leather tome with yellowed pages: the very first copy of the *Malleus Maleficarum*. It was priceless, and not even Nero took it out of its airtight container as far as Sherman knew. In this hall, modern technology rubbed shoulders with ancient wisdom, all to the greater good of humankind.

Nero took his seat on a large chair with armrests, then motioned for Sherman to sit in the smaller chair opposite. The nosebleed had just about run its course, and Sherman sat with the red-stained cloth screwed up in his lap.

"So," began Nero, "there can only be one topic vying for our attention this week, yes?"

"Arcana," said Sherman.

"Precisely." Nero rested the baton across his knees. "Are we any closer to finding the scum at the heart of their organisation?"

Sherman chose his words carefully before speaking. "I have our best men on this, and they've come up with a possible location for a safehouse. We're making headway."

"Headway … *Headway!*" Nero said through gritted teeth. "I want them tracked down and I want them destroyed, Sherman. Do you understand?"

Sherman nodded. He thought about adding, "We're doing our best," but knew that would cut no ice either. The recent attack meant that they were still on a high state of alert, but it also meant that the public—the people who trusted Sherman and Nero to protect them—were living under the constant threat of terrorism. Even more freedom had been granted to try and put a stop to the Arcana strikes, even more power placed in Nero's hands … if that was possible. Sherman knew that results were needed, or that very same public might just lose whatever faith they had in them. Recent polls showed there was an overwhelming majority in favour of stricter laws and people even suspected of using magick should be stamped out. But if they were seen to be failing the masses …

"This has been going on far too long as it is," Nero continued. "The Wiccan Front, the Followers of Herne, the Church of Crowley … and now Arcana. We're facing the most dangerous threat to civilisation since Hitler and the Occult Wars."

That didn't bear thinking about. If Hitler's fascination for the occult and dabblings in witchcraft hadn't been picked up on by their own counterparts in Germany in the early 1930s, he might well have dominated the political landscape and dragged them all into a second *World* War. As it was, he had enough followers to mount an offensive using magick against those who opposed him.

"We don't want a situation in this country where they stand in a position to openly attack us," Nero said, driving home the message.

"But that would never happen, surely."

"We must make certain it doesn't, Sherman." By we, Sherman knew he meant him.

"I'm confident that the leads we're chasing up now will result in arrests sometime this week. The public will be assured that we are on top of things."

"I hope you're right." Nero caught his eyes flicking across at the book encased in glass, the centrepiece of the "museum." "You feel drawn to it, don't you?"

"I'm sorry?"

Nero smiled that off-kilter smile again. "The textbook on which all our work is based, Sherman."

"Ah … Yes. I have my own copy of course, but that one …"

Nero stood and strolled over to the book, hands behind his back—baton jutting out of one fist. "The original, in its own language. Sweated over, and even containing information that wasn't deemed fit for subsequent editions. For example, did you know that there is a book that *they* covet, too? A sacred 'black bible' written by the first of them in a much darker age. It contains every single spell in their original forms, not the half-casts that so many of them use today, passed down through generations and garbled like Chinese Whispers. Unspeakable power … Imagine. To possess that book would mean a defence against them. An end to their scourge for all time."

"Obviously I'd heard the rumours, but … Are you telling me that Sprenger and Kramer allude to this in the *Malleus Maleficarum*?"

"Oh, they do more than allude. They *verify* its existence."

Sherman sat back in the chair, amazed. "And where is the book right now?"

"Now that," Nero replied, "is the question, isn't it? Not even they knew that back then."

"So how can you be sure—?"

"Are you questioning their writings? Or their word, Sherman?"

He shook his head vigorously. "No, of course not. It's just that if nobody's ever seen it …"

Nero turned, walking back over to Sherman. "What would you say if I had evidence to suggest that this book, this mythical bible, was in the hands of Arcana? That they plan to use the most deadly of spells against both the population and us? That if they wield that power they would be unstoppable?"

"How do you know this?" The question slipped out before Sherman realised what he was saying. (And what he actually meant by it was, how did Nero know when *he* didn't?)

Nero bent so that his face was inches away from his second-in-command's. "You forget who you are addressing, I think."

Sherman bowed his head. "I'm sorry."

"That's more like it." Nero pulled back and stood upright.

"But why are you sharing this with me now?"

"Because I want to impress upon you the importance of finding those involved in Arcana." He sat back down in his chair. "To make you aware of what's at stake."

"If we find Arcana, we find the book," said Sherman, catching his drift.

"Exactly!" There was that lop-sided smile a final time.

They went on to discuss strategy for a little while, facts and figures, tables and graphs, but Sherman had trouble concentrating after the bombshell Nero had dropped. Soon enough the meeting was at an end and Nero was escorting Sherman back to the entrance of the hall.

"So I'll expect progress soon, shall I?" Nero asked.

"Without a doubt."

"Good."

Neither were keen on goodbyes; for one thing it was not in their natures, for another it was a question of authority. Nero's. Instead Sherman gave a curt nod and turned to leave.

"Just one more thing," Nero called after him.

"Yes?" said Sherman with a crack in his voice.

"How is he progressing?"

Sherman thought for a second or two, then it dawned on him what Nero meant. "Oh, fine, fine. At the moment it's all pretty much standard stuff."

"Then I think it's about time he was given something a little more challenging, don't you?"

Sherman nodded. "Whatever you say."

"Yes," Nero said, "that's right. Whatever *I* say."

Sherman left his boss to his thoughts, passing the robed figures with staffs, ascending back to ground level, picking up his weapons and his bodyguards at the same time. Then the Commander in Chief walked down the steps to his car and got in. He barely noticed his surroundings on the way out, which wasn't unusual. He had too much on his mind after the meeting.

And as the car pulled away from the Centre, he produced his mobile phone. Without looking back, he began to punch in numbers.

CHAPTER SEVEN

For the last two days, they'd been handling fairly routine tasks.

"It can't all be as exciting as it was the first day," Gibson said as they'd cruised the roads. "It can get pretty boring sometimes."

Which would certainly explain why his partner took such great delight in anything that involved a possible arrest or detention. Take that afternoon when they'd been sent to investigate a lock-up belonging to a market trader in the West sector, which they'd had a tip-off might contain stashes of Henbane. "If that stuff ends up on the streets, who knows what kind of potions it'll wind up in," Gibson explained. They'd cranked open the corrugated doors to find it full of cardboard boxes. It looked a little like Callum's apartment … only tidier.

They'd checked the consignments, which at first glance appeared to have imported dolls inside them. But then Gibson found several plastic bags in the bottom of one. "Bingo!" He flipped open a pocket knife and punctured the packet. Then he smelt the sample. "Urgh … It's worse than we thought. Extract of Deadly Nightshade. Supposed to aid in divination, but you take too much of it …" They called in for a crew to confiscate the merchandise, then paid a visit to the market where the merchant was reportedly trading. After talking to the other stall-holders they discovered he hadn't showed up that day, nor the previous one. "Must have been tipped off," Gibson spat. "Son of a bitch!"

Yesterday they'd been called out to a house where a woman had been spotted talking to animals out in her back garden.

"I chat to the birds when I feed them, yes," admitted the overweight woman. "What's wrong with that?"

Gibson consulted his notepad. "You were also seen conversing with a neighbour's dog."

"I stroked it and said, 'Who's a good boy?'" the woman told them, folding her arms.

Gibson mulled this over and said, "I'm afraid we'll still have to take you in for questioning."

Callum had felt like saying something, then. This was ridiculous, the woman had only been feeding birds and petting a Golden Retriever for Heaven's sake! But he knew what Gibson's reply would be: "We can't be too careful, they could be her familiars. If she's innocent, then she's got nothing to worry about, has she?" This wasn't the Middle Ages, though.

So that had been the size of it. Dead ends and wild goose chases. But at least that meant Callum hadn't had to witness anyone else burning to death in front of his eyes.

Wallis had been pleased with his progress, except he'd had another close call the previous morning when the Super almost caught him yawning again. Even Gibson had commented on his tiredness that day.

"You can't keep burning the candle at both ends, it's going to catch up with you," was his sage advice. His antidote was to get more coffee down Callum in the mid-morning break.

It was hardly surprising he was worn out. Callum hadn't managed more than about twenty minutes of sleep once he'd got back to bed, and once he knew the Hodgsons were fine—especially little Sam. He'd checked on them again the following morning and they'd told him the cream had done the trick.

"The rash is virtually gone," Tina informed him. "I'm really sorry we disturbed everyone."

"I'm just glad he's all right," Callum said.

He considered going up and knocking on Ferne's door that morning, too, but thought better of it. She'd probably be sleeping in after her late shift. He'd try and catch her later. But a delay on the monorail that evening meant he was late getting home, and missed her leaving for work.

She'd been on his mind all evening, as he made a start on unpacking at least some of the boxes, although he didn't actually get around to putting any of their contents away. What he'd seen, or *thought* he'd seen, was a vague memory now. *There* hadn't *been a glow coming from her palms, how could there have been?* the rational part of his brain kept saying. She was trained to handle situations like these all the time, and had just done her job. So what if he hadn't heard of a particular technique for resuscitation? It wasn't like he kept up to speed with developments in the medical world, was it?

Little wonder then, that she appeared even in his dreams. Callum remembered one particularly vividly. He was on a bridge, suspended between two rock faces. The rickety wood didn't look safe at all, yet he was still crossing. There, at the other side, was Ferne. She was beckoning to him, one finger crooked. The way was dangerous, but if it led to her ... There was so much he wanted—no, *needed*—to know. Tentatively, he took one step, seeing if the old wood might stand his weight, then he took another. But he was being held back by something, hands on his shoulders, invisible hands he couldn't see. What he *could* see at the other end was Ferne, being grabbed by shadowy things. They had a hand over her mouth and were dragging her backwards. She reached out, pure terror in her face. Callum tried to speed up, but the wood began to give way beneath him. There was a mighty crack and one slat splintered right down the middle. The rope he was holding on to was fraying. He tried shouting to Ferne, but she was receding from him, taken away by the shadow things he couldn't quite make out. He didn't know exactly what they were, but knew she was in trouble, terrible trouble—and that he had to help her. It was what he did: help people.

The bridge finally collapsed, pitching him forward. Callum looked down and found nothing beneath him, not even a river running between the two rocks. Now he was falling, disappearing from sight. He was the one reaching out for help, but there was nobody there to give it. Down he fell, down … Then a million sets of eyes opened up in the gloom.

That's when he woke, his pillows drenched in sweat. Callum breathed in and out heavily, resting on one elbow, a shaky hand out in front as if still reaching for help.

He felt like he was still being watched, not by all those eyes … but by one set. There was somebody in the room, he was sure of it. Over in the corner, watching him. He'd learnt the lesson from the other night and had already unpacked his bedside lamp, so he snapped this on, hoping to catch whoever had broken in. The light made him blink, but he forced his eyes open, not giving whoever it was a chance to escape. But, of course, there was nothing in the room. No sign of anyone—just a hangover from the dream.

No, from the *nightmare*.

Callum found his way to the bathroom and splashed water on his face, then drank some straight from the tap. The dream images were fading, but what he *was* left with—and that was even more ridiculous—was a very real sense that Ferne was in danger.

And so was he.

The following morning he'd thought about knocking on her door yet again. But what would he say? That he'd been dreaming about her, that ever since they'd met she'd never been far from his thoughts, not even at work, and now he was afraid for her but didn't know why? It was stupid, chick flick stuff at best. At worst, grounds to get him locked up in the cells back at the station.

Callum had begun walking down the corridor towards her apartment, when he did an about-turn and headed off in the direction of the stairs. *Screw it*, he thought.

But fate wasn't going to let him off that easily. When he got to the lobby, there she was, checking the letters in her mailbox: one of the lockers stacked in rows near the entrance. She was thumbing through post and didn't see him until he was almost upon her. When she did look up, she gave a start.

"Hey, sorry. I didn't mean to frighten you," he said. Callum's hands were out to steady her, but he withdrew them before they touched her; something he hadn't thought twice about the night Sam was sick. Back then it had been a whirlwind of confusion and adrenaline, now it was a chance meeting and he wasn't the one in charge.

"You didn't," she replied, the tone hard at first, then mellowing. "I was just preoccupied."

"Mail that interesting?" Callum said, then realised he hadn't meant to sound so nosey. Before she could tell him to mind his own business, he added quickly, "All I've had since I arrived has been junk. I think I've won about three million in cash and four cars."

"Lucky you."

"Ferne, listen, I've been hoping to bump into you since … well, since you did what you did for Sam."

"I did what any other nurse on the scene would have. Nothing more." Her reply was defensive, as if she thought he was accusing her of something.

"You did a lot more than that."

"I—"

"You saved that kid's life." He smiled. "That's quite a special thing."

"Callum, I told you, if that gets out I could be in real trouble."

"And I told *you*, forget it. I'm not about to tell anyone. None of the people on the floor saw anything much. Even if they did say something, I'd testify that you were just a concerned citizen giving a helping hand. How could they pull your license for that?"

"You'd do that for me?"

"Sure. Like I said, you saved his life."

She smiled back, head tilted slightly. "So, you're a cop, Callum."

"Don't hold it against me," he said. "I'm really an okay guy." *Yeah, an okay guy with a partner who sets people on fire, and is training me up to do the same.*

"Never been friends with a policeman before," she admitted.

"Is that what we are? Friends?" *What a stupid question …*

She nodded. "I hope so."

"Then how would you like to go out for a drink sometime with your new friend?" *Too much, God you're out of practice at this kind of stuff. Hell, have you ever been* in *practice?*

Ferne looked even more coy. "Maybe. We'll see." She began to walk off, up towards the lift.

"Wait, Ferne." He chased after her. "I know this is going to sound like a really strange question, but is everything okay?"

"What, because I won't give you an answer right now about a drink?"

Callum shook his head. "No, that's not what I meant."

"I just need a bit of time to mull it over, that's all."

"No, I meant generally. Is everything okay?"

She frowned. "You mean am I happy with my lot in life? A job that pays peanuts, that wears me out, and I only do because of the satisfaction of seeing people leaving St. August's Hospital hopefully feeling much better than when they went in? That's when Med-fee Cover lets us treat *anyone* at all, of course. I'm venting, aren't I? Sorry."

"It must be tough," said Callum, trying to sound sympathetic.

"It's no picnic. Must be the same with your job, though, no such thing as state funding for that, either, is there?"

"Well, no … But my particular division is kind of self-funding anyway."

"Your particular division?"

"I'm an M-forcer." *Okay, you've got past the fact you're police. Now wait for the ventriloquist act.*

"Oh … right." Ferne's eyes flitted around his face; he'd never seen this reaction before, it was more Harpo Marx than Pinocchio. When her eyes settled, she said, "I definitely haven't met one of those."

"No." He smiled again. "I'd be surprised if you had. I'm pretty new to the job, this week in fact. New place, new job. Before that I worked on normal cases back in London. At the moment I'm … as my Superintendent keeps on saying … learning the ropes."

He was aware of her backing off, eager to get to the lift. "I'd better let you get to work," she said, pressing the button.

Callum looked at his watch. "Yeah, actually I had. You take care of yourself, Ferne."

"I will," she told him, before stepping into the opening lift. "Always do." The doors closed.

All the way to the station he went over and over this encounter. He shouldn't have gone into any details about what he did; if he'd had any sense he'd have known it made people nervous. With Gibson taking folk in for questioning about talking to birds, that was hardly surprising. It was one thing to follow up people like Temple, who they knew were involved in the craft, it was another to pester people who were so obviously not. In this state of paranoia and suspicion, he couldn't blame Ferne. Maybe if she agreed to go out for that drink he'd be able to explain his reasons for wanting to work for this division. Perhaps then she'd understand. Dammit, wasn't he protecting the public just as much in his own way? Why should he have to justify it *at all*? But there had been a definite change when he'd mentioned it, a … closing of doors.

Even though he got home early enough that night, Callum didn't see Ferne leaving for her shift. Either she'd gone off early, or she'd stayed at home. Or even done a swap, which would explain why she'd been up that morning checking her mailbox.

And Callum didn't dream, but he still couldn't shake the image of all those eyes.

Nor the feeling he was being watched.

CHAPTER EIGHT

There was something different, something in the air on that fourth day.

Even before he arrived at work Callum could tell. He'd had a restless night, with no dreams again thankfully, but on waking found himself experiencing a strange mixture of apprehension and excitement. For all he knew, it would be another ordinary day of enquiries; they hadn't seen any real action since that first outing, and he'd been too stunned by Gibson's behaviour anyway to fully take anything in.

But as he got off the monorail and walked to the station, that feeling of anticipation grew, and the fact there were more officers in the car park than usual only added to his suspicions. When he buzzed himself in, Gibson met him at the door, already kitted out.

"Get changed, quick," he told his young partner. "And bring your helmet."

Two more officers ran past Callum in the corridor. "What's going on?"

"We're working on a tip-off. Plain clothes snoops have come up with an address where they reckon members of Arcana are planning their next attack."

"*What?*"

"You heard—now get your arse in gear!"

Callum had never dressed so fast. His uniform was on in seconds, belt strapped round him, vest over his shirt. When he emerged, Wallis was in the corridor talking to Gibson.

"Ah, here he is. I was just saying to Gibson, I want you to stay well back and observe on this one, McGuire. Let the men do their work, don't get in the way, but take note of everything that's going on. Because in the not-too-distant future that'll be you, lad."

Callum wanted to tell him that he was ready now, that he'd never felt more ready in his life, but he knew Wallis wouldn't listen. He was still new to this division, untried and untested. Maybe it was for the best to hang back a little, watch and keep his mouth shut.

As all the officers waited outside for transportation, Callum asked Gibson where exactly they were going. "Dunno yet, hotshot. They're keeping that very quiet. I guess we'll know when we get there. That's when we'll get the lowdown from whoever's in charge."

It wasn't long before the vans arrived—four in total—to take them to their destination. Callum and Gibson climbed in alongside half a dozen or more men, all helmeted. The back of the vehicle was lined with equipment. As their transport set off, they were assigned their weapons: Heckler & Koch HK53 or HK33 assault rifles, Browning high-powered pistols, gas and stun grenades. It wasn't the first time Callum had handled a gun—he'd done his stint as an armed response officer, which this job required—but it was still breaking new ground. He had absolutely no idea what to expect from this raid.

Looking over, he noticed that Gibson had taken something out of his pocket and was rúbbing it with his fingers. It was a yellow stone, cast in an oval. Gibson looked up and laughed. "Amber," he said. "Traditional protection against magick. You can't have too much of that when you're going up against sparkies." He slipped it beneath his vest, into the top pocket of his shirt.

The van rumbled along, jolting them from side to side. It took them at least an hour to reach their destination, which meant they were a fair way from home.

"Must be a co-ordinated effort. They've pooled all available resources on this one so they don't mess it up," Gibson said.

"Sending in the ground troops first more like, because it's too dangerous for anyone else," said another officer to their right. He had a cross and chain wrapped around his fist, and every now and again he'd kiss the cross.

"I wouldn't worry about it, Harris," said Gibson, "once those sparkies see your ugly mug coming, they'll surrender in droves."

Harris held up the hand with the cross around it, and raised his middle finger. Gibson laughed and nudged Callum. "No sense of humour these New Church of Benediction boys."

The van sat idling for a good five minutes, then at last the back doors were flung open by an officer Callum didn't recognise. "All right, out you come. Move yourself, move yourself!" He waved an arm to guide them from the vehicle and Callum saw when he clambered out that they were on a street that had been cordoned off, in quite a run-down area. Their vans plus a number of others had massed on the place; had to be about sixty or more officers there, all armed to the teeth—some holding dogs, others cradling battering blocks or hefting flamethrowers. An army. Gibson nudged him again, nodding towards one of the squad cars positioned well away from the vans. "Looks like this isn't a drill. Even the top brass are here. That's Commander Sherman Pryce," he told him.

"No," said Callum, gazing over the heads of the other troops. He could see a man sitting in the car, with two guards standing outside. "It can't be."

"Either it's him or his twin brother," Gibson said.

"All right, all right," butted in another man, a heavy-set plainclothes detective wearing a raincoat, "time for yacking later, gentlemen." Then louder, to the rest of the group: "I'm Chief Inspector Ian Cartwright of Braintree Sector, I'll be leading the raid on No. 13, Widow's Way, which is in the street running parallel to this one."

"Number 13," muttered Gibson. "Unlucky for some … but us or them?"

"I told you people to can it," shouted Cartwright. "Okay, so we have reason to believe that the coven operating in this area has definite links to Arcana. How we know this isn't your concern. What *is* your concern is that we're going to be storming that house and I want every single one of you on full alert. Got it?"

The officers told him they had.

"Good. Now, earlier on this morning—under cover of darkness—we evacuated all the people that we could from this patch without drawing too much attention to ourselves, including this street. Told them it was pest control; wasn't strictly a lie." He snorted. "Luckily, there are a fair amount of empty houses around here, including the ones on either side of Number 13. Probably why they chose it in the first place. We have snipers covering the front of 13, so *we're* going to be entering through the back gardens of these houses directly behind it, in a sort of pincer movement." Callum had seen this kind of layout before, lengthy gardens back-to-back, separated by fences. "With a bit of luck our perps shouldn't have any idea that we're coming, but they might well have someone on look-out. So if you see any movement at the windows, signal back along the line. Officers with battering blocks will move in first, covered by my armed assault units who'll be entering the back garden of Number 13 from both sides. You lot," he said, addressing the men from Callum's station, "will be bringing up the rear, leading the second wave. The rest of the men you see here will form a perimeter in case any of our marks somehow slip the net and make a run for it."

One of the officers raised a hand. "Excuse me, sir, but how many sparkies are we talking about, exactly?"

"I don't much care for that name, officer. To my mind it makes light of just how serious these criminals are. And make no mistake about it, gentlemen, these *are* hardened criminals, plotting to take innocent lives. But, to answer your question, it's not known exactly how many might be here at this precise time. We estimate it could be anywhere between five and fifteen, though, each one with Level Seven abilities or higher."

A gasp spread through the assembled officers. Callum knew the ratings system all too well, and that was pretty high. The most skilled and dangerous of magick users.

"Be prepared for any kind of transformations, flight—although if you keep them pinned down in an enclosed environment, you should be all right—energy bursts, or trying to make you see things that aren't there. Keep focused and you won't go far wrong; fire first and ask questions later. But, and this is very, very important, gentlemen, we need at least one of them alive to talk. We know a little about what they're planning, but it would be extremely useful if we could get some names out of whoever we capture. With this in mind, go for leg or shoulder shots if you can. But where absolutely necessary …" he lowered his voice, "… fry the fuckers. I lost two of my men in the Silver End incident, and I reckon it's payback time. Right, so is anyone not clear on what we're doing?"

No one spoke up.

"Good—then my men with me, to the back of these houses." He pointed left and right. "Team two, bring up the rear." Cartwright pulled out a large Browning BDA9 from the holster at his hip, and motioned for his teams to fan out.

When it came time for them to set off, Callum caught Gibson by the arm. "I thought Wallis wanted me to stay well back on this one."

Gibson gave a chuckle. "He also told you to observe. You can't do that from back here, can you? What's the matter, getting cold feet?"

"No, I …" Callum shrugged.

"Look, I felt the same my first time. Thing to remember is you're not on your own out there." Gibson patted his shoulder. "Now come on, you heard what the man said: we're the back-up."

Gibson hefted his rifle then trotted up the path of the centre house, which was directly behind 13, with the men from his station. Callum swallowed dryly, before running after him. When he caught up, he saw the house's back garden—which looked like it hadn't been mown in months—filled with armed M-forcers. A handful were scaling the tall fence at the far end, being given a leg-up by their colleagues and then quietly slipping back down on the other side: into the back garden of Number 13. Callum joined Gibson, who was crouching next to a lop-sided shed.

It wasn't long before it was their turn to go over. Gibson shouldered his weapon, put his foot in the makeshift stirrup of a bridged pair of hands, and suddenly he was gone. Callum hesitated briefly, then did the same: holding onto the wood at the top and swinging his leg over slowly. Just before dropping to the ground at the other side, he took in the sight ahead of him. The garden of Number 13 was even more unkempt, so it was perfect cover for the M-forcers who'd climbed in from either side, forming that pincer movement. Officers that were now making their way up towards the detached house. The building itself was maybe fifty years old, but looked ancient because of the repairs that needed doing. Slates were missing from the roof, and something had stained parts of the walls. The wooden framework of the windows, once painted white, had turned a putrid yellow, peeling and rotting away in places. The place looked like it had been abandoned a long time ago—the perfect location for a squat, or a base of operations for the people they were after.

Callum hit the ground. The grass came up almost to his waist but when he squatted down, it hid him completely. He pushed forwards, rifle in front of him, as the other men around him were doing, every now and again raising his head to get his bearings … though not too high. It felt like he was in some foreign jungle fighting a war, not a back garden in England. But then, he reminded himself, this *was* a war; just not the kind that's fought out in the open where you can see your opponent. Often, you wouldn't know if you were standing right next to the enemy on the street, or sitting next to them on public transport. That's why this job was so important, to protect the public. He of all people could testify to that.

Callum raised his head again and saw Cartwright, plus a handful of his men, break free of the grass. Hunched low, they headed towards the shabby green back door. Cartwright ushered two men with battering blocks before him, holding his hand flat up to signal that the rest of them should stay where they were. The men took up positions on either side of the door. Their boss gave a sharp nod and they swung into action, pounding on the barricade with the blocks. It took a couple of bashes with the heavy, flat-nosed tools and the door was down, torn free from the rotting jamb at the hinges.

At the same time Cartwright shouted, "This is the police, everyone in the house is under arrest!" and beckoned his other officers forward with a cupped hand. With his other, he levelled his pistol at the doorway.

Squinting, Callum saw a figure peering through that doorway. He couldn't be entirely sure, but he thought the person had their hands raised as they walked towards the light. It was a young man, early twenties, wearing what appeared to be a vest and shorts. Callum reasoned that he must have been in the kitchen, or even the hall, when the raid began.

"Don't shoot," Callum heard him cry, voice wavering. His eyes were wide with fright, hands shaking. Little wonder; there were several men with high-powered rifles aiming directly at him, not to mention a fierce-looking Chief Inspector with a Browning levelled at his head.

"Look out!" Callum didn't know who shouted it, couldn't even tell from which direction the warning came, but the result was immediate. These were men who were used to living on their nerves. Cartwright had even said it himself, "Fire first and ask questions later." When you were dealing with Level Sevens or higher you had no choice. And that's exactly what happened. The young man's eyes opened even wider, then his body was riddled with bullets. He danced in the doorway as if electricity was being passed through his body, arms and legs flailing before turning red, vest stained with his blood.

Then came the fire.

Flamethrowers opened up and suddenly he was ablaze. It made what happened to the lawyer Temple look tame by comparison. Callum was just glad he was some distance away this time, not close enough to smell the flesh as it cooked on his bones. The boy staggered a few feet—a bright, smoking object barely recognisable as a human being—then dropped to the ground in a burning heap.

"Davey! My Davey," came a scream from inside. It was shrill, a woman's voice, and Callum noticed another figure appear where the first one had been. She was older than the boy by a number of years, with streaks of grey in her otherwise long, dark hair. Easily old enough to be his mother. Her long dress swished as she ran towards what was left of the younger man. Another volley of bullets flew through the air, but it was difficult to see through the smoke curling upwards. Callum wanted to get a better look, and crawled sideways till he hit the fence separating this house's garden from the one on the left—then he followed it along. The rifles were still going off and from his new position he could see why.

The woman had held up her hand, a hand that was glowing bright blue, energy sparking from her fingertips. Callum's mouth hung open, but even as shocked as he was, he couldn't help thinking that the name they gave these people was wholly appropriate. The bullets were bouncing off a kind of invisible shield she'd created in front of her, the shells also sparking where they hit and ricocheted off. Her cheeks were wet with tears, her face a mask of rage: teeth clenched, lips mouthing strange incantations.

Then the light from her fingertips spread out, directed at the shooters. It hit the first and sent him flying back a good twenty metres, into more of the M-forcers that were rising from the grass. A second blasted one of the men sideways and through the fence opposite Callum; his body hung in the hole, dark blue clothes smoking. Another man was lifted straight up into the air, landing awkwardly as he fell back down again. Callum winced at the crack of bones. Yet more were simply punched backwards, as if a giant fist had pounded into them.

She stepped fully out of the doorway, but didn't look to her right in time. Cartwright was there, off to the side, pistol at her temple. The woman was aware of nothing as he fired a single shot into her cranium, Cartwright's weapon behind the protective line of her shield. It seemed to Callum that the woman's head just deflated like a punctured ball, but seconds later a wound opened up on the other side and a mixture of blood and brains coated the old door-jamb. Then her entire *body* deflated, collapsing to the ground in a heap. Cartwright nodded in satisfaction.

More officers from the first wave came out of hiding now, but as they did so there came a tinkling sound from above. Someone was smashing the windows in an upstairs room. A hand appeared and it threw what looked like a lightning bolt into the garden. This exploded near to one of the approaching men, sending him reeling sideways. There came another bolt, which landed in the middle of several M-forcers and tossed them easily into the air. Callum could smell ozone, mixed with a coppery odour.

Further lightning strikes were cast from the hand at the window, this time smaller, catching officers in shoulders, arms and legs. Cartwright and a couple of men still fit enough near the doorway ran inside the building. There were flashes of light, the crack of a pistol and the *rat-tat-tat* of machine-gun fire. Callum heard a smashing sound and looked up to see another window pane being broken, this time connected to a smaller room, possibly even the bathroom? A second hand—make that fist—poked through, just long enough to release what it had been clutching. The glowing purple sphere of energy grew as it hurtled across the garden, before exploding in the air above the troops. Droplets of purple rained down on the men, and as it touched them their clothing smouldered. The M-forcers screamed in agony as it burnt through their clothes, pulling off gloves and vests that were melting to their skin. The ground became wet with the purple water, and where it did the earth caved in, the men sinking up to their thighs and waists. Then as quickly as the garden had turned to slush it hardened around them, trapping the troops where they were.

Callum gaped at another such sphere cast directly overhead. Just as it exploded, he felt himself being dragged by the arm. He didn't struggle, didn't have time to. And when a familiar voice screamed in his ear, "Move! Inside—we have to take cover!" he did as he was ordered, finding his feet and allowing himself to be pulled towards the back door of the house. He pulled back momentarily, remembering those flashes inside when Cartwright had entered, but the purple rain left him no choice. It was like acid, eating through anything it landed on. Those trapped inside the garden couldn't move, couldn't escape. The closest one had a chain wrapped around his fist, the knuckles now protruding through the skin as he tried to kiss the crucifix: Harris.

"I said *come on!*" shouted the voice again, tugging him through the doorway, past the body of the dead woman.

Callum whirled round to face Gibson. Sweat beaded the older officer's brow below the line of his helmet. His eyes narrowed as he glanced beyond Callum at the devastation outside. "Looks like we're what's left of the second wave," he said. "Fuck!"

Callum gaped at the corridor ahead, over Gibson's shoulder. It was empty as far as he could see.

"Stay sharp," Gibson told him, raising his rifle, "and stay behind me."

They pushed themselves up against the wall, sliding along it, moving down the corridor. There was an open door to their right and Callum could see inside—into the dingy kitchen, a table knocked over in the centre. It appeared to be deserted, but Gibson was taking no chances. He edged across, toeing the door open a bit more. "Keep me covered," he called back to Callum.

Taking deep breaths, Callum trained his rifle on the kitchen door. *Keep it together. This is why you came here, this is what you wanted to do. Don't think about the men outside, block out the screams. You're here to do a job, here to—*

Gibson stormed inside, did a quick sweep of the room, then pulled back out. "Clean," he grunted, sounding mildly disappointed. They crept up the corridor, until they came to a set of stairs on their left, and another room on their right. The front door ahead of them had been peppered with bullets from the hidden snipers out front; someone had obviously tried to escape and been driven back. Maybe even killed? Though where was the body, outside?

The door to their right was closed this time. It would be the same procedure to clear that room as before, except Gibson would have to kick open the door first. He nodded to Callum, who nodded back, then he brought up his boot and aimed it at the handle. The door flew inwards and Callum gained a glimpse of a couple of armchairs before Gibson burst inside. Callum waited for him to come out again.

He didn't.

"Gibson?" he whispered. "Gibson, are you all right?"

There was no reply.

Callum bit his lip and stepped cautiously forwards, gun poised. He began walking towards the open door of the room. There was a noise from inside, a creaking sound. Callum paused, raising his rifle to shoulder height.

Then it happened.

He was aware of something—some*one*—behind him. At first he thought they must have appeared there as if … as if by magick; like one of those banned underground entertainers who popped up on stage in a puff of smoke. But later, when he had time to look back on it and reflect, Callum would realise there had been nothing extraordinary about it at all. They'd been hiding in the space under the stairs, a tiny cupboard he hadn't bothered to check because he never would've imagined anyone would be crazy enough to get inside.

But not everyone had his problem with confined spaces.

That would be when he *was able* to look back. Right now, all he could do was react, as the person there pushed him up against the wall, crushing him and shaking dust from the ceiling above. All the wind exploded from Callum's lungs and his Heckler & Koch dropped to the floor with a clatter.

It's one of them. *Arcana! And in a few seconds you'll be just like those poor bastards outside.*

No!

Callum brought his head back sharply, the helmet connecting with his attacker's face. The weight behind him suddenly gone, he spun to face whoever it was. The man was about Wallis's age and dressed in civilian clothing; but where his superior was fat, Callum's assailant was bulky. He also had a beard, and enough hair on his head that there was no need for a comb-over. In fact, there was hair everywhere: on his arms, peeping out of the top of his shirt. But there was also wetness, blood from a wound at his shoulder: the person who'd tried to flee out the front and been forced back. And there was that same angry expression on his face the woman had at the door. "Why?" shouted the bigger, older man. "Why did you kill them?"

Callum said nothing.

His voice changed, cracking, and then the tears came. "My David, my Annie. They'd done nothing to you." He took a step towards Callum.

"I … Stay back!"

"Why?" the man simply asked again, his voice softer this time.

"Because you're hurting people," Callum replied. "Because you have to be stopped."

The man's laugh was bitter. "We're hurting *no one*!"

Callum thought about the men back there on the lawn—Cartwright's men, his colleagues, Harris—and shook his head. The man took another step, almost upon Callum again. The young officer reached for his pistol, but couldn't get it out of its holster in time. The bigger man flattened him against the wall once more.

"What's … what's the use? You'll never listen," shouted the man, who was changing, growing even more hair. Growing larger as well. He was towering above Callum, a snout appearing, claws replacing fingernails on his hands. The man was turning into some kind of bear, teeth extending and growing that could rip his throat out in seconds. His clothes tore and fell away. He roared and Callum could feel the heat of his breath.

Callum flinched, then closed his eyes and prepared for the end.

It didn't come. A smattering of shots from Callum's right blasted into the bear and the oppressive weight was gone. Callum opened his eyes in time to see the body, human again and naked, twitching in its own blood. Gibson was standing at the doorway to the room he'd been exploring.

"Thanks," offered Callum, but Gibson didn't appear to hear it. He just walked over to the body and spat on it.

"Fucking animal!"

There were flashes from the second floor and Callum looked up. Even if there were no more "sparkies" down here, there were still the ones upstairs to deal with. At least two that they knew about. Gibson motioned for them to climb the stairs, so Callum trailed after his partner, drawing his pistol as he went.

The old stairs groaned under their weight, and Callum felt sure they'd give way at any moment. When they reached the top and turned, his mouth fell open again. He thought he'd seen it all outside, but this was something else. One of Cartwright's men had been pinned to the far wall, halfway up it. Arms and legs outstretched, he was held in place by manacles of pure energy. When he saw Gibson and Callum, he tried to speak, but there was a gag made from the same substance around his mouth. Callum saw another M-forcer on the landing, face down. He couldn't tell whether the man was breathing or not.

There were three rooms up here by Callum's reckoning, one on either side of them as they came up onto the landing, and one near the floating officer with its door closed. The only light was coming from both the doorways nearest to them.

Suddenly a figure sprang out from their left. It was a man, mid-twenties, with long hair, wearing a shirt and jeans. A crazed grin was spreading across his face with each stride. "Good, more M-forcer bastards!" he called out gleefully. Without a doubt Callum knew that one of the hands at the window had belonged to him. Gibson wasted no time in levelling his rifle, firing off a volley of bullets in his direction. But he didn't raise a shield as the woman had done; he just stood there and let the hot lead strike him.

Callum was amazed to see the bullets riddle the man, the rest of the clip emptied into him. Gibson waited for his target to fall. Instead, he carried on grinning. Then he ripped off his bloodstained shirt, holding it up to examine the holes that had torn through it, back and front. He screwed up the material and wiped away the blood on his torso, before tossing it to the floor. Where before there had been entry wounds, some of which you could see right through, now there was nothing. Not a mark on him. The holes had healed over completely.

"That all you got?" goaded the man.

"Nope." Gibson dropped his rifle, and tossed an incendiary grenade at him, then shoved Callum up against the wall. A blast of heat engulfed the figure. The carpet caught light and the wallpaper was seared off the walls. But when the blast cleared, the man was still standing there smirking: no burns, no blisters, not so much as a patch of red skin. He patted down his jeans, which were still smouldering.

"I'm not so easy to torch, pig," he said with a sneer. Then he raised his hand and from the fingertips white lightning danced.

"Gibson …?" Callum managed, his voice cracking.

"Get down," screamed his partner. "Get down *now!*"

Callum dived to one side as tiny shards of energy shot from the man's digits, more deadly than any bullets. It ripped through part of the banisters at the top of the stairs; most of it missed Gibson, who flung himself flat to the floor. The officer hanging from the wall was not so lucky. Eyes wide in terror, his scream was muffled as the darts embedded themselves in him. He spasmed for a few moments, then his head dropped.

"Congratulations," said the man who'd just electrocuted their colleague. "*You've* just become our way out of here. But we only need one of you ..." He pointed with his finger, first to Gibson on the floor, then Callum. "Eeny ... meeny ..."

"McGuire," cried Gibson, pointing himself.

Callum's eyebrow's knitted together. Then he saw what Gibson was trying to tell him. On the man's belt hung a small bag. Callum dived, snatching the bag before the guy could stop him.

"*No!*" he yelled, but it was too late. He turned, trying to grab it back. But Gibson was up, yanking a length of cord from his belt that already had a loop in it. With practised skill, he slipped it over the man's neck, then kicked him over the rail, winding it quickly around the wood as he did so, pulling it tight. The man dangled above the stairs, swinging from side to side, while Gibson tied off the noose.

"Who's smiling now?" he shouted down to the man who was reaching for his neck. But the strange thing was, the man *did* still have that stupid grin on his face. In fact he was laughing ... and rising up at the same time. The noose went slack as he levitated up towards them. "Shit," mumbled Gibson. "I hate it when they do that."

Gibson motioned for Callum to hand him the bag he'd snatched. Fumbling inside, he took out a stone that had markings on it. "Talisman. I thought so. Let's see how tough you are without this." The M-forcer took out his pistol and tossed the stone into the air, then let off two rounds which shattered it. The man below wailed, then cried out when Gibson turned the gun on him. This time the bullet entered the man's chest and stayed there. The wound didn't heal over, and he flopped back down, the noose tightening again. Blood dripped from the bullet-hole onto the stairs.

"Drop … drop your weapons," said a voice off to their right. It wasn't an order; it sounded more like a plea. And it was garbled. Gibson and Callum turned, to see a young woman with short, blonde hair; the other hand at the window. But her hands were full right now, holding the barely conscious body of Chief Inspector Ian Cartwright, who'd spoken the words. She was somehow controlling him, because he had his own gun in his mouth, finger on the trigger.

"Do as the man says," she told them, attempting to sound tough, yet she was far from convincing. "Or he'll kill himself."

"Look, you're not going anywhere," Gibson told her. "More police are coming, you might as well surrender."

"Surrender?" she said as if she'd never heard the word before. "What, so you can take me off to one of your 'installations' and question me? I'd rather die right here, right now."

"Your decision," Gibson snapped back. He raised his smoking pistol.

She shook the Chief Inspector, and he shoved the gun that bit further into his mouth, saliva dribbling down the sides. "I mean it! I'll get him to shoot. It'd be a pleasure. He … he killed …" She couldn't finish the sentence.

"So? Go ahead. The poor sod knew the risks when he joined the force. Every one of us does. But we're willing to give up our lives to get rid of scum like you!" Gibson held the pistol at arm's length now, aiming straight at her.

"Gibson," said Callum. "Gibson, hold on a minute."

"Shut up."

Gibson's finger tightened on the trigger. The woman closed her eyes and she muttered something under her breath. Gibson's gun changed shape, lengthened and coiled around his hand, then his arm. What had been the barrel seconds ago now hissed and blobbed out a forked tongue. Gibson looked down at the snake, and shivered. "Christ!" He flung it to the floor immediately before it could sink its fangs into him. The viper slithered out of reach before transforming back into a pistol.

Cartwright suddenly snapped awake—it was as if the woman couldn't concentrate on two things at the same time, and had lost her grip on his mind. He pulled the gun free and wrenched himself from her grip.

Callum caught the change in expression on her face, from someone relatively in control to total fear. Cartwright was levelling his weapon at her, shouting for her to freeze. She pulled out a knife and for a moment Callum thought she was going to try and fight Cartwright with it. Then he saw what she really had in mind and ran towards her. She drew the blade across her throat, digging deep into the flesh, making sure she cut the jugular. Callum made it over just in time to catch her, hoping he could stem the bleeding. But it was useless, the blood was pumping out too fast. She whispered something; another incantation? No, as he held his ear closer to her face she said one word: "Arcana."

Then she died.

"Well, that's just great! That's just fucking great!" Cartwright barked. "*None* of them left alive, nobody left to question."

"Sir," said Gibson. "I don't think that's strictly true."

"What?"

"Her eyes kept flicking over there."

"Over where?"

Gibson nodded. "Towards that closed door."

He thought for a second. "Well spotted, officer …"

"Gibson."

"Officer Gibson."

He wouldn't be saying that if he'd heard what Gibson said a minute ago, thought Callum. *That he was prepared to let the man kill himself.*

Cartwright wiped his pistol on his trouser leg, then began walking up the length of the landing. Gibson did the same, picking up his weapon as he went, stepping over the bodies of the M-forcers there, the second one having dropped off the wall now that the spell had run its course. The two men stood outside the door, guns at the ready. Cartwright held up three fingers, then folded one down, then another. When there were no more fingers, Gibson kicked in the door.

"Jesus," Callum heard Cartwright whisper.

"You can say that again," Gibson added.

Callum left the body of the blonde woman and rose. He rushed over to Cartwright and Gibson in the doorway, not quite able to believe what he saw when he got there. Out of everything he'd witnessed that morning—the things he could never, ever forget—this surprised him the most.

There, inside the room, and inside a circle of crystals that had been laid on the floor, were three people, two of which were children. The little boy, only about five years of age, was crying. The girl was closer to eleven … and had her mother's blonde hair. She was standing with her arms around the lad, holding him, trying desperately not to cry herself.

Which left the other person inside that protective circle.

Ironically the baby in the cot was the only one, it seemed, who was not in tears.

CHAPTER NINE

They needed special drilling and cutting equipment—twice blessed—to get through the circle, so strong was the field around the children and baby.

Within minutes of finding them, more M-forcers had stormed the house, Cartwright asking where the fuck they had been earlier. They swept the building from top to bottom, finding nothing but old spell books, potions and ingredients, which were all bagged and taken away. Wider sweeps of the area were being conducted with those trained sniffer dogs, but it seemed unlikely anyone from that morning's siege had escaped.

Siege? thought Callum. *It had been more like an out and out battle!* Looking through one of the back windows, the one the blonde witch had used to cast her purple rain spell, he could see the devastation in the garden: smoking holes that looked like small meteors had landed, men still being cut out of the earth and treated for severe burns. They were lucky the cost hadn't been higher, that no one had been killed. The felled man on the landing had still been alive—albeit in a comatose state—and even the officer struck by the energy darts had survived, just; he was now in a critical condition in hospital.

But hadn't they themselves drawn first blood? The young man in the doorway, half-naked, shot and torched by trigger-happy officers.

Who knows why that warning had been shouted, or what might have happened if it hadn't; would things have gone any differently at all? Then the woman, probably the mother, shot in the head by Cartwright.

"I mean it, I'll get him to shoot," the blonde witch had said, talking about the Chief Inspector. *"It'd be a pleasure. He … he killed …"*

Who? Her mother, her aunty? Someone she loved and cared about, definitely. If they hadn't been related, then they were all as close *as* family. But the little girl was definitely hers. The child had the same face, the same hair.

What would any mother do to protect her daughter, her family?

Callum squeezed his eyes shut. No, he couldn't allow himself to think like that. Had to remember what had really happened here today, how many injured. Remember Harris as he kissed his crucifix.

"You all right?" Gibson asked from behind him.

"I will be," Callum said.

"That was good teamwork with the talisman back there … partner." He clapped him on the shoulder. "Wallis will be proud."

"Have they got the kids out yet?" Callum enquired, turning.

"Almost."

"I want to be there when they do."

Gibson smiled. "You and everyone else in a three-mile radius. I hear even Sherman Pryce is coming to check them out."

"What's going to happen to them?"

"Why're you so concerned?" Gibson frowned. "Oh, right, I get it … the whole orphan thing. Look, don't worry, they'll be taken care of. But first …"

"But first, what?" Callum allowed his voice to rise just a little too much, though Gibson appeared to ignore it.

"Well, we need information from them." Gibson didn't bat an eyelid.

Callum heard the mother's voice again. *"What, so you can take me off to one of your 'installations' and question me? I'd rather die right here, right now."*

"For God's sake, they're just kids."

"They're not what you think," Gibson warned him. "They might be children but they're still sparkies. Still Arcana, for all we know. They breed all that shit into them early."

"They're just kids," Callum repeated.

"They're *dangerous!*" Gibson made to walk off back onto the landing, but Callum grabbed his arm. "What?" Callum reached into Gibson's vest and felt around. "Hey … hey stop, that tickles. What the hell are you doing, McGuire?"

He pulled out the amber stone and held it up. Gibson looked at it, then at Callum.

"Yeah, so what?"

"So what's the difference between this and that talisman *he* used back there?" Callum nodded his head to indicate the man still hanging from the banister rail.

"What're you talking about? There's a world of fucking difference. This," he said, snatching back the amber, "is for protection."

"So was his. Protection against *us*."

Gibson didn't answer, just turned away and walked out of the door. It might have been five or ten minutes before Callum heard the voices on the stairs, men's boots on the landing. He looked out to see an entourage accompanying Sherman Pryce, surrounding him as best they could, like a rock star being delivered to a concert. There was the minutest of gaps and the man himself turned, looking in Callum's direction. Their eyes locked. Pryce paused and the whole entourage paused with him. Callum stared back; he couldn't shake the feeling that they'd met before. Sure, he knew what Pryce looked like—everyone did—but this was more than that. For the briefest of moments, Callum was certain Pryce felt it as well. Then the moment passed and Pryce's bodyguards led him down the landing to the room at the far end.

Callum followed, but couldn't get anywhere near the doorway because of the guards. He could hear what was being said, though.

"… need to ship them out as soon as possible," Sherman was saying.

"Of course." That was Cartwright.

"And you must be … Grayson?" Pryce said.

"Gibson, sir," replied Callum's partner with a nervous lilt in his voice.

"Good work. *Excellent* work, in fact."

"I wasn't alone," Gibson told Pryce.

"Ah yes. Where is McGuire?" asked Cartwright.

That was his cue. Callum pushed past the guards, telling them he was the man in question, forcing his way back into this small room. There were still a couple of techies inside with the equipment they'd used to get inside the circle, but the crystals themselves were now gone. Instead, Cartwright, Gibson and Pryce encircled the three youngsters, the older two now on their knees. As Callum looked more closely, he saw that what appeared to be padded mittens had been placed on the boy's and girl's hands. Around their wrists were chained handcuffs, the kind reserved for the most heinous of criminals. In addition, their mouths had been taped over with black duct tape. Thankfully, they'd spared the baby in the cot all this, reasoning that it couldn't form words yet or conduct magic through its fingertips. The children looked up at Callum with doleful eyes.

"I was just saying, good work," Pryce broke in. "*All* of you, good work."

Callum looked at him again. "Sir … is that really necessary?" He pointed to the chains and gags.

He thought he saw the corners of Pryce's mouth raise, just slightly. "Oh yes."

"You'll have to excuse McGuire, Commander. He's new to the job," Gibson explained.

"Indeed," Pryce replied, looking Callum up and down.

"It's like I explained to him before, they're dangerous."

"They're Arcana." Pryce practically spat out the word.

"They're children," Callum whispered under his breath, but Pryce heard him.

"Don't be deceived so easily, Officer … McGuire, wasn't it?" Pryce walked over to the blonde-haired girl and, bending, placed his gloved hand on her shoulder. Callum could see the terror in her eyes. "They have the potential to become even more powerful than those you fought today. Have more than likely already been trained up to a

Level Two, perhaps even Three or Four? Wouldn't you concur, Chief Inspector?"

Cartwright nodded his head curtly. Callum got the impression that if he'd just suggested that the children were in fact hallucinations brought about by stress he would have agreed.

Callum bit the inside of his lip. "So what happens to them now?"

Pryce laughed, stroking the girl's blonde hair. "They'll be taken to The *Penitent*-iary." He emphasised the first bit deliberately.

Callum had heard about The Penitentiary. Nobody knew exactly where it was, or at least nobody on his clearance level, but Pryce certainly did. After all, it was he who'd founded the place. The Penitentiary was the primary facility for the incarceration, interrogation and expiration of those with magickal abilities. When he thought about it, he would have expected no less for those "suspected" of being Arcana. But children …

Still under Pryce's close scrutiny, he risked asking, "And then?"

"Then they will be asked a series of questions about their group. Who else is involved and where we might find them."

"And if they don't know?"

"Officer McGuire!" snapped Cartwright. "You forget your place."

Gibson had his head down and was shaking it.

Pryce rose and held up his hand to indicate that it was all right. "I like an officer who takes an interest in the system," he said, half-smiling. It was a chilling sight; like he wasn't used to it at all and hadn't the first clue how to make it look real. "They will come to no harm, if that's what you're thinking."

"I want to go with them," Callum demanded, the words tumbling out before he'd had a chance to check himself.

Gibson's head snapped back up, a look of complete shock on his face. Cartwright's eyebrows were raised in surprise. Nobody ever spoke to Sherman Pryce that way—at least nobody they'd ever heard of. Which meant nobody who'd ever stuck around for very long.

Pryce was silent for a few moments. He closed his eyes as if communing with a higher being. When he snapped them open again, he said, "Very well. I think you've earned that right, Officer McGuire. They *are* your prisoners, when all's said and done."

Gibson and Cartwright exchanged glances. Now they could see Pryce wasn't going to order Callum's immediate termination—from the force—they wanted in. And Pryce knew it.

"Of course the invitation extends to Chief Inspector Cartwright and Officer Grayson." Gibson opened his mouth to correct him, but swiftly closed it again. "Look on it as my way of saying thank you for what you've achieved here today. You might have saved countless lives with your courage." Pryce's gaze lingered on Callum a fraction too long, then he swept towards the door, ordering three of his men to bring the captives and to take the utmost care when handling them. "We leave for The Penitentiary in ten minutes," he called back.

Suddenly Gibson, Callum and Cartwright were the only ones still left in the room, all struck dumb by Pryce's words. Then they raced through the door, not one of them willing to miss out on this trip to the fabled Penitentiary.

CHAPTER TEN

The old man knew he would have visitors long before he heard the footfalls approaching. They echoed down the corridor to his ears, and he blinked, the lids closing over his milky white eyes. The cards were positioned to his right in a stack and he patted them comfortingly. They had been good to him over the years, allowing him to pull back the curtain, to unlock the mysteries of past, present and future. Both his mother and father had possessed the ability to read the cards, which meant its strength was two-fold inside him. The cards allowed him to channel his gift. It was what had led them so far down this road, and what would lead them to its inevitable conclusion.

The footsteps stopped and a familiar excited and frightened breathing took its place.

"Come inside, Gavin. I have been expecting you."

The young man entered, almost bumping into a candle holder to his left. Even with the bonus of eyesight, some people just couldn't see what was right in front of them. "Master? Master I—"

As he so often did, the old man held up his hand to silence the boy. "I know what you are about to say. I have seen it, like everything else. Just as I know we're not alone in this room today. Why don't you show yourself, Michael."

Gavin looked around but saw nothing. Then a pair of eyes lit up the shadowy corner, flickering and reflecting the gas-lamp's glare. A bearded man stepped out of the gloom, the curve of his jaw and curls of his hair catching the light. He was in his mid-thirties, and so the old man knew that Gavin would be in awe of him. Anyone over the age of twenty-one was a veteran to his young servant.

"Master Unwin," said Michael, not appearing surprised that he'd been discovered.

"You are always welcome here, you know that. There's never any need to spy," Unwin told him. "Although I know you often do."

"I wasn't spying, I was …" He couldn't finish his sentence, so he changed the subject. "You're aware of what's happened, I take it."

Unwin nodded. "Just as I was saying to Gavin, who ran all the way here to inform me of the situation."

"Then you also know what we have to do?" Michael came further into the centre of the room.

"Yes. We wait."

Michael's eyebrows knitted together. "Wait? For what? For the M-forcers to come? For every single one of us to be slaughtered just like David, Annie, Ben. Like Rhea and Jez? We must warn people, we—"

"*We* will wait, Michael." There was a finality to those words, but the bearded man persisted.

"It was bad enough that Victor was taken. That Ferne put us all in danger … But now this!"

"Everything is so black and white to you, isn't it?" Unwin said. "She saved a child's life."

"She upset the balance. She exposed herself!" Michael shouted. "To him, to the fair-haired policeman. He was there this morning, you know. He's partly the reason why they now have the children. We should do something, try to rescue them, warn the other members of Arcana."

Unwin shook his head. "We wait."

Michael clenched his fists. "You know what they will do to them?"

The old man didn't speak.

"And if they discover the truth about the baby, what then?"

"Michael, I have seen the future, but I cannot prevent it from happening. Events must play out the way they are supposed to. So it has been foretold."

"What, the end of us all?"

Gavin watched this exchange like it was a spectator sport. Both Michael and Unwin seemed to have forgotten he was even there.

Unwin picked a card from the deck and turned it over. The Wheel of Fortune; the card that indicated fate and events beyond human control. "It is all in here."

Michael took a step up to the table, teeth gritted, and swept the deck of cards aside with his hand, sending them scattering everywhere. "After all these years of persecution, it is time we acted! Took the fight to them!"

The old man glared at him with those white orbs of his, seeing nothing yet everything. Michael held the gaze as long as he could, then had to look away, shaking his head.

"I think you should go now," said Unwin, pulling a face like the words had soured his mouth. "You have worn out the welcome I gave to you."

Michael retreated. "Perhaps I should." Then his form seemed to shimmer, taking on a glow. He became translucent almost, as he walked right through the table like a ghost. Gavin put his hands up to ward the man away, but Michael simply passed through the youth as well. Gavin turned, but already Michael had vanished.

Unwin sat back in his chair and let out a deep sigh. His servant rushed over and began to pick up the cards that were on the floor.

"Thank you," Unwin said to him.

As he was on the ground rescuing the tarot deck, Gavin finally plucked up the courage to ask, "Master, is what he said right? Is this the end of us all?"

The old man's smile was bittersweet, as he took one of the cards from the boy. It was The Star. "What if it is, young Gavin? Do the cards not teach us that after every end comes a new beginning?"

Gavin looked petrified, so the old man put down the card, laid a hand on his shoulder and patted it gently. "Do not worry, my faithful friend. Things will not work out in quite the way Michael thinks." Then the old man looked up towards the ceiling. "The Universe has a few tricks of its own up its sleeve."

CHAPTER ELEVEN

Callum and Gibson rode in the back of one of Pryce's trucks, while a blindfolded Chief Inspector Cartwright journeyed with Pryce himself in his black chauffeur-driven car behind tinted windows.

There were four of Pryce's personal guards in the truck with them, plus the children. The baby was being cradled by a female techie they'd commandeered for the purpose. Callum was seated opposite the little blonde girl, who continued to look at him with those huge, pleading eyes. A couple of times Gibson had clicked his fingers at the side of Callum's head, frightened he was being hypnotised by her.

"You want to watch that," his partner told him. "It's how they get to you."

But it was nothing of the sort. The girl wasn't putting him into some kind of trance, merely begging him with her eyes to help. When Callum glanced over at the boy all he could see was a reflection of himself at that age: a snivelling little kid, feeling sorry for himself because the Universe had shit all over him and left him alone. Except Callum had been given a home, and something he could believe in. Something he *still* believed in … didn't he? It had also given him purpose and a reason for doing what he was doing. Callum couldn't help wondering if this poor wretch would be quite so fortunate;

whether what had been done to him could be undone and he could live a normal, happy life. What kind of people dragged kids into this in the first place, anyway? What had they been thinking?

Maybe they had no choice? What else were they supposed to do with them, when they themselves were being hunted? Callum put those thoughts out of his mind: they were dangerous, especially for an Enforcement Officer.

The truck rattled along, taking them at least half as far again as they'd come that morning. It was a good thing Pryce had cleared their jaunt with Wallis or he'd wonder where they were. Not that he would be getting *any* of his men from that morning back in a hurry. Again, they couldn't see anything of the outside world during the journey, nothing that would give away where they were heading. The Penitentiary was secret for a reason, and Pryce definitely intended it to remain that way.

Finally, just as it seemed they were never going to arrive, the vehicle pulled up. But they weren't inside yet. A flap at the front of the truck slid open and the driver—another of Pryce's men—shouted, "We're at the gate. Security check."

The back doors of the van were opened from the outside and two men dressed in body armour peered inside then relieved them of their weapons, before giving them the all-clear. The doors shut and Callum imagined a set of gigantic gates opening, taking them inside a compound before the van stopped for good this time.

When he was allowed out, Callum found it was pretty much how he'd imagined it. The open space of the yard was enclosed by a huge fence, almost certainly electric. Whether it was to keep people out or in, Callum didn't have a clue, but he guessed it suited both purposes. Behind them was a building low to the ground, with only one storey. It was long, though, and Callum figured it went back quite a way. It would also probably be like a maze inside, even if you knew your way around. Pryce's car was parked not far away and the driver had got out to open the door. Cartwright emerged first, pulling off his blindfold, taking in his surroundings and whistling—suitably impressed. Then came Pryce, smoothing down his uniform.

The rest of his men were climbing out of the back of their truck, bringing the children with them. A team of people in light green jumpsuits were already making their way across the yard with instruments and silver cases. One of them was wheeling a plastic tank, like the kind premature babies rely on. They began to look the girl and the boy over, tilting their heads this way and that, squeezing limbs. A young man relieved the techie of the baby and placed it inside the clear tank, where it rolled around, oblivious to what was going on around it.

Callum tapped one of them on the shoulder. "What are you doing?"

The man in green appeared bemused, then looked over at Pryce who nodded his okay for an answer. "Checking they're all right, that they haven't sustained any injuries. Head traumas, that kind of thing."

"And?" asked Pryce.

"They all look healthy enough, but we'll have to do more tests of course to make sure," replied the man.

Callum relaxed slightly. This wasn't what he'd been expecting at all.

"Not quite as barbaric as the rumours would have you believe, eh?" said Pryce.

"See?" said Gibson. "The kids'll be fine with them."

The younger officer watched as the medical team took the children away, the little girl looking back over her shoulder at him, eyes still pleading.

"You'll see them again later," Pryce promised. "In the meantime, allow me to show you around a little." He waved his hand like a circus ringmaster introducing his show. "Welcome all of you … to The Penitentiary."

They were taken in through a door at the side, which had a crew manning it from behind security glass. Everyone was checked *again*, even Pryce, and they all had to pass through what looked like a metal detector.

"Hey, I've read about these," Gibson said, nudging Callum, "they pick up on magick residue. There was some talk a while back of bringing out hand-held ones, but the cost was too high or something." His partner was like a kid in a natural history museum gawking at all the cool dinosaur skeletons.

Callum shrugged and stepped through. The alarms immediately went off. Several guns were suddenly swung in his direction. Pryce gestured for the guards to back off slightly, but they didn't lower their weapons.

"These men have just been involved in an ... incident where Level Seven enchantments or above were used," he explained. "I can vouch for them." The guards nodded, then silently withdrew.

So that's what it had been, Callum thought to himself, *an incident? Not a skirmish or battle at all. Just an incident.* To Pryce, maybe, who had been a good distance from the action.

The Commander waved Gibson and Cartwright through, alarms still sounding, then one of the crew turned off the machine. "Now then, if you'd follow me," said Pryce. He took them up a long corridor, under close scrutiny from CC-TV cameras, to another set of doors: this time constructed from iron bars. Pryce took out a key from his pocket and undid the lock. "Technology is all well and good, but ..."

"But sometimes the old methods are the best," Gibson finished for him, then looked at Callum.

Pryce nodded. "Quite so."

Passing through these, into the inner part of The Penitentiary, they walked alongside glass windows. Callum guessed they were all reinforced, but they were also webbed with a metal grid. They afforded the visitors a view of a quadrangle outside. A number of shiny metal booths were lined up in the centre of the square. Torpedo-shaped, they looked like missiles on a launch pad ready to fire, except they had clear frontispieces. Pryce caught Callum staring at them. "Waste disposal units," he said, grinning.

Cartwright laughed at Callum's puzzled expression. "Less dangerous than burning at the stake, son. Microwaves, am I right?"

Pryce nodded. "Quicker than incineration, too. Times do move on, whether we like it or not."

Now Callum understood. The chambers were just big enough to fit a person inside.

"Only for the more … extreme cases. People we can do nothing with who still pose a threat to others, for example those responsible for the death of your own men at Silver End." Pryce turned to Cartwright, who now stopped laughing. "They ended up in there. The units *are* sanctified," he added, looking at Callum, as if that made them somehow more palatable. Their superior pivoted and continued walking up the corridor. Callum was left gaping at the units. He closed his eyes and tried to imagine what it might be like inside one of them, how someone trapped in there might press their hands up against the glass, if they were able, pounding on it as the temperature rose. And then—

He jumped as Gibson laid a hand on his shoulder. "Come on," he said, pulling Callum by the arm, "catch up."

Pryce and Cartwright were waiting for them at the bend in the hall, below more CC-TV cameras, ready to make a left turn. On either side, Callum could see doors to rooms that were shut away from sight. "Cells," Pryce explained, "to house the prisoners here at The Penitentiary." He paused at one of the doors, pressing his hand to a screen at the side. A red line scanned the palm and then flashed green. Heavy gears whirred inside and there was a hissing sound as the seal on the door was broken.

Callum, Cartwright, and even Gibson held back, but Pryce assured them it was all right and pushed open the door. Cartwright stepped in first, followed by Gibson, then Callum last. A camera swivelled round above the entranceway, training on them. The room was bright, and very clean: that was the first thing which struck Callum.

It was also uninhabited.

"You didn't think I was going to bring you into a cell that had a prisoner in it, did you?" Pryce shook his head. "Too much of a security risk, I'm afraid."

Callum took more of the room in. There was a bed with one sheet, a small toilet, a sink and a window, covered again with that same mesh from the corridor.

"But, as you can see," Pryce continued, waving his hand around, "the facilities are no worse than a standard prison. Better than most, I'd say. The inmates are given three square meals a day while under our supervision, and allowed to clean themselves daily. They are under constant surveillance. But then *everything* is here. Probably not quite what you were expecting to see, am I correct, Officer McGuire?"

Callum had to admit, the facilities did seem humane.

"Too good for pieces of shit like them," mumbled Cartwright. Gibson nodded his agreement.

"We *do* live in a civilised society," Pryce reminded them, but somewhere, deep down, Callum knew the man concurred with Gibson and Cartwright. He led them back out of the cell and locked the door again. Then took them down to the far end of the corridor, turned left, then right, then left again. Callum mentally patted himself on the back for guessing correctly; the place *was* like a maze. "You're going to see now where we interrogate the prisoners and suspects," Pryce called over his shoulder. "We have trained teams of psychologists and psychiatrists on hand during all the questioning sessions, but for everyone's safety the subjects have to remain cuffed, drugged, and under close scrutiny by armed guards. I'm sure you understand the importance of not taking their ... talents for granted, especially after what you witnessed this morning."

Pryce entered another room, this one unlocked, and nodded hello to a handful of men and women in white coats seated next to a window. No, not a window. Callum recognised the basic set-up of an interview room: the two-way mirror allowing these people to see what was going on next door, but not allowing those inside to see them. The people in white were making notes on a subject. Callum stared through the mirror to see two people seated at opposite ends of a table. One, a man with dyed hair, wore a dark suit not unlike Pryce's, and was flicking a switch on a recorder. The other was a man in his late forties perhaps, with a patchy beard and silvery locks, strapped to his chair with an I.V. drip attached to his wrist. He had a glazed expression on his face, but certainly wasn't incoherent. Two guards stood in the corners of the interview room that Callum could see, high-powered Colt Commando rifles by their sides, poised to bring them up and fire if necessary. They'd take no chances, as Pryce had explained, with a prisoner who could throw thunderbolts from his fingers or cause you to choke with a single incantation.

"This one has been with us a few months," Pryce told them. "A fascinating study, and stubborn with it. He has held out for quite some time, even when drugged. But we're beginning to get through to him, we think."

"You're safe now, Victor, you know that," the man with dyed hair was saying, his voice like ice water. "You're away from that place where they held you captive. Back with your friends. Friends like me."

Victor nodded. "Yes, I'm safe."

Callum drew closer to the mirror, watching the conversation closely.

"Remember … remember we were talking about the house on Widow's Way? I was going to visit, say hello to some more of our friends?"

The older man nodded again.

Callum let out a gasp. It was this man's information that had led to the raid. He'd given the name of a street, a house number, in one of these sessions and they'd been the ones to follow up on it.

"Well, they said to tell you they need to get in touch with the others. They have something they need to say to them. A warning." The interrogator leaned back, waiting for a response. "Where are the others? Where can I find more of our members? The members of Arcana?"

Victor seemed to be having more of a problem with that, perhaps something in the tone of the man's voice signalled that this was no friend. He struggled against the leather straps on the arms of the chair.

"Where, Victor? Where are they?"

Victor shook his head.

"But they're in danger, *so* much danger."

The interviewee struggled more forcefully, backwards and forwards in the chair. "No …" he moaned. "No more."

"Tell me where, Victor. Then I can save them, just like I saved you."

"No … *not* safe! *Not* safe!" shouted Victor. He was almost tipping the chair over.

Callum looked up at the other people scrutinising, enjoying the spectacle of seeing the man squirm.

Dye Job sighed. "You're placing them all in great jeopardy, Victor, can't you see that?"

"From you. From you!" Victor repeated, and Callum could have sworn his eyes looked a little less glazed. He rocked once more and his interrogator pressed a button on the table. Within seconds, two men entered and injected Victor with something. His head slumped forward, chin touching his chest, spittle running down over his beard.

"And it was going so well," said Pryce. "But I did say he was stubborn. We'll question him some more later."

Victor was removed from the room, the suited man following behind the doctors and guards. Similarly, the men and women in white coats in the observation room picked up their clipboards and left.

"Well, I trust that you've enjoyed seeing at least some of our operation here today," Pryce said. "You definitely earned it. Now, I have a great deal of work to do in the aftermath of this morning's activities. I'm sure you do, too. I'll see to it that you're dropped off at your respective station houses."

Callum frowned. "What about the children?"

"What *about* the children?"

"Will you be drugging them to get information?" Callum persisted.

Pryce hesitated before answering. "The children will be taken care of, as I said before. If they can tell us anything, that's good news. If not … All I can say is that not a hair on their head will be harmed."

"You said we could see them before we left."

"McGuire." Gibson said his name as a warning to hold his tongue.

"No, no, he's right. I did say that." Pryce bid them follow him, up and down more corridors, which felt like they were doubling back on themselves, until they arrived at what looked like a small infirmary. The people in green who had taken the children had gone, replaced by a team wearing blue scrubs. The baby was still in its isolation tank at the far end, with two members of the team flitting around it. The boy and girl were on opposite sides of the room, in beds, their eyes closed, curled up under the covers. Monitors had been attached to them that showed their heartbeats and blood pressure. If he hadn't known better, Callum would have sworn they were just ordinary kids asleep in any hospital ward.

"They've been sedated, of course," Pryce told him, "at least until we have a chance to assess how much of a threat they are." Seeing them like this, Callum found it hard to imagine they could be any kind of threat at all. "But they're being well looked after, as you can see."

Callum and Pryce's definition of "looked after" obviously differed wildly.

"Who knows, perhaps in time they might even be rehabilitated. They could end up in a state-run orphanage."

Callum looked directly at Pryce, but said nothing. Did the man know? How could he? It was just a coincidence that he'd mentioned the place of Callum's childhood. The place where it had been drummed into him to hate the people he'd been fighting that morning, the people these children belonged to. If Pryce was right, they could end up hating their own kind in years to come.

"Now, if there's nothing else …" Sherman Pryce prompted. Callum shook his head slowly. "Then allow me to accompany you to the exit."

Pryce led once more, and they followed: Cartwright, Gibson and, finally, Callum. But he risked one last look at the boy and girl, and over at the baby in its isolation tank. Then he walked out of the room, letting the door swing shut behind him.

CHAPTER TWELVE

The freeze frame threw back an image of that look. It had captured the scene perfectly and remained fixed for the last few hours.

The camera in the corner of the room transmitted it as clear as crystal. In fact the cameras throughout The Penitentiary had tracked his every movement, the line feeding not only to the security personnel at the prison, but also directly to a bank of monitors here, where it could not be traced. He'd sat and watched as Sherman Pryce had taken the three men through the security checks, past the execution chambers, into the cell and observation room. To end up back with the children they'd taken captive that morning. He'd studied the young man's face, listened to everything that had been said with great interest. Now he sat back and examined the resigned look on that same face.

Callum McGuire might have been leaving the children behind in The Penitentiary, but they would still be on his mind for some time to come.

Too much emotion. Too much compassion. Too much empathy. He had hoped that they'd purged most of it from his system at the orphanage. God knows the boy had been given enough reason, enough motivation to become what he eventually became even before that. But this … what would you call it, lapse? Not a good sign.

If the reports from the Widow's Way operation had come in on their own, he would have seen it as cause to feel jubilant. McGuire had apparently acted bravely, aiding his partner in dispatching three members of Arcana that were in the house: one shot, one hung *and* shot, the other forced to take her own life. It wasn't a bad day's work, particularly the first time out as back-up for a major swoop. True, he hadn't expected the officer to be placed directly in the line of fire—had expressly given orders for him not to be—but the situation had called for it, and McGuire had not been found wanting. In fact, he should be commended for it.

But what had followed at The Penitentiary had disturbed the viewer, making him shift about, ill at ease in the leather chair. Maybe McGuire should have been transferred earlier from London? Perhaps he'd spent too long dealing with ordinary crime and it had infected him somehow, diluted his spirit.

No, it was McGuire himself who had put in for the move; he still hankered after the position he'd dreamed about as a boy. All the wait had done was stoke his fire. So why all this? Why the doubt?

The children had thrown him off-guard, that was all. Clouded his judgement. McGuire saw parallels to his own childhood when what he should really have been seeing was the spawn of Arcana, to be used, to have information plucked from them by any means necessary. Christ, if this was McGuire's reaction to the toned down version of The Penitentiary, imagine what he would say if he saw what *really* went on there! Realised what a sick fuck Sherman Pryce actually was.

He knew that man had only been following orders by taking McGuire to the facility. When put on the spot, Pryce had been given no option but to say yes to McGuire's request. What else was he supposed to do? And to leave the children's fate to the young M-forcer's imagination would only have made things worse. At least now he'd seen them being treated, could tell himself they'd be okay. Then get on with the job, learning from Gibson and Wallis. Getting back that desire to purge mankind of their enemies for all time. This had been a minor hiccup … not even a test.

The real test was yet to come.

Nero Stark rubbed his closely-cropped beard as he stared at the face of Callum McGuire. He saw big things in the young man's future, very big things. When the time was right, the boy would make the right decision, he was sure of that.

Wasn't he?

Before today there would have been no doubt whatsoever. Now there was a nagging voice whispering in his ear.

What if he fails? What if he's not strong enough to do what must be done? What if he betrays everything he stands for? And, by that same token, betrays you*?*

The answer was simple, though Nero didn't like to contemplate it. At that point Callum McGuire would have to be destroyed. Nero Stark would personally see to it. He would simply be too much of a threat.

Nero shifted about in the chair again, looking for something, *anything* in the young Enforcement Officer's eyes that revealed the man he knew him to be. But, as before, he came away with no firm conclusions. Nero would wrestle with this until he knew the answer one way or the other. Until the choice had been made.

And the time was coming.

If it wasn't already here.

CHAPTER THIRTEEN

No sooner had Callum and Gibson arrived back at their station and filed their reports than Wallis had sent them home, though not without quizzing them about the Penitentiary.

Callum could see the gleam in Gibson's eyes as he related what they'd seen, embellishing on certain facts for the sake of theatricality. After what had happened that morning, they'd returned to a hero's welcome, and the invite to that famous prison by Sherman Pryce himself had sealed the deal.

"You two should feel very privileged," Wallis told them. "It's not everyone who gets to see where Arcana prisoners end up."

"Yeah, we do. Don't we?" Gibson said, nudging his partner.

Callum gave a slow nod of his head.

"As for you, young McGuire," said Wallis, beaming, "you've lived up to all our expectations, I reckon, and then some. Now go and get some rest; you've earned it."

Throwing a half-hearted smile back, Callum headed off in the direction of the lockers, leaving Gibson and Wallis to chat more about the day's events.

On the monorail home, he slumped against the window, watching the city as it passed by. When they went through a tunnel, he could have sworn he'd seen the reflections of the boy and girl from that house, from the Penitentiary, staring back at him accusingly—their mouths covered in tape, hands bound in chains. They had that same terrified expression on their faces. Tears were still tracking down the boy's cheeks. When the train emerged from the tunnel, the reflections were gone. Callum checked behind him and saw only the other passengers on seats.

What was wrong with him? He'd done a good thing today, helped to protect the people out there, in that city, even the people on this monorail. He was on the side of the good guys, doing something he'd always dreamed about since he was a child himself. So why did he feel like shit? Why did leaving those kids back there feel like the wrong thing to do? Callum pictured Pryce running his hand through the blonde girl's hair, then imagined him gripping it more tightly, winding it round and round in his fist, yanking her head back until the cords in her neck were stretched taut.

Callum shook his head. Thoughts like that could drive you mad. He remembered what Gibson had told him on his first day: "You start to question yourself in this job, you make mistakes. Those mistakes get yourself and everyone around you killed."

The children would be taken care of, Pryce had promised him that.

But they wouldn't be all alone in the world right now if it wasn't for you, a little voice in his head reminded him. *You, Gibson and Cartwright. You murdered their family.*

Another shake of the head.

They were Arcana, a second voice told the first, *and Arcana must be stopped. They're killing people.* They're *the murderers.*

But now, as they passed through a second tunnel, Callum saw the man from the house in the black reflection, the one who'd sprung out of the space beneath the stairs. "We're hurting *no one*!" he'd shouted. It was a weird thing to say when everybody knew what Arcana had done in the past, the people they'd sacrificed for their cause. They were terrorists, pure and simple. Were the children of terrorists responsible for what their parents did too? How far did the sins of the fathers, and mothers, extend?

Callum shook his head a third time. Perhaps Gibson had been right back in that truck. Maybe the kids *had* done something to him with their staring, planted something in his mind to ensure he wouldn't forget their faces.

Or maybe it's just your own guilt? the first voice replied.

Callum got off the monorail a stop earlier than he'd meant to, but the walk home cleared his head a bit. By the time he'd climbed the stairs to his floor, though, he found he was exhausted. He made for his flat, then suddenly found himself continuing past it, on up the corridor.

Before he could stop himself, he was knocking on Ferne's door. Nobody answered at first. He'd completely lost track of what shift she was on, so had no idea whether she was even in or not, but Callum hoped … *needed* her to be home. The second time he knocked, the door opened. Ferne was in a pair of jogging bottoms and an old jumper, black hair hanging loose over her shoulders. He preferred it like that: natural, free.

"Callum?" she said, eyebrows raised.

"Sorry," he offered. "I'm not sure why I just did that."

"Are you all right?"

He laughed, but there was no humour to it. "No, I'm really not. I didn't get you up or anything, did I?"

She shook her head. "Day off. Besides, I'm on more regular hours this week. I get to sleep when everyone else does for a change. You, however, look as if you haven't slept in days."

Callum laughed again. There was an awkward gap which he felt he needed to fill with something, so he said, "I don't suppose you'd consider going out for that drink with me, would you?"

"What, right now? At half four in the afternoon?"

"Yes."

She thought about it for a second, then shook her head firmly.

He sighed. "That's okay, I just thought I'd ask." Callum turned away and was about to leave her doorstep when she put a hand on his arm.

"I'm not going *out* anywhere, and neither are you in that state.

But we can still have a drink. You definitely look like you could use it."

He smiled a thank you as she held open the door for him to come inside. Her place seemed much bigger than his, probably because she wasn't in the midst of unpacking. There were no boxes scattered around, just a rose-coloured couch and two chairs, a rug with a glass coffee table on it in the centre of the living room, and a TV in the far corner. Ferne had been watching a movie when he'd knocked, it seemed, and she'd paused. It was a black and white film: a couple were on a train station platform and the woman looked upset.

"An old weepie," Ferne explained, pointing to the tissues on the floor next to the couch. "I have a weakness for them." She picked up the remote and aimed it at the TV.

"Don't stop on my account," Callum told her. "I'd hate to ruin your day off."

Ferne flicked the set off. "I've seen it a million times. It was just getting to the sad bit anyway, so probably just as well. This way I can pretend that everything works out all right in the end."

"Wouldn't that be great," Callum said.

"Hmmm?"

"If everything always worked out okay."

Ferne said nothing, just pointed him in the direction of the couch, then disappeared off into the kitchen. A few seconds later she called back, "You want a beer?"

Ordinarily, that would have been enough for him—he wasn't that big a drinker—but today was different. "Do you have anything stronger?"

"I have wine, and I think I might still have a bottle of whiskey one of my patients gave me once as a present."

"Whiskey would be great. I thought patients weren't allowed to give presents? Med-fee policy," he said as an afterthought.

"They're not, but this one kind of insisted," Ferne replied. "Heart attack; he would have died if I hadn't kept the muscle going until the crash team could take over. He was pretty grateful. Now where did I put it . . . ?"

"Must be very rewarding, what you do," said Callum, easing back slightly into the soft material of the couch.

"Sorry?" Ferne's voice sounded muffled, like she had her head stuck inside a cupboard.

"I said it must be rewarding sometimes, being a nurse."

"It has its moments." She returned with two glasses, one filled with white wine, the other with a measure of golden brown liquid. Ferne handed Callum the whiskey.

"Cheers," he said, clinking his glass with hers. As she sat down on the couch, leaving enough of a space between them for comfort, he took a gulp of the alcohol and sat forward, coughing.

"Easy," said Ferne, placing her wine down on the coffee table, then shuffling up and patting him on the back. "I don't want to have to take you into work on my only day off this rotation."

Callum turned and they locked eyes, just for a moment. It was Ferne who looked away again first.

"So, you want to talk about it?" she asked, moving back along the couch.

"What?" he croaked. In his head, Callum was still looking into her eyes.

"About whatever happened today that made you knock on my door."

"That wasn't the *only* reason I knocked on your door," Callum informed her.

Ferne didn't bite. "It's the reason why you have that look, though."

"Look?"

"I see it sometimes in the trauma department at St August's, on the faces of doctors who've been fighting to keep someone alive … and lost." Ferne took a sip of the wine. "It's your work, isn't it?"

He nodded. "Today I was involved in … an *incident*," Callum said, stealing Pryce's description.

"What kind of incident?" Ferne looked at him sideways, and sipped more of the wine.

"I can't tell you that." Callum wasn't even sure he wanted to.

"So what *can* you tell me?"

"There were deaths," he said bluntly. "People died, Ferne."

She blinked and nodded. "Okay."

"And there were children involved."

Ferne brought up a knee and shifted round to properly face him on the couch. "Children? What do you mean? They're not the ones who—"

Callum shook his head. "No, no—they're all right." There wasn't much conviction in his voice when he said the last bit.

Relief washed over Ferne's face. She took a deeper draught from the glass. He knew very well how she felt about children, had seen the way she'd been with the Hodgsons' child. If she realised the full extent of what had happened today … "I—I don't know what to say to you, Callum."

"Not sure there's much *to* say." He drank more as well, taking it a little steadier this time. The burning liquid made its way down into his stomach.

"Were you hurt?" Ferne asked him. "Is there anything you want me to take a look at?"

"No, I wasn't hurt … not really. But some of my colleagues were."

"Then you were lucky."

"Yeah, that's me: lucky McGuire." Callum drank some more of the whiskey.

"Can I ask you something?" Ferne said.

"Sure. I'll even answer if I can."

"How did you end up being an M-Forcer? I mean, it takes a certain sort of person to … well, you know."

"Track down witches and warlocks? You can say it, you know." Ferne looked at her glass. "Sorry," Callum added. "I realise it makes some people uncomfortable to think about it. If I'm honest, it makes me uncomfortable sometimes."

Now she looked directly at him again. "Then why?" Ferne repeated.

Callum shrugged.

"That's not an explanation."

"All right," he said, his voice taking on a more serious tone. "You really want to know?"

Ferne gave a small nod.

"It's because of my parents."

"I don't understand."

"They … passed away when I was very little, a baby. I can barely remember them." Callum hung his head.

"I'm … I'm so sorry." Ferne reduced the gap between them again, and placed a hand on his shoulder. "But I still don't—"

"I tell everyone that they died of natural causes, Dad before I was born, Mum of cancer when I was two."

"You … tell everyone …?" Ferne still couldn't grasp where he was going with this.

"They …" Callum was struggling with the words. "They didn't die that way."

"Tell me," said Ferne, the hand squeezing his shoulder lightly.

He held her gaze, not blinking. "They were killed in one of Arcana's very first protests, not long after I'd been born. Out for the night, celebrating their wedding anniversary in a restaurant when …" Callum turned away and drank what remained of his whiskey in one go; he didn't cough this time. Holding up the glass, he asked, "Is there any more where this came from?"

Ferne nodded, but seemed reluctant to leave the couch. She eventually did though, tearing herself away, placing her glass on the coffee table and heading for the kitchen. Moments later, she returned with the bottle, still more than three quarters full. She gave it to him so he could help himself.

"Thanks," Callum said as she settled back down on the couch. He poured himself a generous measure, and immediately took another gulp.

"You were talking about your parents," Ferne prompted, then shook her head. "I'm sorry. I shouldn't—"

"It's okay," Callum told her, half-smiling. "It's about time I told someone about all this. They'd been out that night, celebrating," he continued, looking down, "not a care in the world. Then a group of three people burst in. They took the small restaurant hostage, there couldn't have been more than two dozen people inside. They … made demands, threatened everyone inside. The police were there pretty quickly—who knows who called them, maybe the members of Arcana, maybe that's what they wanted? Anyway, things … escalated. Magick was used and the next thing everyone knew they were looking at a fucking hole in the ground where that restaurant had been." Callum glanced over at Ferne. "I'm sorry."

"No need," she assured him.

"It just makes me so …" He took another drink of the whiskey, his hand shaking, before going on. "There were no survivors. This is all from the reports at the time, which I saw later."

"God, that's …" Ferne couldn't finish the sentence. They sat in silence for a while, then she asked, "What happened to you after that?"

It took him a second or so to answer, but then: "I've been told that an aunty on my mother's side took me in. I have vague memories of her, nothing distinct though. *She's* the one who died of cancer when I was two. Her husband was already dead by the time I came along. She was the only family I had left."

"And afterwards?"

"Church-funded orphanage."

Ferne pulled a face. "I've heard about those places. They can be very … strict."

Callum shrugged. "They taught us right from wrong, I guess. Taught us about the history of the conflicts, about how it all began, and about how it must all be stamped out." He polished off that glass, and poured some more.

"And … what about the other side of the argument?" Ferne ventured.

"What other side? There *is* no other side," Callum snapped.

"Well, there are those who say that witches have been persecuted throughout the ages, that all they really want to do is follow their own religion. That innocent people have been wrongly accused of witchcraft and died because of it."

Callum stared at her. "You mean heretic propaganda?"

Ferne held up her hands defensively. "Just playing devil's advocate."

"They're in league with them, Ferne, spreading their lies. Magick exists. Witch … witchcraft is evil. It must be … must be …" His speech was slurred.

"You say the words, you learnt them by rote. But I can see the doubt inside you, Callum."

He frowned and looked away. "I … There's no … no doubt." Callum took another drink.

Ferne reached out and touched his face, turning him back towards her. "Yes. Yes, there is. What happened today, Callum? What *really* happened?"

"I've told you I can't—"

"What did you *see*?"

Callum started to get up, but the whiskey was having more of an effect. It suddenly felt like his whole body was made of lead. "I—I think I shhhould go."

"No, wait. I'm sorry." Ferne pulled him back down and he fell awkwardly, his face inches from hers. "Don't," she said, and there was something in her voice that made him want to stay.

"Who … whoo are you, Ferne?" he asked.

"Who are *you*, Callum McGuire?"

Ferne stroked his cheek and it felt good. "I … I asked firsht." Her beautiful features were blurring, his eyelids growing heavier by the second. As his head lolled towards her, exhaustion claiming him, he felt her lean in closer, whispering in his ear.

"I'm not who, or *what*, you think I am."

That was it, Callum was gone, and blackness was all he knew.

When she was sure he was asleep, Ferne rose from the couch and looked down at Callum. She picked up her wine glass and took a sip. He looked so peaceful lying there, oblivious, like the baby he'd once been when he lost his parents. Listening to his story, she could understand why he'd ended up this way. The thought of vengeance, coupled with the doctrines of the orphanage, had done their worst. Like so many, his views, his understanding of things, had been warped by a corrupt regime. In a way she almost felt sorry for him. Left alone, told that Arcana had murdered his parents, what else was he supposed to do? But then she thought of what he'd become. The things M-forcers did made her shiver. If he was a part of that arm of the law it automatically made him her enemy, didn't it? And after what had happened today …

"Why don't you just get on with it?" the voice said behind her.

She whirled, spilling some of her drink on the rug. "Michael! I didn't realise you were here."

"Few ever do." The bearded man with dark hair approached, looking down at the sleeping figure as she had just been doing. His hands clenched into fists, balling at his sides. "It would be easy, so easy." He held up one of those fists, lips moving almost silently. Sparks of lightning crackled around it until the whole hand looked like one glowing mass of raw energy. "All I'd have to do is—"

"No!" Ferne placed her free hand on his chest and he shot her a look of confusion.

"Why, because you'd like to do the honours?" His hand returned to normal, the lightning subsiding. He waved it in front of her as an invitation. "Be my guest. If anyone deserves the right, it's you. Take his life, feel the power—the hatred—welling up inside you and let it out in one, swift—"

"No," Ferne said again. "This is not the way. It's not *our* way."

Michael grunted. "Who are you to say what our way is?"

"I think you know the answer to that question. She was *my* kin, wasn't she?"

"They were *all* our kin," Michael retorted. "If the roles were reversed, he would do the same to you," Michael assured her.

"You know that for a fact, do you?"

"I know where he was this morning, what he did. That alone should be enough to make you want to vanish him. Though not before inflicting a little torture, perhaps."

Ferne threw the rest of the wine in his face, tossing the glass away. Michael was so shocked all he could do was splutter. "How dare you?" she said. "That's *their* way. I could never …"

Michael wiped the wine from his eyes with the back of his hand,

and snarled. "It's *his* way too!" He pointed to the sleeping man on the couch.

"No, I don't … I don't believe it is."

"You don't *believe*?" Michael threw his hands up in the air. "What's going on here, Ferne? I heard you, there on the couch. You're a very good actress, I'll give you that. To be able to sit and talk like that to a man you know has just—"

"That's enough!" Ferne folded her arms like a little girl who couldn't get her own way. "I don't need to hear it again."

"Unwin said I shouldn't tell you and he was right. You're too stubborn to listen. Or maybe …" Michael looked from the sleeping Callum to Ferne. "No, not even you would be that … Don't tell me you—"

"What?" snapped Ferne.

"You and him? Please tell me that you don't … You can't!"

Her mouth dropped open, but she didn't answer Michael.

"My Goddess! I'm right, aren't I?"

"I … There's good in him, that's all I know."

"How can you say that? Him and his kind killed five of us today."

"We don't know the full story yet. Not even you can be everywhere."

"I know all I need to! You sound just like Unwin, do you know that?" Michael moved closer to Callum and bent over him. "He's been to The Penitentiary, you know. Recently as well."

Ferne put her fingers to her lips. "How …?"

"You forget, Ferne." His eyes looked big and sad. "When you've spent time in that place, you never, *ever* forget the stench. He reeks of it, almost as much as he does of guilt."

"The children? Are they there, Michael?"

He sighed. "I'd say so, yes."

A single tear ran down Ferne's cheek.

"And *he* put them there!" spat Michael, about to grab Callum's throat. Ferne covered the short distance between them and gripped his wrist with both hands. Callum didn't so much as twitch. Shaking his head in disbelief, Michael said, "Still you aren't prepared to do what's necessary."

"I'm doing what's *right*," argued Ferne. "Please believe that. After all these years, trust me."

"No, trust *me*, little Ferne. Come back with me where it's safe."

She shook her head. "*Nowhere* is safe these days, Michael. And I'm not your 'little Ferne' anymore."

Michael snatched his hand away and stood back. "You'll regret not doing what was needed," he told her. "Sooner or later he will lead them to you. Then you'll think of this moment and wish you'd chosen another path."

"We can only the walk the paths that are given to us, Michael."

"Then I pray for you on yours," he concluded.

"And I for you."

Michael bowed his head, his form shimmering, blending in with the surroundings, fading to a spirit-like state. Then he was gone; she knew that because she knew Michael. He wouldn't hang around here much longer if he didn't think she was listening to him. Ferne hadn't even been expecting him to return after their previous encounter. He'd warned her then, as he had now. Part of her wanted to heed it, knew that it was crazy to put her trust in the man asleep on her couch —he'd been brought up to detest witchcraft and all it stood for, had requested a transfer from ordinary duties to M-forcer. But he clearly believed he was protecting the public against a threat, from the people who had killed his parents.

Believed he was doing some good.

But what of the children? Had he really handed them over at The Penitentiary—as Michael said—so easily? No, she didn't think so. There was guilt there, she sensed it, but not about the deaths. They had not been at his hand, she was certain of that. The smell of guilt was on him because he'd left the children in that place of nightmares, when all he really wanted to do was grab them and run.

They were children of Arcana, he'd been told. *Probably even told him they'd been suckled by pigs*, thought Ferne. That had stirred conflicting emotions in him. Of duty, of loyalty. But most importantly those feelings of being alone will have come flooding back from when he was an orphan.

Michael was right about one thing, however: Ferne was a good actress. She'd had to be, living the life she'd led. And she would carry on pretending until she didn't have to anymore.

Or she was discovered.

Again, she stared down at the unconscious Callum McGuire in his self-induced coma. Would she really regret not killing him?

"There's good in you," Ferne said quietly. "I know there is. It's not too late."

Then she sat down in one of the chairs and watched the M-forcer sleep.

CHAPTER FOURTEEN

His dreams were feverish.

They began on the bridge again, with Ferne. Once more she was beckoning to him, even more desperately than the last time. But he couldn't reach her in time before she was snatched away. Callum ran across the bridge as fast as he could, not even noticing that the environment had shifted, as it often did in dreams. Instead of the bridge, he was in a corridor: one of the bland, stark corridors of The Penitentiary. He felt eyes watching him, beyond the obvious CCTV cameras mounted at every turn. Callum ran down first one passage, then another, never stopped by the guards or any security systems. He had free run of the place. Callum thought he saw a glimpse of Ferne at the end of the corridor he was in, then she was gone. Racing up it, he scrambled and slipped into the next one, the maze-like turnings folding in on themselves like a funhouse.

Then the doors opened behind him, releasing the prisoners one by one. There was the lawyer, Temple, his flesh blackened and burnt to a crisp. Behind him, in the next cell, was the guy Callum had chased on the street: the conman using cards and sleight of hand to trick people. He was covered in welts and lacerations, blood pouring from a cut over one eye. "I ain't done nothing," he moaned, shambling along, holding out his red hands. There were more to come, though, such as the young man from the house on Widow's Way. Unlike Temple, he was still alight, burning like a human torch, but still moving down the corridor. The older woman Cartwright had shot in the head wasn't far away, either, the hole still visible, bits of blood and brain dripping out of the exit wound on the left side. She was still wailing for her Davey. The man Gibson had noosed on the stairs was here, too. He was half-levitating, half-hanging from a rope that was dragging him down the corridor towards Callum, his body riddled with bullet holes now that his amulet was gone.

"That all you got? That all you got?" he chanted as he swung, black tongue lolling from his mouth, feet inches off the floor.

Callum backed away, but something burst out of the cell on his left, pushing him into the opposite wall. It was the big man from under the stairs at Widow's Way, the bear-man. He was still part-human at this point, but had claws, and they slashed at Callum. "Why?" the man roared, saliva cascading from his maw. "Why did you kill them?"

"I—I didn't," Callum tried to explain, but his attacker was having none of it.

"We're hurting *no one*!" the bear-man bellowed. It seemed a ridiculous statement, given he looked like he was about to savage Callum.

Callum gazed at him, looked sideways at the approaching prisoners, and slid along the wall to escape them.

"That all you got?"

"Why did you kill them?"

"I ain't done nothing."

"My Davey!"

The cacophony was deafening. Callum put his hands to his ears, but continued to inch up the wall until he came to a door with a handle. He tried it, but the door was locked. Pulling did nothing and, looking over his shoulder, he saw that the inmates—now numbering in their dozens—were almost upon him. One last try … Nothing.

Callum turned around, facing the hordes, ready for whatever they wanted to do to him. But just as they got close enough, he fell backwards through the doorway into a terrible darkness. The door slammed shut. Callum felt around for a light-switch, but there wasn't one. However, the worst thing about the dark was it seemed like it was closing in on him. He stuck out his hand and felt a wall on his left, right, in front and behind. Callum began to panic. He banged on the walls with his fists, but they continued to close in. He screamed at the top of his voice. Again, nothing happened, except the walls moved closer.

"No … No, Miss Havelock! Please let me out. *Please!* I promise never to do it again," he shouted. "Please just *let … me … OUT!*"

Just when he thought he would be crushed alive by the blackness, a light appeared on Callum's right. A long strip of light, illuminating the two-way mirror of an interrogation room. Callum looked around and found that, sure enough, he was in the observation room next door. There was no-one in here today, though, except him.

Callum walked slowly towards the glass, placing his fingertips on the pane. The table was there, with chairs either side. But today Pryce was sitting on one side, with the little blonde girl on the other. Instead of being hooked up to an I.V. there was a metal collar around her neck, and her arms were manacled to the chair. There was a huge guard behind her wearing a jump suit, his hands resting on what looked like a wheel.

"Tell me what you know of Arcana," Pryce was asking, steepling his fingers and touching his mouth. "I want names."

The blonde girl shook her head.

"If you do, I will make this go easy for you. If you don't …" He nodded to the guard, who pulled on the wheel like he was steering a ship. The metal collar tightened around the little girl's neck and she let out a choking sound.

"Do you see?"

Callum pressed both hands against the glass.

"Do you see what will happen if you don't tell me? And this is only the beginning." Pryce smiled that unsettling smile of his.

The girl attempted to shake her head, but couldn't properly because of the collar. Her cheeks were the colour of tomatoes.

Another nod of Pryce's head, and the wheel tightened again. This time the little girl's face turned the colour of beetroot. Pryce got up and walked over to her, then began to stroke her hair. Callum found himself banging on the mirror, pounding on the toughened glass, but it seemed as if no-one on the other side could hear him. Or maybe they just didn't care.

"You *will* talk eventually," promised Pryce. Then, out of nowhere, he produced the little boy from the house. The girl's eyes went wide as Pryce placed a hand on the boy's shoulder and brought out a knife, holding it to his throat.

Looking round, Callum spotted one of the chairs the psychiatrists had been sitting on. He grabbed it and swung it against the glass. It didn't even crack.

He banged and shouted as Pryce started to draw the knife across the boy's throat. But the scene had changed slightly. Now the girl on the chair was a woman: the woman who'd taken her own life at the house; the woman he suspected was the mother of these children. And the collar was no longer around her neck. As Pryce cut deeper into the boy's throat, a slit appeared at the woman's neck instead of his, blood pouring from the gash. She made gurgling noises, bringing an unfettered hand up to her throat.

She looked over at Callum, pleading with him for help. Though it was obviously agony for her, she mouthed the words: "For Arcana."

"Callum," said a voice from behind. He recognised it instantly and, spinning, saw Ferne there in the shadows at the back of the observation room. "Callum, help—"

Her words were cut off by gloved hands on her shoulders, forcing her down to her knees. The figure was almost completely in darkness, and from where Callum guessed the mouth was came the words: "Don't believe their lies."

Then the hands took hold of Ferne's head, twisting it sideways quickly with a loud crack. "*No!*" Callum screamed. He ran towards the figure, but it was already retreating into the darkness. In fact the whole room was growing dark once more, closing in. Callum's breaths came in short bursts, the air evaporating. There were walls surrounding him again, but this time there was something different. When he reached out in front of him he felt spikes. He wrapped his hands around one barb, trying to push it back, but it was no use. A final surge, and the spikes found their way into him.

He let out one last shriek then—

The beeping of his mobile snapped him awake.

Callum shielded his eyes from the light in the room, sitting up. As he did so, the blanket around him dropped to his waist. The surroundings were unfamiliar and his head was throbbing. Where was he? The phone persisted, so he dug his hand into his pocket, fishing it out.

"Where the bloody hell are you?" Though garbled, Callum knew the voice was Gibson's.

The first word out of his mouth was a croak, then, "I-I was just wondering the same thing."

"You've missed the start of your shift," said Gibson, "by a couple of hours."

Callum gazed around, still confused. He swung his aching legs over the edge of the couch, saw the bottle of whiskey—with only a small amount left in it—and remembered at last where he was, though even that seemed to pain him physically. There was a note next to the bottle, which he reached over and read:

Had to go to work. Let yourself out. F.

"I'm sorry," Callum said, not really sure whether he was talking to Gibson or the absent nurse.

"I covered for you," Gibson informed him.

"Thanks."

"But you need to get yourself down here pronto. In fact, no. Where *exactly* are you?"

Callum almost told him, but said instead, "I can meet you outside my place, corner of Claremont and Hale."

"What happened, tied one on last night?" Gibson sounded amused.

"Something like that."

"At least tell me there was a woman involved."

"Something like that," Callum repeated.

"Well, you'd better get your shit together, McGuire. You have a spare uniform at home?"

"'Course. Why, what's—"

"I'll explain when I pick you up." Gibson switched off his phone, leaving Callum still gazing about him. He could remember knocking on Ferne's door, having a drink while he bent her ear about his parents, but only fragments after that. Had he really spent the night on her sofa? God, he was a prat. What must she be thinking of him?

And a dream? Hadn't there been a dream?

More like an alcohol-fuelled nightmare.

He didn't have time for this. Callum had to get ready to meet Gibson, that meant a quick wash and getting changed. He stood, but really wished he hadn't. This was why he didn't drink, his constitution really couldn't handle it. Shaking his head, which was also not a good idea, he took steps towards the door like a toddler learning to walk.

There had been something urgent in Gibson's voice, similar to how it had been yesterday morning. Callum hoped today wasn't going to be quite as … eventful.

But somehow he had a feeling it just might.

CHAPTER FIFTEEN

When he got downstairs, the squad car was waiting for him outside. Gibson tapped his watch when he saw Callum enter the foyer, and the young officer ran across, then out through the door.

"I've been here ten minutes," Callum's partner shouted through the open passenger window.

Callum slid in beside him. "Sorry."

"Here," said Gibson, passing over a polystyrene carton. "Figured you wouldn't have had time to eat."

Callum opened up the box and there was a burger inside, tomato sauce spilling from its innards. His stomach rolled over and he put a hand to his mouth. He passed the carton back to Gibson and stuck his head out of the window.

"Boy, you really did hit the bottle last night, didn't you?" Gibson commented, taking the container from him, discarding it, then biting into the burger. "Waste not, want not, eh?"

Callum looked back over at Gibson chewing on the bun. Then he quickly gulped in more air from the window.

"That's fair enough, it was a rough day all round. But one thing you'll find on this job is that when the heat's on there's not much let-up, kid," said Gibson with a full mouth, spitting bits of bread everywhere. "So you'd better pull yourself together before we get there."

"Get where?"

"Tip-off. This one comes from the top, though. Seems we've got a nice juicy member of Arcana in our very own district and we didn't even know about it."

"Where ... did ... the ... information ... come ... from?" Callum gulped down air in-between each word.

"Beats me, but I'd say it's more than just a coincidence that we pulled in those Arcana brats yesterday, wouldn't you?"

"They were just children, Gibson," Callum reminded him, bringing his head back inside.

"You keep on saying that, but you and I both know that they weren't. They knew things all right, overheard conversations—and Pryce must have got them to talk a little. Guess he asked them nicely."

Vague flashes from the nightmare returned: the girl in the collar, the boy having his throat slit. Callum pushed them aside.

"In any event, the big boys asked for you and me personally to check it out, so we must have done something right," Gibson said, grinning.

"Who's the suspect?" Callum asked.

"No name, just a location. We've got our work cut out for us, McGuire, but we do have four other officers meeting us. Which is why we don't want to be late and miss all the fun." Gibson put his foot down on the accelerator, speeding through a light that had just turned red.

Callum spent the rest of the journey trying not to throw up. This megalopolis was still new to him, so he would have had trouble following Gibson's route even if he'd had landmarks to go by, but it was nigh-on impossible when his partner was racing through the streets and it felt like his belly was denouncing him. Callum almost asked him to slow down, but he'd been the one who'd made them late. It was his fault, so he had to put up with it.

When Gibson turned the final corner, Callum's eyes opened wide in disbelief.

"Here we are, St. August's Hospital."

Callum didn't need Gibson's announcement, anyone could see where they were. The building was plastered in white crosses on a red background, with that trademark sign below each one: the Med-fee seal of approval. As for St. August himself, he was one of the saints of the New Church of Benediction who, in his time—specifically the 19th Century—had driven evil spirits from the hearts of infected people (for a price of course) before putting them to death afterwards to make certain the demon had been vanquished. In the end, he was himself accused of being possessed by the evil he fought and gave his own life to stop it spreading. Or that was how the legend went, Callum remembered. Small wonder that this hospital should take his name, a person who sought to relieve the suffering of others, though the treatments it offered had come a long way since St. August's day.

"The suspect is inside there?" Callum pointed.

"You're quick today," said Gibson. "Glad to see the hangover hasn't affected that keen intellect of yours."

Already there were two other squad cars waiting, the officers still inside them. Gibson parked up behind, then got out. Callum was slower, only just getting out of the passenger side as Gibson was banging on the roof of the car in front.

"Herring … Metz, look lively. Out of the car." He moved on to the next one, banging again; the noise went right through Callum. "Roberts and Webb, are your arses glued to those seats or something? No wonder you didn't get the shout yesterday."

"Yeah, we really missed out … Besides, you're the ones who're late," Metz argued, a female M-forcer in her 30s with short ginger hair tucked into her cap.

Gibson ignored the remark and waited for everyone to disembark.

"You all know why we're here. You all need to be armed. Like as not, the suspect will run when they see us. If that doesn't happen, we've got a long day ahead of us weeding them out. The aim, no matter what your gut tells you, is to incapacitate rather than dispatch."

"It's a big hospital, Gibson," complained Webb, whose skin was so blotchy it looked like he should be a patient inside. "Lots of people."

"Brilliantly observed! Are you related to McGuire by any chance?" He laughed. "I guess we'd better get started then, instead of standing around here gassing all day." Gibson walked back over to Callum, then round him to pop the trunk. He tossed Callum a vest, utility belt—complete with Browning handgun in the holster—and baton, then some extra clips of ammo: armour-piercing, as per usual.

"I … look, I know someone who works here. A friend. She lives in my block," Callum told him.

"Good for you."

"She's a nurse."

"In a hospital? *No.*" The sarcasm oozed out of Gibson. "Wait a minute, this the 'friend' from last night?"

Callum ignored the last question. "She might be able to help. You know, narrow down the search."

Gibson pursed his lips in thought. "Okay, it's worth a try, hotshot. Lead the way."

Callum strapped on his belt and made his way up the steps, with the others close behind. All eyes turned as they walked through the doors. People were used to seeing uniforms in here, but not this kind. Callum still hadn't got used to the reaction these clothes attracted. Not even when he'd been a street cop in London had people stopped what they were doing and shrunk back; trying to hide, trying to pretend they weren't even in the same room. It was probably because of the powers Enforcement Officers had, to run anyone in, question them … or more, all without fear of reprisal.

Callum walked up to the reception desk, the others moments behind. The bespectacled young woman behind the glass looked up and froze on the spot. Then she apparently decided that if she didn't say something soon, that might look suspicious, so she attempted a, "Hello, officer."

Callum nodded. "Could you tell me where I can find a nurse called Ferne Andrews? I believe she's on duty."

The woman stared at him blankly.

"Look, Miss, we're in kind of a hurry," Gibson said, and she snapped out of her daze.

"Andrews, you say?"

"He did." Gibson sighed heavily as she tapped the name into her computer.

"Aldis, Allen … Ames, Amner … Abernathy … Ah, here we are: Andrews, F. Nurse Andrews is on the wards today. Would you like me to make an announcement?"

"If you could just tell us which ward," suggested Callum.

"Right, yes," the woman replied, flustered. "Smedley Ward."

"And how do we get to that?" Gibson butted in again, his voice rising.

"Er … straight down the corridor, through the double doors, up the stairs on your right and down that corridor. You should be able to follow the signs from there."

Callum smiled. "Thank you."

They set off. It reminded Callum far too much of The Penitentiary in here, all bright tunnels and doors.

"How do we know it's not her?" a thickset Herring said, coming up the side of Gibson, "the woman back on reception. She looked terrified of us."

"*Everyone's* terrified of us," Gibson replied, annoyed that he had to field such stupid questions. "But it's the ones with good reason you can spot a mile off. You should know that by now."

"I would have taken her in anyway," Roberts—who was the opposite of Herring, stick thin and all gangly limbs—piped up. "Just to be on the safe side."

"We haven't time for fun and games today, this is serious." Gibson looked over at Callum. "This friend of yours had better be able to help us."

"I'm sure she can," Callum said confidently. "In fact I'm certain of it."

When they reached Smedley Ward, they had to deal with yet another woman on a desk. This one didn't appear quite so fazed by the six M-forcers.

"Nurse Andrews is currently on a break," she told Callum bluntly.

"Terrific!" Gibson threw his hands up in the air, drawing glances from the patients. "We've marched through the whole of this place looking for her—might as well have sent a flare up announcing we were coming to the person we're looking for—and when we finally get here, she's off smoking a fag or something."

"She doesn't smoke," Callum told him over his shoulder. "At least I don't think so."

"Oh, that close, are you?"

"Close enough. Look, can we save this till later?" Callum turned back to the woman on this desk. "Where can I find her right now?"

"Try the staffroom."

"Thanks, and that is . . . ?"

The woman gave them instructions: out into the corridor, turn right, down the hall and round the corner. Callum thanked her once more, ignoring the groans from Gibson, and they set off again.

The door to the staffroom had a round glass window which Callum looked through. The room itself was quite long and filled with chairs covered in a hideous orange plastic. Scattered here and there were nurses, doctors with white coats on, and people dressed in scrubs.

"See her?"

"No."

"For Christ's sake!"

"Hold on, yes. Got her." Callum saw Ferne across the far side of the room, sitting in one of the chairs, alone and reading a newspaper. "Look, let me talk to her first. I don't think she's all that comfortable with what I do for a living."

"I don't give a shit," Gibson told him. "We're here to catch a criminal, and she's going to help us. End of story." He put his hand on the door to open it, but Callum barred his way.

"Don't want to spook the woman. Let me talk to her first," he insisted. "She'll be a big help, I promise."

Gibson chewed it over for a second, then nodded. "Your call, hotshot."

Callum thanked him and walked through the door. Even in this room of professionals, all wearing uniforms themselves, he got a reaction. Heads turned, people stopped talking or eating and just gaped.

It's fear, Callum said to himself, *they're all terrified of me. Why? I'm here to protect them, can't they see that? I'm here to arrest a dangerous terrorist. Why are they frightened of* me?

Ferne, however, didn't see him until he was almost upon her. Then she raised her eyes from the newspaper, mouth falling open.

"Hi," said Callum. He could feel the blood rushing to his cheeks under her scrutiny.

Ferne didn't say a word.

"It's okay, I get that a lot."

Still nothing.

"First time you've seen me in my uniform … Bound to be a bit strange, I guess."

Ferne nodded, very slowly.

"Look, I'm sorry about last night. I—"

"W-What is this, are you stalking me now?" she said, suddenly finding her voice.

"No … No, it's not like that at all." Callum sat down beside her on one of the orange chairs. "I'm … The truth is, Ferne, I'm here officially."

"What are you talking about?" The newspaper fell from her grasp onto her knees.

"You know this hospital inside out, the people, staff, patients," said Callum. "Has anybody been acting … I don't know, suspiciously at all?"

Ferne frowned. "What, you mean pulling rabbits out of hats, that sort of thing?"

"This is serious. People's lives could be at stake."

Her eyes fell. "I'm sorry."

"We have reason to believe there could be a member of Arcana operating out of this place."

She looked up again as soon as he said that word, then repeated it herself. "Arcana?"

"Yes, so you can see why we're … What is it, Ferne? What's wrong?"

"You said 'we.'"

"Myself and my colleagues." Callum thumbed back towards the door where more uniformed officers could be seen through the round glass.

Ferne swallowed dryly.

"It's okay, we're only here to help," Callum assured her. "We won't be questioning anyone who doesn't warrant it."

"Does that include me?"

It was Callum's turn to frown. "I'm asking for your help, Ferne. That's all."

"Sooner or later he will lead them to you," she whispered under her breath.

"I'm sorry?"

"Look, Callum, we don't have much time." She took his hands. He felt hers trembling.

"I … Ferne, I don't understand. What—"

"Be quiet and listen to me," she said. "I know who you're looking for."

"How … how could you know?" he managed. But he didn't even need to ask the question. He knew: deep down, he knew. Callum tried to pull his hands away, but she wouldn't let him. "No. Jesus, it can't be. Not you. This is a joke, please tell me it's a joke."

"Callum, listen, it's not what you think. You know me—"

"I thought I did." *But do you really? How long has she been in your life, Callum? Best friends can turn around after years and it's like you don't really know them at all. You've known Ferne, what? A couple of weeks?*

The tragedy was that he thought he'd found one of those people you really do connect with, like you've known them before in some other life.

"Am I really capable of the horrific things they say?"

Now the roles had been reversed and Callum couldn't find the words to reply.

"I work here, I see death every day. Do you really think I could inflict that pain on anyone else?"

Callum's mouth was moving, but still nothing emerged.

"I use my powers to heal, not to hurt others."

"The Hodgsons," he said suddenly.

She nodded. "Their son wasn't breathing."

"You brought him back to life."

"No. I don't have *that* kind of power. Only one of our kind ever did."

Callum was desperately trying to think, but his brain wasn't co-operating. "You have to give yourself up," he said finally. "If what you're saying is true, you won't be harmed. I'll see to that."

Her face hardened. "What, like you did with the children from Widow's Way?"

He was stunned that she even knew about them, especially as the details hadn't been released to the public. "They weren't harmed."

"No? You sure about that?"

Callum couldn't answer her. Snippets of the nightmare came back again. Of Pryce and the little girl, cutting the boy's throat.

"Callum, there are forces at work here that you can't even begin to imagine," Ferne informed him. "You have to trust me on that."

"Trust you?" He was amazed she'd even ask him. "When you've been lying to me about who you really are. And to think I was starting to …"

"What?"

He shook his head. "I'm going to have to tell them."

"Tell them what?" The voice made them both jump. It was Gibson. They'd been so preoccupied with their own drama neither of them had seen him enter and walk over. The rest of the M-forcers were inside the staff room as well, standing by the door.

"Er …" Callum was caught off-guard and was lost for words again.

"Proper little conflab you seemed to be having over here. Thought

I'd come and find out what was so interesting." Gibson said, smirking. "So, what are you going to have to tell us?"

"Miss … Nurse Andrews … she's—"

"I'm willing to co-operate with the investigation," Ferne said, doing a good job of keeping her voice level. "Officer …"

"Gibson. Tully Gibson. So, has lover boy here explained the situation?" Gibson placed a hand on Callum's shoulder, then clapped it.

"He has."

"And you think you might be able to help?"

"I … Yes, I'll definitely do my best, Officer Gibson."

"Good. Then you can start by telling me where I can find the rest of your merry little band, you fucking sparkie parasite." Gibson had his hand on his belt. In one smooth motion he drew his hand-noose and lassoed Ferne around the neck with it. One tug saw the noose tighten. Ferne struggled to her feet, kicking over her chair, the newspaper flapping to the floor. She grabbed the length of noose with both hands. All eyes in the room swivelled in their direction.

Callum rose. "Gibson, what are you—"

"We've met before, haven't we, love? Years ago," he said, pulling the noose even tighter. "'Cept her hair was down back then, and she was going under the name of Tracy Evans."

"What?"

"I should have twigged. She was working in a halfway house for the homeless back then. There was some trouble, somebody died in suspicious circumstances and I was called in."

"I—I was … taking away … his pain!" Ferne choked out the words. "The man … had terminal … cancer."

"You took away his pain, all right," Gibson said through clenched teeth. "You escaped that time, but I never forget a face. You knew my name even before you asked it, didn't you?"

Callum looked from Ferne to Gibson.

"Get these people out of here," Gibson shouted to the other cops, who began to usher the medical staff from the room. "Now, tell me where we can find the rest of your lot," Gibson demanded, then hit her across the face with the back of his hand. Ferne's head rocked sideways, and blood sprang from the corner of her mouth. She dropped to her knees in front of him.

"Hold on," said Callum. "I'm sure we can—"

"Tell me!" shouted Gibson, yanking again on the noose. Ferne could hardly breathe, let alone tell him anything.

"Gibson, loosen it. She can't get any air."

Instead, he slapped her face with his palm and her head flipped the other way.

"Stop it," said Callum, barely a whisper at first. When Gibson pulled Ferne to her feet and punched her in the stomach, Callum's voice rose in pitch: "I said, *stop it!*"

Gibson paused, facing his partner. "What?"

"This … this isn't how it's supposed … She's got rights."

Gibson shook his head. "She's Arcana. She *has* no rights."

"What about her rights as a human being?"

"I gave you the benefit of the doubt yesterday with those kids," Gibson grumbled, "but now you're pushing it."

"There are other ways of getting information," said Callum.

"These people are bloody fanatics. This is the *only* way!" Callum looked at Ferne, and Gibson caught it. "Oh, I see. Got a bit too close to her, did we? More than just a quickie?"

Callum's face scrunched up. "You're disgusting."

"I'm not the one who's been screwing a sparkie, me laddo. Or …" Gibson's face suddenly altered, like he'd just realised something. "Or maybe you knew all along?"

Callum touched a finger to his chest. "Me? You're accusing me now?"

"It'd make sense. You suggested we find her as soon as we got to St. August's, ask her help. Maybe to deflect attention away from her, eh? Then you wanted to speak to her on your own. To warn her, I'll bet."

"You've lost it," said Callum.

"It'd be the perfect cover, wouldn't it? M-forcer?" Gibson yanked on the noose a final time, pulling Ferne towards him. "Is that right? Is he with you and your lot?" He took out his baton and brought it backwards, ready to smash Ferne in the face with it. But something was holding his arm in place.

Callum had grabbed Gibson's wrist.

"Enough."

Gibson looked into his eyes, saw that Callum meant business. "You don't want to do that," he warned the younger cop. "It's not too late. If you really don't have anything to do with this business, if it really was a mistake—"

"The only mistake I made was in not stopping you from hitting her the first time," Callum told him. Then he snatched the baton and jabbed the end into Gibson's ribs. Winded, the man bent over double, releasing his grip on the noose. Ferne staggered backwards, coughing.

Callum brought the baton down across Gibson's shoulders and he fell over sideways onto the floor. Already Metz, Roberts, Herring and Webb were rushing over, but Callum had his pistol out before any of them could react. "Stay back," he called out. "I'm warning you."

Ferne got a finger, then two and three, under the noose, freeing her neck enough to gasp for air. She pulled it over her head and threw the line away.

"Is there another way out of here?" Callum asked her.

Coughing, she nodded, pointing over towards the other end of the room. Keeping the four officers covered as best he could, Callum backed up towards Ferne, then they both backed towards the area she'd indicated. Behind a partition lay another set of doors that led to a different wing of the hospital. As soon as they were through, Callum said, "Run!"

They started off up the corridor, but Ferne was still having trouble breathing. The pair were barely twenty metres away from the door when the rest of the M-forcers burst through, Gibson in tow. They all had their weapons drawn, but there were too many people in the corridor to fire. As soon as they saw the cops giving chase, though, the crowds parted; some shouted, others screamed. But it wasn't long before the officers could get a bead on the fleeing couple.

A bullet whizzed past Callum as he dragged Ferne round a corner.

She coughed hard, wheezing something to him that he couldn't quite catch. When he tugged on her arm, she resisted.

"We have to go. They're right behind us!" he said.

Ferne brought up a hand and rubbed her throat where the noose line had bit deep. She began to mouth something, croaking out the words. As panicked as he was, Callum watched, fascinated, while the flesh there began to glow as orange as the chairs they'd been sitting on just minutes ago. Spilling out from under her palm, it turned a yellow colour, then faded completely. When she removed her hand the skin at her neck was completely healed—and Callum knew that the damage on the inside had been repaired as well.

"Handy trick," he said.

"It's much more than a trick," she said, her voice restored to full strength.

A bullet grazed the corner of the wall they were pressed up against, reminding them of their pursuers. "Come on," said Callum, pulling her down the hall.

Gibson and the others rounded that corner seconds later. "You won't get away, McGuire!" he shouted after them. "You've turned on your own, and for that we'll hunt you down till doomsday."

Callum ignored the threat, leading Ferne to a junction ahead. He was about to drag her to the right, when she said, "No, this way."

He bowed to her superior knowledge of the place, but was surprised when he saw they'd turned into an empty dead end.

"What're you playing at?"

"Getting us out of here," she said, pointing to a door on their left. Quickly, she opened it. Callum's face fell.

"It's a storage closet."

She nodded. "I can't do this in a large open space."

"Do what?"

"You'll see." Ferne pulled on his arm, but he stood stock still.

"I can't go in there."

"What do you mean? We'll both fit—look."

"I … I'm claustrophobic."

Ferne stared at him. "Please Callum, we *have* to. We won't be inside for long."

The group of uniformed officers negotiated the last bend and suddenly they were there in the same corridor, guns raised. Gibson stepped forward. "Nowhere left to run, McGuire."

Ferne ducked inside, eyes pleading with him to join her. He looked from the woman to Gibson, then made a move towards the closet. A hail of armour-piercing bullets rained down on him as he fell into it, and Ferne slammed the door behind them. She held on to a slumped Callum and reached inside her uniform, pulling out a key wrapped in a red ribbon.

"Hold on," she said, though she didn't know whether Callum could hear her. Clutching the key in her free hand, she gripped the cloth of Callum's sleeve with the other. "I thank the powers that be … That returneth me … To the place from which I received this key."

Outside, Gibson approached the closet cautiously, his gun still raised. The other officers hung back behind, also ready to fire.

The gaps in the frame seemed to swell with light, just for a moment. Then it was gone. He took hold of the handle and turned it, pistol still out in front of him. Gibson pulled the door open. There was nothing in the closet except a few stacked boxes.

"Shit!" he said. "A fucking teleport." Turning back to the others, he let out a long breath. "We need to let Wallis know about this, and he's going to be far from happy. Not only did we lose the Arcana, but his fucking golden boy has switched sides." He punched the wall. "I showed him friendship, took him under my wing, and this is what I get. But I tell you one thing …" He let the sentence hang in the air for while in front of the others.

"When I do catch up with the little runt, he's dead."

CHAPTER SIXTEEN

"He's dead."

Callum heard the words but couldn't be sure who was saying them. The voice was male, but unfamiliar. His vision was blurred—verging on non-existent—and the pain he'd felt when those bullets struck him had turned into a kind of numbness. He couldn't feel his arms or legs, let alone his fingers and toes.

"No. But he's very badly injured." Now *that* voice he recognised.

Ferne: the reason why he'd just betrayed everything he'd ever believed in. His late parents, the teachings of the orphanage … The badge. Though did that mean anything anymore when people like Gibson were wearing it? The man had the audacity to say *he'd* given Callum the benefit of the doubt; it was the other way around. Callum had excused Gibson's actions since he'd been partnered with him, telling himself that at least it was for the greater good. They were protecting the innocent from scum like Arcana.

Scum that you've just helped to escape.

No, not Ferne. She wasn't like that. He couldn't believe …

And just *how* had they escaped anyway? The last thing he remembered was falling into the closet, Ferne closing the door and mumbling something.

There were hands on him, detaching his vest, unbuttoning his clothes; pulling open his shirt and taking off his trousers. The hands pressed his side and it felt warm. Then the pain returned as the nerve endings registered the bullet wound there again.

"He's lost a lot of blood." This was the first voice again.

"Not nearly enough!" This was a third person's, gruff and mean. Pure hatred. "What were you thinking, bringing him here? Are you insane?"

"Shut up," Ferne told this one. He felt her hands searching again for more holes. Her touch was light and warmth flooded through him once more.

She's doing what she did to her throat, to the Hodgson kid. She's healing you, Callum told himself. *She's healing bullet wounds! How about that?*

"He's not worth expending your energy on." The gruff voice again.

"He saved my life!" Ferne snapped.

"But brought them to you in the first place," the man reminded her. "I told you—"

"And I told *you* to shut up, so I can concentrate on what I'm doing."

Ferne felt around some more; God, he was covered in the things. He *should* have died by rights. But he knew he was in safe, and quite remarkable, hands. The more work she did, the better he began to feel, but Callum was still too weak to move. By the time she was finished, he could see again, but it was all he could do to keep his eyes open. The figures above him were still more than a little blurry—and he had no chance of identifying where in the hell he was—but he knew this was only a temporary thing. He could see the closest of the three people, though. Ferne's face hovered above him. She was pale and the top of her uniform was stained red.

"You need to rest now," she told him, and put one of those hands over his eyes. Callum didn't know whether it was just sheer exhaustion, or if she'd done something to make him sleep, but sleep he did.

And this time there were no nightmares.

When Callum awoke, he felt better than he had in a long while.

The first thing he noticed was that the dullness of the hangover had gone, and he was hungry. Light filtered in from an open doorway, but he still couldn't see much of the room. Lifting his head, he found he was lying on a small camp bed barely wider than himself. He was covered with a blanket, but underneath that he was naked apart from his boxers. Callum checked himself over: his sides, his back. There were no bullet wounds to be found.

He sat up, the metal of the bed creaking, and was about to stand when a voice said: "You were very lucky."

Callum retreated back on the bed, pulling the covers up to his chin—like a child who thinks it will protect him from the bogeyman.

There was a small laugh. "Don't worry, it's not the first time I've seen you like that."

Callum squinted into the dark recesses of the room. "Ferne …?"

A figure rose up from the outlines of a chair and walked over. Her black hair was down again now, free to fall onto her shoulders, and she'd changed out of her nurse's uniform into a long, dark-blue dress. "How do you feel?"

"I feel … odd," said Callum honestly, letting the blanket slip. "But fantastic."

Ferne laughed again, and sat on the edge of the bed. She felt his head, ever the nurse. "Your temperature's normal, anyway."

"Have you been here all this time, watching over me?" he asked.

"Don't look so surprised. You made yourself my patient when you got yourself shot to pieces."

"Yeah," breathed Callum. "I remember. How did we get out of there?"

"I … sort of teleported us."

"What?" Even after everything he'd seen, Callum had trouble with that one. "You can do that?"

Ferne shook her head. "Not usually, but I do know a good spell to get me home."

"Is that where we are, home?" he asked, sounding lost.

"You'll find that out in good time. You're not regretting what you did, are you?'

He hesitated slightly before giving a shake of the head. "It was the … right thing to do. At the time," he added.

"But now? What about now?"

Callum closed his eyes and opened them again. "I don't know what to think. Part of me is wondering if I should be turning you in. There are still good men in the division."

"You really believe that?"

"Yes. *I* was one of them," he argued. "I believe in protecting innocent people against—"

"Against the likes of us?" Ferne looked away, towards the light at the door.

"If you want to put it that way, yes." A silence passed between them and he felt the need to justify what he'd just said. "Listen, Ferne, I know you have your beliefs … But the fact remains that Arcana has been responsible for some of the worst terrorist acts known to man. You are Arcana, aren't you?"

She turned back, a defiant look on her face. "I am, and proud of it! But Arcana is not what you think."

"Oh? You're telling me they don't go around killing people now, like that shopping precinct the other week?" he barked, just as angry at himself as them. "It would have been much worse if the security people hadn't stopped two of them. Then there was the business at Central Airport last year. The monorail disaster from a few Christmases ago."

"I'll admit there are radicals—"

"You mean fanatics."

"Let me finish!" Ferne shouted back. Callum blinked and let her continue. "We weren't responsible for what happened at *All Seasons*."

"Then who was?" asked Callum.

"We don't know. They claim to be Arcana, and for all I know they joined the cause in order to instigate trouble."

Callum sniffed. "So you're saying that Arcana aren't the ones doing these things? I suppose you'll be telling me next I imagined them fighting with us back on Widow's Way?"

"If *you* were being hunted down and exterminated like vermin, wouldn't *you* fight back?" She was only crystallising what he'd thought himself at the time, but it was still hard for him to hear. "Our kind have been persecuted for centuries. Hunted down and burnt at the stake, dunked in water with no way to survive the test. The ridiculous rumours that were spread about us and our Sabbats, that we communed with demons and kissed the buttocks of a goat-headed devil! Do you know that some people still believe all that crap to this day?" Ferne was fuming, and intent on venting her frustrations. "We hurt no one, we never have done. You have your religion, the New Baptists and others, we have ours. We pray to The Goddess, serve her in the best way we can. And we practise magick. That's what you people can't get your head around, the fact that we can do things that you can't. When it all comes down to it, you're jealous. That's why you hate us so much. That and the fact you don't understand how we have the power do such things. Am I right?"

Callum thought back to how he'd felt when he first realised magick was real as a child, rather than a fairy-tale to scare children. That there were people who could fly, alter their appearance, control people's minds. They'd been told that to use these skills, they needed to sign their souls away in pacts with the dark side of nature. But hadn't there been just a tiny part of him that was envious? If it was possible to fly, to be as strong as ten men, to transport yourself to another place without having to drive or take the mono, wouldn't that be worth some kind of sacrifice?

"I can see by the look in your eye that I'm right," she said, with no small amount of satisfaction.

"Perhaps," he confessed, "but I prefer my soul to remain intact, thanks."

Ferne laughed again. "Is that what you think? We're damned for all eternity because of what we do? What utter nonsense! Our powers are gifts from The Goddess, and we try to use them wisely in everyday life. Besides which, if you really believe that then you're tainted now as well."

"How do you figure?"

"Because I healed you, Callum." She smiled. "By your reasoning, you're just as damned as I am."

He hadn't thought of that.

"Those other M-forcers think you're in league with us anyway. They thought it, whether it was true or not. Do you see how that works, how quickly it spreads?"

Callum had to admit that she was right. Gibson had been ready to condemn him, even before he'd heard an explanation.

"It's how you … how *they* always work. Spreading suspicion, using the population's fear to justify what they do. Which is basically cold-blooded murder."

"It's no more than some members of Arcana are capable of," he countered.

Ferne sighed heavily. "I thought I'd explained that. We wouldn't hurt anyone. It's against our beliefs to take a life, unless in self-defence."

"But isn't that what Arcana claim to be doing, defending themselves against a corrupt police system and government?"

"You're twisting what I'm saying." Ferne moved closer. "Yes, in the beginning Arcana did seek to get our message out to the population, to try and inform them that there was nothing to be scared of. Remember the Palace protest?"

"Vaguely," said Callum, who'd only been in his early teens back then. He recalled that members of Arcana had gotten past the security systems at the King's Palace and were climbing up the side of the building before guards could get to them.

"That's because it hardly got any coverage at all," explained Ferne. "It was pulled from TV stations almost as soon as it aired, the story distorted in all the newspapers. That's how much power these people have. What I can do with my hands pales into insignificance compared to that."

Callum looked puzzled. "But Arcana were trying to kill the King, weren't they?"

"That's what you were told. It was a peaceful protest, our people had banners they were going to hang on the outside of the Palace. That's why they were climbing up the side. But they were shot before they could attach the first corner. Ask anyone who was there at the time, there were plenty of eyewitnesses to report that security fired without provocation. Except, of course, all the people who saw that were bundled off into vans never to be seen again."

Callum rubbed his forehead. "I don't believe that. Why would they—"

"It's a form of control, can't you see?"

"So, if you're right, *that* protest was peaceful. But what about all the others? What about what happened to my parents?"

Ferne looked down. "I can't say for sure about that, I was very young at the time. But if those people really were Arcana, then I'm pretty certain things didn't happen the way the reports stated."

"This is a lot to take in, and I'm not even sure I should be listening to any of it."

Ferne took his arm and lowered it. Then she placed his hand on the middle of his chest, with hers on top. "Forget what's up there," she said, nodding at his head. "What does this tell you?"

"I don't know."

"Think about everything you've seen as an Enforcement Officer, and then think about me. Am I a menace to society, Callum? Would you see me hanged or burnt to death, just for who I am? For who I was born to be?" Her tones were soft, seductive.

Don't believe their lies! The voice came to him but he didn't know where from, the remnants of a dream, he thought. He remembered how the woman back on Widow's Way had been able to control Cartwright, manipulate his mind and perception. Was that what was happening to him, what had been happening since he first met Ferne?

"How do I know you're not doing this to me, making me act this way?" said Callum. "I've seen it before."

Ferne pulled her hand away from his, stung. "If you think that then you're even more of a fool than Michael says you are. Or maybe I'm the fool for thinking you'd believe me." She got up to leave, but he reached out and grabbed her wrist.

"Ferne, wait. I'm sorry."

She looked down and he let go. Then she held his gaze. "Do you know, Callum, I could have just run away and hidden as soon as I knew you were an M-forcer, just like I did when Gibson was after me before. But I didn't. Do you know why?"

Callum shook his head.

"I believe you're different. I believe you're someone who fundamentally knows right from wrong. Someone who's not blinded by smokescreens or constricted by rules and regulations. You're a moral person. You proved that when you didn't turn me in after I helped the Hodgsons' boy. And you showed me again today when you stopped Gibson from hurting me. I couldn't have forced you to do that if I'd tried! Believe it or not, you have a strong sense of self-purpose, Callum. You know what you should or shouldn't do." Ferne drew in a slow breath and let it out again. "Something inside you is aware that I'm telling the truth, it knows I haven't done anything to beguile you—"

"Oh I … I wouldn't say that," Callum replied with a half-smile he hoped she would reciprocate. But she kept to the subject.

"You saved my life today; I've now returned the favour. And I've fought your corner when there were people who would gladly have sent you off to some isolated spot and just left you there to die."

"This Michael you mentioned?" asked Callum, wondering if it was the same person she'd been arguing with when she was healing him.

Ferne ignored the question. "The important thing is, you've earned yourself a chance."

"To do what?"

"To make a difference, to see things from the other side. To put something right that has gone terribly, terribly wrong."

There was a soft knock at the door, and they both turned in its direction. A small figure stood there and when he spoke, Callum recognised it as the other male voice he'd heard as Ferne fixed him up. He was a teenager, about seventeen if Callum had to guess.

"What is it, Gavin?" said Ferne.

"Sorry, I didn't mean to interrupt."

"That's all right, you weren't." Callum raised an eyebrow at that one, but Ferne didn't see it.

"It's just that Master Unwin has asked to see the prisone … the guest. If he's recovered, that is?"

"He has. Tell Master Unwin I will bring our visitor to him as soon as possible."

Gavin nodded, looked once at Callum, then withdrew from the doorway.

"So, who's this Unwin guy, then? Your leader?"

Ferne laughed softly again. "Things do not work in the way you think they do here. We're not some kind of army, Callum." When she saw he was still waiting for an answer, she tacked on, "Master Unwin is the oldest and wisest of us all. He's a seer."

"Excuse me?"

"He can see the future."

"Right, sure he can." Callum got up from the bed, standing intentionally in front of her with just his boxers on. "At any rate, I can't meet him looking like this, can I?"

This time, because she could see he wasn't embarrassed, Ferne blushed and looked away.

Callum smiled. "What's the matter, it's not the first time … right?"

Ferne went over to the corner where she'd been sitting, stooping to gather something. When she returned she threw clothes onto the bed. "These looked about your size."

Callum held up the jeans and shirt.

"What were you expecting, robes?" Ferne asked, walking over to the door. She turned, once, and Callum saw the corners of her mouth raise slightly. "I'll be outside when you're ready," she said.

Then she left him alone to get changed.

CHAPTER SEVENTEEN

Even before the phone rang, Nero knew what the call was about.

He'd been monitoring the official reports from McGuire's stationhouse all day. After being informed of the situation with the children, he'd insisted that the young M-forcer be part of the team that was sent to the hospital. He hadn't listened to Pryce, who thought that both he and his partner Gibson needed a bit more time to cool off, but was rather of the mind that they shouldn't give him any more of a chance to dwell on what had happened.

"You saw the footage from The Penitentiary yourself," Pryce told him. "I don't think he's ready to go into action again so soon. He's questioning himself, and others."

"You have your orders," Nero had informed him. Orders which had then been relayed to Superintendent Wallis via the usual channels.

So McGuire, Gibson, and a couple of support units had been dispatched to chase up the information eventually "given" to them yesterday. What followed had shocked even Nero, so much so that he had to re-read the online report several times just to get it straight in his own mind. He hadn't been expecting the choice to be made quite so soon, or for it to swing so spectacularly against them. What had tipped the balance? he wondered. Had it been McGuire's reaction to The Penitentiary, as Pryce had warned him? His pathetic attachment to those Arcana children? Or had it been the fact that McGuire had known the Arcana member in question? That through a million to one shot, he was actually living in the same apartment block as her?

"You've seen Gibson's report, I take it," said Pryce down the line.

"I have. It's … unfortunate."

"If Gibson's to believed there was something going on with the girl."

"'Now hatred is by far the longest pleasure; Men love in haste, but they detest at leisure.'"

"What?"

"Lord Byron, Pryce. It means that he will regret his dalliance, but perhaps by then it will already be too late."

"He's with Arcana, wherever they are."

"They will attempt to corrupt him," Nero said, grimacing. "I had hoped to avoid that particular scenario."

"You and I both knew he had the capacity for this inside him."

"You know nothing!" Nero bellowed down the phone. His free, gloved hand closed: making a fist, releasing it, then clenching it again.

"It was a mistake to put him in harm's way again so soon."

"Don't you ever, *ever* …" Nero slammed his fist down on the table in front of him, so hard that Pryce was bound to hear it, "… question my decisions, Pryce. Past, present or future." But what was he really angry about, the fact that he'd been wrong, or that Pryce was now calling him on it?

"I'm sorry." Pryce's voice sounded like a mouse squeaking. "*Of course* you couldn't have known about this variable when you sent McGuire to the hospital."

"More like it," growled Nero.

"And …"

"Yes?"

"And on a more positive note, we're getting more information now than ever before. I estimate we'll have a good dozen or more members of Arcana rounded up before the week is out."

Nero smiled thinly. That did take the edge off somewhat. It

meant they were closer to finding the book and, who knows, might even get McGuire back before too much damage was done. He shuddered to think what kind of brainwashing might be going on. *Oh look at us, the poor victims of a ruthless regime. Boo-hoo.* Snivelling wretches. It made Nero sick to his stomach.

"The children have proved quite … malleable," Pryce went on. "They knew things I don't even think they realised. And the more Arcana we have in custody, the more we *will* have eventually."

"Good," said Nero, "then perhaps there is hope after all." A part of him realised Pryce was just telling him what he wanted to hear, to save his own skin, but it made Nero feel better nonetheless. "Keep me up to speed on things," he said, hanging up. It wasn't necessary, he would keep himself apprised anyway. Nero was just reminding Pryce who was the boss. Sometimes his right-hand man had a tendency to get above himself, probably because he was the one out there as the public face of the Magick Law Enforcement Division, while Nero hadn't set foot outside of his keep in years. Well, not officially.

He wouldn't do so until there was cause. Nero had a feeling that day was coming, just as he'd known about Callum's choice. He'd have to make one himself soon, probably the most important of his entire life. But he wouldn't waver or turn his back on what he believed in.

Soon Arcana would be no more, one way or the other.

CHAPTER EIGHTEEN

When Callum emerged from the room, Ferne led him up a dusty corridor with gas-lamps on either side. The walls themselves were partially covered with a faded red velvet, and yellowing wallpaper that was peeling with age.

"What is this place?" Callum asked, agog.

"You'll see," promised Ferne, giving nothing away.

They turned a corner and Callum saw the remains of posters on the walls. One, just as faded as the wallpaper, announced: "*The Turn of the Screw* by Henry James, starring Madeline Beck and Peter Daines." Another advertised Shakespeare's *Richard III* with Victor Johns in the title role. Yet another proclaimed that *Mother Goose* was fun for all the family at "The Valentine."

"A theatre?" said Callum.

"The oldest surviving theatre in the area," Ferne told him. "But there hasn't been a production here in over ten years. Couldn't compete with the multi-entertainment centres. You were resting in one of the changing rooms."

"But surely this place would have been torn down, wouldn't it?" Callum said.

"Not if nobody knew it was here."

"I don't understand."

Ferne waved her hand around. "We mask it from the world, a spell of concealment."

"You mean you've made it invisible?"

"Not exactly. Just made it so that nobody will question why it's here. How many times have you gone past the same building time and again? Eventually it just becomes part of the background and you can't even describe it when you're asked."

It was true. Callum used to walk past buildings as a beat cop in London; after a few months they just blended in with their surroundings. "But someone at the Department of Housing would have queried it by now, wouldn't they? I mean, they could put a block of flats or something where this place is."

"We have someone who owes us a favour working there," Ferne said. "You'd be surprised how many people are sympathetic to our cause. The innocents you claim M-forcers are protecting from us."

They walked past the old ticket office, and the bar area. Callum was aware of eyes turning in their direction, watching him. Maybe a dozen or more people sat on chairs, in the snugs. Members of Arcana. He felt a bit like he was in the lion's den and was grateful he had Ferne beside him, otherwise he might just get eaten up whole.

It was the same when they opened the door that took them to the stage area. Walking up onto the stage itself, Callum noted people in the audience; downstairs, and in the horseshoe-shaped balcony above. Clumps of Arcana members watching him.

As if reading his mind, Ferne said, "Don't worry, you're quite safe. Or at least safer than the people that end up in The Penitentiary."

Callum knew what she was digging at. "Sherman Pryce himself assured me the children would be cared for, otherwise I wouldn't have left them."

"Sherman Pryce is a sadistic bastard," Ferne informed him. "I bet he didn't show you the basement of that place, did he?"

Callum shook his head. "I didn't even know it had one."

"They call it the Dungeon." Ferne's eyes turned to slits. "Pryce designed it himself, based on the old torture chambers from Spanish Inquisition days."

"No," said Callum, "I don't believe you. Those kinds of methods were banned long ago."

Ferne shook her head. "That's what most people think, but behind closed doors it's another matter entirely. Like your friend Gibson said, we don't have any rights. We're scum as far as Pryce's concerned, so he's free to do what he wants with us. To rape, molest, torture, then dispose of."

Callum swallowed hard.

"Come on," said Ferne, taking his hand. "Master Unwin will be waiting." Down behind the stage, they walked along a corridor and descended more steps. She noticed Callum looking nervously at the walls and remembered what he'd said about confined spaces. "It's okay."

"No," said Callum, "it's really not."

She took his hand and squeezed it, whispering under her breath. He felt the heat again from her palm. "Yes. Yes, it is."

Callum did feel better somehow. *There really isn't anything to be scared of down here,* he told himself. *I don't know what I was thinking.*

"That's incredible," he said, grinning.

"It's only temporary, I'm afraid, but it should get you through the meeting with Master Unwin."

"Why does this Unwin want to see me, anyway?"

Ferne shrugged. "I'm not privy to his reasons, but I would imagine he has something to tell you."

"Let me guess, about the future?"

"Or the past. Or even the here and now," Ferne clarified.

"Has he ever told you anything about yours? Your future, I mean?"

Ferne didn't answer, just guided him towards a door at the end of the corridor. "Here we are." Ferne gestured for him to descend into the basement, which must be located somewhere under the stage, Callum guessed.

He took a step into the room, then turned and waited for Ferne to follow. "Aren't you coming?"

"Master Unwin hasn't asked to see me," was her reply.

Callum looked disappointed and more than a little terrified, not of the confined space this time, but rather what he would find inside it.

He took a deep breath, and ventured inside.

It was gloomy in the room, the light coming from a single small gas-lamp. As far as Callum could make out, though, this place had once been used to house the various props and costumes from the plays performed here. There were trunks lurking in corners, racks with cloaks and other clothes draped over them, some with hats on top too. In the half-light it looked almost as if scraggy figures were hanging there, limp and lifeless. To his left Callum spotted a sword leaning against the wall, and an axe beneath it. Various other bits and pieces littered the space, including fake telephones, dummies, and old painted façades, used for scene changes.

"Well, don't just stand there, young man," urged a voice from the back of the room. "Come inside."

Tentatively, Callum made his way further into this Aladdin's cave. And quite by chance he saw a lamp that must have belonged to that particular character, stacked on top of a mound of counterfeit gold coins inside a tea chest.

Then he saw who the voice belonged to. A man who looked as old as time itself, sitting at a table. He was shuffling cards as if about to ask Callum to pick one so he could guess which it was. The closer Callum drew, the more details he spotted. There were no pupils in the man's eyes, just the thick webs of cataracts that must have made it impossible to see anything. They matched the thin wisps of white hair that fell from his crown over his shoulders. His face was a map of lines, some fine, some deep as trenches. His neck was no less wrinkled, skin folding upon itself in layers. When he smiled, the mouth revealed the stumps of rotten teeth that looked like they hadn't been brushed in months, maybe even years. Callum pulled a face, letting out a small sound of disgust.

"Does my appearance upset you?" asked the old man. Callum shook his head, then realised the fellow couldn't see it. Before he could answer, though, Unwin said: "This is not the place for lies, to spare my feelings or anything else, young man. I can remember looking upon my grandfather and feeling a similar revulsion. The old remind us that we are not immortal. That time catches up with us all in the end."

He continued to shuffle the cards, with hands that looked arthritis-riddled, but showed more dexterity than someone of Callum's age. It was almost as if the deck was keeping his fingers nimble. Like it was linked to him, giving the old man strength. Then, as the shuffle grew faster, it seemed to Callum that the cards took on a life of their own and Unwin's hands were just the means via which they moved.

"Hello, Callum McGuire," said Unwin. "I've been waiting a long time to meet you."

"I'm … I'm afraid you have me at a disadvantage."

Unwin laughed. "That is what everyone says."

"They're right, it seems."

The old man chuckled again. "A sense of humour, I like that." He stopped shuffling for a second and held out his hand for Callum to sit opposite him.

Once he'd done so, Callum said, "Okay, you know who I am. Who are you?"

"They call me Unwin."

"That much I do know," Callum informed him. "And the small fact you're supposed to be a seer."

The old man continued to smile his stumpy smile. "My vision isn't hampered by reality. I'm not distracted by the world you see around you every day. It helps me to focus on … what's important."

"I'm not sure that I understand," said Callum truthfully.

"Do you believe in other worlds?" Unwin suddenly asked.

Callum opened his mouth to speak, then hesitated. Finally, he said, "Are you talking about little green men from outer space?"

Unwin shook his head. "I mean other *possible* versions of this world. There's a theory, and it has been around some time, though the men who came up with it were silenced very quickly, their notions too much like magick … This theory," he said, getting back to the point, "suggests that there are many different Earths. Many alternatives in which every single choice we make is played out. Imagine, Callum, if you could go back and change your mind about something, go left instead of right, hold back when before you rushed in. That's what you're wondering right now, isn't it?"

Unwin took a card off the top of the deck and laid it on the table. It showed a man in a dark cloak, head bent, looking at three spilled goblets on his left; on his right, behind him, were two goblets with wine still in them.

"The Five of Cups," Unwin explained, though Callum had no idea how; some kind of braille? "It indicates unhappiness with how some event has turned out, or a feeling of missed opportunity."

"I'm still not sure I follow."

"Remember, this is not the place for untruths. It is futile—the cards know all."

Callum remained silent.

"You're wondering if you should have just let Gibson take Ferne into custody, aren't you? Whether you made the right decision. Then perhaps we shall discover that together, eh?" He turned over another card: The Seven of Pentacles. "Ah, you may yet achieve what you were born to do, young Callum, though perhaps not quite in the way you had expected."

"I think it's pretty unlikely now that I'm a fugitive," Callum sniped.

Unwin tapped the Five of Cups. "You're concentrating on the spilt goblets, but there are untouched ones behind you that you're ignoring."

"What are you saying? That I should count my blessings? I turned on my fellow officers and helped a criminal escape." Callum rose to leave. "This isn't fortune telling, this is useless mumbo jumbo."

"Sit down," said Unwin.

"I'm sorry, I'm going now." Callum made a move to walk away.

"I said, *sit down!*" Unwin's tone caused him to freeze up completely. It wasn't any kind of magick, it was simply fear. Not specifically of Unwin. More that if he ignored what was being said to him now, there wouldn't be another opportunity to listen. That if he didn't take heed then something terrible might happen. Callum sat back down again stiffly.

"I'm sorry," he repeated, but actually meant it this time.

"Better." Unwin smiled. He flipped over another card: it was the King of Swords. "Some say he looks like he's sitting in judgement. But over what, I wonder? You're a strong-willed man, Callum. Powerful and well suited to a position of authority. But at the same time you're fiercely independent and can't abide being constrained in any way. Am I right?"

Callum shrugged, then realised again he needed to answer out loud.

"I'll take that as a yes," said Unwin before he had the chance.

"How did you—"

"And although you think you were destined for great things in the ranks of the Enforcement Officers, it is nothing compared to what you might achieve as … something else." Unwin held up a finger. "However, the path is not completely blocked for you. If it is truly what you desire, then there is a way for you to return to what you once were."

"How?" said Callum. "I turned a gun on my fellow officers. I hit my partner with a baton, for Heaven's sake! I'd say that particular career path was closed off, wouldn't you?"

"There *is* a way, I tell you."

"How?" Callum asked again.

"You can betray us all."

There was silence. Callum's brow creased as he took in what Unwin had told him. Yes, it made sense. The only way he'd ever be accepted back would be if he could prove his loyalty. And to do that he'd have to hand over some of the major members of Arcana, give Wallis or Pryce the location of their base. It would work, Callum was sure of that, but why would Unwin put the idea in his head?

The old man looked Callum up and down with his ruined eyes. "There is always a price to pay. That price is our deaths. The question you must ask yourself, therefore: Is that particular ambition worth our lives?"

Callum quietly regarded the seer.

"You have seen how M-forcers operate now, their methods and procedures. There is no law but the ones they make for themselves. There is no escape for the innocent or guilty alike. They will not stop until every single magick user has been eradicated. And what then? Already, the Division are using information given to them by the captured children to target more of our kind, as they did with Ferne. I know the doubts you had back at Widow's Way, at The Penitentiary. You have no reason to trust us, nor believe what has been told to you about Pryce. But you know more than you think you do."

This time Callum really didn't understand, and he told Unwin so.

"Your dreams, my young friend. You've been having more and more lately, haven't you?"

"How did …" Callum realised it was pointless to keep asking that of this man, so asked instead: "What have they got to do with this?"

"A great deal," Unwin assured him. "Just as my cards open up the past, present and future to me, so your dreams do the same for you. You may not understand them yet, but they are speaking to you nevertheless. Tell me what you saw when you dreamed of The Penitentiary."

"I don't remember. I was drunk and—"

Unwin waved a hand in front of him. "I think that you do. Tell me."

Unwillingly, Callum reached down into his memories. He could recall the occasional snippet, but nothing more. Finally, he shook his head. "No, sorry."

"You're protecting yourself from the truth, but it will find a way out," Unwin warned him. "See … even now your subconscious is showing you. The children, remember what you saw happening to the children."

Then he *did* remember: the chair, the wheel that was being tightened, choking the little girl with the blonde hair. The threat of slicing open the little boy's throat to get her to speak. Callum gasped.

"You saw what Pryce was doing to them, didn't you?"

Callum shook his head. "It was just a dream. Only a dream."

"You believe that about as much as I do. Tell me what else you saw."

"The woman who died at Widow's Way, and Ferne. I saw Ferne."

"And someone else."

"Yes. Someone in the darkness. A figure, holding Ferne. Telling me not to believe the Arcana."

"Nero," whispered Unwin.

"Head of the Enforcement Division? But I don't even know the man. He hasn't been seen in public for years. Why would I be dreaming about *him*?"

Now it was Unwin who remained silent. The answers would come eventually, this old man knew, and they would come in time.

"So, *do* you believe that we have been lying to you?" Unwin asked, at last.

"I don't know what to believe anymore," moaned Callum.

"You acted instinctively when Ferne was being attacked. Part of you thinks that was because you have feelings for her." Callum raised his eyebrows. "Part of you knows it was to stop an injustice from being carried out. Like the ones you've seen your partner commit even in the relatively short space of time you have known him. Tell me if I am wrong."

Callum bit his lip.

"Your dreams reflect your doubts about the role you have to play." Unwin peeled another card off the top of the deck and held it up in front of him. This one said at the bottom: "The World." "A significant change in the querent's life," said Unwin.

"No shit," Callum whispered.

"You remember what I was saying about there being many worlds, many possible dimensions?" his elder asked.

Callum nodded.

"I've seen them. Seen them all."

Callum laughed. "What, in a crystal ball?"

Unwin grinned. "No, in the cards." He reached out and grabbed Callum's hand, so fast he didn't have time to pull away, then rammed the last card he'd chosen into Callum's palm. The young man jolted upright in his chair. The room around him was gone, replaced with a vision of a world at peace, with meadows and forests: nature living in tune with humanity. He saw himself and Ferne there, walking through fields, holding hands, stopping to kiss every now and again. Children, a boy and a girl, came running up behind and Callum grabbed the lad, swinging him up into the air as the little girl hugged her mother.

"And in all the worlds I've witnessed, I've never seen the barbarity of what's happening in this one." Unwin's words drifted through the vision. "Picture it, Callum, a world where people aren't arrested or killed just for what they believe in. For who they are. Where people who practise magick actually perform in places like this, are revered by the public for their skills. Where people aren't constantly suspected of crimes whether they're guilty or not. And children's books have wizards and witches as their heroes. Their *heroes*, Callum! Not something to be scared of or demonised, but ordinary, everyday things, accepted and loved. In most worlds your kind—the M-forcers, the finders—were stamped out long ago, when people realised what they were doing was wrong. But not here, not in this one. Here their power only grew stronger; Hopkins saw to that. Leaving us to hide away like criminals, to try and spread the word the only way we can."

Callum blinked away the vision, throwing down the card. "But what you're doing is hurting people. Is killing worth the price of 'spreading the word,' as you call it?"

"Never," replied Unwin without missing a beat. "Life is sacred to us, especially our own. That's why no true Arcana would ever have done the things you're talking about."

"What about the girl back at Widow's Way? She took her own life," Callum argued.

"Rhea did what she did because she knew she was dead anyway."

"So, you deny it's your people who have been carrying out the attacks."

"I deny nothing. All I am saying is that things are not what they appear to be, Callum."

"You're talking in riddles. Either it *was* your people or it *wasn't*. An Arcana cell maybe? One that you have no control over?"

He shook his head. "You're not listening. No true Arcana would behave in such a manner. We are in tune with this world, its balances. It is forbidden to interfere with them."

Callum frowned again. "Then what—"

"You spoke of Rhea before."

"I never knew her name, but yes." He nodded on the last word.

"You remember what she could do."

"The purple rain?"

"No, no, no. That was a simple trick, self-preservation … and no-one was killed, if you recall."

"Wasn't for the lack of trying."

Unwin sighed. "No, I meant to the senior policeman."

Callum pictured Cartwright with his gun in his mouth, so far in he was almost gagging on the barrel. "She was controlling him."

"Not really controlling, as such. Not Rhea." Unwin smiled. "And she only did what she did in order to escape; to secure the children's safety when she had no other choice. But imagine if someone actually did have such persuasive powers and used them in a malicious way … with a certain intent."

"You're saying someone might have been controlling the terrorists like that?"

"In a manner of speaking."

Callum's head hurt. Before he'd walked in here, before Ferne had teleported him to this long-abandoned theatre, things had been so simple. He knew what the sides were, which one he was supposed to be on.

"But did you, *really*?" Unwin questioned.

"You can read my mind as well?"

Unwin's smile broadened.

"But who—"

"Who would have the most to gain by demonising us?" Unwin let the words settle before continuing, giving the accusation the weight it deserved. He didn't answer it himself, nor did he wait for Callum to offer his suggestions. "Rhea was as close to Ferne as a sister. They grew up together. The boy and girl who were taken were like her nephew and niece."

Callum's mouth fell open. "Jesus," he whispered.

"I do not tell you this to make you feel guilty. Not even Ferne herself blames you for what has happened. You had no choice, either. Not really, not then."

"Then why?"

"Because it is important for you to understand that things happen for a reason."

"And you know what those are, I expect. You hold all the cards." The sentence still wasn't without a healthy dose of sarcasm, but Unwin answered him plainly:

"Yes. Without what happened at Widow's Way, you would not be sitting here. Without what happened you wouldn't have knocked on Ferne's door last night. The M-forcers wouldn't have come for her, and you wouldn't have helped her escape. You, young Callum, have an important role to play in events to come."

He touched his chest. "Me? I doubt it."

Unwin turned over a final card. There was a figure of a child riding a white horse, with a walled garden in the background. High above was a beaming sun, from which the card took its name.

"The child represents simplicity and innocence in the human race," Unwin revealed. "Without the sun there would be no life on Earth. It's the power of nature, Callum, can you feel it?'

Callum didn't have a clue what Unwin was talking about.

"The child is making the transition from the known to the unknown. Soon it will be filled with self-knowledge. It will know its purpose, its true potential. At the right moment, Callum, so will you." Unwin breathed out heavily, eyelids dropping. The reading had taken its toll, that was plain to see. As he began to fall forward in the chair, Callum got up and held him by the arm. Unwin raised his head and patted Callum's hand. "You have no idea who … *what* you are, do you?"

"I'm Callum McGuire," he said.

"A name, nothing more."

There were footsteps behind him and Callum turned to see the boy who'd been sent to fetch him and Ferne. Something told him that … what was his name? Gavin, that was it … Something told him Gavin was the one who looked after Unwin, so Callum offered the arm to him.

"Thanks," said the lad, as Unwin began to cough.

Callum backed away from the scene, feeling like he needed more. More information, more clarification of what had been said (he still didn't understand half of it).

And more reassurance.

That last one was the most important of the three. But he knew he wasn't going to get any of them now.

Just before he turned to make his way out of the basement room, Unwin called out his name. Callum paused and saw the old man stand up, with Gavin's assistance. "Be ready," Unwin wheezed. "The time is approaching when you must take that final step. Do …" Callum waited for him to finish, but it seemed like Unwin wasn't going to complete the last bit of his farewell.

"Yes?" he prompted at last.

"Do not be scared," Unwin murmured, though the echo carried it to Callum's ears. "It is your destiny."

With that, the lights in the basement dimmed, and Callum, still frowning, retreated up the steps and headed for the surface.

CHAPTER NINETEEN

Peter Finlay hated the mornings.

His body just wasn't equipped for getting up at 6:00 a.m. First he'd sleep through the alarm, which earned him a swift elbow in the ribs from his wife, Janice, woken up by the beeping (though she could stay in bed until gone nine, crawling out in time to watch the reality talk shows). Then he wouldn't be able to get his eyelids to open; it was like they were glued shut. Sleep was good, sleep was fine. He loved everything about the act, the dozing, dropping off into deep, untroubled oblivion. And the dreams; they were his favourite part. In them he lived out his ultimate fantasy from when he was a kid. He was a superhero who could fly and had super-strength, just like in the comics, shooting laser beams from his eyes, trying to save the world from mad villains with ray guns. In his little homemade adventures, he would leap tall buildings with a single bound, be resistant to fire, bullets and the cold.

He could make absolutely anything happen.

"I don't know whatever you do in your sleep," Janice would say, tutting. "The state of the duvet in a morning, it's a complete mess."

Unlike some, Peter never had nightmares, or at least he couldn't remember any. Sleep was his refuge from the daily grind of work and homelife, neither of which he was happy with anymore. That was probably why he'd take so long waking, Janice having to virtually push him upright and force him out of bed to get ready for the long trek into the city.

Every morning he'd stumble across the bedroom, banging into things because he still hadn't managed to prize his eyelids apart. In the bathroom he'd tug on the light-cord, but not even the glare from that could get him to open his eyes fully. Even as he ate his breakfast, inevitably spilling the juice and milk as he poured them—one into a glass, the other onto his Wheaty Flaky Oates—his eyes were still only a third of the way open.

Yawning, he'd walk to the nearest monorail station, adjusting his tie several times as he waited on the platform. It was no good buying a magazine or paper, because he wouldn't be able to read it, not at half seven in the blessed morning. And as the monorail began its journey, the monotonous juddering of the wheels on the tracks didn't help when it came to staying awake.

The major problem, of course, was that he knew the monorail terminated at his stop. That was fatal. The train would halt, he'd get off, and he'd trundle to work where he'd watch as a another bunch of morons tried out sofas, easyboy recliners and tested the springs on the mattresses, while Peter looked on longingly at the latter, wishing he could just climb in and grab forty winks.

Which was probably why he woke when the monorail stopped that morning, expecting, as usual, to get off and go to his job at the furniture store. But they were not at the end of the line yet. Peter looked out at an unfamiliar station.

People in the seats around him looked at each other. Those holding on to handles dangling from the ceiling exchanged glances, too. Mutterings about works on the line began and how the monorail wasn't value for money these days, not that it ever really had been. But that wasn't the reason they'd stopped.

Squinting down the aisle, Peter saw a commotion at the doors, which had opened automatically as they'd pulled into the station. Folk were moving back, making room for more passengers, he assumed. But these were no ordinary commuters. Dressed in their distinctive uniforms, with their caps, vests and boots, he recognised the garb of M-forcers straight away.

Oh my God, thought Peter, opening his eyes finally. *What's going on?* He'd seen the news lately, knew of the attacks that were becoming more and more frequent … everyone did. He just got on with his life; you couldn't let a handful of maniacs stop you from going about your business, could you? Except right now he'd have been quite happy to let them do so. Wouldn't have needed much coaxing to remain in bed today.

Now that the M-forcers were getting closer, Peter was about as far from sleep as you could get.

"Everybody, remain calm," shouted the lead officer, wielding a hefty machine-gun. "This is official MLED business."

Peter looked nervously from left to right, and spotted a man opposite wearing sunglasses, sweating profusely. His hands were in his lap one minute, then separated and on his knees the next.

See? See what you miss when you're asleep? Suspicious-looking characters on your very own monorail, Peter!

But did the man really look dangerous? Plenty of people on the train were sweating; whether they were guilty of something or not was anyone's guess. In fact … Yes, didn't that guy with the leathers on standing not ten feet away from him look just as dubious? Bald head, with a trimmed goatee beard.

No, the M-forcers had already checked him and were moving down the aisle.

Then they stopped. One of them was looking right at him. The man held up a gloved hand for the other officers to halt, too. Raising his rifle, he ordered Peter not to move. "I repeat: remain in the chair, Peter Finlay!"

There was no mistake about it, these people were talking to him. How could that be?

"I—"

"Keep your mouth closed until we reach you, or we will use deadly force. Repeat, deadly force!'

What the hell are you talking about? he wanted to say. *You've got the wrong man!*

"Peter Finlay, we have reason to suspect you are a class eight magick user and, as such, will accompany us. Now, there's no need for anyone to get hurt if you'll just come along quietly."

A class what? Peter was shaking, all vestments of sleep shrugged off.

"Now stand up, slowly, keeping your hands where I can see them."

Peter did as he was told. His hands were trembling, his whole body following suit.

"Good, that's good. Now walk towards me. Again, nice and slow."

Peter put one tentative foot in front of the other. He had to trust that whoever was in charge would sort this mess out. He was no more a magick user than Janice.

As if on cue, the officer shouted, "We have your wife, as well. We know what the pair of you have been up to, Arcana scum."

Janice? Up to? We haven't been up to anything. He'd always been scared of this, though, hadn't he, scared of … of being caught.

"Come on," continued the man, beckoning him with his crooked finger. "Just a little further, sparkie."

It was then that the trembling in Peter's fingers, legs and feet grew into movement. His body crackled with energy seemingly sucked up through the floor. He was on the first officer before the guy could even let loose a round. Peter had grabbed the weapon and pushed it back into his face, breaking the man's nose.

The M-forcers behind were quicker to fire and, although the carriage had people inside, they pulled the triggers of their machine-guns, sending passengers diving for cover. The stuffing of the seats exploded, windows shattered.

Peter flew—literally—at the other officers, hitting one and sending him sprawling into more, so hard that they all landed up at the other end of the carriage. As they recovered, he ripped a seat from its housing and rammed them with it, making sure they stayed down.

What … what the hell are you doing? he was asking himself. There was no answer. This was instinctual, he knew that much: this was survival. He felt free, awake in more ways than one. Peter felt like he always did in his dreams, when he used his powers against the villains.

Was that it? Was this another dream, different this time? If so, why was he fighting the Enforcement Officers? They were here to protect honest and law abiding citizens like him, weren't they?

Two more officers ran through the open door and he turned towards them, his eyes burning bright. Before he knew what was happening, two laser-bright bolts shot from them and pounded into the M-forcers, sending them flying backwards onto the platform. Peter rose off the floor, his mouth muttering strange incantations he didn't recognise. Drifting out of the doorway, he saw more police, all incredibly well armed. They opened fire as soon as he was out in the open, but while the inner Peter cowered, the one who faced them did nothing of the kind.

Bullets struck him and bounced off, as if his body was made from some sort of metal. Trails of energy snapped and popped along his arms and legs. He let loose with more of the beams from his eyes. Not killing, merely wounding the nearby officers.

I still don't understand. I am *dreaming, aren't I?* Again, there was no reply, but just the trace of a memory. Janice, astride him in bed, swinging an amethyst crystal and chanting:

"Listen to the words I say, forget the night, embrace the day. Let your other half hold sway."

My God! thought Peter, although that sounded wrong. *Goddess! My Goddess!* Yes, that sounded better. He had no real idea who he was, but had some notion of what had happened to him, why he'd been so reluctant to wake up in the mornings. He'd been placed into a deep sleep by Janice, who herself wasn't what he'd thought. Peter's world was upside down, the dreams real, and the reality … Perhaps he'd been such a security risk she'd had to tuck away the real *him*—the one who could do these incredible things; had the gift of making his fantasies come true—during the daytime at least. It would also explain *why* he was so tired, because he had a whole other life that he lived at night. The dreams were his mind's way of dealing with this incredible power, or maybe the power was feeding the dreams?

Another two M-forcers came at him from the right, one pulling a noose and trying to throw it over his head. Peter grabbed the line and yanked the man towards him, before knocking him unconscious. The other officer he picked up under the chin and threw into the air, to land awkwardly on a bench.

More bullets flew, and even a gas grenade was tossed in Peter's direction. He swatted it away, barely coughing.

This is easy, he thought. Why hadn't they just come out into the open before, taken the battle to their enemy? (As more of them attacked, he was having greater difficulty thinking of them as guardians of peace and justice.) He could take whatever they threw at him. Whatever—

Another gas bomb—or so he thought—was tossed at him. Except that when he tried to bat this one away, it smashed, and the liquid from inside covered his arm, chest and part of his face. It burnt like acid, but some part of Peter's mind recognised what it really was. A concoction of liquid mugwort, angelica, and rowan bark; ancient protections against magick and witches. Peter shook, then screamed out loud: the energy he'd been channelling was fizzling out.

Have to get out of here. Have to ...

With all the power he could muster, he made one last-ditch attempt to fly away. His feet lifted a good few metres off the ground, but before he could get anywhere something attached itself to him; was able to now in his weakened state.

Something with wires dangling from it.

The Taser delivered a charge which made his magick look like a static shock from a car-door handle. Peter jerked, falling and crumpling onto the platform. Officers were all over him immediately as he continued to twitch, foaming saliva spewing from his mouth. One of the men kicked him in the stomach with his hard-tipped boot and laughed as Peter groaned. Another took out his baton and pounded Peter's back.

After a while, they cuffed him and—noose finally around his neck as a deterrent—dragged him off towards the car park and the waiting vans.

Peter fought against unconsciousness, would give anything not to face the oblivion of sleep he'd been craving before. In the end he could postpone it no longer, but he knew that he still wouldn't have nightmares. For those only really existed in the waking world.

And he knew the next time he awoke he would find himself in the most horrific one of all.

Meg Tierney always went food shopping early on a Thursday to avoid the rush, just before work. It was her routine and, even though she was between jobs right now so could choose to visit at any time of the day, she didn't see any reason why she should break with her habits.

But for some reason, this particular morning, there were more people in here than usual, pushing their trolleys up and down with that dazed expression on their faces. The place was obscenely bright as well, in spite of the fact it was light outside and had been for a good couple of hours. The powerful strip panels irradiated everything with a bleached, sterile blanket.

She blinked and pushed her own trolley up the rice and pasta aisle, heading towards the freezer section. As she walked, she caught the strange glances people were giving her. Not obvious looks, but the kind of thing you see out of the corner of your eye.

Meg reached the freezers, leaning over to pick up some ready meals. The saddo meals. She looked up again, to see a couple gawking across at her, who promptly turned their heads.

What? Can they tell? Can they see that I'm unemployed? Unemployable? She knew she should have worn a dress instead of the tracksuit bottoms and long-sleeved T-shirt she was so used to lounging around in. *Yeah, so what? So I messed up at the coffee shop, spilt hot cappuccino in someone's lap by accident. Am I supposed to pay for that the rest of my life?* And her hair, maybe she should have done something with that, too. For thirty-eight, she didn't look too bad when she was all glammed up—which was almost never these days—but without make-up or having even dragged a brush through her hair, she could imagine what they were thinking. *She's let herself go a bit. Pity really, I can remember when she used to shop in here not long ago. She looked really pretty back then. Pretty and—*

And in love.

That was at the root of all this, wasn't it? Why she'd not been concentrating when she brought over that drink to the customer, why she wasn't really paying attention now: just doing the ordinary, everyday things on automatic pilot. Life simply wasn't the same anymore, without her.

Without Tawny.

They'd met in a bar one Friday night, back when she had known how to glam with the best of them. Tawny had been on the dance floor, twirling and spinning like a short, blonde-haired tornado. She was a force of nature, and the minute they'd locked eyes that had been it. They'd sat and watched the sun come up after having no sleep at all the previous night, then kissed as the clouds gave way to streaks of sunlight in the sky. The ten months they'd spent together had been the best of her life. Tawny had brought the magic into what had always been such a dull existence. They walked hand-in-hand by the river in the rain. They went to see trashy movies and complained about the acting and storylines. They drank wine, then wrote and read poetry to each other; Meg still had some of it back at the flat. And they made love like wild things, furious and full of passion. None of the men Meg had ever wasted her time with back in her teens could ever compare with Tawny. She pressed buttons no one else, man or woman, ever could.

Those days had seemed like they would last forever, yet were over in an instant.

What had kicked off the argument that led to their split? Meg still couldn't figure it out. All she'd done was ask Tawny to move in. She'd had it all planned: a romantic, candlelight dinner (certainly not a ready meal), music … She would ask her in the form of a poem she'd memorised:

Without you here, by my side,
My life is poorer, but by
Saying yes, it would mean the world.
And I would give the world
To you if I could.

The thought of it still brought tears to Meg's eyes. *Though not here, keep it together in the supermarket, girl!* Tawny had arrived early and insisted they forego the meal, dragging her off to the bedroom instead. Afterwards, Meg had gazed up at the ceiling and asked her there and then. No meal, no poem, just: "Tawny, will you move in here with me?"

Tawny turned her head on the pillow. "What?"

"Come and live with me."

She'd looked at Meg like she was insane—a little like some of the shoppers were doing right now—and replied, "Oh baby."

"I love you," Meg had blurted out.

Tawny shook her head. "I hoped it wouldn't come to this. I thought we were keeping things casual."

"It's been almost year."

"So?"

"So, doesn't that mean *anything* to you?"

Tawny pulled off the sheets, climbing out of the bed. "Means I've been around too long. Time to say goodbye."

"No!" Meg pulled at her hand as Tawny made to gather her clothes.

"Let me go," said Tawny, and Meg obeyed, knowing it was futile to plead with her.

"At least give me some kind of reason." Meg was in tears, the salt-water stinging her eyes.

Pulling on her jeans, Tawny looked across at her. "It's for the best, Meg. Trust me. There are things you don't know."

"So tell me!" Meg shouted, crawling over the bedsheets to get closer.

Tawny looked away and pulled on her T-shirt. "I can't."

"*Please!*"

"I'll be seeing you, Meg," said Tawny, and blew her a kiss as she let herself out. Meg had crumpled up like a car in a crusher, her body racking with sobs.

She'd made excuses at first, that Tawny was a free spirit who didn't want to be tied down. Or maybe if Meg had been stronger and insisted that they have the meal first, then she could have read her poem and maybe that might have made a difference—instead of letting the words dribble out in the aftermath of sex like the rest of their bodily fluids … and just as off-putting. Or was it the way she'd acted clingy, begging Tawny instead of playing it nice and cool?

Then followed the anger, especially when she couldn't get through to Tawny on her mobile. She'd never told Meg where she lived, so she couldn't even go round and rant. Instead, family members and work colleagues, back when she still had a job, bore the brunt of that fury. After anger came depression—the feeling that nothing really mattered anymore. Meg was barely sleeping. For hours she'd lay awake wondering what Tawny was doing. Imagined her with dozens of women.

When she'd eventually lost her job, it gave her even more time to mope. She didn't have a TV, so would read books, but found that she wasn't taking anything in. It was at times like these that she'd pray, just mouth a line or so to God, offering anything in exchange for just seeing that beautiful face one more time. They were never answered.

Until now.

As Meg was walking past the cheese counter, heading for the fruit and veg department, God finally saw fit to grant her that wish. Today, of all days, when she looked like shit. Today she bumped into Tawny, basket hanging over one arm and squeezing an orange. Meg had to look twice. No, it couldn't be! It was a cruel trick of the eye. This had happened before, a couple of weeks after Tawny had vanished. Meg rushing up to people of the same height with blonde hair on the street, only to discover they looked nothing like her lover up close.

But this time it was different. Inside, Meg *knew* that it was Tawny. That same tingle she always felt when her former lover was around, when Tawny was about to knock or ring. Meg hesitated at first, for one thing unable to catch her breath, for another not having the faintest idea what she'd say after three and a half months. In the end it didn't matter because it was Tawny who saw her first. She put the orange down.

Please don't run. Please don't run away, Meg prayed again. *I just want to …* She realised she had no idea what she wanted to do. This was the woman who'd walked out on *her* after she'd gone to so much trouble that night, after she'd stitched her heart well and truly to her sleeve. The woman she'd cursed for weeks, who'd lost her the coffee shop job. Could there be a way back? Did Meg even *want* her back?

Who was she kidding, of course she did! She'd never felt as alive as when she'd been with Tawny. If there was a chance she could feel like that for just one more day, one more night, she'd take it gladly and suffer the consequences.

Meg pushed the trolley towards her, angling it slightly to try and cut off any escape, no longer bothered by the looks the other shoppers were giving her. She needn't have worried. Tawny remained where she was, waiting for her, ready to face the confrontation.

Meg opened her mouth to speak, but nothing came out. It was like one of those nightmares when you couldn't cry for help.

"Hi," Tawny said first, her lips accentuating every letter. Meg didn't realise quite how much she'd missed those lips until then. "How are you?"

How are you? Was that it, after all this time? Like two old school friends meeting or whatever. It was the opening line of someone who'd never even experienced what they'd had together. Someone who didn't care that they'd left her world in pieces.

"I'm fine," she found herself replying, the bitterness creeping back into her voice.

"Good. You look …" Tawny paused.

I know how I look, thanks very much. Don't say it, don't you dare say it!

"You look … well."

There, she said it! I can't believe she said the corniest line ever.

"I'm glad I've seen you," Tawny continued. "There's something I wanted to say."

Oh, thought Meg, *what's that? Did you leave an earring at my place or something? No, it's more serious than that. Look at her face. Look at her eyes.*

"Yes?" said Meg.

"I wanted to tell you that I'm sorry."

"You're sorry?" Meg couldn't believe what she was hearing.

"Yeah, I should have handled things better than I did. But I didn't have a choice, you have to believe me."

Meg scowled. "Choice? There's always a choice."

"Keep your voice down," said Tawny, looking left and right.

"Come on then, why?"

"What?"

"Put me out of my misery after all this time. Why? Why didn't you have a choice, why did you run out on me? There was someone else, wasn't there?"

Tawny bowed her head, shaking it.

"Makes perfect sense now I think about it, the way you'd be gone sometimes for days on end. The way you'd disappear early in the morning."

The blonde woman looked up again. "No, nothing like that. There was never … There's never been anyone but you."

Now it was her turn to say: "What?"

"You remember what you said to me that night?"

"Remember?" said Meg, raising her voice once more. "How could I ever forget? I've been replaying it on a loop in my head ever since."

"You know, that thing you said."

"That I loved you?"

"Yeah." Tawny stared at her without blinking. "Well, it was mutual. *Is* mutual."

That word again: "What?"

"I love you as well."

Meg put her hand to her mouth, shocked. Then the anger returned. "That makes perfect sense. I tell you I love you. You love me too, but walk out for almost four months, never get in touch, never answer your fucking phone!"

"I had my reasons," Tawny assured her in a steely tone. "I was protecting you. I never meant for it to go as far as it did. I just couldn't help myself. I didn't mean for you to fall in love with me, Meg. I didn't mean to fall in love with you, either."

"It's what normal people do, Tawny. They meet, fall in love, and live happily ever after—or hadn't you heard?"

"That's just the thing," said Tawny. "I'm not normal."

"What are you talking about?"

Tawny sighed, then pulled Meg closer. "You want to know

who … what I really am, why I couldn't tell you all this before. Okay." Looking over her shoulder to make sure she wasn't being observed, Tawny picked a grape and held it in her palm. Meg bent, puzzled. Tawny pointed with her index finger, whispered something, and a spark of energy passed between her and the fruit. It began to float, at first a couple of millimetres above her hand, then an inch or so. Tawny ticked her finger sideways and the grape began to spin. She pointed at it and there was another crackle of energy before the grape stopped, hanging in mid-air. Then she spun it the other way.

Meg's jaw dropped. "How …?"

"How do you think?" Tawny replied. "It's a kind of magick."

"Magick? You mean you're …"

Tawny let the grape drop into her palm. "What you didn't know couldn't hurt you, Meg. You used to wonder where I went when I wasn't with you. I was with some friends of mine. They're like me."

Meg shook her head, as if trying to force the information back out again. But it was no use, now it was inside there was very little she could do to eject it. "So you're a—"

"You can use the word, it's not dirty or anything. I'm a witch, yeah."

Another shake of the head. "This can't be happening. You can't be …"

"Oh, I am. Didn't my little demonstration convince you? Shall I do it again?"

A firmer shake. "No, please. I can't get my head around this." Meg turned to walk away from Tawny, but the blonde woman caught her arm.

"I'm still the same person I was when I was with you, Meg," Tawny whispered in her ear. "And I've thought about you every day since I left. It tore me up to walk away, but I *had* to. Don't you see?"

Meg looked into her eyes and knew that everything she'd said had been the truth. Tawny had fallen in love, then walked out to protect her from what she was: a magick-user, a "sparkie" as they were known. But it was the same woman in front of her, wasn't it? The same person she now wanted to slap with one hand, cup her face with the other and kiss those lips again.

"You should have told me," Meg said, hurt.

Tawny snorted. "And what would you have said to that? 'Oh, by the way, Meg, I'm a member of Arcana and can make you levitate above the ground.' 'That's nice, Tawny. Now let's read some more poetry to each other'?"

"Arca—?" Meg almost shouted the word, but Tawny had a hand over her mouth before she could get it out. She looked furtively around, but apart from a couple of glances from other shoppers they hadn't attracted much attention.

"Keep your voice down," she warned, taking her hand away.

Meg's eyes were bulging. "You're with that group on the news. The ones who tried to blow up the mall?"

"It's not what you think."

Meg laughed. "Explain it to me then."

"We don't have time right now. That's part of the reason I came back. You're in trouble."

"What?"

"It's my own fault. I've put you in terrible danger." There were tears welling in Tawny's eyes.

Meg trembled slightly. "From them, from Arcana?"

"No, from the people who want to kill us all."

"The authorities?"

"They might be yours, but they're not mine. I answer to a higher authority than that." There was pure venom in Tawny's voice. "Look, can we just go somewhere and talk about all this?"

It was then that Meg noticed all the other shoppers in the supermarket, slowly but surely, seemed to have congregated in one aisle: theirs. To the left, the right, at the back and in front. Whereas before they'd been spread out, now they were all in the fruit and veg section. Meg looked at Tawny, who'd noticed it too.

"What are they doing?"

Tawny didn't answer.

The odd expressions the shoppers had worn on their faces grew even stranger. Not so much judgmental now, but shockingly serious. One man was reaching inside his tweed coat, a woman doing the same inside her handbag. Another wheeling a pushchair was digging inside that, the child clearly a doll.

Oh my God, thought Meg, *it's a trap. It's a trap for Tawny and … and I'm the bait.*

"Hands in the air!" one of the shoppers boomed. "Both of you!" Suddenly there were guns everywhere. Pistols, aimed at them.

Tawny pushed Meg behind her, tossing her basket away. She kicked Meg's trolley at the undercover M-forcers in front, who fell over it. At the same time, Tawny spread her arms out at the sides, calling forth her magickal energy like she was summoning flocks of birds.

Meg ducked, glancing round as most of the contents of the stalls rose up. Apples, oranges, coconuts, pineapples … all flew into the air. Similarly, potatoes, swedes, cauliflowers, lettuce, tomatoes and ears of sweetcorn joined them, then began spinning.

In no time it was as if Meg and Tawny were in the middle of a tornado, the fruit and vegetables whirling around them, hitting the Enforcement Officers and jarring their aim. Even those who were quick off the mark fired wide, the food hitting them like missiles, thumping into forearms and chests.

Tawny grabbed Meg's wrist and dragged her through the maelstrom. She shouldered cops out of the way, pulling Meg into the next aisle. A bullet whizzed past as the man at the cheese counter unfolded his arms to reveal two automatic pistols. Tawny reached out a hand and the mass of dairy produce on display suddenly leapt up and overpowered him, Edam smacking him in the face while shards of Cheddar and Wensleydale powered into him.

The couple who'd eyed Meg up earlier on were standing at the head of this aisle now, both with weapons drawn. Tawny pointed at the tins on the shelves, which flew off en masse and buried them under their weight. Meg couldn't help feeling a hint of satisfaction.

"Come on," said Tawny, guiding Meg towards the check-outs. The women on the conveyor belts had nestled in behind them, though, machine-guns drawn from underneath. Even from this distance, Tawny could cause the magazines that were on sale at each till to flap around in front of them like birds.

The more Meg saw of this, the more she understood why Tawny had run away from her. This wasn't the life she would have chosen for herself, *if* she'd had a choice that is. But she felt like that free spirit again, just as she had when she'd been going out with this woman. It was exciting and a million miles away from what she was used to. So what if Tawny was a witch? They could get past that. A member of Arcana? If she explained it, maybe she'd join the cause. Now she realised that Tawny had only been trying to keep her safe, it placed a whole new complexion on things. There might be a future for them after all … providing they got out of this alive.

Skidding through one of the check-outs, they made for the exit doors.

It was as they passed through these that an electronic grid was triggered. A mesh caught them and knocked them backwards. Meg shuddered on the floor, foaming at the mouth. She looked across and saw that Tawny was the same. She wouldn't be pulling any tricks out of the bag this time. The imaginary future she'd envisaged for them was fast slipping away.

The officers surrounded them, guns jammed in their faces.

"Put these sparkie bitches in the van," said one of the M-forcers, and Meg realised just why Tawny had endangered her life to find her. They thought Meg had powers. Not only had she been the bait, they figured she was a magick user as well—or at least in league with Arcana. As the officer neared, kicking them in the stomach and pulling them up by the hair, Meg almost wished she was. Tawny would never hurt anyone, she was the woman Meg loved. And that meant Arcana was definitely not what she thought. Not what *anyone* thought.

But she would never have a chance to pass on that knowledge. Meg knew what happened to those accused of using magick, let alone fraternising with a member of a terrorist organisation.

As they were dragged through the doors, the electric field deactivated, she reached out a hand for Tawny. The blonde woman reached out too and they touched fingertips for a second. Then the contact was gone and Tawny was separated from her grasp a second time.

As they were loaded into the van—disguised as an ordinary

delivery vehicle—Meg wondered where they would take her, and whether it would be the same place as Tawny. She'd claim to be Arcana just to stay with her. Just to *die* with her. After all, the life she'd been living hadn't been a life at all, simply an existence.

But she doubted whether they'd ever see each other again.

She tried to tell herself it didn't matter, but she felt cheated. A future, a life together … it would no longer be a possibility. Taken away from her not by Tawny, but by those who hunted her.

Meg, seething as she was tossed into her van, understood why these people were Tawny's enemies, just as they were hers now. They didn't care about individuals or feelings or anything else. They only had one goal: to wipe all magick users from the face of the Earth.

Now they were a step closer to achieving it.

Only one thing consoled her as the van trundled off, taking her to God knows where, and that was the fact Tawny loved her after all. What Meg had viewed as callousness had been protection, from men and women like this. They didn't want to hear explanations or reasons, and Tawny knew that. She couldn't place Meg intentionally in harm's way, so she'd fled. But she'd come back again to try and save her, that was the thought Meg held onto even as the bag was placed over her head, even as she was manhandled through endless corridors and asked endless questions she couldn't answer. Even as she was put through ordeals she could never have imagined, she held on to that thought, that love.

And she prayed again. Not to see Tawny's face one last time, she knew that would be impossible. No, this time when she prayed, Meg was praying for the end of her life to come quickly.

So that she and Tawny might be together again in the next one.

The animals were restless today.

Keeper Angus Carson had noticed this on his morning tour of the zoo. The monkeys had jumped from their tyres to the bars of their cages, the lions and tigers had been roaring in unison, while the elephants trumpeted and stamped their feet. Even the usually placid horses in the stables were whinnying madly. It wasn't that they were hungry, because they'd all been fed. It was almost like they were trying to tell him something.

Of course, if anybody might understand what, it was the man beside him: his assistant, Nate. Angus glanced over at the young man with the pony-tail and knew he sensed the animals' discomfort as well. How could he not? In all his years at the zoo, Angus had never seen anyone have such a rapport with the beasts as Nate. So much so that he'd earned the nickname Doolittle. It was almost like he could communicate with them. A word or two, a gesture of the hand, and they'd behave themselves, or come forward for their feeds. Angus recalled the time not long ago, when Betsy the tigress had cut her paw open and was trailing blood. She hadn't let anyone get close enough to look at it, even with two darts in her. But before Angus could stop him, Nate had hopped into the sealed-off part of the enclosure. Now, it could have been that the sedatives were starting to take effect, but Betsy let Nathan come right up to her without complaint. It was the damnedest thing Angus had ever seen. There she was, one of the most dangerous creatures in the animal kingdom, and she was suddenly acting like a playful kitten. Nate stayed with her until she was asleep and they'd been able to carry her off to the clinic.

"I really should discipline you for that," Angus had told him. "It was a stupid thing to do."

"Sorry," said Nate. "But she was in pain, and she was scared. I couldn't just stand there and watch."

It was true, he couldn't. Ever since he'd arrived a little over a year ago, Nate had wanted to be involved with every aspect of looking after the animals, from cleaning out the enclosures to helping when any of them needed treatment. He spent hours in the reptile house, not the most pleasant of places Angus had to admit, and handled the spiders with relish. For some of the keepers this was just a job, but it was more of a vocation for Nate. Angus understood because it was that way for him, too.

"Why did you want to work here then, son?" Angus had asked him over a cup of tea one break-time, eager to know more about his background.

Nate shrugged. "I've just loved animals since I was little. I used to read those books, you know the ones I mean? With pictures of wild animals in them? I spent hours flipping through them and wondering what it would be like to see a lion or a bear in the flesh. Now I get to see them every day."

"Yeah, not many places in the city you can," Angus had said, chuckling.

Nate took a sip of his tea. "Sometimes, though, I wonder if they might be better off in their natural environment. Like they were in those books."

It was an argument Angus had heard time and again, and he offered the same reply as always. "They're well looked after, and for some of them that natural environment doesn't even exist anymore. Look at the orang-utans from the Rain Forest that's being cut down. We saved them from that."

"But didn't put them back into another forest," added Nate.

One of Angus's eyes narrowed. "You're beginning to sound like one of them there animal rights people. I love those creatures out there."

Nate nodded in agreement. "I know you do. They know it, as well. I just don't think any intelligent creatures should be caged because of what they are."

"You'd prefer it if they were running around loose?" said Angus, laughing again. It was meant as a joke, but he seriously thought Nate was going to come back with a yes. He waited for it, and when it didn't materialise he continued, "Sometimes things are done because it's for the best, son."

"I suppose so." Nate nodded, and it was the last he'd spoken on the subject. Nevertheless, the conversation had stayed in Angus's mind. Was it really cruel to feed and look after the animals the way they did? Treat them like they had when Betsy slashed her paw open? What would she have done in the wild if that had happened? And with the world the way it was, there might come a day when the *only* places you could find these creatures was the zoo, bred in captivity.

But it was more what Nate had said about the animals knowing Angus loved them. That man had such an affinity with them, so perhaps he really *did* know how they felt about being behind bars? It was a prison when all was said and done, no matter how well the prisoners were treated. Was that what was rattling them today, thought Angus as he wandered around, had they finally decided to stage a riot?

"Something's definitely spooking 'em," he said to Nate. "What do you reckon it is?" His assistant said nothing, he was too busy looking around him. In his own way he resembled those that he cared for, ears twitching at the faintest sounds, sniffing the air.

As they rounded the corner of the llama enclosure, Angus saw three uniformed men not far away. Their dress was similar to your average policeman, but slightly different. He recognised the outfit of an M-forcer when he saw one. When he was younger they'd carted off one of his neighbours and the entire street had come out to watch. Nice bloke, Angus had thought: quiet, but always polite. You just never could tell. But what were they doing here in his park?

They're after somebody. But who? One of the visitors? One of the staff? Angus turned to see what Nate thought, but the lad was gone. He frowned.

Oh God. It's him, isn't it? Nate? He's the one they're looking for. No wonder he could bloody well talk to the animals, he was using magick! Angus began to look for him, but one of the officers shouted, "Freeze!"

"He's gone that way," Angus replied, pointing back up the path. "The man you're looking for, Nate. I … I didn't know." They grabbed him by the collar and forced him to lead them, calling in for back-up at the same time.

They were passing the first enclosure when Angus noticed there was something wrong. He looked to the side, and saw it was empty. Then he spotted the door was wide open, energy still crackling at the lock.

"He's opened the cage!" Angus warned them.

"What was in there?" asked one of the cops, weapon drawn.

"It's the leopard enclosure," Angus told him.

The other M-forcer slowly peered round the keeper, but there was no sign of anything. It wasn't until they took a step along the path again that the attack came. All Angus saw was a flash of spots, and one of the officers was down. His gun went off, but didn't hit the animal tugging on his clothes.

The other cop drew a bead on the large cat, but before he could fire, a second leopard moved into their field of vision. Angus put a hand on his arm. "No sudden movements," he cautioned.

But the man took no notice, levelling his gun at the leopard. It sprang and bit into his arm, knocking him backwards as well. Angus ran, off up the path, plugging his ears at the screams. It was the same story at every cage he passed, doors hanging open, their locks crackling.

"Lord Almighty," he murmured. A family came round the corner and he shouted at them: "Run, the animals have escaped!" They must have thought him crazy, but he *was* wearing a keeper uniform.

There was more gunfire up ahead, and though all his instincts were telling him to take flight, Angus had to see. He raced towards the centre of the zoo, an open space where people usually sat to eat packed lunches, or burgers from the refreshment area. There were no people here today, though. Just animals, side by side, virtually every animal in the zoo it seemed. They stood shoulder to shoulder, lions next to tigers, horses next to apes. Not fighting, as one might expect, but lined up as if all on the same side. Sitting on one of the elephants, like Hannibal, was Nate.

Angus couldn't help himself. "Stop! Nate, stop what you're doing to them! Let them go."

From his perch, the youth cried down, "I already *have*. They're as free as you or I now. But they've made up their minds to stay, to fight with me."

Angus shook his head.

"They told me so themselves. Guess they recognise a kindred spirit when they see one." Nate smiled. "I don't want to be caged, either."

It was then that Angus saw the other "army" approaching. Groups of Enforcement Officers taking their positions, flooding the numerous paths that converged on the centre of the zoo, armed with pistols and automatic rifles.

Nate looked down again at Angus. "If it means anything, they forgive you. And they love you, too," he told the keeper.

When it happened, it happened quickly. The cops fired off the first salvo, but the smaller animals were already moving towards them, picking their targets and ducking under the bullets. Chimps rolled into officers, snatching weapons and tossing them away. The gorillas and orang-utans were less polite, picking M-forcers up and throwing *them* instead. Horses from the stables kicked out, breaking arms and legs. While the lions bounded up, leading the way for the other big cats to follow, including the leopards that had caught up.

Nate rode his elephant—Angus recognised it as a female called Sheila—through the chaos, trampling a couple of officers. When he was close enough, he cast a spell aimed at the reptile house and arachnid lair. Boa constrictors, cobras, and vipers poured out, closely followed by orange and black tarantulas. One boa climbed up an M-forcer's leg, wrapping itself around his body and squeezing until he dropped the gun, collapsing into a heap. Someone ordered a retreat, but the animals chased after the fleeing officers. Angus, keeping back just enough to see, ran after them all.

As Nate led his troops towards the exit signs, they rounded one corner and found themselves face to face with armoured vehicles that had water cannons mounted on top. The sheer force of the water hit the animals like a wall, pushing them backwards. Angus ducked behind some bushes to watch the rest of it. The big cats ran away from the blast, as did the apes, but Nate ploughed on through with Sheila. Angus actually found himself rooting for his animals in the end. They were his after all, and had been long before Nate came along. He'd fed and nurtured them, some from being tiny. This was his zoo and he was proud of the way they'd fought.

But now the tide was turning. A blast from the cannon dislodged Nate from his seat on the elephant, and a barrage of bullets thudded into Sheila, some from high-powered Remington shotguns. She was bleeding from several places, but still had the strength to butt one of the armoured vehicles and tip it over, virtually collapsing on top of it.

"*No!*" screamed Angus, coming out of hiding. One of the officers let off a round in his direction, but a rogue gorilla pushed him out of the way in time, taking the bullets for its keeper. Angus shouted out again as the huge ape fell, its glassy eyes lifeless. From his position on the floor, he looked up to see three or four officers descend on Nate, viciously beating him with batons. The lad held up his hands to protect himself and Angus heard the loud crack of bones breaking. The animals behind were desperate to protect their friend, but were being held back by a constant volley of bullets. And now any M-forcers from the previous skirmish that were still able had picked themselves up and were attacking from behind.

The fight was over. Nate lay bleeding on the ground, unconscious; a wounded Betsy loped up to lay with him, licking the blood from his hands. The police were joined by other members of zoo staff, who were ordered to dart the animals still alive. Angus rose to his feet and surveyed the devastation, the creatures who'd fought to protect this one man either dead or dying. And the way the M-forcers had behaved made him think that there was something fundamentally wrong somewhere.

They'd probably take him in for questioning too, but Angus knew nothing and would probably be let out again. Nate, on the other hand, obviously knew a lot.

"I don't want to be caged," he'd told Angus. But he would be now, and his captors would treat him worse than any animal.

Angus shook his head, and wasn't in the least bit surprised when tears started to flow down his face.

He placed them on the table, one after the other.

The first card showed a man in a carriage being pulled by two sphinxes: "The Chariot." The man inside had awoken on his journey, realised he was the person he'd always dreamed he could be, just before disaster struck. In the next one "The Queen of Wands," a witch had fallen because of her love for another. Peeling off the top card he found the symbol that represented "Strength." But it was the picture that was important on this occasion: a man closing the jaws of a lion … or was he talking to it? All represented people on this reading, members of Arcana who were lost to them now.

But the cards went on: "The Hanged Man," a barman noosed in his own establishment; "The Two of Swords," a blindfolded woman with her back to the ocean, holding two swords, became a dock worker the M-forcers had taken into custody, though not without a struggle; "The Ten of Pentacles," another family—man, woman and fifteen-year-old boy—swooped on and brought down while they were eating dinner together; "The Ten of Swords," a prone figure with the blades sticking out of his back, standing in for one of their number who'd died of his wounds on the way to The Penitentiary. There were more; the list went on. A co-ordinated operation to weed Arcana out of society completely, based on the information given to them by the children. Fragments of names overheard, even subconsciously in sleep, details of places like the hospital at which Ferne had worked.

They were safe here for now, as none of the children had ever seen the theatre and a powerful spell was in place to ensure that no Arcana could speak about it outside these walls. The only way would be if an outsider told the MLED. An outsider like Callum McGuire. Unwin had given him the opportunity, even the idea. Now it was up to him. Of course, he already knew which option the young man would choose. Which path he must take, and what it would mean for the rest of them.

Like "The Ten of Swords," some wouldn't make it through this alive, people he cared about: Unwin knew that as well.

But sadly the future was not his to change.

Only to foresee.

CHAPTER TWENTY

He'd had plenty of time to think.

Lying here in this old dressing room, Callum had been going over his encounter with Unwin.

Be ready. The time is coming when you must take that final step. Do not be scared.

He'd already taken enough steps to last him a lifetime, turned his back on everything he'd believed in. Or had that faith been an illusion? Callum remembered the glee on Gibson's face when tackling a sparkie, even on a small scale. Somehow for that man—and many others—it had changed from protecting the innocent into a vendetta, an extermination.

Or maybe it had been like that from the start?

And what about your parents? You owe them. Shouldn't it be a vendetta for you as well? Isn't that why you became an M-forcer, to avenge them?

Callum had to admit there was truth in that. But after all he'd seen, the injustice, he couldn't excuse it anymore. Couldn't turn a blind eye while these people—men, women *and* children—were taken off to The Penitentiary to be tortured and killed.

You didn't see anything like that there. Just in your dreams, he reminded himself. *You only have Ferne and Unwin's word for it.* Yes, incineration for the most dangerous subjects, but it was only the same as the death penalty for murder. Whether it was by knife, gun or magick, did it matter how the deed was done? People still died in the Arcana attacks, he shouldn't forget that.

But there was the argument that no Arcana can kill. It didn't tally with what was happening out there in the world, yet Unwin and Ferne made a very convincing case. If she hated normal people, why did she save the Hodgson boy? Why work in a hospital? A good cover, but there was more to it than that. Ferne cared, anyone could see that.

Callum shook his head. *You mustn't let how you feel affect your judgement. Do the right thing, it's what you've done all your life. Do the right thing, Callum.*

And he would … if only he could work out what it was.

Sound drifted through the open doorway, a sort of distant chanting. Callum rose, walking to the crack of light. There was no guard at his door; he'd discovered that after Ferne had brought him back, and his meals had been left just outside. He was free to leave the room at any time, it was only fear of bumping into members of Arcana that kept him prisoner. Fear of the unknown. They all knew what he'd done in the raid, he was sure of that, and he wasn't convinced they were as forgiving as Ferne and Unwin. He'd thought about talking to her on their walk back here, asking about the woman Rhea, about the children, but decided against it.

No one had been to check on him in a long time, not even Ferne, and he couldn't just stay here driving himself nuts deciding what to do. So, in a way, he was glad of the distraction of the noise, something to force him out. At heart he was still a cop, with a cop's curiosity.

Callum inched open the door and the chanting grew louder. He followed it up the passageway, past the posters. He hesitated when he came to the old ticket office and bar area but, after sticking his head out, found that there was nobody in sight. Following the voices led him to a door on his right: the entrance to the main body of the theatre. Carefully, he opened it and slipped inside.

It was dark, except for the light that came from the stage itself.

That was brightly lit with candles of varying sizes. Here, on the back row, Callum was tilted high enough that he could see the candles were arranged in the shape of a ringed pentagram. At each corner of the star stood a member of Arcana, also holding a candle, while others were just inside the circle. The only one he recognised was young Gavin, Unwin's aide. Squinting, he could see that in the centre of the pentagram, and indeed the stage, there was an altar. Upon this was a chalice, a scroll, and two more candles with a ribbon wrapped around them. The chanting, in a language Callum had never heard before, grew even louder. He felt his way along the back row and quietly sat on a seat, leaning forwards as the ritual continued.

Two people, a man and a woman—both hooded—climbed the steps to the stage. Callum had to remind himself that he wasn't watching some kind of production; this was real. The figures entered the ring and stood next to the altar, their backs to Callum. The chanting hushed as they removed their hoods, the woman sporting long, dark hair, the man's brown and short. The latter reached for the scroll and undid it, reading aloud.

"This is the great altar of all things," spoke the man. Callum recognised the voice from somewhere, but couldn't quite place it. "For in Ancient times, Woman was the altar and so the altar was made and placed. This is a sacred place at the centre of the circle, and we have been taught in the past that it is the origin of all things. We are sworn to adore it, sworn to protect it, as long as there is breath in our bodies."

There was a slight smell wafting towards Callum, and he noticed that smoke was coming from sticks of incense placed at the side of the stage.

"Oh, mighty Goddess," the man continued, "watch over those who are lost to us, especially those who have been taken by force this very day by our enemies. Protect them, as they sought to protect you and your name. Marvel beyond wonder, yours is the soul of infinite space. Therefore by seed and root, stem and bud, leaf, flower and fruit, and the powers of nature, do we invoke thee. Oh, Queen of Space, Jewel of Light, we offer our very lifeblood to thee in your honour—and to give thanks for the gifts that you have bestowed upon us."

The man put down the scroll, and suddenly produced a large, very old-looking dagger. He held it aloft. The woman turned, and Callum saw it was Ferne. The man opposite held up the dagger, as if ready to plunge it into her chest. Callum stood bolt upright, hands clutching the seat in front of him. He was too far away to do anything about it, even if the man *did* intend to stab her. Callum was about to cry out when he saw Ferne take the chalice from the altar. Holding her free palm up, she allowed the man to draw the dagger across it. Blood dripped slowly into the chalice. Then the man turned to his own palm, cupping it and drawing the blade across his skin. Squeezing his fist, his own blood dribbled into the chalice to mix with hers.

Callum was experiencing a jumble of emotions. Adrenalin had started to pump as soon as he saw the dagger—he knew the correct name for it, *athame*, just as he knew there would be symbols on the hilt—but something had held him back. Now, seeing Ferne take part in such a personal rite as this one, her blood mingling with this man's, he felt something else.

Jealousy.

It was stupid, irrational, he realised that, but couldn't help it. Some part of him actually wished that it was him up there with Ferne on the stage, looking into her eyes as the chalice was passed around the others so that they might add their own blood.

Callum watched as the chalice returned to Ferne and the man. Taking each other's hands, they placed it on the altar together and bowed.

"Open for us the pathway, the secret way," the lead pair said in unison, closing their eyes. "Of intelligence beyond this mortal presence. Beyond light and dark, day and night, sense and time. Behold the mystery aright. Blessed be."

"Blessed be," repeated the others, closing their own eyes.

There was silence. No one moved. The candles flickered as if a draft had just been let in. As Callum watched, tiny sparks of energy crackled between the flames that formed the circle, that formed the pentagram. The sparks increased their intensity, hopping from candle to candle. The electricity began to wind around the group, coiling around their bodies like snakes, linking them all. It sprang from the figures at the pentagram points and those inside the circle, onto Ferne and the man in the centre, their heads still bowed. They began to shake, and Callum saw Ferne clutch the man's arm for support as the energy flowed around … and *into* them.

But something else was happening at the altar. The energy was forming a shape, coalescing into a rough figure. The longer it went on, the more detail Callum was able to make out: flowing hair crackling with lightning; breasts moulding themselves around a network of veins; arms and hands that reached out for the chalice, holding it up before drinking. And a pair of glowing white eyes which caught Callum's gaze while the members of Arcana kept their eyes firmly shut.

The energy being didn't move its mouth to speak, yet Callum heard her voice clearly. Part of him knew it was inside his head, and he felt sure he must be hallucinating.

"Don't be frightened. You know me, Callum McGuire," she said, the timbre unique. The closest thing he could compare it to was the plucking of harp chords, a musical rhythm to the voice which echoed inside his mind. "You've just forgotten. But we have met before, haven't we?"

Callum found himself nodding involuntarily.

"I was there with you in the dark, and I brought you light."

There was a blinding flash and Callum was back at the orphanage, locked in the cupboard as punishment for asking too many questions in class again. He was shaking so hard he thought his teeth would fall out. He'd shouted and shouted for Miss Havelock to free him, but she didn't answer, probably wasn't even there anymore. He'd banged on the cupboard door until the sides of his fists were bloody and grazed. Then he curled up in a ball, rocking to and fro.

"Hush," that same lyrical voice had said. "Don't be frightened. Everything is going to be all right." It should have made him more scared, but for some reason it didn't. Callum's breathing slowed and he realised there was more light in the cupboard than he'd thought. Or at least there was now.

The small space, which had been so black, the darkness so dense he could feel it pressing down on him, was now lit with a sort of blue glow. Callum looked around, but couldn't trace the source.

Must be coming from under the door, he told himself. *Or a gap in the walls?*

But no. As Callum looked down, he saw exactly where the light, the energy, was coming from. He held up his hands in front of him, tiny sparks of light bouncing from fingertip to fingertip.

It was then that the door opened and the stern face of Miss Havelock was standing in its place. She dragged him out, as he was still looking at his hands. Now, though, in the light, they appeared normal again. "That will teach you," she said. "Now run along before I decide to use the cane as well."

Callum had run all right, out of the classroom and down the corridor. Out of the orphanage's doors to the tree he often sat under when he needed to think. Callum slumped against it, gaping at his hands. It had been an optical illusion, a trick of the light. As the days passed, he'd blanked it out of his mind, shut it away. Nothing like it had ever happened afterwards and he'd never heard that voice again … until now.

"Yes. You remember, don't you? And rightly so. Nothing is ever what it seems in this world, my child. Nor in any other. You are more special than you could ever comprehend."

"No!" Callum cried out, squeezing his eyes closed now. "Leave me alone. Leave me alone!" There was quiet again and, after a moment or two, he opened his eyes again.

The people on the stage were all looking directly at him. The lightning was gone and both Ferne and the bearded man beside her were staring across the sea of seats. They were still holding hands.

"Callum?" Ferne practically mouthed the name.

"How dare you!" raged the man, dropping her hand like it was a hot coal. "How dare you spy on our most private of ceremonies!"

"Michael," said Ferne, reaching for his arm once more.

That was it: Michael. Callum remembered where he'd heard the voice now. When he first got here, telling Ferne she should just let him die.

Michael turned to her. "You see, what did I tell you? You brought an M-forcer here, have allowed him to wander around of his free will, speak to Master Unwin—"

"Master Unwin *requested* to see him," Ferne corrected. "Didn't he, Gavin?"

The boy on her right nodded.

Michael pulled away, holding up the dagger. "It's blasphemy, that's what it is." He strode out of the circle and down the steps.

"What are you doing?" Ferne called after him.

"What I should have done at the start of this."

Michael marched up the left-hand aisle towards Callum, athame poised. Callum slipped out to meet him.

"You and your ignorant kind, you're responsible for so much," Michael spat. "People have died today, others are missing. Taken by people like you."

"Look, I don't know anything about that," Callum began, "but—"

"In the Goddess' name I'll make you pay!" Michael ran at him with the dagger. Callum side-stepped his attacker, but was elbowed in the face when Michael twisted round. Callum fell, rolling and standing again as they'd taught him in training. He touched his lip with his finger and felt the wetness there, tasted the copper in his mouth. Michael came at him again without warning, but Callum was ready this time. He ducked, pushing his shoulder into Michael's stomach and using the man's own momentum to flip him over. As Michael tried to stand, Callum kicked the athame out of his grasp.

Michael stood, and leapt at Callum again. The former cop took a swing, but his hand passed right through Michael. Just as Michael passed through Callum—leaving a bewildered expression on his face. Behind him now, Michael solidified, wrapping his arm around Callum's throat. He heaved backwards, causing Callum to choke.

By this time Ferne and some of the other Arcana—including Gavin—were running towards them. "Michael, stop this right now!"

His response was to tighten his hold on Callum, who clutched at Michael's forearm for release.

"Let him go!" Ferne ordered.

Michael laughed bitterly. "Every minute he spends here puts us all in more danger, can't you see that? Every second he remains alive."

Ferne walked up to Michael and slapped him across the face. His head rocked to one side. He released his grip on Callum, who dropped to his knees, gasping for air.

Michael stepped back, rubbing his cheek. "I'll pretend you didn't just do that."

Ferne shrugged, which enraged Michael even more.

"You stand in for the High Priestess now. Your loyalties should be to me, to Arcana."

"They are," Ferne assured him.

Michael pointed to Callum on the ground. "He will betray us all; Master Unwin said so himself."

Ferne looked from Callum, who was rubbing his throat, back up at Michael. "And how do you know that?"

"I was … I was in the room when Unwin saw him," admitted Michael, drawing a gasp from Gavin.

Ferne snorted. "Then you're a fine one to talk of spying."

"It was necessary."

She stooped to pick up the athame. "I suppose using a sacred weapon to kill in cold blood is necessary as well."

He said nothing.

"Michael, you're worse than those who give Arcana its bad name. None of this was necessary, it never is."

"You are a healer," said Michael. "What do you know?"

Ferne crossed the distance between them, grabbed his hand and slapped the ceremonial dagger into it. Then she curled his fingers around the blade and forced him to hold it to her throat.

"W—What are you doing?" said Michael.

"You wish to take a life, even though it is against everything that we stand for. So, take mine. I give it gladly."

Michael's expression was a mixture of surprise, confusion and anger. With a wrench, he tugged away the athame. "Act your age," he said through gritted teeth. "And start taking some responsibility for what's happening to us all." He gave her and the coughing Callum one last glare, then made his exit from the auditorium the same way Callum had entered.

Ferne let out a groan, bending to help Callum up. Gavin joined her at the other side, holding him steady. "I'm sorry," croaked Callum.

"What for?"

Callum tried to speak but couldn't.

"Come on, we'll take you to my room and I'll have a look at that throat. It's a specialism of mine, you know." Ferne smiled awkwardly and dismissed the rest of the worshippers. The ritual was over, the "sacrifice" made. But Callum doubted whether any of them would forget what had happened.

Gavin and Ferne took an arm apiece and helped Callum out, though he looked over his shoulder back down at the altar.

Then he looked down again and, as he had done once as a child …

Callum looked at his hands.

CHAPTER TWENTY-ONE

Sherman Pryce looked out of his office window and beamed.

As he surveyed the compound of The Penitentiary, he saw yet another truck roll in. How many prisoners would be in this one? Two, three, maybe more? It would be like a snowball effect now: the more people they swooped on, the more information they'd be able to glean, leading to more arrests. Who'd have ever thought that the key to all this would be a couple of brats? It was a good job they didn't have the strength to hold out like some of the more adult members of Arcana. The children were ripe for picking. You just had to know which buttons to press to get them to talk. Or which handles to turn …

Drugs had helped as well, of course, and even hypnosis. Through this Pryce and his team had gained unprecedented access to their psyches, coming up with places, names—or enough of them to make educated guesses—and even future plans. Children were usually seen and not heard, but that didn't mean they heard nothing themselves. All in all, Pryce was delighted with the progress made so far.

Or he would be if it wasn't for one major fly in the ointment: Callum McGuire. Pryce would be lying if he said he hadn't seen the potential for him to go rogue. The man just asked too many questions, something that had followed him through his education and even his training back in London. Questions were a dangerous thing. You ask them of other people, you ask them of yourself. And sometimes you might not like the answers to either.

Nero still had faith in a positive outcome, but then, didn't he always? He still saw a way this situation could resolve itself without leading to the death of McGuire. Pryce was less certain. That young man was a loose cannon as far as he was concerned. Sure, he was just one guy, but if he'd been brainwashed by the broomstick brigade, he could prove very dangerous indeed. McGuire was Nero's blind spot and Pryce would just have to make sure that he took care of things if the need—and the opportunity—arose.

He'd bury all this so that the mind readers couldn't find it, naturally, before the next time he had to see Nero. One day they'd look back on the operation with satisfaction, knowing that they'd wiped out every scum-sucking sparkie in the country. Maybe even Europe, and then the world. Britain would set the example others should follow. Zero tolerance.

Pryce knew of communes that lived freely under some of the less … effective regimes abroad. The mountains of Switzerland, for instance, or some of the more obscure regions of South America. But there'd come a time when nowhere would be safe for magick users. They could run, but they couldn't hide forever.

The prisoners were bundled out of the back of the van: four in total, all with sacks over their heads. But he could see, even from a distance, that a couple were women. Pryce rubbed his hands, licking his dry lips in anticipation. He looked forward to dealing with those personally. Downstairs, out of sight, where only a few of his most trusted people had ever ventured.

For the time being he'd put the problem of McGuire out of his mind.

The endgame would be played soon enough, and then … Well, then they'd just have to see who'd emerge victorious.

Wouldn't they?

CHAPTER TWENTY-TWO

Gavin shouldered open the door to Ferne's quarters, angling himself so he could take the bulk of Callum's weight. They managed to get him across to the bed and he slumped down on it.

Ferne went to a small chest not far away, taking out a black bag. Opening this, she removed a bottle of green liquid and unscrewed the lid.

"I would have done this the easy way," she explained to Callum, "but the ritual took a lot out of me, and on top of healing your wounds before … Soon as I can I'll—"

"S'okay," croaked Callum. "Thanks anyway."

She lifted his chin to examine his throat. "It's not too bad," Ferne told him. "Could've been worse, at any rate."

Gavin stood and watched as Ferne applied some of the lime-green liquid using a cloth. He held his nose at the smell.

"I know, I know—but it'll take out the bruising quickly. It's a little recipe of my own reserved for home patients only." She gave a small laugh. "If I'd used this at the hospital it would have stunk the place out." Callum hacked and coughed again, and Ferne put an arm around his shoulders. When she caught Gavin staring, she removed it. "You'd better inform Master Unwin about this."

"Master Unwin will probably know already," Gavin said. "He usually does."

"Nevertheless," Ferne told Gavin, her voice firmer, "go and tell him."

Gavin took the hint and left, pausing only briefly at the door as if to tell her something, then deciding not to.

"He's a good boy, but sometimes …" Ferne shook her head, rubbing more of the liquid into Callum's throat. "How's that feel?"

Callum nodded. "Better." His voice was a little stronger. He looked around the room, taking in the desk on the far side, complete with phone on top, and filing cabinets in the corner.

"It used to be the manager's office," Ferne explained. "Not as nice as my other place, I know, but beggars can't be choosers."

Callum smiled. "And now *you're* the manager, right? High Priestess?"

Ferne shook her head. "Only temporarily. Our previous Priestess, Helen, was taken."

"And Michael?"

"He took over when Victor, our High Priest was—"

"Wait a minute, did you say Victor?"

Ferne frowned. "Yes, he was lost to us a few months ago. Why?"

"I've seen him," Callum said solemnly. "At The Penitentiary. He was the one who gave them the Widow's Way location."

"Never!"

"They've been drugging him, Ferne, messing with his mind. He thought the people there were in danger." Callum shook his head. "They were in a lot more after he'd given them up."

"But he's alive? You're sure of it?"

"He was the last time I saw him."

Ferne let out a breath, fingers to her mouth. "Then there's a chance Helen might still be as well."

"You were … close to them?"

She nodded. "You wouldn't understand."

"Is it like Rhea, the woman at Widow's Way? The one who was like your sister?"

Ferne got up off the bed and stood in front of him. "You still don't understand anything about us, do you?"

"Try me," said Callum, coughing again.

"The *whole* of Arcana is our family. All we have is each other. But yes, Helen and Victor are special. They were as close to me as any mother and father."

"But what about your real parents?"

"They disowned me when I was very young, when we all became aware of what I was. For my eighth birthday they gave me a puppy called Trixie," she continued. "I loved that dog so, so much. I'd just turned ten when she got sick with kidney disease. She was dying."

"And you couldn't let that happen."

"I already had some power, a gift from The Goddess, though I didn't know much about her back then. She … called to me, that's the only way I can explain it. Just like she does with anyone who has inherent magickal tendencies."

Callum rubbed his chin, his mind flashing back to what had happened during the ritual. Those memories …

"What?" asked Ferne, mistaking his look for disbelief. "It's not something just *anyone* can learn, regardless of what you've been told. I mean anyone can say the words of a spell, of course, but … We're born like it, with this … spark in us. It's not a drug. We don't go out seeking the power, getting high on it, like some might have you believe. There isn't a choice. We're *chosen*. Anyway, it was like I just knew how to make Trixie better, where to place my hands. My parents caught me, and rang the authorities. They came and took Trixie away—and would have done the same with me if I hadn't escaped out of my bedroom window and run. I'm lucky I didn't end up locked away back then. I hid, lived on the streets for a while—oh, I could tell you some stories!—until I was eventually found by Helen and Victor. I owe them everything. They gave me my name, gave me focus. Showed me how to hone my skills, developing them through the structures of magick. Helped me understand my own particular strength. You see, the magick flows through us and we can all tap into it to do certain, general things. Simple stuff, like manifesting that energy. If we're taught how."

"Like the way you got us here, with the key?" he asked, casting his mind back to the teleport.

She nodded. "But each of us has one particular thing we're naturally gifted at: a specialism if you like."

"Yours is healing," said Callum, and she nodded again.

"Victor and Helen helped me to channel that power correctly, and I can never thank them enough for it. Rhea …" Ferne steadied herself, careful not to show any sign of weakness. "She was their birth daughter, but they loved me just as much as her."

"So who were the people with Rhea?"

"Her partner's family. All dead now, thanks to the raid you were a part of." There was an accusation in the sentence, but not in the tone of Ferne's voice.

"And the shelter Gibson talked about?" asked Callum, changing the subject.

"My way of helping some of those who gave me a hand when I was living rough. In spite of what you hear, not everyone out there is rotten to the core. Some have just been … unlucky. There, so, now you know my story."

"Hardly," Callum said, shifting his weight on the bed. "There's still a lot about you I don't know, or understand. That ceremony, for instance."

Ferne walked across to the desk and leaned against it, increasing the space between them. "You people follow your religions. We follow ours. We give thanks for our strength and power, asking The Goddess for guidance."

"But you thank her by shedding your own blood," Callum pointed out.

Ferne held up her hand to show him. There wasn't a mark on it. "The Goddess heals us, Callum. She doesn't want to see her children in pain. But it's important for her to see that they are willing."

"To do what?"

"Sacrifice," Ferne said simply. "Give ourselves fully to her."

"Sounds very much like fanaticism to me."

Ferne groaned. "Ever the Enforcement Officer. Perhaps Michael *was* right."

Callum pulled a face. "The guy's a lunatic."

"You don't have the right to talk about him like that," Ferne scolded.

"I see," he replied softly, eyes finding the carpet. "So you two are—"

"Was he right about what Unwin said?" Ferne broke in, changing the subject. "Will you betray us all?'

Callum looked up again. "That's not exactly what the old man said."

"Just answer the question."

"I can't," said Callum, honestly.

Ferne turned away, hugging herself. "The arrests have escalated. Many of our kind have been taken into custody."

"I gathered from the prayer."

"People just like Helen, Victor, Rhea … the children."

"I know."

Ferne turned and stamped towards him. "Then help us! In The Goddess' name, please help us!"

Callum let out a long, weary breath, only coughing slightly this time. "What would you say if I told you I'd seen her?"

"Who?"

"Your Goddess."

Ferne took a step back again. "What are you talking about?"

"I saw her during your … you know, back there. She appeared to me. Spoke to me." Callum shuffled about, obviously uncomfortable.

Ferne shook her head. "You can't have. Not even … The Goddess *never* appears to us that way. I mean, She exists in us all, She is the lifeforce that gave birth to the galaxies, the stars, and us—because we are made from the stuff of stars. She's reflected in the face of all women—"

"She appeared to me," he repeated. "When you had your eyes shut, bowing."

"That's impossible!"

Callum nodded. "I thought that as well, at first. Look, I can't explain it; maybe it was some side effect of what you did to me?"

Ferne came and sat beside him. "I don't think so. No one's ever reported anything like it before."

"Then perhaps I'm a first," he said, laughing.

"Tell me what you saw." There was an urgency to Ferne's words. So Callum told her what he'd witnessed, the woman forming, taking the chalice and drinking. He paused.

"There's more, isn't there." It wasn't a question.

"Yes," Callum confessed. "I've seen her before. Or at least I think I have."

Ferne gasped. "This is incredible. I can't believe it."

"I'm having a hard time with it myself."

"When?"

Callum coughed again. "It's all a bit muddled really."

"Please," begged Ferne. "I have to know, it's important."

"Okay. It was when I was little, about the age you ran away from home. Our teacher used to … punish us by locking us in a cupboard in her classroom. It was so black in there. The others just used to sit it out. But me, well, you already know my trouble with confined spaces."

"She appeared to you when you were locked in this cupboard?" Ferne was desperate for the next part of the story.

"I guess. Like I say, it's all a bit muddled. Until today I'd forgotten all about it."

"Did she give you a message? What was it?"

Callum looked across and saw that Ferne was clutching his hands. This time she didn't pull away. "I … She spoke to me, told me everything was going to be okay."

"This is …" Ferne shook her head a final time. "It's just unprecedented. What then?"

"Then nothing," said Callum, and he pulled *his* hands away.

Ferne looked at him sideways. "There's something you're not telling me, Callum."

He examined his palms, his fingers. "No. Nothing."

"Are you sure?"

Callum looked her directly in the eye. "Quite sure. Look, I think I'd better be leaving you to get on with … whatever it is you're supposed to be doing." He began to get up off the bed, but she reached out for his arm.

"You can't just go like that, not after what you've told me. We have to talk."

"What about?"

She was searching his face. "For one thing, if what you're telling me is true, you're the only person who's seen the true face of the Goddess and not gone stark, staring mad ... or blind."

Callum thought about Unwin with his white eyes. "Or a little of both?"

"Sit down, Callum," she said softly. "There's something I think you ought to know."

He swallowed, then did as she asked.

"It's not going to be easy for you to hear this, but I think I'm going to have to be the one to tell you."

"Tell me what?"

"There's a prophecy that—"

"Hold it, hold it," Callum said, raising his hand. "I think I've had enough of those from Unwin, thanks."

"Will you just listen to me?" she snapped, infuriated.

He nodded. "All right. I'm sorry. Go ahead."

"It's been passed down from generation to generation, since the very first of our kind. It's become a sort of fable, really. A story told to children to comfort them at bedtime. I used to tell it to Maria and Jonathan, Rhea's children. I don't think anyone takes it seriously anymore. I certainly didn't ... at least not until now."

"Ferne, what are you—"

She took his hands in her own again. "All our struggles, all our hardships and centuries of persecution, they were foretold at the very beginning."

"I'm not sure I understand."

"By Master Unwin's forebears. The whole line has had the power of second sight, down the ages."

Callum blinked a couple of times. "But what's all this got to do with me, and what *I* saw?"

"As the prophecy would have it, a defender was supposed to come to us. A stranger among our kind. A non-believer, in fact. He would face many tests, and in the end would make his choice. He would lead our people to salvation. By The Goddess' will, he would save all of us."

Callum laughed out loud. "You think that's me? You think I'm here to save Arcana?"

"Not just Arcana, but the whole of magick-kind."

"Oh, come on, that's just a children's story. You said so yourself."

Ferne gripped his hands tighter. "I'm not finished. The legend says that this person will be able to commune directly with The Goddess, that he will be her representative on Earth. Her son. She will keep him safe no matter what, protect and guide him through all kinds of difficulties."

Callum shook his head. "I don't want to hear anymore."

"It is also said that this person will be the most powerful of us all. That he will possess the abilities of every single one of us combined. That time and space itself will eventually open themselves up to him, and then nothing will stand in his way."

"Ferne!" he shouted. "Stop!"

Callum rose again and walked towards the door. "If you're looking for another leader, I'm not your guy. I was a police officer up until a couple of days ago. I'm just someone who wanted to see justice done. Give the gig to Michael, he's obviously dying for the role."

This time Ferne got up and barred his way. "Callum. There's a part of the prophecy you haven't heard yet."

"I'm not sure I want to," he replied, reaching for the handle.

"It is prophesised that this person will fall in love with one of us. A High Priestess. And that she will help him understand and wield his power." She hesitated for a moment before continuing. "It was also foretold that she would fall in love with him, too ..."

He sighed. "You said yourself, you're not a High Priestess—"

"No matter how obstinate he might be. And no matter how much her head tells her not to get involved." She grinned. "I made that last bit up, by the way."

"Ferne, I—"

She kissed him, her lips pressing against his. For days now since he'd first met her, he'd hoped for this, though never under these circumstances. But Callum's arms wrapped around Ferne, pulling her close to him. They fell back on the bed, collapsing onto it, hands in each other's hair, touching each other's faces.

"Wait," he said, pulling away. "Are you sure?"

"You saved my life, Callum," Ferne replied.

"You saved mine, as well, but—" he began, and stopped when she put a finger to his lips.

"I've never been so sure of anything, *ever*." She moved the finger and assured him with another kiss. He responded eagerly, tongue meeting tongue; energy sparking between them. In moments they were undressed, losing their clothes without remembering removing them.

Their fingertips explored each other, crackles of electricity heightening the pleasure. He reached down and Ferne let out a gasp, bucking beneath his touch. When she did the same, finding him, he moaned with excitement and expectation. Then, suddenly, they were together. As one. Callum above her, looking down into her eyes. She stroked the back of his neck as he moved inside her.

The moment called for them to both let go and, uninhibited, they made love like they were the first couple on Earth to do so. At one point, they sensed what each other was thinking, the turmoil that raged inside both of them. But for as long as they held one another, that didn't matter.

All that was important was their union, a haven set aside from the hurt and pain of this world. Tomorrow was another day and they'd face the consequences of their actions when the time came.

But, for now, they had each other.

And that was all they needed.

Eyes in the corner of the room watched the naked, writhing bodies.

It made Michael physically sick. How could Ferne do such a thing to him, and with an M-forcer pig she'd brought to their home? He'd known her for such a long time, had such high hopes for her. Was she just basing her entire actions on an old legend or were they real feelings? It made little difference. Each moan, each sigh, felt like she was taking a dagger to his heart.

He stayed a moment or so longer, then drifted out of the room, tears filling his eyes. Why couldn't Ferne see what this man was, what he could do to them? To Arcana? When Michael attacked him after the ritual, he'd been ready to kill the bastard. Maybe that hadn't been the right thing to do, but what if it meant their survival? Michael strode away, brooding. Ferne, Unwin … none of them had what it took to finish this. Only he was in charge of his senses, thinking clearly.

He'd allow them all their time, but soon the moment would come when they'd have to choose. When they'd see who was on their side and who was truly their enemy. Arcana's number was dwindling by the day, and something had to be done.

Turning a corner, Michael faded again into nothing. It reflected how he felt right then. In his present state he could go anywhere, do anything.

Yet he felt truly helpless.

He was a ghost among the living and there was nothing he could do about it.

CHAPTER TWENTY-THREE

It seemed like a very weird thing to do.

Leaning against the railings of a fence, Carl had seen the silver car pull up from a distance: a fairly new model, certainly not one anybody would leave unlocked or unattended in this part of town, near to one of the biggest conglomerations of night-clubs and bars in the area. He'd watched as—bizarrely—the driver had got out, looking left and right, before slamming the door and walking off up the street. Nudging his mate, Addy, Carl nodded towards the vehicle. Addy nudged the much larger Jay, who in turn elbowed Nick, who then did the same to Kels. The last youth thought they were passing round the cigarette Jay had lit a few minutes ago.

"What?" he asked, the first one of them to speak, and Nick nodded again towards the car. "Oh."

Carl shook his head in despair. He'd been with this gang since being expelled from secondary school a year ago. The night was relatively young and they hadn't had nearly enough alcohol to serve their purposes. For one thing they'd only been able to lift a couple of bottles of cider from the off-licence, and those had long since been drunk. Life was about living for the moment, that was their creed, and they stole just enough to implement it most weeks. Carl was a nobody, one of those "teenage tearaways" the system had turned its back on and left to fend for themselves. He stood no chance of getting any kind of job—even if he lied about his age—looking like he did. Carl didn't really want one, anyway. His hair was shaved in strips, which made his head look like a mowed lawn according to the foster parents he'd crashed with before squatting. He wore a cap, hooded sweatshirt, jeans that had seen much better days, and dirty white trainers with the laces loose, verging on undone. Carl looked like the archetypal teen yob; there was no way anybody would take him on.

But that didn't mean he was stupid. Far from it. He was clever enough to get by on the streets. He'd had to be, there was no such thing as benefits for him and his mates. No nice Med-fee cover or handouts for the likes of them.

So he continued to doss around with this group of like-minded individuals, no-hopers but happy to be so. Existing just shy of the law, they got by on their savvy and adrenalin: a wallet here, a handbag there. The cops had other things on their minds usually, like tracking down all those freaks. The fucking sparkies. Carl couldn't see what the fuss was about, personally. Every so often they'd do something big, like that *All Seasons* thing, but who cared if a bunch of rich shoppers got it in the neck? If the cops left them alone, maybe they wouldn't even do that much. But still, if it kept the heat off *their* backs … He'd only ever come across one of their kind before, being taken down by a couple of Enforcement Officers in an alley. Hadn't looked that dangerous to Carl, just an average bloke who they chased down then shoved against the wall to search. Carl had been expecting something to happen then, something spectacular. A free lightshow, a levitation, maybe even for the man to turn the M-forcers into *real* pigs. That would have been cool. But they'd whacked the sparky across the back of the legs before dragging him off to their car at the entrance to the alley. It was all a bit anti-climactic really; if only he'd seen *something*.

"So?" asked Addy, his wired-up teeth glinting in the streetlight. "Fancy a spin?"

"Hhhmm?" Carl wasn't sure. There was still something niggling him about the way the motor had been left. "Dunno."

"We could always just check it out," Jay offered. "No harm in that, is there?"

"You ask me, it's a gift, man," said Nick, puffing on the ciggie and handing it to Carl. "They're asking for it to get nicked." He realised what he'd just said and let out a loud laugh. "Nicked by Nick, geddit?"

"Funny guy," said Carl. "But don't you think it's a bit … I don't know, weird?"

"If they're stupid enough to leave it just lying around," said Kels, which was the pot calling the kettle black. Carl suspected that if Kels ever came to own a car—which was highly unlikely—he'd probably park it in a scrap yard then be shocked to come back and find it crushed.

"So …?" said Addy again, but it was clear he'd already made up his mind. He was walking off towards the vehicle, beckoning the rest of them to follow, which they did: Nick loping up the street, followed by Jay and Kels. Carl was the last one, moving cautiously towards the car. By the time he got there, his companions were all over the car like bees swarming near a flowerbed. While Nick kept watch, Kels and Jay shielded their eyes and looked through the back windows, like prospective buyers in a showroom.

"Nice," whispered Jay.

"Looks comfy," chimed in Kels.

It was Addy who tried the driver's side door, though, popping the lock easily and sliding inside. Carl was looking left and right, as the owner had done when he abandoned the car in the first place. Something about this just didn't sit right.

Addy got out again, and leant on the roof. "The silly twat's only gone and left the keys in it."

"*Adrian,*" Carl called out to him. He'd listen if he used his real name. "I really don't think we should be doing this."

Addy frowned. "But it was your idea."

Carl touched his chest. "Me? It was never."

"Yeah it was. You nodded at the car."

"Only because there was something funny going on," Carl responded.

"Look," Jay said, "we're here now, let's get in and take it for a burn."

Carl shook his head.

"Christ, what's the hell's wrong with you?" Nick shouted. "Get in!"

"You lot go if you want. I'll meet you back at the squat," said Carl.

"Fine," Addy snapped, swinging back inside the car, ready to start her up. As Jay, Kels and Nick piled in too, Carl stepped back. It was then that he saw the glow coming from the boot.

Puzzled, he drew closer. The light, faint at first and hard to spot because of the streetlamps, was growing brighter, spilling out from the gaps where the boot came down. "Guys," began Carl. "Hey, guys, I think there might be something—"

Addy had started the engine and was revving it, drowning Carl out. Nick stuck his head out of the passenger side window and cupped an ear, guffawing and shaking his head.

Carl approached the boot and tried lifting the lid. It was locked. He took out his knife, opening it up and sticking it into the lock. In seconds he'd jimmied it, but wished that he hadn't.

There, in the boot, were three glowing spheres, crackling with energy: one yellow, one purple, and one pink. They were growing bigger by the second. Soon they wouldn't even fit inside the trunk.

Oh my God, thought Carl. *Oh my God!* This was one of *those* times, when the sparkies were doing something big to prove a point. The magic in that boot would not only obliterate them and the car, but most of this entire neighbourhood. All those nightclubs and bars, all those people. *Well, you did say you wanted to see something. Now's your chance!*

Unless he could stop it happening somehow. Get him and the lads out of here quickly, call the authorities. Carl skidded back around the vehicle, grabbing Nick by the scruff of his neck.

"We have to get out of here, right now!"

Nick slapped Carl's hands away, looking at him like he'd gone mad. "We ain't going nowhere, 'cept for a little ride."

"I—In the boot," Carl babbled, "c-c-colours ... magick."

Kels and Jay looked at each other in the back, then burst out laughing. "You didn't have *that* much to drink, mate," chuckled Jay.

"We *have* to call the cops," Carl insisted.

"Oh, yeah. Nice one," said Nick, "why don't we just drive ourselves to the station and hand ourselves in?"

Carl backed away. "Sod you, then. Bloody well *sod you!*" He turned and began to run away. It was now that Addy turned off the engine, realising there really *was* something wrong. Through the rear-view, he could see the back of the car lit up like a neon sign.

"Out!" he shouted at the others. "Get out!"

But it was too late, the spheres had already swelled to such a size that the boot could no longer contain them. They seemed to suck themselves in, then suddenly blew outwards. Kels and Jay were the first to vanish in the flash; there one minute, gone the next. Then it swept over Addy and Nick in the front, catching them in a frozen moment of opening the doors. Within moments there was nothing left of the car or the street, nor the street beyond.

Carl knew he wasn't running nearly fast enough, then he tripped over the laces of his dirty white trainers. Flying forwards, he landed awkwardly. He could hear the crackling of the energy as it caught up and, rolling over, saw the wave streaking towards him.

There was nothing he could do as it hit him, only accept the inevitable. The one consolation was that he'd be headline news, no longer a nobody, a teenager that society had forgotten. Maybe in some strange way these people, even after all the deaths they'd cause tonight, had done him a favour.

Carl had to think that, hold on to that hope. Because it was the only thing stopping him from going crazy in the final few moments of his all too brief life.

The magic bombs which exploded, killing Carl and his gang, were just one of a series of attacks across the megalopolis that night.

At Bishops Stortford Arena, thousands had shown up to see the first night of a reunion tour for The Nervejanglers, the biggest experimental rock group in the world who had split up during the late twentieth century because of creative differences but were back together now because the royalties from their hits and the market for their "Best Of ..." albums had dried up. At a pre-concert press conference lead singer Kirk Monroe had expressed his delight that the band were attracting a new audience with their recent singles, as well as bringing the old fans back into the fold. Or at least he'd started to express his delight before the other members of the group—guitarist Razor, bass guitarist Rob Getterman, and drummer Sandy White—had all chipped in.

Nevertheless, it did reflect the age ranges of the audience that night. People who were shocked when, during one of their most famous numbers called "Not Getting Nearly Enough Lovin'," the Janglers were thrown up into the air, the stage exploding beneath them in a flurry of colours. Moments later, smaller magic bombs were detonated in the crowd, killing the carriers—who had somehow managed to smuggle the orbs inside—and many more besides. Innocent men, women and kids.

In the North of the city, near Sandringham, a truck rammed into a government office block at speed, detonating a high volume of magickal devices it had on board and destabilising the structure so that it toppled into the block of flats beside it. Hardly anyone was at work at that time of night, but many records were lost in the attack, as well as the people unfortunate enough to be living next door.

Not too far south of Great Yarmouth huge waves suddenly rose up from the ocean, out of nowhere. What few survivors there were claimed this was initiated by a group of people standing on the beach who, in their own words, called out to the sea. Giant tsunami-sized walls of water succeeded in flooding the area, drowning hundreds in the process. Houses were virtually washed away, even those who thought they were safe up on the cliffs.

To the west of Cambridge magickal charges exploded in the sewer system, which not only tore up a number of roads, killing more than twenty people and injuring another fifty, they reached into homes, exploding toilets and sinks, terrifying many households enjoying a peaceful night in. One father reported on the news, tears still in his eyes, that his young daughter had been cleaning her teeth at the time and had been blown backwards into the wall by the force of the blast. He didn't know whether their Med-fee would cover her stay in hospital.

At the same time a flight coming in to Luton airport from France was forced to divert by three people on board claiming to be members of Arcana. They waited until the plane—which was carrying something like eighty passengers—was near Ipswich before activating the magic bombs they'd created on board. Their last words, recorded by the staff on duty at Luton, were: "This is in retaliation for our brothers and sisters who have been illegally detained against their will. For Arcana! For Freedom!" Then the plane crashed, killing and injuring hundreds.

When looking at the map, experts on the TV proclaimed that they saw more than just a superficial link to the attacks, including the magical car bomb that had devastated the nightclub district in the centre. One even took a highlighter pen and moved it over the locations of the strikes.

"There, as you can see," said a man wearing spectacles. "The points form an almost perfect pentagram."

The host of the news programme nodded gravely, then asked what Sherman Pryce, and indeed Commander Nero Stark's, response to all this might be.

CHAPTER TWENTY-FOUR

Callum was the one who woke first, rolling over on the pillow and looking across at Ferne's beautiful face, her raven hair spread out like a fan.

He watched her breathe, wrapped his arm around her, careful not to wake the woman, and drifted in and out of sleep himself. When he woke again, she was staring into his eyes, and he opened his own wide, terrified of what she might say.

"Hello," was the worst she could muster, "you okay?" It was a strange question, under the circumstances. Was he all right? Let's see, he'd attacked his colleagues on the force, helped a fugitive escape, almost been killed himself in the process, and communed with The Goddess these people worshipped, which had led to being attacked by that madman Michael. The only thing he could think of that might make him okay—more than okay—had been the moments they'd spent together in this bed.

"I'm … How about you?" he asked, turning the question back on her.

Ferne smiled. "I'm happier than I have been in a long time."

"Good," said Callum. "That's good … I'm not who you think I am, you know." He blurted out the last bit, as if guilty about what he'd done. Taking advantage of a person who thought he was something he couldn't possibly be.

She seemed to take in the information, then nodded. "I know it's hard for you to accept—"

Callum sat upright in bed. "Hard? That's an understatement. Last night you were telling me I was some kind of superbeing, some sort of God."

Ferne leaned on her elbow and rubbed her temple, giving a slight shake of the head. "Callum, do you know what most of those people would think of me if they knew what we'd done?"

"I can imagine," Callum told her.

"I don't think you can. Like Michael, the majority still think of you as an Enforcement Officer. But I know different. I know who you really are."

"You *think* you do," he said. "Ferne, you know how I feel about you, that should be pretty obvious. But the simple fact is I'm not your saviour, nor anyone else's. I can't even save myself! I'm just some idiot who let his feelings get in the way of his job."

Ferne dipped her eyes. "Your feelings for me."

"Look, that didn't come out the way I meant it to."

"I don't know what else to say, Callum. I've told you about the prophecy; what I believe. If that won't convince you I don't know what will."

There was no answer to that. Looking awkwardly around, he cast his eyes to the side, spotting a pocket-sized black book on the make-shift bedside table. Callum picked it up, turning it over in his hands. "What's this?" he asked, flipping it open and skimming through the handwritten pages. "A diary?"

Ferne made to grab it, but he turned away. "Please, Callum. It's my book of spells."

"Book of …" His sentence trailed off as Callum slowed down his flicking through the pages.

"We all have one. They're personal spells, gathered over time. Unique to each magick user, and mainly bound to their particular talents. They choose us as much as we choose them."

"You talk like they're living things," scoffed Callum.

"In a way they are," she said in all seriousness.

Callum's brow creased. "But these spells … they must come from *somewhere*?"

"Some say they originate from the great book that contains them all."

"You're telling me there's a big book somewhere that has every single spell in it?"

Ferne nodded. "And a way to counter them."

"My God, if Pryce ever got hold of that … Where is it?"

"Nobody knows."

"Not even Unwin?" enquired Callum. But before Ferne could answer, the book in front of him fell open at a particular passage. "A spell to bring forth my one true love …"

Ferne made another grab for the book, but failed. "Give me that!"

Callum shook his head, reading out loud. "'Bring me the love that is right for me. Bring us together so that we may be happy. And give me a sign so that I might recognise him.'"

Ferne's cheeks were flushed.

"Have you ever cast this spell?" asked Callum. "Is this how you attracted me? How you made me feel the way I do?"

Ferne folded her arms. "How can you even ask that? Don't you know your own heart, Callum McGuire?"

He hung his head. "I want to believe, but I just don't know what to think anymore."

She pulled on his shoulder to get him to face her. "Look at me. I didn't need a spell to make you want me, Callum."

Ferne had a point there, he would have to have been blind not to be drawn to her. To desire her. "But you're a healer, I—"

"Don't you see, it did heal. It healed *me*. Made me whole. The spell simply revealed the right person, that's all. You. I knew it the moment I saw you."

"How? How did you know?"

"Because I'd seen your face many, many times, even before we met. I saw you in my dreams, Callum."

"In your dreams …" Callum remembered his own night-time visions. The bridge, the struggle, the way they always ended.

"I allowed myself to hope. But when I found out what you were, what you did, I thought something must have gone wrong. You were an M-forcer, one of the people sworn to wipe us out. Why would the spell, The Goddess, bring an enemy to me? At the same I couldn't deny my feelings, or my own heart."

Callum groaned. "This is all so confusing."

"I understand that. My way of life is new to you. Perhaps it would help if I told you that our magick is like hypnosis. We can't get anyone to do anything against their will."

"What about Rhea, then? She got Chief Inspector Cartwright to shove a bloody gun in his mouth."

"If she was in contact with you, Rhea had this way of getting you to see the truth of things, to see clearly; that was her gift. All I can say is that he can't have believed in this crusade either, deep down. To murder those he hunted."

Callum thought back to what Unwin had said, about the fact Rhea hadn't really been controlling Cartwright. But then said, "Even if that's so, and I'm still not convinced it is, he *did* kill your kind."

"Revenge had clouded his mind," explained Ferne.

He heard Cartwright's speech again now; the one he'd given before they commenced the mission. "He'd lost people of his own before Widow's Way."

"Exactly. And yet," Ferne went on, "he allowed himself to be 'taken over.' Would you have done the same thing?"

Callum set his jaw firm. "Absolutely not … at least I don't think so. I'd definitely fight it, that's for damned sure!"

"There. You've answered your own question. You would never have been so weak-minded as to follow orders blindly."

He shook his head.

"So why would your heart follow such orders just as blindly? It has to go its own way, no one can make it feel something it doesn't. Not even with the strongest of magick."

Callum was at a loss for words. He knew that Ferne was right, that he wouldn't have fallen in love if he hadn't really wanted to. "So, what is this?" he asked.

"A test," came the answer, "to see if you'd side with the right, or the wrong."

"I've always liked to think I'm in the former camp."

"As have I," Ferne said. "We both have to do what we feel is right, even if everything is screaming at us that it's wrong." Callum closed the book and gave it to her. "Thanks. The power of The Goddess runs through us even before we know what a spell is," she reiterated.

"What, like Michael, you mean? Has he always been able to do that little trick of his?"

Ferne nodded. "He can pass between this plane and another, switch between the physical and the intangible at will. But, like me, he didn't know how to use it properly until he joined Arcana. Until he was given focus. Those whom the Goddess has chosen are given special talents for a reason, whether we realise it or not." She looked directly at Callum when she said this. "We just need to focus."

"You're talking about me again," he said. "I keep telling you I'm not what you think I am."

"But," Ferne said, "by your own admission you *have* talked to our Goddess. You can commune with her directly, which is more than the rest of us can."

"No, I—"

"If you still doubt, then answer me this. How could you read what's in my spell book? It's written in our ancient language." She showed him the pages again, and it was true, it was now in a tongue he couldn't decipher. "It's how you understood *Her*. Your subconscious mind remembers, even though your conscious mind fights it."

"I didn't ask for this!" said Callum, a little too loudly.

"None of us have, that's what I've been trying to tell you. But the gift has been given. You should be proud of that fact, not resentful."

"I'm sorry, but how can I be proud of something I don't understand? Something I don't believe in?" argued Callum. "I've not been brought up this way. I have no idea why The Goddess is talking to me, or what she's trying to say. If anything."

"In time She'll reveal that to you." Ferne put down the book and held his hands. "It's a sin to reject Her, Callum, and to reject what She has shared with you. We each of us contain a little piece of Her, remember."

Callum tried to pull his hands away, but she held them fast.

"You felt it, didn't you? Felt it coursing through you. When you held me, when we made love?"

"I felt a lot of things," replied Callum. In spite of himself a slight grin played at the corners of his mouth.

"Why do you make jokes when I'm trying to be serious?" Ferne's lips were tight in contrast. "What are you so frightened of? That if you accept the truth it would mean everything you ever trusted was a lie? That you are, in fact, one of the things that you have hated all these years, even fought against? Why do you struggle with what's deep inside of you?"

"You really want to know?" Callum snapped, the smile fading. "Really?"

"Yes."

"Because I'm frightened of what I might become. Frightened that I'll be brainwashed into killing innocent people, like my mother and father."

Ferne tutted. "I've already tried to explain that. We're not what you think we are, either. We're not killers."

"But you can't vouch for *all* of your kind, can you? What about Michael? Can you say the same about him? He was ready to kill me yesterday."

"Michael's judgment is also clouded."

"Because of the way he feels about you?"

"And because of how he felt about Rhea, his sister."

Again, Callum saw the woman slitting her own throat, her head on his lap as the blood jetted out. That was Michael's sister! Was there any wonder he hated him so much? He blamed Callum for her death. "I had no idea."

"How could you?" Ferne looked like she was holding back a tear. "That's why Michael and I can never be. We were brought up together. I love him, but not in the way he wants me to. Like a brother, nothing more." She gripped Callum's hands even tighter, looking at him directly as the tear finally broke free and rolled down her cheek. "Besides, I love someone else."

"Oh, Ferne. I—"

"Sshh, don't speak." She was crying freely now. "You never have to worry about becoming the thing you hate most. Because I know what's inside your heart, Callum McGuire. Just as you do."

Where she was holding his hands, the energy started to crackle again. Some of it was from Ferne, but some of it was definitely his. They leaned in towards each other, lips about to meet again—

When there was an urgent knock on the office door. It came again, not even waiting for a reply. They let go of each other and the energy dissipated. "Who is that?" shouted Ferne, wiping away the tears at her cheeks with the back of her hand.

"It's Gavin," came the response. "Ferne, you have to come quickly and see this."

"All right, all right. I'll be out in a minute, just let me get dressed."

There was a pause at the door and Callum could imagine what Gavin might be thinking. He'd left them together hours ago, and it was a small theatre. It wouldn't take a genius to put two and two together. Nonetheless, Ferne whispered to him to stay here in the room out of sight, as the mad scrabble for clothes continued.

Now dressed in a pair of slacks and a blouse, Ferne went to the door. Before she opened it, she made sure Callum was out of the line of sight. "What is it, Gavin? What's the big emergency?"

"I ... Just come, Miss Ferne. Please, hurry!" Gavin pleaded.

She turned and looked back at Callum once more, careful not to let Gavin see her, then Ferne was gone. Callum heard her footsteps as she followed Gavin up the corridor. Then he got dressed himself and sneaked out, trailing the pair of them at a distance.

CHAPTER TWENTY-FIVE

Callum didn't have to follow Gavin and Ferne very far.

He could hear the noise of the TV drifting up to meet him even before he reached the bar area, though he couldn't quite make out what was being said. Creeping along to the entranceway, he hid, peering inside at the group of assembled Arcana. All the people who'd been involved in the ritual, and many more: newcomers who must have done the same as Ferne, held their keys and returned to this temporary haven. They probably wouldn't be the last after this day. There must have been about forty or fifty people crammed into that bar room, but they weren't watching the television as such.

Callum saw that one of their number was projecting an image onto the far wall, her index finger lit up, acting like a projector in the darkened room. Her mouth was open and the sound was coming from it, a news report as far as Callum could make out.

The projection was throwing back images of a stadium in ruins, and if the commentator hadn't mentioned the fact it was Bishops Stortford Callum never would have recognised the place. The footage then cut to aerial shots of a devastated town by the sea, flooded, with people clinging on to their belongings, being evacuated from their homes. Then clips of a building that had fallen into a block of flats, the streets and houses destroyed by the sewer explosions, the wreck of an aeroplane, and what was left of a popular nightclub and bar district which, the narrator explained, was the result of magickal terrorism. It was this last report that really struck a nerve with Callum, especially as they kept showing the remains of one particular restaurant.

"It would seem that their tactics have stepped up a notch," the newscaster was saying, stating the downright obvious. "For those of you just joining us this morning, we're leading with the series of attacks that took place across the city last night. Six in total, resulting in hundreds dead, many more injured. It is feared that the death toll may rise, a deadly response to the growing number of arrests made of Arcana members over the past couple of days."

The wrecked plane footage was played again, but this time the recorded message was played over the top: *"This is in retaliation for our brothers and sisters who have been illegally detained against their will. For Arcana! For Freedom!"*

Callum put a hand over his mouth. He felt like he was going to throw up. How could they have done this? After everything Ferne had told him, she'd almost had him convinced. And Unwin with his talk of how no true Arcana could ever kill, about parallel worlds.

The screen flashed to a drawing of a pentagram, just like the one they'd used in the ceremony he'd witnessed. It had been bullshit, all of it. He'd been sucked in by it when he should really have just let Gibson take Ferne and the lot of them! Callum balled his fists, breathing in and out quickly through his nose.

"Representatives of the New Church of Benediction have condemned the violence," the newscaster carried on, "as being the work of inhuman, unfeeling monsters. The Honourable Reverend Harding, spokesperson for the Church, even went so far as to say, and I quote, 'I hope Arcana burn in Hell for all eternity!'"

"Oh my Goddess," Callum heard Ferne say when she saw the images, leaning on Gavin for support. "How could this have happened?"

"It has happened," came a familiar voice, "because some of our kind have had the guts to do what is necessary." It was Michael, of course, rising up near the front—his features highlighted by the projection on the wall behind him. "We have taken the war to them at last, and I for one applaud it."

"How can you possibly say that?" Ferne practically screamed at him. "Look how many people have been killed! This is not what Arcana is about, Michael. You know that!"

"Then perhaps it is time it should be."

Someone in the middle called for them to quiet down so they could hear more of the report.

"We take you now to an emergency press conference, where an official response is about to be given."

Another face familiar to Callum appeared. Sherman Pryce stood behind a podium, his face sombre, his tone controlled yet seething with hatred.

"Ladies and gentlemen of the press, viewers around the world. You'll forgive the lateness of the hour, or should I say the earliness. But our country faces a serious threat today, more serious than it has ever faced before." He paused to mop his brow, though it was more for effect than anything. "These attacks show just how low Arcana will stoop in order to cause the maximum disruption to our everyday lives. Every single arrest we have made thus far has been a legitimate one, based on evidence we have received that these individuals are dangerous and should be removed from society. The reply to this, as you have seen, has been more serious than we could ever have imagined. Arcana care not for freedom, or even for human life. They care only about their lust for power. Their own twisted existence. And they are prepared to kill to preserve it." There was another pause, this time while Pryce looked out over the assembled press, then directly into the camera. "I am here, under Nero Stark's orders, to say to you that we *will not* be bullied. We *will not* give in to threats of a terrorist nature. All Arcana has done tonight is to reveal themselves as the murdering scum we already knew them to be. The cowardly scum," he banged his fist on the podium, causing a whine from the mike, "that are even now hiding from us in a secret location somewhere in this very city. So if anyone out there has knowledge of the whereabouts of individuals they suspect might be connected with Arcana, we would ask them to come forward and tell us immediately." There was one final pause, then: "I have one message to pass on from Commander Stark: we're coming for you, Arcana. And we will destroy you: each and every one of you! We cannot go on as a society with this threat hanging over us, ladies and gentlemen. So again, I ask if there are any—"

The woman projecting the image shut her mouth, shaking her head. She couldn't listen anymore to the vitriol coming from Pryce.

"Do you see the result of this now?" Ferne said, aiming her accusation in Michael's direction. "How it all escalates? There will never be an end to this as long as there are rogue members of Arcana willing to do such things, to involve themselves in such wickedness. The Goddess would never condone these actions, She is the womb of *all* life!"

"But would She see Her favoured ones tortured and killed by the M-forcers?" Michael threw back at Ferne. "See children like my nephew and niece taken to be used against us?"

Callum had heard enough. He pulled back from the entranceway, unnoticed this time. He ran into the foyer, glancing left at the doors. There had to be something protecting them, something to stop him getting out or he wouldn't have been given the run of the place. No, too obvious.

He remembered the phone in Ferne's room—the old manager's office. *"If anyone out there has knowledge of the whereabouts of individuals they suspect might be connected with Arcana, we would ask them to come forward and tell us immediately ..."* Pryce's words echoed in his mind, as if he was talking to Callum alone, and they were accompanied by images of the attacks that had been made on the city. Maybe Ferne didn't hold any truck with them, but it was obvious Michael did. And if he did, why not other members of Arcana? Perhaps they needed stopping for their own good?

Callum retraced his steps to Ferne's quarters, letting himself inside quietly. The phone stared at him, and he remembered Unwin's words about making a choice. He looked down at his hands, ones that had crackled with energy as they'd held Ferne, as she'd held them and confessed how she really felt.

He closed his eyes and shook his head, striding over to the phone. Who knows, it might not even be working.

But fate wouldn't let him off that easily. There was a dialling tone.

Callum used one of the fingers he'd been staring at to press the first button.

CHAPTER TWENTY-SIX

Nero Stark had watched the broadcast several times by now. He'd never needed much sleep anyway, and tonight he would stay awake until the morning light.

He had to hand it to Pryce, he was one hell of a public performer. Nero doubted whether he himself would come across quite as well. All those years of purposely staying out of the public eye was bound to take its toll; the only company his own, and occasionally Pryce's. He was happy to let someone more experienced bait the trap. This was the only way that he could see of bringing Callum back into the fold, appealing to him directly. Provided, of course, he was in a position to see the broadcast at all.

Nero knew that this was his only hope, his *final* hope. It was Callum's choice, naturally, always had been, but Nero knew in his heart of hearts he'd make the right one. Everything had been leading up to this moment, to this day.

"Softly, softly catchie monkey," whispered Nero. He walked up and down in his underground lair, looking at the original *Hammer of the Witches* encased in glass. It wouldn't be long before he owned its counterpart, the book that contained all the original spells in the magick-user's arsenal. The only thing he needed was the location of

Arcana's base. Just that one piece of information the other members of the group had withheld, no matter how much torture they'd endured.

Soon … soon …

It was at that moment the phone beside him began to ring.

CHAPTER TWENTY-SEVEN

It was another one of those days, when something was about to happen. Maybe not right away, but certainly in the very near future.

Not only could Callum feel the change in the air, but every single member of Arcana could too, from the lowest of spellcasters to the most powerful of their kind. The whole world had woken that morning to find newspapers and TV reports full of damning evidence, fanning the flames and backing up Sherman Pryce's vow to do something about this threat once and for all. Call centres hummed with leads from suspicious members of the public: some far from genuine, some showing real promise.

Throughout the morning and into the afternoon, more and more members of Arcana—those who had not already been rounded up by the continuing MLED operations—returned to the nest: men, women and children. Even though they could not speak of the theatre to anyone else, they knew how to get back to it in an emergency. There was a sense that they were being driven to ground, society's hatred of everything they were and stood for now complete. One way or another, this heralded a final stand. There was no way to co-exist now.

The arguments continued long after the meeting, with Ferne and

Michael at the eye of the hurricane. Those who agreed with her and those who sided with him took their stance and said their piece. In the end it got them nowhere, simply adding to the growing sense that Arcana was falling apart, and with it the entire race of magick-kind in all its forms. The meeting fell apart too, with Michael storming out, vanishing through a wall.

When Ferne eventually got back to her room, she found Callum had vanished as well. Not in quite the same way as Michael, but just as effectively. She looked around, as if expecting him to be behind the bed, office table or filing cabinet. Ferne considered going to find him —she so needed to be with him right now—but instead sat on the bed they'd shared together with her head in her hands.

Below the theatre, Master Unwin sat at his table. It would be facile to say that he knew what was coming, as he'd known for some time. Just not exactly when. He held in his hand one single card: a card unlike any other in the world. It was a card that didn't strictly exist, but appeared in his pack occasionally when the need arose. The picture showed a woman whose face was the pure essence of beauty. Hair long, golden locks flowing over her shoulders, down her naked breasts. She was part of the background, the blackness of space filled only with stars, yet she was at the forefront as well, shifting, ever altering. She was standing with her hands open, symbolising that she was willing to commune. At the bottom of the card was written: "The Goddess."

Unwin nodded, inclining his head from time to time, the silent communication between them for no ears other than their own. When they were finished, Unwin placed the card back in the deck, where he knew it would promptly disappear, as if it had never been there at all. He closed his milky white eyes, sadness reflected in his old face. Unwin knew now that Callum's choice had been made. Whether it was right or wrong would remain to be seen. By the rest of Arcana, that was. He, though, had served his time—served The Goddess well over the years.

Unwin's eyes snapped open sharply, then he smiled. "Hello Gavin. Come down here, my boy."

The youth, who had also served in his own way, was standing at the top of the steps, out of view. He'd tried not to make a sound as he'd opened the door, but should have realised by now that Unwin would feel his presence. He descended, coming into the old prop room where he'd spent many a day watching Unwin shuffle the cards, predicting the future.

"If you've come to tell me of the events that unfolded last night, I'm afraid you've had a wasted journey."

"No, Master," said Gavin, drawing to a halt alongside him and biting his lip. "I've come to ask what's going to become of us. Of me."

Unwin raised an eyebrow. For once, he had not seen such a question coming. But perhaps that was a good thing. He gathered up the pack of cards, shuffling them one last time, then asked Gavin to hold out his hand. "Here," he said, handing them to him, still smiling. "Why don't *you* tell *me*?"

"Master?" asked Gavin, bemused.

"I want you to have my cards, young Gavin. You've earned them."

He gaped at the pack of tarot in his hand. "But Master Unwin, I'm no seer."

Unwin laughed. "I once said exactly the same thing, Gavin, to my father. I, as you know, have never been blessed with children. After generation upon generation, the line—for better or for worse—ends with me. You, though, have been like a son to me. You have cared for me, fed, clothed, and bathed me when I wasn't able to myself. And for that, I thank you. The Goddess thanks you, too."

Gavin was slack-jawed as he continued to stare at the cards.

"Well, don't just stand there admiring them. Try them out for size," urged Unwin.

Slowly, and as carefully as if he were handling bone china, Gavin attempted a shuffle. It wasn't half bad for a first attempt, and Unwin told him so. The youth had another go, finding that the cards were actually shuffling themselves this time, allowing their new owner to slide them back and forth quite easily. Not only that, Gavin could feel the texture of them, like living things, and they were all speaking to him: dozens of voices at once, clamouring for attention. He could see the mouths of the painted characters moving fast and furiously.

"I … it's too much," said Gavin, grimacing. Unwin thought he was going to drop the deck. "There are too many."

"Give it a minute, let them settle down. They're just excited," Unwin replied, talking about them as if they were a bunch of puppies all eager to lick his hands. "Cards!" Unwin was right, they did die down, especially after his admonition. "Sometimes you just have to remind them who's in charge."

The voices separated, and Gavin could hear some above the rest. Those that didn't have anything to say right now muted, while those who had a bearing on the present became clear and crisp. Now he could pick them out, tell them apart from each other. Experimentally, he dug into the pack and plucked one of the loudest out. It depicted a building being struck by lightning, on flames, its inhabitants diving from the windows. "The Tower."

"Misery, distress, adversity, deception and ruin," said Gavin.

Unwin nodded. "You *have* learnt well, haven't you? A time of unwelcome change, Gavin, for all of us."

Quickly, the boy chose another card. It was one Unwin had pulled from the deck when this whole business began. "The Devil," whispered Gavin.

"Even now, he draws his plans against us," Unwin said. "But he has had help."

One final card, and Gavin gasped out loud. He knew the skeleton wearing armour and riding his white horse usually didn't mean death, but the card was telling him otherwise on this occasion. And one in particular.

Gavin looked at Unwin. "Master …"

"There is no need for words, Gavin." He reached up a bony hand and touched the side of his aide's face. "My time is soon at an end. This has been drawing close for a while and I have already made my peace with it. I'm sick and old, and the future belongs to the young." In spite of his words, moisture glistened in Unwin's eyes. Gavin felt the tears swell in his own. "Now go. I must prepare myself for what is about to befall us." When Gavin lingered, Unwin shouted: "*Go!*"

The young man dashed from the room, clutching the cards to his chest. He ran up the stairs and out through the door, leaving Unwin bowing his head in silent prayer.

But, as Gavin ran back along the corridor, salt-water in his eyes, one card was screaming at him from the pack, so loud he had to stop and delve into it again. It was another one of the cards Unwin had picked just before Gavin came to tell him the news of the *All Seasons* attack. (But how could he know that?)

A man in robes standing at an altar. Above his head a figure of eight weaved around, the symbol of Infinity. He was holding a wand aloft, and in front of him was a sword, a staff and a goblet.

This man was The Magician. The one person who might yet be able to turn this around, fix things, and save them all.

There was hope, Gavin knew that now. That was when he heard the first shots being fired.

And two hands grabbed him from behind.

CHAPTER TWENTY-EIGHT

The first they knew of the attack was when gas grenades were fired through the doors of *The Valentine*.

Members of Arcana were scattered throughout the building, some in the seating area of the theatre, some in sleeping bags in the bar and lounge, some in the offices. There was no alarm here to be raised, no high-tech security system in place like there was at The Penitentiary, just the screams of men and women, families scrambling to get their children out of harm's way.

Rushing into the foyer, one man with tight curly hair stood in the middle of the gas and breathed in deeply, the crackle of his magickal energy aiding him as he sucked the lethal mist into his expanding lungs. Once it was all gone, he dropped to his knees, screwing up his eyes as his body converted the gas into pure oxygen and he breathed it back out. As he began to get up again, a hail of bullets sent him dancing backwards until he hit an old billboard, which came crashing down to the floor with him. As he died, he saw the black shadows of Enforcement Officers holding machine-guns, approaching the entranceway with gas masks on. The fact that he had bought the others some time comforted him as his eyes glazed over.

The M-forcers looked at each other, wondering what had

happened to the clouds of white smoke they'd pumped inside, but not removing their masks in case it was some sort of trick.

Like ants, the men in black moved in, rifles swinging first one way, then the other. A line of Arcana members rushed out of the bar to meet them, prepared to defend themselves. As one of the lead officers opened fire, a ginger-haired woman held up her crackling hand, turning all the bullets into daisies. The surreal vision of white and yellow flowers falling to the ground caused the shooter to hesitate and another member of Arcana threw an energy bolt his way, literally turning the man's limbs to jelly. Unable to hold the rifle, or even stand properly, the M-forcer toppled sideways into the wall, collapsing in a rubbery heap.

The daisy woman was not nearly quick enough when more bullets were fired their way. These took out not only her, but two other members of Arcana on her left. "T—There are children here," she choked through the blood. But the troops were beyond listening, even if they could hear through the balaclavas and gasmasks. Their answer would have been, "There were children in the flats near Sandringham, on the plane that was brought down in Ipswich, in the houses that were flooded along the coast." They'd been normal kids, of course, not freaks like the ones these people were hiding: the next generation of Arcana resistance fighters, heads filled with rubbish, fists filled with magic.

A large man with a shaved head cast a spell that turned both his crackling fists into lump hammers. He used these to knock the rifles from the hands of two M-forcers, before striking a third behind them. Another man was able to move so quickly he could flit between the officers unnoticed, relieving them of their weapons and making the hammer man's job that much easier.

One touch from a young woman, who'd moved up to the front ranks, was enough to add years onto the M-forcers' lives, turning them into geriatrics in seconds. A further spell caused the carpet in the foyer to ripple so badly that the enemy forces were flipped up into the air before landing back down awkwardly on the ground. The reply to that was another wave of uniformed figures, not bothering with masks, bashing down what was left of the old theatre doors and pushing forwards with toughened see-through shields. They rammed Arcana left, right and centre, lashing out with batons and noosing any they could get close enough to. One woman was dragged several metres down into the bar area, choking and coughing, before the M-forcer who'd lassoed her knocked her out with a kick to the face.

One man dressed in denim clambered onto the bar, bottles in his hands. He tossed them at the officers nearest to him, then blew fire from his mouth to engulf them in flames from head to toe. At the other end of the scale, a woman with silver-blonde hair froze half a dozen M-forcers in their tracks simply by blowing on them. They stood in the middle of the room, statues around which the others fought.

The authorities pushed forwards past the ticket office, crouching and shooting up the corridor as spheres of pure energy were tossed back at them by more members of Arcana holding their ground. One ball hit an Enforcement Officer in the face and turned into a squid, covering his eyes, mouth and nose. Another unleashed a plague of large rats that attacked the troops, biting their legs and arms and hands. A third spread itself out and transformed into a murder of crows, which descended upon the cops, pecking at heads and faces.

Another group of M-forcers entered the fray, this time bringing with them water cannons. It worked for a few minutes, knocking back several Arcana, but as soon as the silver-blonde lady was close enough, she just froze the water with her breath. For her trouble, an officer came up from behind and, before she could fully turn, smacked her in the side of the face with his baton, breaking most of her teeth. After that, Molotov man did his best to turn the water cannon ammunition to steam, but a stray bullet caught him in the thigh and his leg gave way under him, causing him to fall from the bar.

It was becoming increasingly clear that the Arcana in the bar area were outnumbered and outgunned. Soon, Enforcement Officers were picking off their targets one by one, keeping them alive where possible, dispatching when the opposition was deemed too dangerous. Officers were also making good headway up the main corridor, under the direction of one M-forcer who obviously had experience of this kind of thing. The rats were trampled underfoot and the crows swiftly machine-gunned; clearing at least enough to be able to make it through the door at the back of the main theatre.

Inside, they found more members of Arcana staked out, using the seats as cover to mount a defence. The troops could only come into the theatre proper two or three at a time, which meant that they could be held off initially by energy bombs tossed at the door. One last-ditch attempt to keep them out even saw a spell cover the doorway in a thick, mucus-like glue, that stuck to any M-forcers who might be coming through. It took several minutes for others to clear this with bolt-cutters and knives, but gain access they did, continuing to pick off more magick-users in the stalls.

At the same time, police had made it down to the other entrance at the head of the corridor, and so could pin their enemies down from two angles. There was no escape and the last stand took place there, with Arcana being overrun between the seats by swathes of M-forcers. The faded velvet was no protection from pistol and machine-gun fire, and in the end the majority of them simply held up their hands in surrender.

One officer, who'd led the men successfully down the corridor—effectively signalling Arcana's downfall—hopped onto the stage, motioning for his men to follow. There was a trapdoor back there, and he found it right away, as if he'd known it would be there.

He led his people down another passageway, beneath the stage itself, aware that there could be booby traps at any point. But in the end they reached the darkened doorway, shone their torches onto the steps, and entered the room below.

The lead M-forcer descended, swivelling his machine-gun left and right. The others were happy to let him go first, carefully treading in his footsteps.

"If there's anyone down here," said the man, "I'd advise you to give up right now and come along quietly."

Silence greeted him.

"I'm warning you!"

"Your threats," came an echoing voice, "mean nothing to me."

Torches were trained on the source of the noise. It took a moment or two for them to find it, but when they did they saw an old man sitting in the dark, wizened and stooping, barely able to hold himself upright. Yet he stood now, and seemed proud of the fact he had. When the torches caught his eyes, the men saw the orbs were as white as the light itself.

"Don't trust what you see," the man in charge told them. "*Never* trust what you see."

"That is where you fail," the blind man informed him. "I have always trusted what I see."

There was a ripple of laughter from the men behind, their guard dropping regardless of the warning.

"Surrender, and keep your hands where we can see them," ordered the M-forcer he'd been talking to, stepping closer.

"I've seen this. Seen it all," he said, grinning, "and do you know something? I know how it ends." With that, he loped towards the officer.

"Stay back!" shouted the cop, raising his rifle, steadying the hilt against his shoulder. "I said—"

The old man brought one of his hands into view, clasping the other one around it. He hefted the sword he was holding above his head, ready to strike. The *rat-ta-tat* of the machine-gun was all that echoed now, its muzzle flash brighter even than the torches. The old man stopped, weapon falling from his grasp, and stared out past the M-forcer who had shot him. As he fell, another chilling smile played over his lips.

Rifle still jammed into the crook of his shoulder, the lead officer crept nearer to the body. It wasn't moving. More troopers piled into the room behind, one of them skirting the body, crouching and picking up the sword. He showed it to the first man.

"It's … it's made of wood," he said.

As more torches filled the place with light, they saw that this was where the theatre props had been kept. Kings' crowns and cloaks, suits of armour and tuxedos, they were all here. He'd been right to tell them not to believe their eyes. It had all been staged, if you'd pardon the pun: the whole scene just one more in this production.

The first cop frowned. "He *wanted* to die. The crazy old sparkie wanted us to kill him."

There was a faint crackle of radio static. "Officer Gibson," came a voice from behind him, and the lead M-forcer turned, his reverie broken.

"Yes?"

"You're wanted. We've located more of the subjects upstairs."

"Well," said Gibson, kicking the old man on the ground. "What are we waiting for? Let's go bag some more of these fuckers."

With that, they left the body of Master Unwin to cool in the basement he had once called home.

CHAPTER TWENTY-NINE

When Ferne heard the smashing of the doors downstairs, the initial shots alerting her to the attack, she ran out into the corridor of the office upstairs. By the time she'd got to the other end, there were already footsteps on the stairs: heavy and booted. Ferne recognised the uniform sound they made and retreated, the screams of her fellow Arcana reaching her ears from the foyer. But she knew she could do them no good by simply walking into the arms of their enemy.

How had this happened? How could they have found this place? It was a question she could not possibly know the answer to, but asked herself anyway. The bootfalls grew louder, along the hallway now. She hid back inside her room, immediately regretting it. She'd cut herself off completely.

The heavy footsteps were louder still, and stopped outside her door. Ferne put a hand to her mouth, trying to steady her breathing. Her eyes flashed around. Somewhere to hide, somewhere—

The bed!

She slid onto the floor as quietly as she could and slipped beneath it. Ferne wrestled with her breathing again, but it was coming in short, sharp bursts. If she covered her mouth it still escaped through her nose. And she couldn't prevent a small yelp as the door to the office burst open, creaking on its hinges. From her hiding place, she saw a pair of boots stride into the room. Ferne followed their progress as they clumped about the place, searching for the room's occupants. Now she found she *couldn't* breathe, as the boots came back round to the side of the bed and stayed there.

Move on. Just go. You've searched the place, there's no one here. You can tell your superiors that you've looked.

One boot was replaced by a knee, the dark material of the cloth straining against the carpet.

Oh no! Oh, my Goddess, he's bending down to look under—

Callum McGuire's head poked beneath the bed, and she'd never been so glad to see anyone in her life. "Ferne?" he said, and she finally let out her breath.

"Thank the Goddess, I thought you were . . ."

"No, it's just me," he told her, holding out his hand to help her from under the bed.

"What's happening?"

"Same thing as Widow's Way. MLED are storming the place. Your people are trying to hold them off, but they're fighting a losing battle."

"But how—"

"Time for that later," said Callum. "Right now we've got to get out of here. They were on the floor below this when I crept up, checking all the dressing rooms. Won't take them long to reach you." As Callum went back to the door and looked out, she grabbed her spellbook. He nodded that the coast seemed clear. "Come on," Callum urged, then immediately drew back. "Hold on, they're coming up the stairs. I can hear them. Ferne, is there any other way out down the far end of the corridor? A fire exit? Access to the roof?"

She shook her head.

"I don't suppose you have another one of those keys on you?"

"What would be the use? We're already here," she pointed out. "Wait!"

"Yes?"

Ferne smiled. "There is a possible way out. We can—"

"Tell me as we go," said Callum, gesturing that they should move in the opposite direction to the stairs. When they got to the dead end, Callum turned to her. "Okay, I'm all ears."

Ferne pointed at the right-hand wall.

"What?" Callum couldn't see anything. No, that wasn't true. There was a raised edge that had been painted over, the coat admittedly peeling now. He traced the ridge with his fingers. "What is this?"

"It's a hatch. Used to be for workmen to gain access to the platform above the stage, before a door was added on the balcony. It was filled in years ago when the theatre was still open."

"So what use is it to us?" asked Callum, risking a glance down the corridor where he was expecting the see troops at any moment.

Ferne placed a hand on the wall, clutching the spellbook to her chest with the other. Her fingertips started to glow. "Because," she said through clenched teeth. "I can heal more than just people."

Callum looked on in awe, as the small hatch lit up. Ferne was whispering incantations. The edges revealed themselves fully, a handle growing back that had been torn off over a decade ago. When the process was completed, she slumped backwards. Callum put an arm around her. "That was … that was amazing!" he told her. Raised voices interrupted the moment, and Callum pulled on the door handle. Inside, it was narrow and pitch-black. "All right," he urged Ferne, "in you go."

He had to virtually lift her inside, and by the time she was in the M-forcers had made it to the top of the stairs. Callum looked from the small crawlspace back up at the men with guns. For a second or two it really was a tough choice. When the first of the bullets whistled up the corridor, though, smattering across the left-hand wall, he chose the lesser of two evils. Closing his eyes, he jumped in through the open gap of the hatch, pulling the door shut behind him.

The string of police headed up the corridor, some breaking off to check the office room for stragglers. But by the time they got to the hatch, it was as it had been before Ferne touched it, her magick deliberately fleeting this time.

He froze in the darkness.

Above, below, and to the sides were walls, closing in, suffocating him. There was barely enough room for one person, let alone two. What in Heaven's name had he been thinking coming in here?

You were thinking that it would be quite nice not to get shot, Callum reminded himself, *again!* That didn't help the way he felt right now. It couldn't be as enclosed as he imagined, it was only his irrational fear making things worse. But knowing and acting on it were two different things. His hands began to shake, his breathing erratic.

"Don't be afraid."

At first he assumed the voice was Ferne's, ahead of him somewhere, weakened by the spell she'd just performed. But the timbre was completely different, more musical, like someone tinkling on a piano keyboard. It was also inside his head.

"You know what you need to do," said the voice.

Callum shook his head. No, he couldn't do *that*—the thing he'd done before with his hands back in that cupboard at school—no matter how much illumination it might provide.

"*I* am the bringer of the light. *You* are my vessel," the voice corrected.

He balled his hands into fists, partly to try and stop the shaking, partly to keep the energy building in his fingers from leaking out. "No," he whispered.

"Trust in me," spoke the lyrical voice again. "Trust. In. Me."

Against his better judgement, Callum began to open his fists. There was light there, tiny sparks of lightning jumping from fingertip to fingertip, and the patterns they created were beautiful. Suddenly it was brighter than ever, and there was no need to be scared. Light flooded the crawlspace and features formed in front of his eyes. "Goddess," Callum mouthed.

But then he saw that they were too solid, too *human* to be that deity. Though he'd been told she was reflected in every woman's face, this one wasn't Hers. It belonged to the woman he loved: Ferne Andrews.

The light flooding in from behind her was the other hatch she'd just pushed open, and it spread, obliterating the sparks coming from his own hands. Callum closed them again, cutting off the power.

"This way," Ferne said to him. "Hurry!"

They emerged on a platform high above the stage, the wooden slats protesting as they stepped onto them. Callum held the bar, but felt more relieved now he was out of the shaft. Heights didn't bother him nearly as much as being trapped. From their vantage point they could see the battle still raging below, Enforcement Officers picking off those Arcana hiding between the seats. On the balcony, it was a similar story. Callum spotted one magick user hurling a blast of pure energy at a group of cops on the other side of the great horseshoe. When the inevitable machine-gun fire came back in retaliation, the member of Arcana ducked behind the balcony rail. Risking another chance to throw a bolt, he stood up again, only to pay the price this time. The bullets riddled him, causing him to dance for a few seconds, then fall over the rail into the auditorium below.

"Vincent!" shouted Ferne, without thinking. M-forcers were looking up, to see where the scream had come from. Callum pulled her back behind the curtain, fearing it might be too late. They knew someone was up here now, so they'd come. "Who? *Who* could have done this?" Ferne was asking. "No true Arcana would have given them the location of the theatre."

Her question still went unanswered. Holding her by the arms, Callum asked: "Is there another way to get out from here?"

"Along the lighting platform, we can get to an exit on the other side … providing the M-forcers haven't beaten us to it."

"So, let's find out." Callum took a step onto the shaky platform which ran the length of the stage. The wood creaked again and Callum actually thought it would give way.

"Be careful," said Ferne.

"The thought had occurred to me … Wait there till I'm sure it's safe." The platform wobbled as he made his way across it, holding onto the railings at either side. The stage looked a long way down from here, but it was safe enough for Ferne to start along behind him he thought. Callum turned—

And saw an M-forcer holding her, pistol to her head. There were two more of them on the platform behind her, figures in shadow. They must have come up from the door on the balcony.

"Ferne!" he shouted. "Let her go or I'll—"

"Or you'll what?" The question came from one of the figures behind her. Stepping forward, and positioning himself on the other side of Ferne, the man pulled back her hair till she screamed out in pain.

"Please, don't hurt her," gasped Callum.

Letting go of Ferne's raven locks, the man pulled off his helmet to reveal more of his face.

"Gibson!"

His former partner chuckled. "I have to admit you're looking quite good for a dead man, McGuire. Was that down to her? The nurse? Give you special treatment, did she?"

Callum pulled a face. "Just let her go."

"Why would we do that? She's the reason we're here, along with the rest of those maggots. The bulk of Arcana, taken down in a single swoop. I'm just glad they assigned me to the job. Must have been our little adventure at Widow's Way, eh? We had some fun that day, didn't we? Seems like so long ago now." There was genuine sorrow in Gibson's voice. He raised his own pistol, aiming at Callum. "What do you think? A single bullet to the head? Doubt whether even your girlfriend could fix you after that." Ferne struggled and Gibson pulled her hair again.

"You bastard!" she snarled.

"Easy, bitch. If I had my way that's what would happen. The kid and me have got a score to settle. But the powers that be … Well, they want him alive. Now why do you think that might be?"

Ferne glared sideways at Gibson.

"Let's see now, could it possibly be because he was the one who gave us the location of this place? *The Valentine Theatre.*"

Her eyes flitted from Gibson to Callum, who looked down at the platform.

"I'm only guessing, of course. But it makes sense, if you think about it. Former cop, struggling with his conscience, especially after all those attacks last night by your lot. Bet some of those are even here right now, aren't they? Some of the people who planted those magic bombs?"

"Callum ..." Ferne didn't need to ask anymore, her eyes, wet with tears, did the rest.

He looked up. "It wasn't me. I'd be lying if I said I hadn't thought about it, even began ringing them. But then I thought about what fuckers like Gibson would do to you, to old Unwin."

Gibson laughed. "Unwin? Was that his name? I wouldn't worry about him anymore."

"What are you talking about?" said Ferne, struggling again, in spite of the gun on her.

"He's dead. I killed him," said Gibson, with a certain amount of satisfaction.

"*No!*" she screamed.

"Afraid so. Prick came at me with a sword. What was I supposed to do?"

"You ..." Callum couldn't find the words. "He was an old man, blind, half-crippled. He wouldn't have hurt a fly."

Gibson shook his head. "What *have* they done to you? You used to think like an M-forcer, you had such potential."

"I was *never* like you," Callum spat.

"Oh, that's right. Too many fucking morals, that was your trouble. And far too susceptible to the skirt. Well, let me show you something about this particular pretty ..." Gibson grabbed hold of the back of Ferne's head and turned it towards him. He pressed his mouth against hers, slobbering all over her. She bucked, but the M-forcer at her side held her fast.

Suddenly Gibson let out a wail, springing back. There was blood on his bottom lip where Ferne had bitten him. In spite of her predicament, she grinned.

"Fucking whore!" said the M-forcer, dabbing at the lip with his sleeve. "You'll pay for that." Then he paused, thinking, smirking to himself. "You and me go back a long way, don't we? Maybe Sherman Pryce will let me conduct your interrogation personally?"

Ferne's smiled faded.

That was it. Callum ran back along the platform, charging

towards them. "He's mine," said Gibson. The M-forcer gestured for his men to take Ferne away, and they did, with her kicking and screaming. Some small part of Callum recognised this scenario. This was it: the dream; the bridge. Unwin had told him that his dreams had been trying to deliver important messages. Perhaps he'd be able to change things, stop them from taking Ferne from him.

Only Gibson stood in his way.

The cop strode towards Callum on the platform, gun raised. But the younger man was too quick for him, slapping the pistol out of his hand and sending it flying out into the theatre somewhere. Gibson tried to reach for his machine-gun, slung over his shoulder, but it too clattered to the platform, then disappeared below. Callum grabbed Gibson's wrists, wrestling him this way and that.

"I … really … thought we … were a … team," Gibson grunted.

"This wasn't … what … I signed on for," came Callum's reply.

Gibson brought a knee up, winding the blond man. The old wood of the platform splintered at one end. Callum righted himself, only to receive a headbutt from Gibson. He was quick enough to turn and catch it on the cheek rather than the nose, but it disorientated him enough to send him reeling backwards. The top half of the theatre spun around him, then he saw Gibson's fist heading in his direction.

Callum ducked, giving his opponent a rabbit punch to the ribs which caused him to cry out. The men backed off from each other to catch their breath.

"You swore an oath to protect the innocent, McGuire."

"But the lines have become blurred," said Callum. "In fact, the lines are barely there anymore. *You're* the very thing you set out to fight."

Gibson snarled. "Hardly. I'm not a freak who uses magick to hurt ordinary people."

"No, you're a sadistic cop whose taste for power has gone to his head."

Gibson drew his baton. "Okay, so taste this." He swung it at Callum's face, but missed, pitching him off-balance. Callum grabbed hold of his arm, forcing him to drop the stick and brought his own elbow up sharply under the man's chin. He heard the crack of a jaw. Gibson staggered backwards, wiping his bloody mouth for a second time, and spat out a mouthful of redness onto the wooden platform. Grinning, his teeth stained crimson, he held up his hands and beckoned Callum to come at him.

Callum looked over his shoulder, considered finding the exit and trying to get to Ferne that way. But when he glanced back he saw the way was blocked by other officers who'd been sent to help. He was more trapped than he'd ever been in the shaft.

The only option was to go *through* Gibson, so again he ran at his ex-partner, underestimating him wildly. Gibson waited until just the right moment, then whipped out his noose and expertly flung it around his neck. Gibson yanked hard on the wire-like twine, dragging Callum forwards into his fist, catching him on the jaw-line now. Gibson tightened the noose, causing Callum to cough out a breath. The M-forcer wound more of the noose around Callum's neck, though the younger man attempted to get his fingers between the twine and flesh. Callum twisted round, on his knees.

"Not so clever now, are we?" said Gibson, who had Callum in a strangle-hold. "Wishing you'd bet on the right horse, eh?"

Callum squirmed, attempting to shake Gibson loose, but the man held on tightly. In spite of what his superiors had said to him (and just why they'd said that was a mystery), Callum got the distinct feeling the man might just risk choking him to death then claim it was an accident.

Callum hoisted himself up slightly, crouching. His vision was blurred even more than the line he'd been talking about. He only had minutes, perhaps seconds, to do something or he'd be dead. Or in custody. He couldn't quite decide which was worse. Perhaps it would be better to just let Gibson strangle him, for all this to end. Two things prevented him from giving up. One was the thought of Ferne, now in the hands of people who'd do God … Goddess knew only what. The other was that the darkness might be even more oppressive than being in that shaft, in that cupboard. It was no way to spend eternity.

He reached backwards and grabbed Gibson's arms, then leaned

forward, ensuring that if the man held onto the noose he'd have to follow him. Callum mustered all of his remaining strength and took Gibson's weight on his back, then pitched the man over the rail. The M-forcer's body flopped over, but kept hold of the noose. Callum's head was dragged towards the edge of the platform, scraping the wood. If Gibson was going to drop to the stage, he was taking Callum with him.

The veins in Callum's neck stood proud as he tried to pull Gibson back up. It wouldn't be an answer, he knew, but would at least allow him to breathe. No use; Gibson was just too damned heavy. He had no knife, so couldn't just cut his partner free. After all he'd seen, though, Callum would have done it happily.

There is another way, he told himself.

A true Arcana would never take a life, or so they claimed … But he wasn't Arcana, was he?

"Remember," a tinkling voice echoed in his mind. "This is self-preservation."

Callum took the opportunity. *And were* they *self-preservation, the attacks last night? They asked you to protect them from their enemies.*

The voice was quiet, and Callum didn't have time to wait for it to reply. He clamped his hands round the twine, and squeezed as tight as he could. This wasn't letting the power flood out, just using it to sever the bond between him and Gibson—in more ways than one.

The energy crackled inside Callum's grip. Gibson gawked up at the miniature lightning display.

"You're … you're one of them!" he spluttered, not quite able to believe what he was seeing. "You're a fucking sparkie!"

Callum grimaced, though to Gibson it may well have looked like a grin, then the twine snapped. The M-forcer let out a blood-curdling cry as he dropped to the stage below. His body bounced then crumpled, limbs splaying out at odd angles. His eyes gazed upwards at Callum, still unbelieving even in death.

Callum unwrapped the noose, conscious of the fact there were still M-forcers to his left and right, but also knowing that they were under orders not to kill him. Bullets rained over his head, intimidation more than anything else, but Callum wasn't about to let himself be captured.

He spotted a rope not far away, and got up, leaping across for it, not caring what the consequences might be. Callum screamed with pain as he began to descend, his hands burning—ironic considering the energy that had burnt the noose twine. But was it his imagination, or was his descent slowing, the rope slipping through his fingers, his palms, that much slower. The red curtain that had been down on the front of the stage now rose, and Callum landed awkwardly, rolling as he lost his footing on the stage boards.

He lay there, looking over at the body of Tully Gibson. Was there just an ounce of regret that things hadn't worked out? If so, the moment was lost when a hail of bullets shredded the curtain above. Callum rolled over to see another group of Enforcement Officers heading up the stage steps towards him. He climbed to his feet and met the first one head on, grabbing the muzzle of his smoking machine gun, ignoring the pain and lifting, smacking it into the man's face. The next he kicked squarely in the chest, causing him to fall backwards into his colleagues. More shots from his right, and Callum saw a handful of cops climbing the stage there as well.

He couldn't fight them all, certainly not if what remained of Arcana couldn't. He had nowhere near their power. That meant he had to escape somehow and figure out how to rescue Ferne later. Callum ran backstage, behind the backdrop that had once been painted with various hillsides and night skies for a multitude of productions. Now, like everything else, it was faded and useless.

Callum took a moment to gather his thoughts. There was no point heading down below the stage; Gibson had already told him that they'd been there and he'd murdered Unwin in cold blood. Besides, he'd only be cornering himself. As it was there were only two ways to go, left and right, and when Callum looked both those ways he saw M-forcers appear as if responding to a prompt, blocking both exits.

"Shit!"

Callum looked up and saw police there as well, standing where he'd been not long ago, looking down and pointing their automatic weapons in his direction.

Nowhere to run.

He looked down at his hands. Perhaps that was the only way, to unleash whatever they'd all been talking about: Unwin, Ferne, the Goddess …

Okay, I'm ready, he told himself, not believing a word of it. *Let's go! You wanted to channel yourself through me, so be it. Just get a bloody move on!*

Nothing happened. No energy crackling at his fingertips, no magic flowing through him. Had it all been his imagination? The light in the cupboard, in the hatchway, the energy that had severed Gibson's noose? Or had it simply abandoned him right when he needed it most?

Callum girded himself, but again nothing happened. He looked left and right again. "Er … hi guys," he said. "How's it going?"

Then he felt a hand on his shoulder, pressure there, squeezing hard as if forcing him to get to his knees.

And he knew that it was all over.

CHAPTER THIRTY

Callum felt strange, as if he was no longer in control of his own body.

He was standing backstage yet he wasn't. He watched as the officers who had been coming from either side crashed into him, then passed right through and into each other, like characters in some sort of cartoon. They bounced off one another, falling backwards and toppling into the people behind them like dominoes. When the ones who'd fallen picked themselves up again, they looked around, bewildered, not appearing to see Callum, who was standing right in front of them.

He still felt the hand on his shoulder, a firm grip, though not as hard as it had been initially. Callum turned his head to see who it belonged to. A dark-haired, bearded man glared back at him.

"Michael—"

"Shhh," came a voice from the other side of him. Callum looked over his other shoulder and saw Gavin. Michael held him by the left wrist. "They can still *hear* you," the youth added, whispering.

Michael pushed on Callum's shoulder, urging him to go forwards. He shook his head, knowing that if he did that he'd hit the backdrop of the stage. Another push, and Callum was moving, if only to stop himself from falling over. Michael virtually shoved him towards the backdrop, and Callum put up his hands to protect himself from the inevitable collision.

Except it never came.

One minute he was backstage, the next on the stage itself. Just as the M-forcers had passed right through him back there, so he too had passed through the backdrop. Now Callum was noticing that the world around him was distorted. Everything seemed to have less colour, as if he was looking at things through a filter on a camera, bleaching the hues of the tatty old curtains even more than the years had done.

Michael marched him over the stage, past Gibson, past police rounding up what was left of Arcana. Callum felt Michael's grip tighten when one of the officers kicked a prisoner on the floor just for fun. The three of them shifted sideways suddenly, through the wall of the playhouse and out into the corridor to witness the aftermath of the battle. Injured officers, those who had borne the brunt of Arcana's defence, were being treated by medical personnel, while the dead and dying Arcana who had been shot were pretty much left to bleed on the carpets. Callum paused by one of them, but Michael still urged him on.

"We have to do something to help," Callum said in hushed tones.

"You've done enough, don't you think?" Michael growled back. "Keep moving."

"Where? We'll never get out of here," whispered Callum. "Do you expect to just walk out the front door?"

"Don't you get it yet? That's *exactly* what we're going to do," Michael informed him. "Now keep quiet."

And they did, moving through the troopers at the ticket booth, gathered in the foyer, out through the main entrance—though not before Callum had a chance to look sideways and see the devastation of the bar area: the wood riddled with bullet holes, the smoking patches of carpet. Arcana had put up one hell of a last stand, he had to give them that.

Now he, Michael and Gavin were out in the open. Callum had never seen so many squad cars assembled, not to mention the more heavy-duty armoured cars. Widow's Way had been impressive, but this show of force was something else. Prisoners were being loaded into the backs of trucks like the ones they'd used to take the children to The Penitentiary. But, as much as he looked around, Callum couldn't see Ferne anywhere.

"Forget it," Michael told him, as if sensing his thoughts—and for all Callum knew, he probably could. "She's already been taken. They didn't waste any time with the most important ones."

They moved through the throngs of Enforcement Officers, and Callum heard some of the conversations between them.

"… got what was coming to them, fucking sparkies …"

"… didn't know what hit 'em …"

"… putting in for a vacation after all this is over …"

If he'd still been one of them, he would have been expected to join in with the banter. But for the first time since saving Ferne from Gibson back at the hospital, Callum felt truly ashamed that he'd ever worn the uniform, or stood for what the badge meant. This had been a massacre; Arcana hadn't stood a chance. But then he reminded himself about what he'd seen on that projected screen last night, the attacks that had prompted this retaliation. The M-forcers take Arcana into custody, Arcana make a grand gesture by killing innocent people, so the M-forcers attack their base of operations. Where would it all end? Here, probably. There couldn't be many members of Arcana out there still free, not between the arrests and the assault on the theatre. But there were always more groups forming, ready to take Arcana's place and make another stand. Neither Pryce nor his boss Nero Stark would be happy until every single magick user on the planet was either dead or behind bars.

It was then that he spotted Pryce himself, as usual hanging back behind all that muscle, not willing to risk getting hurt. He was talking to another familiar face, Chief Inspector Cartwright. They were all here today to witness the final gasp of Arcana.

That little scene had almost been enough to take Callum's mind off the fact he was walking through the bonnet of a squad car. He'd just about figured out what was happening now. Somehow Michael had extended his power to include himself and Gavin. Because he was touching them, they too could pass through the real world like wraiths without anyone seeing them. *This,* thought Callum, gazing around, *must be the other plane Ferne talked about.* Michael had given them a glimpse of what it was like to be him—disconnected, detached—and it made Callum shiver.

As they came within metres of Pryce, Callum thought he saw the man look over in their direction. It was only a momentary thing, but it also coincided with the man talking about him.

"McGuire *must* be inside somewhere," Pryce was saying to Cartwright. "He can't just have disappeared."

Cartwright raised an eyebrow as if to say: we're dealing with magick users here, of course he could—we're just lucky the whole lot of them didn't do exactly the same thing!

They didn't, thought Callum to himself, *because they had nowhere else left to run. You made sure of that.*

Callum, Michael and Gavin walked through the rest of the vehicles, through the cordons put in place to seal off this street, and left the theatre behind. Though he hadn't been there long, Callum was sad to go. He wondered where Michael was taking them, where they could possibly hide now they were wanted by every station in the city. They couldn't stay like this forever. Sooner or later they'd have to become solid again.

Then what? Unwin was gone, Ferne was gone.

As Callum was forced up the road, he knew one thing for certain, more so now than before.

Nothing would ever be the same again.

CHAPTER THIRTY-ONE

The *somewhere* Michael took them turned out to be a lock-up a few miles from the theatre. It was in an isolated part of town, one of a row of privately let storage facilities used by businesses or people moving to smaller places who couldn't bear to part with the belongings they'd amassed over the years. Michael pointed them at the third one, pushing Callum and pulling Gavin along. They passed effortlessly through the locked metal doors, coming face to face with total darkness. There were no windows in this place (why would there be?) and Michael shoved Callum, letting go at the same time.

The wrench back into reality almost caused him to be sick. Waves of nausea swept over him and he doubled up, his stomach cramping. A flick of a switch and there was light from a single 40W bulb hanging above. Callum saw Gavin at the wall, doing the honours.

"How did you know where …?"

"I just did," said Gavin, shrugging. "The cards told me."

Unwin's cards. *He must have passed them on before his death,* figured Callum. Looking around, he saw hand-labelled cardboard boxes lining the walls; the contents of a life. It reminded him of the boxes still in his flat that he hadn't even unpacked yet. Memories, things from his past he'd probably never see again. He was grateful for the light, but in some ways he felt even more claustrophobic, because he could see the amount of space they had in this glorified shoe box. He could see no sign of Michael, however.

"Come on, show yourself," demanded Callum.

"If you insist," came the reply.

There was a hand at his throat, pushing him into a pile of boxes that toppled over and fell to the ground. Something sharp was sticking into his cheek and, as Michael continued to solidify, Callum saw that he had the sacrificial knife again, ready to finish the job he'd started the previous day.

"Michael!" shouted Gavin. "No!"

"It's all right, no one will hear."

"That's not what I meant," said Gavin. There was something different about the boy, Callum could see that. An air of confidence that hadn't been there before.

"If you wanted me dead, why did you save me back there?" asked Callum.

"Because," Michael grunted, tightening his grip on Callum's throat, "I wanted the pleasure of doing it myself. This is all your fault, M-forcer."

Michael took the knife away from his cheek and drew it back, preparing to plunge it into Callum's chest.

"You contacted them, didn't you? Brought them to our refuge? And now …"

Callum shook his head. "It wasn't me."

"Now they're either dead or have been taken. Ferne's been taken. You used her, then betrayed her."

"Used …" Callum realised what Michael was implying. "You sick bastard. You were there? In the room?"

"I had to leave. I couldn't stomach anymore."

Callum gritted his teeth. "But you heard what she said about you? She doesn't feel the way you want her to, *Michael*." Somehow Callum managed to make the man's name sound like a swearword.

Michael let go of his throat, pushing his forearm up against it instead. He raised the knifepoint so that it hovered just over Callum's right eye. "That doesn't stop me from caring about *her*. Loving *her*," said Michael, and for a moment Callum almost felt sorry for the guy. He already had Ferne's love, something Michael would never experience; at least not that way. The sympathy vanished with Michael's next sentence. "Maybe if you hadn't come along … Or maybe if I'd just killed you that night in your flat, in your bedroom."

"Jesus," gasped Callum. "You've been watching me all along, haven't you?"

"I've seen enough to know who you really are inside. I saw my sister's last moments."

"You were there at Widow's Way as well?"

There were tears in Michael's eyes. "I saw her take her own life rather than be carted off by you. I saw my nephew and niece get dragged away, again by you."

"But you still walked away from it, just like you walked away from *The Valentine*. Why didn't you help more of your kind to escape?"

Michael's eyes boiled with hatred. "I only have *two* hands! Gavin is important to the survival of Arcana. He is Unwin's successor. And you—"

"He is more important than any of us," Gavin broke in.

"No, he's a dead man."

"I didn't tell the authorities about *The Valentine*," Callum repeated. "Are you listening to me, Michael? It. Wasn't. Me. But you … You had both the opportunity and the motive."

"How dare you! What motive could *I* possibly have had?"

"To stitch me up, prove to Ferne and the rest of them that you were right about me? Only something went wrong, maybe you cut a deal and they reneged on it. Who'd you make it with? Pryce?"

Michael leaned more heavily on Callum, crushing him against the boxes and the wall of the lock-up. "No true Arcana can speak about *The Valentine*'s location."

"No, but you could have led the way. Besides, you reckon no true Arcana can kill, right?" Callum's voice was croaky. "But that's exactly what your lot did last night, Michael, and you were proud of them for it. Maybe the old ways have been forgotten somewhere down the line. Maybe Arcana has become the thing the M-forcers have been warning about all this time? I mean, look at you now. You're ready to kill me, aren't you?"

"That's different. You're one of *them*. They all deserve to die." He loosened his hold on Callum a little.

"And the people who could potentially turn you in to them? Where do you stand on killing them? Any flexibility in that department?" The knife in front of him wavered. "You see, it's all part of the same thing. It's a vicious circle, Michael. Neither side can ever win."

"Let him go," Gavin ordered, and this time Michael did as instructed, stepping back from Callum but keeping the knife poised. "He's telling the truth. It wasn't him who betrayed us."

"It wasn't me, either. I'd never do such a thing," Michael argued.

"Yes," Gavin said, nodding. "I know that too. The cards have shown me everything." He shuffled them expertly, his hands both guiding them and being guided *by* them.

"Then who?" asked Callum, rubbing his sore neck for the second time in two days.

Gavin stopped shuffling, looked down at the ground then back up again, delaying what he had to say.

"Tell us!" shouted Michael, stomping towards Gavin. Callum actually thought he might threaten him with the knife as well.

"It was Master Unwin," Gavin finally said.

"What?" Michael said in disbelief. "That can't be."

"It's the truth." Gavin sniffed back a tear. "At first I didn't want to believe it, either."

Michael's body deflated; it looked like someone had let all the air out of him. "But how? He's Arcana as well? He couldn't—"

"The rules never really applied to him," said Gavin.

"I don't understand. Why? My Goddess, all the people killed and captured today … Ferne … Why would he do that?"

Callum had to admit he was having trouble with this himself. Why on Earth would Unwin betray the very thing he believed in to his core? It didn't make any sense.

"He knew what would happen, but it had to be done. Events have played out just as the cards told him they would," Gavin explained, however vaguely.

"You talk just like him," Callum said. "In riddles."

"It was necessary in order for The Magician to awaken." Gavin pointed at Callum. "He did it to convince you."

Callum touched his own chest. "Convince me of what, that he was insane? Well, it worked."

"Master Unwin …?" Michael said, shaking his head. Then he looked at Callum. "Don't you see, he did it because he believed in that idiotic prophecy, just like Ferne. They think you're going to save them all, but they've got it wrong. How could he of all people have been so stupid?'

"I kept telling *them* that," Callum offered, as if it might make everything all right. "They've got the wrong guy. I told them—"

"You commune with The Goddess," Gavin said simply. "Michael, you must have heard him tell Ferne that?"

"To get her into bed," Michael muttered. "To defile her."

"Hey, it takes two to tango mate." Callum jabbed a finger at him. "And I never *defiled* anyone. Ferne knew what she was doing."

"She was deluded, just like Unwin."

"Nothing is hidden from the cards," countered Gavin. "And now they hide nothing from me. Ferne loves Callum, Michael."

"I'm sure she *thinks* she does, but she's wrong about him. I've said as much to her."

Gavin shook his head. "No, she isn't. Neither was Master Unwin."

"Then I agree with *him*." Michael thumbed back at Callum. "Unwin must have taken leave of his senses. Look at all the people who lost their lives; that blood is on his hands. All because of a crazy fairy tale."

"To some, might not what you do—passing through solid walls, vanishing before their very eyes—seem like something from a fairy tale, Michael? Yet it's as real to you as eating or breathing." The words were far too wise to be coming from Gavin's mouth, but somehow it seemed like he'd been destined to say them all his short life. "A sacrifice was needed, for the good of all. For the Favoured Child to realise his potential."

"Whoa, whoa," interrupted Callum, waving his arms, "hold on. I'm with Michael, I'm not a favoured *anything*, let alone child."

"You are a Child of The Goddess. But if you still refuse to acknowledge what you are, then maybe it *was* all in vain," Gavin said glumly.

"I didn't *ask* for this to happen. I—"

"Your choices have led you to this point, Callum McGuire." Callum felt the hairs on the back of his neck prickle. This couldn't be same the wet-behind-the-ears kid who'd come to fetch him a couple of days ago. The same kid Ferne had dismissed from her quarters the night they made love?

"What's happened to you?" Callum asked.

"Nothing, compared with what will happen to you," was Gavin's response. If Michael had said those words, they would have sounded like a threat. But coming from Gavin it was more like a caution.

Callum shook his head. "I'm not some half-baked messiah. I don't have the power to save your people. I'm no hero ... So where does that leave us?"

"Right back where we came in." Michael scowled, raising the knife again. "Whichever way you look at it, it's still your fault all this happened. If Ferne hadn't gotten involved with you, Unwin would never have done what he did. Our people would not be dead, or worse. Time for a little retribution."

Callum knew Michael was determined to have his revenge, no matter how warped the reasoning was. And behind most of it was Ferne's love for him. If Callum wasn't around anymore, perhaps those feelings might switch their focus to Michael? That's if they ever saw her again. Callum blocked out images of Ferne in pain. Ferne being interrogated at The Penitentiary, the milky whiteness of her skin as they cut into—

No! He had more immediate matters to contend with, like trying to stay alive. The fight with Gibson had drained him, but even if he was at full strength Callum doubted whether he could take Michael. Gavin shouted after him, but this time the man wasn't listening. He charged at Callum, slashing the knife.

Callum pulled back, but Michael altered course, determined to find a home for the blade. "Keep still, it'll all be over soon," Michael promised. Callum stumbled, almost tripped over one of the fallen boxes. He took his eyes off Michael for a second, but when they returned to him the man was lunging with the knife.

This is it, thought Callum. *I'm going to be killed by one of* them, *after all. Just like my folks …*

But, at the last minute, Michael froze. His mouth opened and he looked down. Callum followed his gaze, wondering what on Earth could have halted his attack. Then he saw.

His hands, down by his sides, were alive with energy. Lightning crackled in his palms, across his fingers, building with each passing moment. Callum's eyes opened wide in surprise. A muscle in Michael's cheek twitched. He looked up again at Callum, shaking his head—as if trying to convince himself that what he'd seen wasn't real—and came at his opponent again. The knife was in line with Callum's heart and was coming towards him with enough strength to force it in, and probably out the other side again. Without even thinking, Callum brought up his hands to defend himself.

With his left, more energy than ever crackling in the palm, he grabbed the knife blade, feeling nothing of its sharpness as he yanked it out of Michael's grasp. With his right hand, now simply a ball of glowing light, he punched Michael squarely in the chest. There was just time to register a look of astonishment on the man's face, before he was sent flying across the length of the lock-up, crashing into the concrete wall. Winded, he slid down it until he came to rest at the bottom.

Callum was aware that the energy was spreading, up his arms and down his torso, so bright it eclipsed the dingy lightbulb's glow. What he must have looked like to Gavin and Michael, he couldn't guess, but they were shielding their eyes, squinting to even keep him in sight.

He was also aware of opening his mouth and speaking, though he wasn't the one forming the words.

"Did you think I would let you hurt him, Michael Sanderson? And with my own sacrificial weapon?" The voice was much higher in pitch than Callum's, and had a definite lyrical quality.

Gavin dropped to his knees. "Goddess!"

"No," whimpered Michael. "No, it can't be."

"Listen to me. Everything you have heard is true," the tinkling voice continued, "and when the time is right Callum McGuire will take his true place as the most powerful of your kind who ever lived. But first, he must possess my book. The one from which all magick stemmed. Find that, and you have my word that your people will be freed. Find it, and the tyranny that has been enforced upon you and your kin will be at an end. Mark me, though, if it should fall into the wrong hands …"

"Where might we find the book, Mistress?" asked Gavin, but it was too late. The energy was burning up, then it was sucked into Callum like a backdraft. He blinked once, twice.

"I … don't feel so …" Callum managed in his own voice.

Then he collapsed in a heap on the floor.

CHAPTER THIRTY-TWO

She only remembered this:

She'd been handcuffed and bundled into the back of the truck at gun point, along with several other Arcana. Rough hands were on her, some even taking the opportunity to paw and grope her. When she'd struggled, one of the M-forcers had deemed her a threat and brought the butt of a machine-gun down on the back of her head, knocking her unconscious.

Ferne had drifted in and out of wakefulness after that, aware of the sensation of the vehicle moving, carrying them all somewhere. They stopped only once or twice, the second time a long pause, and she could hear muffled voices, the unmistakable sound of an electric gate opening. She lost some more time then, because the next thing she knew she was being carried down a long corridor. The handcuffs were gone and she was shoved inside a cell, containing just a bed and a sink. The back of her head was throbbing as she lay on the cold floor, so she reached up with shaking fingertips to feel the gash the officer had made. Summoning as much energy as she could, Ferne concentrated on healing the wound. The area around it felt warm, and seconds later she felt much better … physically. Now there was just the small matter of being locked away in a prison cell Goddess knew where.

No, that wasn't strictly true. Ferne knew exactly where she was: The Penitentiary. She'd listened to Michael's descriptions often enough. And if she sniffed she could smell the aroma he'd talked about, the one he'd said Callum reeked of that night in her flat. It was the stench of misery, suffering, of lost hope and … yes, death. Ferne knew what they did here, the kind of practices they employed. But the first of these torture tactics was obviously to make you wait.

At first she sat on the edge of the bed, saying nothing, staring up at the camera in the corner of the room. They were watching her even now, seeing what she'd do. The longer they held her in these four walls, the more she imagined what was in store. Was that their game? All she knew was it gave her time to think. About what had happened back at *The Valentine*, about what Gibson had said. Callum had denied it, but what if he'd had something to do with turning them in? It was certainly true that, because he wasn't Arcana, he could have given away the location—at least the name. What if it this whole thing was because of him, and, by extension, because of *her*? She'd brought him back to their home, allowed him into their world. Into her bed! Had he repaid her by leading Arcana's enemies right to their doorstep?

The more time that passed, the more she paced up and down in the confines of the cell, biting her lip. *Don't allow them the satisfaction*, she told herself, *don't let them see you getting so worked up.* But as far as the outside world was concerned, she didn't exist anymore. They could do anything to her, and there wasn't a law in the land that could protect her. Even if there were, she was Arcana, part of the group who'd carried out all those attacks. A menace to society.

"I'm just a healer," Ferne said quietly to herself, then, not even knowing whether the camera up in the corner had audio or not, she screamed at it: "I'm a healer! I've never hurt anyone. I never *would*!" Ferne sat back down again on the bed, in floods of tears. All she'd ever wanted was to be left alone to practise her own way of life, to give thanks to the Goddess and look after the sick. When she thought about the amount of patients she'd aided in their recovery without anyone ever noticing, speeding along the natural course of things and—in some extreme cases

—bringing those with chronic diseases along to the point where they could be cured by conventional medicine. If she hadn't thought she'd be caught, she would have restored their health completely. She might as well have done, because now she was in the hands of the authorities anyway.

Ferne thought back to her childhood, to when they'd come for her dog Trixie. She'd climbed out of her bedroom window and run as fast as she could down the road. Then her mind flashed forward to when Gibson had appeared at the halfway house, after she'd healed the man with cancer and been ratted out for her trouble. She'd barely escaped, leaving the name and life of Tracy Evans behind her. Then again, at the hospital, the noose around her neck. If it hadn't been for Callum ... Could he really have betrayed them, someone who had seen The Goddess in person? She wondered what had happened to him after she'd been taken: was he here, a captive just like her? Or celebrating a victory over them?

So many lucky escapes, too many. But her luck had run out today for sure. Possibly forever.

Ferne lay back on the bed, arm over her eyes. She had no way of knowing how long she'd been in here already because they'd taken her watch away, along with her belt and shoe laces. If she was going to hang it would be on their terms, not hers. It seemed like hours, though. She was beginning to grow hungry, having hardly eaten anything in the past twenty-four hours. It was an odd survival instinct, designed to keep her alive: but there were so many things stacked against that.

Finally, they came. Two big men wearing the jump-suit uniform of the prison rather than the full M-forcer outfit. They had utility belts just the same, though, a pistol on one hip, baton on the other, and probably a noose—though this was hidden out of sight.

"Now, you're not going to give us any trouble, are you?" said the first, a burly man with a barrel chest who looked like he could wrestle an alligator and win. "Or are we going to have to gag you?"

"Naw," said the second, completely bald, with a moustache to compensate for the fact and show that he could grow hair somewhere. "I don't think this one will be a problem. After all, you'd never hurt anyone, would you?" He laughed, obviously referring to her little outburst for the camera.

Ferne allowed them to put another pair of handcuffs on her: these more solid, more like thick metal bracelets connected by a rod instead of a chain; no room for manoeuvre. She hung her head as they walked her out into the corridor.

The burly man coughed; a rough, grating sound.

Ferne cocked her head. "You know, you really should give up the cigarettes. They're killing you."

"Shut it, sparkie," said his bald companion.

"And you," Ferne closed her eyes and inhaled. "That liver's not going to hold out much longer if you don't give up the booze."

Baldie drew his baton and was about to strike her when Burly held his wrist. "They want her unharmed," he said, then whispered, "Remember what happened to the officer that hit her when they put her in the van."

Baldie nodded, sufficiently warned.

So they needed her unharmed? But for what? Ferne tried not to think about that. It at least gave her some leeway if they couldn't hurt her.

"You know," she said over her shoulder as they pushed her down the corridor, "I could help. Fix your lungs. Fix your liver so you could drink till the cows come home."

They both looked at her blankly.

"You saw me on the camera back there. You know what I am, what I can do. I've done it before, to people in hospital. I can *heal* you."

Baldie sneered. "We don't need some fucking sparkie voodoo messing us up."

"No," said Ferne. "That's right, I forgot. You're doing a great job of messing yourselves up, aren't you?"

"Just keep walking," Burly told her.

"Wait, look, I really can help you. You'll feel fantastic afterwards. Here," Ferne turned and placed her hands on Baldie's stomach, mouthing a few words. The area glowed momentarily and he stopped in his tracks, knees buckling. Just as Burly was about to restrain her, she turned and lay both her hands on his chest. His shirt, and the flesh below it, was illuminated. Burly dropped to the floor, with Baldie not far behind, all the strength in his legs finally gone.

Ferne took her chance. She ran off up the corridor, no thought for where she might be going, nor the fact that there were four times as many cameras trailing her here as there were in her cell. That didn't matter, this was another shot at escape. To run, just like she'd done as a kid, at the halfway house, at the hospital. She rounded a corner and found a barred door confronting her.

"Dammit!"

Ferne retreated, not really left much option but to carry on back up the corridor. Burly and Baldie were getting to their feet now, the effects of her treatment wearing off. But worse than that, they'd been joined by a solid wall of guards dressed like them, along with a couple of people in white coats. They weren't running towards her, just waiting. Because they knew there was nowhere left to run. Now they began walking slowly in her direction.

As a last-ditch attempt, Ferne went back and shook the bars of the door. She spouted incantations, her hands glowed, but there was nothing to heal here. No secret hatches like the one back at *The Valentine*. These bars were new, and they were strong. The designers had made sure there were no weak points that could be exploited.

The hands were on her again. Securing her, holding her down, as she was injected with something.

"Check on those two idiots," she heard someone say. "She did something to them. They may be contaminated."

All she'd done was what she promised, fixed their problems, to buy her time to get away. They'd been tainted, though, "poisoned" with magick. They'd be lucky to keep their jobs, let alone their freedom. Ironically, now that they could smoke and drink to their hearts' content, those simple pleasures would probably be taken away from them.

Guards' faces, male and female, swam around her. Ferne tried to bring up her hands, to purge her system of whatever muck they'd pumped into it, but her captors held her down fast.

"I'm a healer," she told them, slurring her words. "Woooouldn't … huurt … any … ooone …"

Then, for the second time recently, consciousness slipped out of her grasp.

This time she dreamed.

She was in a meadow, somewhere peaceful. The sun was blazing down, beating strongly on her face. Not far away a field of barley swayed in the light summer breeze. *Is this heaven?* she wondered. *Is this the eternal resting place we all go to when we die?* It was so beautiful, like the places her parents had taken her before she started to display her powers. They'd gone on walks, had picnics. Been a real family.

There was a figure in the distance, a mere speck at the moment. But the more she concentrated on that tiny dot the closer it came, jumping metres with each blink of the eye. As it came into focus, she recognised the build, the fair hair, then finally the face of the man she loved.

Callum.

He was running, as fast as he could towards her. She found herself running as well, bouncing on the springy grass, each footfall bringing her closer to the man she'd been forcibly separated from. Then suddenly she was in Callum's arms. He was holding her, stroking her hair, telling her everything was going to be all right.

"How … Where are we?"

"The Goddess has allowed us this time," he explained, pulling away briefly.

"Where are you?" Ferne asked him.

"I can't tell you that. They're going to be asking you the same question." He kissed her softly on the lips. "But you have to be strong, Ferne. Do you hear me?" Callum cupped her face in his hands. "And don't believe what they say. You were right about me."

The picture grew dull. Ferne looked up and saw dark clouds covering the sun.

"Callum," she said, holding onto his arms. "I'm scared."

There was a billow of thunder on the horizon; it sounded like a giant stomping towards them. Callum brushed a strand of black hair out of her eyes. "Me too."

A flash of lightning, more thunder.

"Listen," Callum said with some urgency. "We don't have long. Whatever you do, don't forget what I told you, Ferne. I know how difficult it is to remember half of what you see here, I doubt whether I'll wake up knowing what I do right now. But …" He held her hands tightly. "You have to hold on to this. You were right about me. And I'm coming for you."

"Callum—" There was a bright flash of lightning, then everything went white. The dreamscape had suddenly melted away, to be replaced by somewhere completely different.

The light was shining directly in her eyes.

Ferne tried to blink but someone was bending down, holding her eyes open. First one, then the other, flashing something into them. She tried to bring her hands up to either shield them or knock the light away, but found she couldn't move. She saw red circles, but when the brightness was taken away she caught a glimpse of a man in a white coat. She was awake again, back in the real world. Ferne tried to recall what she had seen when she'd been asleep, but only vague memories had made the journey back with her.

"She's fine," declared the doctor. "Coming round nicely."

"Good," said another voice. Even when the white-coated guy moved out of her field of vision she had great difficulty bringing the other man into focus; partly the after-effects of the pen-torch that had been jammed into her eyes, partly the contrasting murkiness of the rest of the room. This was a place deliberately filled with shadows. That smell was stronger here, too. People had definitely died in here.

The doctor spoke next. "Would you like me to stay, just in case?"

"No, that will be all."

Ferne heard the first man move off behind her, then rap on a door to be let out. There was a creak of hinges, a slamming sound, and she was left alone with the enigma. As her eyes adjusted to the dim surroundings, Ferne tried to look down. She couldn't; there was something around her neck. Not a noose this time, something more substantial. It felt cold against her skin. She swivelled her eyes downwards and saw her wrists were held tight by more metal clasps, attached to the chair arms. In front of her was a table, and it was at the other end of this that the man sat.

It was some kind of interrogation room, she guessed. Michael had described one just like it with a mirror running the length of one wall so people on the other side could watch. It must have been a new experience for him.

Finding she could move her head left and right, albeit with a limited range, Ferne looked for the mirror, but couldn't make one out —though it was too dark to tell for sure.

"Welcome back," said the voice, and she faced forwards again. The figure's features were still covered in folds of black, and she knew the lights had been angled precisely to create this effect. He didn't want her to see his face until he was good and ready.

"Where …" began Ferne, wincing because the metal grating against her throat hurt when she spoke. "Where am I?"

"That's not really important. It was a silly thing you did outside your cell, you know. If you hadn't … well, there might not be the need to restrain you like this during our little chat."

"Who are you?"

"I think you know that already, High Priestess."

"I'm not—"

"*Acting* High Priestess, then, if you want to split hairs. We know all about you, Ferne Andrews. We almost had you twice before, didn't we? Once when you were little, then again in your twenties. It's a miracle you got away with practising at St August's for so long without arousing suspicion."

"I was very careful," she said, her tone even.

"I'm sure you were. How many people did you infect with your particular brand of medicine while you were there? Dozens?

Hundreds? They'll all have to be tracked down and dealt with, of course."

"I helped them."

"You *condemned* them," came the harsh rebuff. "Just like you condemned that little boy in your block of flats, the one you cured."

"What?"

"Oh yes, we know about that too. As soon as your identity was confirmed after that little escapade at the hospital, we questioned everyone on your floor. And guess what? A couple called the Hodgsons admitted that you had interfered with their child."

"Interfered ..." The accusation made her sound like some kind of pervert. "I helped him to breathe after a severe allergic reaction." Every word hurt to say, but now Ferne was angry.

"By unnatural means. They agreed with us that the child is now a blasphemy in the eyes of the Lord."

"What have you done to him?"

The man didn't answer.

"You son of a bitch," Ferne shouted, then had to stop because it was too painful. Her next word was little more than a whisper. "Pryce."

"See, you *do* know who I am." As if reacting to some kind of cue, Sherman Pryce stood and walked along the table. He sat down on the edge near to her and, as he did so, she saw him properly. It was the first time she'd seen him in the flesh rather than on some broadcast or in the papers. Those pictures didn't do him justice. His features were so much more severe when they were only a metre or so away. So much more predatory.

"I know *what* you are," Ferne said in hushed tones.

Pryce laughed. "I can see we're going to have so much fun, you and I."

Ferne doubted whether they shared the same definition of fun. "I won't talk," she promised him.

"Oh, come on. I only want to know a few teeny-weeny things." Pryce squeezed his gloved thumb and forefinger together to emphasise the fact. "Like for instance, I don't know, where your male counterpart is, the High Priest?"

Michael? They don't know where he is, so he must have escaped. "I've no idea what you're talking about. We have no High Priest."

"If you say so. All right, how about a person formerly in our employ: one Officer Callum McGuire? You remember him, don't you? You should do, you abducted him a few days ago."

Ferne laughed this time, then winced again as the metal caught her throat, its sides rough and sharp. "I didn't abduct anybody. He came with me of his own free will."

Pryce inched himself up further onto the table. "Then how would you prefer me to put it? Beguiled perhaps? Be*witched*?"

Ferne narrowed her eyes.

"But it wasn't strong enough, was it?"

"What are you talking about?"

He licked his lips. "The call that gave us the location of *The Valentine* came from the theatre itself, Miss Andrews." Though he used her full title, he had a way of still making it sound derogatory. "It was Callum McGuire. You know it and I know it." Pryce leaned in, only inches away from her face. "He must have realised what you and your kind were really like, murdering filth that you are. Or, who knows, perhaps he sampled the goods and that was enough to break the spell."

Ferne spat into his face and he recoiled, wiping his cheek with the back of his gloved hand. Then in the same motion, he brought that hand back hard across her face. Ferne's head snapped sideways with the blow, but was prevented from going too far by the neck-clasp. There was a coppery taste in her mouth and she knew he'd split her bottom lip. Touching it with her tongue confirmed the fact; it was tender and swollen.

"That's right. Painful, isn't it?" said Pryce. "That's just for starters if you don't cooperate. Plus, there'll be no naughty healing yourself this time. So I suggest you tell me what I want to know. The location of your High Priest, of Callum McGuire … and of the book."

Ferne looked at him, genuinely puzzled. "What book?"

"Don't play dumb with me, you worthless sow!" Pryce screamed into her face. He reached over the table and picked something up, brandishing it in front of her. Ferne saw that it was her book of spells, the one she'd grabbed as she and Callum tried to escape. The one that had been taken from her when she'd been captured. "*The* Book. The one like yours here, like the others from *The Valentine* we've burnt or impounded. Except the one we're after contains all the incantations that ever existed in their original form."

"That's just a myth. It doesn't exist."

Pryce smiled. "I have it on good authority that it does, and that Arcana have been hiding it."

Ferne shook her head. It couldn't be. That the Great Book should have been in their possession and she knew nothing about it. Even as interim High Priestess, she should have been told. No, Pryce was feeding her lies. *Don't believe what they say.* "Impossible."

"Nothing's impossible when it comes to your lot," he sniped, poking a finger at her. "You should be the first to admit that."

"Even if I knew anything about it, I wouldn't tell you."

Pryce tutted. "That's a shame, because there's an easy way to do this. And there's a hard way." He got up off the table and, for a second, Ferne thought he was going to hit her again. She even flinched as he passed by. But back where the door must be, where the doctor had gone, there had to be a dimmer switch for the lights as well. Because she heard a clicking, then suddenly she could see the whole room—and its contents.

This wasn't one of the interrogation suites at all. There were *no* mirrors in here. Only the stuff of nightmares lining the walls. Every conceivable torture device known to man, and some that had been kept secret because of their sheer depravity, were present. She recognised a few from books about her kind's history: a square hollow box with poles at either end, standing on four legs. It looked like another table but Ferne was fully aware of its nature—a rack for stretching the victim until either their bones cracked or they talked; a wooden construction that looked like an upside down triangle, but with a further beam running along the centre on which the victim would be placed, also upside down, with their legs spread wide along the "V"; a simple set of wooden stocks; an open Iron Maiden, a coffin basically laced with rows and rows of spikes; and several pokers resting in a giant metal furnace, that was thankfully not lit. Plus there were some contraptions she had no clue about, and wanted no instruction as to how they worked: a large pole with a circular wooden wheel; what looked like a set of gallows but had a large metal hook hanging from them in the centre; a cage-like device with metal poles attached, running up the length of it like a cattle-grid; and something that resembled an old fashioned mangle, except it had bumps moulded to each of the rollers.

Then there were the smaller items that hung from the stone walls themselves, in-between the sets of chains and manacles: various assortments of whips, ranging from the ordinary leather affair to a cat-o'-nine-tails, and even one which had hooks and spikes on the ends, to cause maximum pain; a set of thumbscrews; a large iron hoop, hinged in two halves, meant to bring the chest to the knees and secure the victim like that; a warped variation of a scold's bridle headpiece, studded with small spikes; cleavers of various shapes and sizes, some of which wouldn't have looked out of place in a butcher's shop; and a serious assembly of metal instruments including knives, scalpels, tongues, forks and scissors. Ferne had never seen such a collection, even in her days as a nurse.

But there was no discrimination against the modern in Pryce's torture chamber. There were electric saws, small handsaws and hand-held chainsaws, just perfect to lop off fingers, toes, or other parts of the body. What looked like a miniature flamethrower rested in the corner, big enough to generate quite a blast of heat, but small enough for the user to direct it at a specific area. Alongside this was a common welding torch, complete with gas canister to power it, allowing for an even more precise burn. And electric drills, more powerful than those used in any dentist's: for teeth, bone or anything else that sprang to mind. Beside these was a tray of needles, swabs and other medical equipment, which would be used to keep the victim alive for however long it took to get answers, prolonging the agony as long as possible.

Ferne squirmed in the chair, railing against the neck and wrist clasps, not caring whether they dug into her or not, ignoring the cuts they made.

A hand pressed her shoulder. "Stop," said Pryce. "You'll hurt yourself." She froze up completely, though she was trembling at his touch. "And that's my job. You should feel privileged, not everyone gets to see this place."

"You're sick!" she managed.

"I suppose you're going to heal me, eh? Not this time. Not like that, and with the drugs still in your system."

He pulled the chair back, then came round and stood in front of her, hands on his hips, leering down at Ferne's body. "I'm so looking forward to this, you know. Now," he said, tapping his mouth with a finger, "are you ready to begin?"

CHAPTER THIRTY-THREE

Callum was aware of someone leaning over him when he awoke.

For the third time in as many days, he felt like he'd been dragged around by a wall of death motorcyclist for a couple of hours, then had someone reach down his throat and pull him inside out.

"How do you feel?" asked Gavin.

He was tempted to say, "You tell me, you're the one with the pack of cards that knows everything" but instead he just mumbled, "I feel like crap."

Callum tried to sit up, but didn't get very far, so Gavin helped him. Now he was at least semi-upright, he realised what a mistake that had been. He felt woozy, his head spinning. What the hell had happened to him?

"Michael says it was a manifestation of the Anima," Gavin stated.

Callum didn't bother asking how the boy knew what he was thinking, it would be a waste of time, so he just asked: "And that is?"

"The buried female element of your psyche."

"But you don't agree with him, do you?"

Gavin gave a subtle shake of his head. "Of course not. The

Goddess was channelling through you, anyone could see that. Anyone who wanted to, that is."

Callum looked around the lock-up, then regretted that as well. "Where is Chuckles, anyway?"

Gavin smiled. "I'll let him tell you that himself when he gets back. He just said he had to get away from here for a while."

"How long ago was that?"

"A few hours, maybe more."

Callum let out a breath. "I've been out cold all that time?"

"Doing what you did took a lot out of you. You needed to recover."

"Look," said Callum. "I know what you're thinking. I can't explain it myself yet. But it wasn't what it looked like, okay?"

"What, that you blew Michael across the room using magick and then spoke with the voice of The Goddess?"

"Er … yes."

"So it wasn't that at all?"

"No." There was very little conviction in Callum's voice.

Gavin took out his cards and began shuffling them with expert ease. "You're going to have to face up to this sooner or later, you know. For all our sakes."

"There's nothing to face up *to*!" Callum insisted, with an edge to his voice.

"For Ferne's sake," said Gavin.

Ferne. The name sparked a memory inside Callum; it felt like he'd just been with her, talking to her. But he couldn't have been, she was who knows where right now. Nevertheless …

"Callum, are you listening to me?"

He snapped out of his daze. "I hear you. I just don't know what you expect me to do. I can't fix it with some wave of my hand and an abracadabra."

Gavin didn't reply at first, then he said, "But you can do … something, can't you?"

Before Callum could say anymore, he felt another presence in the lock-up, someone who'd just appeared out of nowhere. Michael stood there, hands behind his back. The brooding face had gone now, replaced by … what, a look of grudging respect? He hadn't been expecting Callum to be awake yet, obviously.

"Hello, Michael," said Gavin.

The man remained silent, just kept on staring in Callum's direction. Callum got to his feet, swaying slightly at first, then righting himself. Michael backed up a little. No, it wasn't respect at all. Michael was *scared* of him. Callum decided to test the waters.

"Where have you been?" It wasn't just some casual enquiry and Michael knew it.

Michael opened his mouth to speak, then shut it again swiftly.

"I asked you a question," Callum said.

"I've been … out."

"Obviously," stated Callum. "I asked where?" Was that a flinch?

"I went back to *The Valentine*," Michael admitted.

"You did what?"

Michael was looking anywhere but at Callum. "You heard what I said." So there was still some fire inside him.

"But why?"

"They've all but gone now, just a skeleton crew of M-forcers around in case anybody should return. Not that there are any of us left now, and not that we would after this." He brought his hands round the front, and Callum could see that they were holding two or three newspapers. Michael tossed them in the direction of Gavin and Callum. "Early editions, they're full of it."

Callum picked up one of the papers, glancing at the some of the headlines: "ARCANA DEN CRUSHED"; "PRYCE MAKES GOOD ON PROMISE TO STAMP OUT ARCANA"; "MASS EXECUTIONS ORDERED" It was this last one he dwelled on, scanning the lines saying Commander Sherman Pryce had told the press that in the following days the most dangerous members of Arcana would be summarily executed under Section 1a of the James I of England Act, pertaining to harmful magick users in custody. Gavin left the other papers where they were; he didn't need to look at them.

"Pryce's making good on his promise, all right," Michael continued. "He's ensuring there isn't a single one of us left."

"They're going to start killing Arcana?" Callum said.

"What did you expect them to do, slap them on the wrist and let them go?" Some of Michael's old defiance was creeping back in. "It won't be long before they've murdered all the prisoners. And no-one out there will take any notice because it's just a bunch of lowlife sparkies."

"That's because the population see it as revenge, Michael." Callum screwed up the paper he was holding and threw it on the ground. "Now do you see why Ferne reacted the way she did to those attacks?"

"So I'm not the only one who listens in at doors."

"Did you have anything to do with organising them, Michael?" asked Callum directly.

Again, no reply.

Callum walked towards him and Michael shifted about. "Well, *did* you?"

Michael's eyes were darting from side to side, looking for a way out. As Callum drew closer the other man began to shimmer slightly. Callum shot forward with a speed he didn't even knew he had, let alone thought he could muster, and grabbed Michael's wrist.

"No you don't," he said. "Not this time."

Gavin watched as the pair flickered out of existence momentarily, then came right back. Michael wasn't going to run away again.

"Answer me!" ordered Callum, shoving his face into Michael's. The man looked terrified, memories still fresh of what Callum had done to him a few hours ago.

"I had *nothing* to do with the attacks." His voice cracked as he said it. "I swear. It wasn't me."

"Then who? Ferne spent ages trying to convince me that you were all good people, just misunderstood and persecuted. Then the next thing I know, Arcana are bombing nightclubs and tower blocks, and that's on top of all the other attacks. You tell me: *who?*"

Michael was shaking; Callum could feel the vibrations travelling up his hand. "I don't know."

"You won't find your answers here," said Gavin from behind them.

Callum looked over his shoulder. "Then where? Back at *The*

Valentine?" He turned to Michael again. "Is that why you were there, looking for answers? Maybe covering up the truth?"

"I was looking for The Book." Michael finally let the words tumble out of his mouth.

"Book? What book?"

Michael raised his eyebrows. "The one you spoke of yourself."

"Me?" Then Callum realised it must have been just before he collapsed. Must have been when he did the things that he couldn't possibly have done, said the words he couldn't remember.

"It was the Goddess who told us," corrected Gavin. "*Through* him."

Callum groaned. "Not that again … Okay, all right. So what did she say?"

"That you must possess The Book, the one from which all spells came." And, as if to demonstrate the fact, Michael reached into his pocket and produced a small hardback—his own book of spells. Personal ones that would be mainly connected with his special talent; that other plane he used.

"Then, and only then," Gavin took up the drift, "will you be able to save us."

Callum let Michael go, shaking his head. "So you've been looking for this stupid book back at the theatre, when what we really need to be doing is … Did you find it?"

"No," answered Michael.

"Right, so that's that," Callum announced with a certain amount of finality. "Can we concentrate on how we're going to free Ferne, and the rest of your friends?" He added the last bit, though it was a bit of a shock to him. Had he said it because he was trying to enlist Gavin and Michael's help, or because he genuinely believed the other members of Arcana should be freed? That they didn't deserve to be exterminated like pests?

"What?" spluttered Michael. "And how do you propose we do that?"

"We're all agreed on where she … they'll be, right? So, we break into The Penitentiary." Callum said it like they were going for a leisurely stroll down by the riverside.

"The Penitentiary!" Michael looked more afraid now than he had when Callum grabbed hold of him. "That's madness!"

"Do you have any better ideas?"

"We'll be killed before we get within five miles of the place," Michael assured him. "That's assuming you know where it is."

"No. I've only ever been once, and it was in the back of a truck." He left out the fact that he was with members of Michael's family at the time. Callum pointed at him. "But Ferne told me you were the only one ever to escape from there. Is that true?"

Michael swallowed. "Yes, a long time ago. But—"

"So, you have to know the location."

"I don't," Michael retorted.

"Then how did you get out?"

"Well, I didn't just walk out. Same as we're not just going to walk in."

"You used your powers?" Callum ventured.

"Not in the way you're thinking. They can detect magickal activity in that place."

Callum nodded, recalling the detector he'd had to go through, then swatting aside the memory of it going off as he'd done so. It didn't prove a thing. "What did you do, then?"

"There are many different levels of travelling." He held up his spell book, tapping it as if to emphasise the point. "The one I use most often, the one I used to get you both out just skims the surface. It allows me to take my physical form with me, only in an altered state. But there is a way to detach the soul from the body, to leave it behind. Essentially I disconnected my spirit from my physical self."

"You … you died?"

"To all intents and purposes, yes. I did it while they were interrogating me. They didn't even get my name. But they still gave me an autopsy to make sure." He lifted part of his shirt to show Callum the scars.

This must have been what Ferne was talking about when she said only one of their kind had ever come back from the dead, thought Callum, giving a little shudder. *No wonder Michael lives his life like a ghost.*

"But to remain on the other side like that for any great length of time is incredibly dangerous. You've only experienced a fraction of what it's like, M-forcer." There was great bitterness in his words. "You become lost. The real world turns to smoke, to fog, and the longer you remain there, the harder it is to find your way back. The worst thing is that you find you're not alone."

"You did, though," said Callum. "Get back, I mean?"

"Eventually. I'm told my body was shipped out. That I was in a truck with several more murdered Arcana, in body bags, on our way to be incinerated en masse. Luckily, it was intercepted by other members of our order and the bodies liberated. Don't worry," Michael said, looking directly at Callum this time, "the driver and guard weren't harmed … much."

"I can remember the rumours about the day he was brought back in. I was very young then," Gavin added. He'd been so quiet listening to the account that Callum had totally forgotten he was there. "Everyone thought he was dead, but then he suddenly woke up. He didn't have long even then, because of what they'd done to him back at The Penitentiary."

"So how did you survive?"

"Ferne," said Michael.

"Ah."

"She healed what they'd done during the autopsy, although there was still only a small chance I'd pull through. I owe her my life."

Callum nodded. "I know the feeling. Which is one of the reasons why we both have to go back there and save her. Heaven knows what she must be going through."

"But how?" Michael asked. "You've said yourself you don't know where it is, and neither do I. Then there's getting inside."

"There's a way of doing both: finding The Penitentiary, and getting ourselves in," Callum told him. "But I don't think you're going to like it much."

Michael waited for him to reveal his grand plan. When Callum spoke again, though, he said only this:

"You're going to have to die again. And this time, so am I."

CHAPTER THIRTY-FOUR

Ferne hung from the wall in chains manacled to her wrists, head lolling forward, feet barely touching the ground. Sweat dripped from her brow, matting her long, raven hair.

She couldn't describe what she'd been through in the last couple of hours, didn't think it was possible to feel such agony (the drugs, Pryce had explained, designed to weaken her whilst still allowing her to feel pain). Her torturer had started off small, taking her hand, her little finger, and inserting a needle-like dart under the nail. He'd smiled as he forced it upwards, causing her to draw in a quick breath.

"I know how much this hurts, so why don't you make it easy for both of us, eh?" But she sensed that Pryce was torn. On the one hand he wanted her to talk right now, because someone was leaning on him for answers. On the other he wanted to take his time with her. This wasn't his first experience of torture, not by any stretch of the imagination, but Ferne was special. Ferne was worth savouring.

He'd done the trick with the needles, a variation on bamboo he'd explained as he was shoving more of them in, before realising that wasn't going to loosen her tongue. They'd moved on from there, but he hadn't taken out the needles. They were still in there now, though the other pain she'd felt had taken her mind off them.

Next, unclamped from the chair, he'd manhandled her to one of the many contraptions she hadn't recognised: a half-moon "sculpture" made from bars, held up by what looked like two solid girders. She'd tried to resist now that she was free, but found she barely had any strength. Her limbs didn't appear to be working, yet she could still feel everything acutely, every pinch and shove as he wrestled her across to the thing, throwing her face-down over the curve and clamping her wrists and ankles to it. The bars dug into her front, but that was the least of her concerns. Pryce had ripped off the back of her blouse, then proceeded to thrash her with what seemed like every single whip he had in his collection. Each delivered a different sensation: the ordinary variety stung in just one place, while the multiple stranded whips targeted several spots at once for the utmost torment.

Ferne gritted her teeth as Pryce brought down the leather again and again, but didn't give him the satisfaction of a scream. At one point she even heard him moan softly to himself, perhaps in lieu of her, or more likely because he was enjoying himself a bit too much.

Stay strong. Just stay strong! She repeated it to herself, though she had no idea where the words had come from. Nor why she was determined not to believe a word Pryce had told her about Callum. *Come on, you can do this. Just Ahhhhhhh!*

When Pryce was fed up, or just plain exhausted, he'd released her from the frame. She was like a doll in his arms as he carried her over to a table and dumped her on it. Ferne's back was on fire, but it wasn't the only thing to feel the heat. Pryce strapped her arms and legs to the table, then held a lighter to her feet. She jolted and hissed each time he burnt her, but worse was to come as he heated up those irons in the recently-lit fire and touched one to her leg, her stomach, the tops of her arms, licking his lips as he did so.

Pryce pressed his face close to hers. "You can make this stop anytime you like, you know." She would have spat at him again, but all the saliva had dried up in her mouth. When the pain got too much, she blacked out, but Pryce would splash water in her face. "Wake up, witch. I'm not done with you yet."

On and on. So much pain crammed into such a short space of time. Finally Pryce used knife blades on her, struck her again with his gloved fists, then left her hanging on the wall to "think."

"When I return, we'll resume our little … conversation," he'd said to her.

So that's where she'd hung, half-dazed, seemingly every part of her hurting, covered in wounds and still not really believing that in this day and age such things went on. She'd known Pryce was ruthless, but the man simply had no conscience at all. No, more than that, he was loving every minute of putting her through this. Recording it with those hawk-like eyes of his, in place of the cameras that were not present in this part of the facility. Recording it so he could play it back later for his own pleasure. The thought made Ferne want to vomit. She felt violated, both physically and mentally.

Ferne attempted to pull against the chains, but her strength was still deserting her. And her powers would do her no good, even if she had the energy to use them. What could she do, make the chains and clasps new again so that they were even tougher to break?

Her head jerked up. No, she couldn't do that, but …

Ferne stood on her toes, balancing herself as best she could and pushing her body back. It was complete agony, and she couldn't maintain that position for long before she fell forwards and let the chains take her weight once more. She almost blacked out again.

Don't give in. Don't you dare!

Breathing quickly, Ferne pushed herself backwards again, angling her good hand—the one without the needles in it—so that she could reach the brace on the wall that held the chain, at least with her fingertips. She brushed one of the bolts before falling back into her collapsed position. A couple more times she tried this, failing miserably, but on the next attempt her fingertips caught hold of the ridge of the brace.

Now, come on. Concentrate, Ferne, summon up every last bit of healing power you have left.

Her fingertips started to glow, as did the metal surrounding the brace. The bolts keeping it in place on the wall squeaked loudly as the energy flowed through them and into the wall. Ferne mouthed the words, screwing up her face in concentration. She ignored the pain in her feet, the whip marks across her back.

Nearly there. You can do it!

One of the bolts gave way as the wall fully healed itself, returning to the state it was in before it had things driven into it. Rejecting the foreign object and letting the top half of the bracket spring free.

Yes, just one more. Just hold on in there, girl.

Ferne grimaced as she sent one last surge into the wall. The second bolt popped, the holes that they once fitted into sealed over now that the wall was "healed." The bolts and brace came away quickly, pitching her forwards so that her full weight was taken by her other arm still attached to the wall. She almost let out a howl at that point, but bit it back.

Don't cry. And don't you pass out on me now. You need to free your other hand.

Ferne swung herself around, grabbing the chain that held her weak hand. It was tempting to try and heal the damage done to her fingers, but she knew she had to work on the other bracket. Two more bolts and she was free. Where she would go, she hadn't figured out yet, but there were plenty of weapons she could use in this torture chamber, if she had the strength to wield one.

Don't think about that now. Get started on the other bracket. Hurry!

Ferne swung on the one arm now, holding herself up so that she could place her hand against the wall, heal that side as well. She stuck her tongue out of her mouth, willing the healing power to come.

No glow, no energy. There was nothing left.

She tried again, another three times—and it was on the last attempt that she thought she saw a spark of something at her fingertip.

It was then that she heard the door ahead of her open.

And it was then that she knew her dreams of getting out of here were well and truly dead.

CHAPTER THIRTY-FIVE

They were dead.

Gavin had felt the pulses himself, felt the men's wrists and their necks. There was nothing, not a single beat. He shook his head, ignoring the facts and remembering that they weren't really gone, that their spirits were somewhere else. The place they'd all been to briefly when Michael had rescued them from *The Valentine*, only deeper, further inside. And their link with the real world was growing weaker by the minute.

He remembered the discussion—or should that be argument?—which had followed after Callum had explained what they must do.

Michael held up his hands in protest. "I'm not doing it again. I can't. And I won't go back to The Penitentiary."

"Then Ferne will die. It's as simple as that."

"She chose *you*," Michael said coldly. "Perhaps that will be her punishment."

Callum had nearly gone for Michael again, but instead let his words do the fighting for him. "And you say you love her. From where I'm standing that love is pretty damned conditional. She saved your life."

"And I tried to save her ... from you. But she wouldn't listen."

"So that's it, just leave her to rot then because she fell in love with someone else?" Callum snorted. "Grow up! If you won't do it for Ferne, then what about your other friends? For the love of God! All right, your Goddess … You have family inside The Penitentiary, Michael."

"That you put there."

Callum nodded. "Granted. But I learn from my mistakes. How about you?"

Michael was quiet for a few moments. He looked at Gavin, who'd been shuffling the cards again, and the boy had nodded as if giving him permission to go ahead. "There's a chance they might recognise me."

"Maybe, but I doubt it. You were just another sparkie to them back then and I'm willing to bet you've changed. Did you have that beard first time around?"

Changing tactics, Michael said, "You know that if we do this, it's possible neither of us will make it back alive?"

"I'm willing to take that risk. For Ferne," said Callum firmly. "You?"

"I'm willing … for Arcana."

A smile broke across Callum's lips. "Right, so what are we waiting for? How do we go about becoming corpses?"

First of all, they had to get to their destination. This entailed Michael taking their arms again, walking them through the door of the lock-up and then all of them catching the nearest monorail … or at the very least, travelling along with it. Gavin took in the greyness of the scene around him: the teenagers kissing on the opposite seat; the man in the suit reading a newspaper with more headlines about Arcana; the woman with the dog that was yapping at something it couldn't quite see in front of it, but knew was there. Grey people, grey lives, even when they were in colour. He felt sorry for them. They'd never know what it was like to be able to see the future, to travel without anyone seeing them, or shoot pure Earth energy out of their fingers.

Why was Callum hanging on to this way of life so dearly, wondered Gavin, when he could embrace what he really was? When he could be greater than all of them put together? Still, it had to happen this way, the cards had told him so. And they'd never been wrong … had they? Not according to Master Unwin, anyway. But what if they really had driven him mad, like Michael said? Gavin looked down at the tarot pack he was clutching in his right hand. What if the power had driven his old mentor insane and now they were off on some suicide mission?

Where is your faith? Have faith, came a voice. It might have been his own, it might have been the cards, Gavin couldn't tell. It even sounded a little like Unwin's tones. Where exactly *was* his faith? Without that, he'd be no more than the blinkered people sitting around him on that monorail carriage. Before he had time to dwell on it anymore, they had arrived.

Callum led the way off the train, with Michael and Gavin tagging along behind. He was still walking down stairs, reaching for door handles—only passing through the doors when he remembered he couldn't grip them properly in this form. In short, he was still thinking like the greys. How could this possibly be the Magician? The one who would liberate them all? He wouldn't even admit that he had a direct line to the Goddess.

They walked along streets unfamiliar to Gavin, yet somehow he knew them all intimately. Even if Callum hadn't been there, he could have guided them; *the cards*—that he was still getting used to, still unsure of—could have guided them if he'd asked. Left, right, continue straight on. And there it was, just opposite the alleyway where they were standing.

"Are you sure you want to do this?" asked Michael again, checking that there were no people around.

"Ask me again when we wake up," came the reply Gavin knew Callum would give.

"All right then." Michael let go of Gavin, and he was jolted back into the real world. He waited a few seconds, then Callum appeared beside him. His eyes were glassy, his body stiff. The man toppled forwards and Gavin slowed his descent to the ground, though he wasn't strong enough to hold him. Seconds later, Michael blinked into existence at the other side … or rather Michael's *body* did. That too was awkward and rigid, and would have tumbled to the ground face-first if Gavin hadn't been there.

This was when he checked their vital signs. They were definitely dead, or dead enough to fool the people they needed to.

Gavin took a gulp of air, then looked across at the building he would soon be walking towards. If he had any doubts now, it was far too late.

Have faith.

Gavin shuffled his cards once more for good luck, then was breaking cover, out of the alleyway and heading to the kerb, placing the cards in his pocket. Two of them were emerging from the front entrance, about to head to their car outside, and Gavin waved his hands in the air.

"Oh Goddess, what am I doing?" he muttered under his breath.

They appeared to wonder that themselves, because they gave him odd looks as they strode over, watching for any traffic on the road.

"Hey there, hello!" Gavin called out when they were in hearing distance. "I wonder if you could help me with something?"

The pair were well built in comparison to Gavin's slight frame, and towered above him when they came across. "What seems to be the problem?" said the first, whose eyebrows met in the middle.

"I think you're going to want to see this." Gavin beckoned them into the alleyway and pointed at the two bodies lying there.

"Oh my God," said the second man. "Look at that one."

"What?" asked the first.

"Don't you recognise him? It's … bloody hell, that's Callum McGuire."

The first Enforcement Officer crouched. "Is he—"

"Don't touch him! It could be a trap," warned the second, turning to grab Gavin by the arm. "What's going on here? Who are you?"

"My name's Gavin." He smiled. "And it's quite safe. They're both stone, cold dead, I can assure you of that."

"How did they … I mean …" The M-forcer turned Gavin round, cuffing him. "Wait a minute, you don't fool me. You're one of them too, aren't you? A sparkie."

"You saw right through me," said Gavin, not resisting at all. *Or you would have done a few moments ago.* "I understand this was Callum McGuire's station house, officer."

"Yeah," said the cop who'd cuffed him. "It *was*."

"Then I wonder if you'd be kind enough to take me to see a … Superintendent Wallis?"

The crouching officer looked back over at his partner. "I think they really are dead. They're not breathing or anything. This is seriously fucked up, Les."

"Tell me about it." He clicked on the radio that was resting on his shoulder. "HQ, come in. This is Officer Les Jenson requesting assistance. We have an … er … emergency situation here. Over."

There was a crackle of static, then: "HQ responding. You've only just left for patrol, how can there be an emergency situation?"

"Just get some men out the front of the station house, will you!" snapped Jenson. "Oh, and tell the Super I have someone who wants to talk to him. Yes, it's important!" He looked at Gavin, who grinned again. "Right, well I hope you have a good explanation for all this, sparkie. 'Cos I wouldn't like to be in your shoes if you don't."

Gavin continued to smile, knowing that this part of the plan was over. It was just a matter of time now.

And whether Michael and Callum would be able to survive what came next.

CHAPTER THIRTY-SIX

The door opened and Pryce was standing there.

He looked over, saw Ferne hanging from the wall by one arm, and tutted. "You've been a naughty girl, haven't you?" Leaving the door open, Pryce walked across. She tried to lash out with her good arm, but could hardly lift it anymore. Pryce easily sidestepped the feeble blow and grabbed her wrist. "You want me to let you go, is that it?" Ferne gave a pitiful nod of the head. To her surprise, he let go of her wrist and undid the other manacle fixing her to the wall. She fell forwards onto her hands, but they couldn't hold her weight and she collapsed, spread out across the cold stone floor. "You'd better get up if you want to leave," Pryce coaxed, but there was something else in his voice. "Come on. I tell you what, if you can make it to the door, I won't stand in your way. You'll be free to go."

Ferne lifted her head and gave him a vicious stare. What was he up to? Surely he couldn't be granting her freedom now, not after all he'd done, not when she still hadn't told him what he wanted—though how on Earth she was supposed to do that was anyone's guess.

"I mean it," said Pryce, knowing she had no reason to trust him. "You make it to the open door there and you can go. Well, what are you waiting for? That's what you want, isn't it? I won't make the offer again."

Regardless of whether he was telling the truth or not, Ferne could see the exit and decided to head for it. There was no way she could walk, the burns on the soles of her feet made sure of that. So she grunted, getting an elbow beneath her and pushing herself upwards. Trying to crawl on her hands and knees was a complete failure, because her damaged hand—the one with the needles still under the nails—continued to let her down. After a couple of attempts, she resorted to using her good hand to claw herself along, using her other elbow as a kind of anchor. It looked like a demented swimming stroke, but got her a few yards closer to her goal before she had to stop and rest.

"Come on, you can do it!" To begin with she thought that might be her inner voice trying to urge her on, but bizarrely it was Pryce again. He bent close to her ear. "Freedom is on the other side of that door, Ferne. Just think, you could feel the sun on your face again, walk the streets. Don't give up, fight for it. That's what Arcana do, isn't it? Fight for what they believe in?"

In a strange sort of way, it did spur her on. Ferne got back up on her elbow and started the "swim" again. The door was growing nearer with each haul of her body, even an inch brought her that much closer to freedom. Little by little, bit by bit, she was going to make it. Ferne reached out an arm, a hand towards the doorway. It had taken her a good ten minutes—which seemed like hours to Ferne—but she was almost at her destination. Just a couple more strokes, a couple more.

Then suddenly, amazingly, she was there. A smile broke across her face, even though it hurt her split lip. *Yes,* she thought, *yes, I've done it. I've shown you, Pryce! If nothing else, I've shown you what I'm made of!*

A pair of legs filled the space of the open doorway—she couldn't see any further up until she tilted her head. A guard, it had to be. She just knew that Pryce wouldn't play fair. It was another one of his games, another torture.

But as she looked upwards, she realised her mistake. The man didn't have the posture of a guard. His body was thin and frail, and he was barely able to hold himself upright. When she got to the face she hardly recognised it, he looked so different. A million miles away from the man who'd practically brought her up, who'd given her the name she used now. His beard was patchy, as if someone had torn clumps out of it, and nowhere near as thick as it had once been. There were bags under his eyes, hanging over protruding cheekbones. His eyes had a faraway look to them, and his silvery hair was thin to the point of falling out.

Ferne could hear Pryce laughing: loud belly laughs, as if he'd just heard the funniest joke in the world. "I told you *I* wouldn't stand in your way. Victor," he managed amidst the guffawing, "why don't you come in and join us?"

The man who'd once been their High Priest, who'd been a surrogate father to Ferne, shuffled into the room, scarcely even noticing her struggling on the floor. Whatever she'd imagined after Callum told her he'd seen Victor, this was so much worse. He probably still had no idea it was information gleaned from him that had caused his own daughter's death.

"Come here," Pryce ordered, wiping away the tears from his eyes with a handkerchief. "Oh come along, don't be shy. We're old friends after all."

Ferne twisted herself round so she could follow Victor's progress across the room. He shambled like a zombie, not really here at all. What had that bastard done to him?

"Vic … Victor," she croaked, but he didn't even glance in her direction. "Oh my Goddess." A tear rolled down Ferne's cheek; it didn't have far to drop to the dirty stone floor beneath her.

"I'm afraid he won't recognise you at present," Pryce explained. "He doesn't really know who *he* is, let alone anyone else." The Commander patted Victor's shoulder. "He's in better shape than his other half, though, aren't you? She couldn't take the treatments, unfortunately. In the end it was kinder to just ash her. So, congratulations, you truly *are* the High Priestess now."

"Helen," uttered Ferne.

"Victor more than made up for it, thankfully. He's been very useful, haven't you? If it hadn't been for him we wouldn't have found

Widow's Way, if it hadn't been for the children … Well, you get the picture."

"Victor," repeated Ferne, more loudly. There was the faintest of twitches in the corner of his left eye. "Victor, you know me."

"But now, ah it's so sad … now that Victor has served his purpose, he's no longer of use to us." Pryce reached into his jacket pocket and brought out an automatic pistol. "To be quite honest with you, he'd be better off this way than just simply existing." Pryce jammed the pistol underneath Victor's chin.

"No," pleaded Ferne, the tears coming more freely now. "Please don't."

Pryce frowned. "But what do you care? You have your freedom now. You made it to the door, witch. All you have to do is crawl through it." He pushed Victor's chin up a little more. "Or have you had second thoughts?"

"Victor! Victor, it's me. It's little Ferne!"

"Tell me what I want to know about Callum McGuire and the Book. Tell me where they both are, and I'll let you and the retard here go. You can heal him, Ferne. Once you've recovered yourself, of course."

"Victor?"

"Tell me what I want to know!" screamed Pryce, his body jerking with each yell, the gun jabbing even further into the crevice under Victor's chin. Victor himself was now looking down, towards Ferne.

"I don't *know* where they are," said Ferne truthfully.

"That's a pity." Pryce cocked the gun and readied to squeeze the trigger.

Ferne reached out towards Pryce this time. "Wait! No, please wait!"

"You have two seconds."

"They're … Callum and the Book, I—"

"You're stalling for time." Pryce's finger was tensing. "Tell me now, or it's going to get awfully messy in here."

"They're …" Ferne caught Victor's eye and was startled to see it wink. "They're in—"

"Too late," growled Pryce. But just as he did so, Victor moved his head back sharply. He bent back further than it seemed humanly possible to do, even for a contortionist. Pryce's gun went off, but the bullet hit nothing apart from the ceiling. Then Victor was snapping back again, grabbing Pryce's arm and pushing it. The pistol flew from his grasp, clanking across the floor out of reach. Pryce attempted a headbutt, but Victor was twisting again, mouthing incantations, his torso turning completely around so that his legs now faced the other way. When he pulled the rest of himself back, he took Pryce with him, dropping him on the floor. Victor's fingers began to crackle with energy, a ball of it gathering in his palm. He threw it in Pryce's direction, but the man dived out of its way.

"Go, Ferne," shouted Victor, twisting in her direction. "Get out of here!"

Ferne stayed. She couldn't leave him, not now.

"Go!" Victor yelled again, and it was only now that she obeyed—beginning her crawl again through the open doorway. Perhaps she could fetch help, free some of the other prisoners? There was a gunshot and Ferne looked back to see Victor dropping to his knees, a patch of red staining the material at his shoulder. He held up his hand, but the energy there was petering out. Pryce, holding the gun he'd retrieved, its barrel smoking, was rising steadily.

"Not nearly as slippery as you once were, Victor. Back then it took a whole division to apprehend you. But I did underestimate your willpower. That won't happen again." Pryce pressed the gun to the back of Victor's head. Victor and Ferne exchanged one last glance before the pistol went off. Ferne shut her eyes tight, forcing more tears out, and heard the thump as Victor's body hit the ground. "Stubborn to the end," said Pryce.

Ferne heard footsteps as Pryce walked over to her. When she opened her eyes again, she was expecting to be greeted with the sight of a gun in her face. But Pryce had put the weapon away. It had served its purpose.

"So, now you know I mean business. And just in case you were still thinking of leaving us," Pryce nodded at the door, "remember, I have Victor's grandchildren as well."

Ferne had a sudden flash of Jonathan and Maria with guns to

their heads. That would be the next step for Pryce, and even sooner if she left the confines of this room.

"So, the question I have for you is: do you still want out?"

She looked at him, then shook her head.

"Good, I'm glad you feel that way. After all, we're just starting to get to know each other. But just to be on the safe side, I think we'll have you back in the chair again for the time being."

Pryce picked up her arm and dragged her across the room. Ferne caught a glimpse of Victor's body as she was yanked along, blood pouring from a gaping wound in his skull. Once more she fought back the need to vomit. Pryce hefted her into the chair and manacled her wrists, though thankfully left the neck brace alone this time. He leaned on the arms of the chair and brought his face close to hers, his predatory features softening a little. He raised a gloved hand and wiped the tears from her cheeks. "Don't spread this around, but I'm not a bad man. Not really. I just have a job to do, you understand?"

Ferne gaped at him, unblinking.

He moved back, face hardening again. "I'm not that patient, however. So when I come back again, I'll expect a few answers." Pryce pulled the chair around so that it was facing Victor on the floor. Ferne turned away, her eyes trailing Pryce as he ambled towards the door. He allowed himself one last, lingering look at her and the dead man, then he was gone, leaving the door of the torture room open.

Ferne fought it, but couldn't help herself. Victor's body was almost crying out for her to look at it. Finally, she gave in and did just that. It was still, not that she'd been expecting otherwise; limbs out at odd angles, even stranger than they had been when he'd used his magick. He would have been the first one to tell her that it was just a vessel, that his consciousness was with the Goddess now. That *She* was looking after him. It was a comforting thought as Ferne sat there, waiting for more tears to come.

But they never did.

And not for the first time she wondered what it must be like to be dead.

CHAPTER THIRTY-SEVEN

Was this what it felt like to be dead?

It was bright, and almost certainly cold. If Callum still possessed a body he would probably be shivering about now, but there was very little else by way of sensation. He felt numb, like the gum around a tooth that's about to be extracted.

After Michael had detached them from their physical selves, he'd felt himself being pulled backwards. The nearest he could come to describing it was like being in a gigantic wind tunnel. He'd had no control over where he was going or where he might end up. Callum had clung on to Michael, though, in the hopes he might be able to navigate this slipstream a bit better. Out of the two of them, he was the one who'd done it before.

But, if anything, Michael seemed even more disoriented than Callum. In fact, the usually confident and belligerent man had been replaced by someone whose expression was frozen in a rictus of pure terror. Callum had tried to say something to him, but found that he couldn't get his words out. So, instead, he'd shaken Michael's arm in an attempt to rouse him. That didn't work either.

It was only when they had been pulled so far back into the tunnel it seemed to Callum that finding a way back would be an impossible task, that he discovered why Michael had been so terrified. The light that had accompanied them to begin with was fading. Like an ink blot soaking into paper, darkness was impinging on the brightness all around. Inch by inch, it was being eaten up by the black. Callum began to experience that familiar feeling of being hemmed in, of walls closing on either side. This time they were metaphysical, rather than solid bricks and mortar, but that didn't comfort him at all. Somehow, in fact, it made things a million times worse. There was at least the hope of escape in the real world: finding a door, someone knocking down the walls. But how do you escape from a darkness that's encircling you, that's eager to devour you along with the light?

And that was before Callum saw the shapes. Just glimpses to begin with, peripheral visions, but he was convinced there was something, or several dozen somethings, alive in that obsidian space. No, more. The closer he looked, fooling his vision by turning first one way, then another, the more of them he could see: there had to be hundreds of the creatures, never standing still long enough for him to get a proper sense of what they looked like, even if they hadn't been the same colour as their background. For all Callum knew, they *were* the background. Maybe there were so many of them that they made up the darkness on their own. Here or there, however, he was granted a flash of teeth, a contrasting yellow-white against the shadows.

This must have been what Michael saw the last time he was in limbo, why he didn't want to go back. He must have blocked out much of it, or why else would he have let them talk him into coming back? "Standing" here, waiting for those things to reach them, Callum wasn't sure anything was worth coming back to this place for.

Not even Ferne? he asked himself. Suddenly he could see her beautiful face, her raven hair, those lips he'd kissed—at first tenderly, then harder as they'd made love. He remembered he was doing it for her, because he loved her. If Michael had returned to this Hell—for that's surely what it must be—then it was only because he had those same feelings, no matter how unrequited.

It wouldn't make any difference soon, because the "eaters" would reach them and all would be lost. Not even the blessed Goddess would be able to save them.

Callum tried shaking Michael one final time, but he was virtually catatonic. So he awaited his fate, a strange calmness passing over him as he resigned himself to it.

And though he had no voice on that plane, his words echoed inside his own head, directed towards the things out there.

What he said was: "Come on then, you bastards. I'm ready for you!"

CHAPTER THIRTY-EIGHT

It had gone pretty much how Gavin had expected it to. But then again, nowadays, what didn't?

He reflected on events as he was sitting in the back of the truck with three armed guards covering him. How he'd been taken to see Superintendent Wallis and allowed to see him alone, as long as two officers remained outside the glass-fronted office. There, Gavin had played his part to perfection so as not to around suspicion. It wasn't hard. Even if he hadn't been told what to do, he knew the script already because of the cards. They were showing him glimpses of the future as he went along, but not the whole picture; not yet. He wasn't ready for that.

"So, you're trying to tell me that you killed them both and handed yourself in?" the overweight, balding man said, virtually closing one eye. The bodies had been taken into storage until it could be decided what to do with them … and with Gavin.

"In the hopes I would be granted leniency," Gavin recited. "But *I* didn't kill them as such."

"Oh?"

"They attempted to escape from *The Valentine* by using magick, by shifting to another plane and walking out. But something went wrong," Gavin told him, as if he was reading a story to a youngster at bedtime. "This was how I found them at the rendezvous point. With no one left, I decided to come here. Callum McGuire spoke about you, has said before that you might give me a fair hearing. Said you were all right … for an M-forcer."

Gavin detected a swelling of the man's chest at that remark, but it soon went down again. "You'd sell out your own grandmother you lot, wouldn't you? As for McGuire, he hasn't been here long enough to know what kind of man I am. Do you know what he did back there? What he did to his former partner, a fine, upstanding officer called Tully Gibson? A man I counted as my friend?"

Gavin shook his head, although he knew full well about the incident above the stage.

"Murdered him in cold blood, that's what," said Wallis, sitting up and slamming his fist on his desk. "And I never saw it coming. I actually paired them up—Tully was supposed to be his mentor. That boy had so much potential." Wallis narrowed his other eye now so that they were both practically slits. "Until you people got hold of him and twisted his mind."

"We did nothing to Callum … to McGuire's mind. The choices he made were his own," Gavin said honestly. "People cannot be forced to do things they don't want to, as you'll show shortly." It still amazed him, how this time yesterday he was barely able raise his voice, let alone answer anyone back. Now, just twenty-four hours later, he was a different person altogether.

"You expect me to believe that load of crap?" Wallis poked a finger into his own chest. "I've got experience of sparkies myself, I know what you are."

"Ah yes, the 'ambush' where you fought three of us at once. And that limp you got in the process."

Wallis's eyes opened a crack, probably because this kid had never even seen him walk. "What of it?"

Gavin eased himself back in the chair on the other side of Wallis's desk. "I think we both know what *really* happened back then, don't we?"

"I have no idea what you're talking about," said Wallis, his eyes now flitting left and right.

Gavin half-closed his own eye. "Oh, come now. What was he, a little younger than I am? He was surrendering, wasn't he, even though you had no evidence that he was a magick user? Waiting in the alley to give himself up. You had your gun on him, were searching him—taking your time, distracted—when you slipped on the wet concrete from the rain earlier on."

Wallis's eyes were fully open now, as was his mouth. "How could you—"

"But you know the worse thing about that day wasn't so much *how* you broke your leg, causing the bone to jut out at the knee. It wasn't so much what you told the officers who answered the radio call which earned you that commendation." Gavin steepled his fingers. "It was the fact your gun went off and caught him in the side as he was running away. It took him almost two hours to die, did you know that? Two hours, Superintendent Wallis."

Wallis swallowed hard, as though he couldn't quite force his Adam's apple to go down.

"And things have a way of coming full circle, don't they?"

"Shut up."

"Perhaps McGuire was wrong about you, after all."

Wallis banged his fist on the table again. "God damn you, I said shut it!" The office was quiet for some time, then Wallis produced Gavin's cards from inside his drawer and placed them on the desk. "What are these? My men found them on your person."

Without missing a beat, Gavin said, "They're what I use to see the past, present and future."

"Oh really?"

"Yes. Care to pick one?"

Wallis glared at Gavin. "I don't need any fortune teller to show me *my* future."

"Then allow me pick one for you." Before Wallis could stop him, Gavin had reached out with his cuffed hands and slipped a card from the deck. He spun it around to show the man, as he didn't need to see it himself. "The Five of Pentacles."

"What the hell's that supposed to mean?"

"See the downtrodden figures in ragged clothes, the leper and the cripple, passing by outside the lighted window, gazing up tantalisingly? One day, you're going to be like them, Superintendent. You're going to be left outside in the cold when your little secret is exposed."

Wallis laughed. "Who's going to tell people, you? You're just another fucking sparkie."

Gavin grinned. "But I'm not the only one who knows, am I? How is Mrs Wallis, these days?"

The Super's face fell. "You leave Evelyn out of this."

"She's beginning to suspect, you know. You can't hide your … tastes from her forever."

Wallis jabbed a finger in Gavin's direction. "You shut your filthy mouth, right now."

"And when she does realise what's been going on," continued Gavin, "she just might want a little revenge of her own. All those years she wasted married to you. Have you never heard the phrase about a woman scorned?"

Wallis snatched back the card, then ripped it in two. Gavin let out a yelp as if he was in pain. "Didn't like that much, did you? How about this?" The policeman ripped up another card, then another. Gavin gritted his teeth, breathing hard. "And this, and this!" Wallis tore up card after card, some into four or five pieces, while Gavin looked on in torment. Finally, there were no more left. Wallis had destroyed the lot.

Gavin looked up at his sweaty features, and whispered, "You'll see his face again, Superintendent Wallis. Just before you take your own life, when you're at your lowest ebb, you'll see the beautiful face of the boy who you followed into that alley. Who you killed. It will take you a good long while to die—longer than him. And then you'll know. You'll see the face of your true creator."

"Men!" roared Wallis, reaching for the painkillers in his pocket. "Get in here right this minute!" The officers on guard rushed in at that point. "Put this scum-sucking sparkie in a cell. I'm going to arrange a transfer for him, along with his two friends."

They grabbed Gavin by the arms and hauled him out. He said nothing more, just stared down sadly at the cards littering the floor. He'd heard the screams as each one had been hurt, felt their individual suffering at Wallis's hands. The fat man deserved his fate when it came.

Gavin had been tossed in a cell for a while, where he waited for the men to come back. Even without his cards, he knew they would. He'd seen it happen. Though after that, things got a little fuzzy. It wasn't long before he was being bundled into the back of a truck, at gunpoint. The arrangements had been made for him to be shipped off to The Penitentiary. The bodies would be travelling separately, but they would still be coming with him. That was the important thing.

The three of them—Gavin, Michael and Callum—were heading into the demon's lair.

Now all Gavin could do was pray their plan would succeed.

CHAPTER THIRTY-NINE

The time Ferne was left alone with Victor's body was more of a torture than anything Pryce had put her through before. It wasn't just his corpse lying there, it was also the thought of what else Pryce might do to those poor children when he came back. But how could she tell him things that she didn't know? She had no idea where the Book was, nor Callum and Michael. That lack of knowledge had cost her adoptive father his life. She just hoped it wouldn't cost the children theirs. Ferne would rather offer herself up to him than witness that.

Just when she thought Pryce might never come back, she heard footsteps again. Definitely that sick bastard's, she could identify them by now. *Click-clack, click-clack* went his boots.

Then he was in the room, standing in front of her. "I have some good news and some bad news," he told her. If he was waiting for Ferne to reply, he was wasting his time. "The good news is you can relax. I no longer need to know the whereabouts of Callum McGuire or your acting High Priest, Michael Sanderson. We have them both in custody. In fact they should be arriving anytime, so you can forget about them charging in here on their white horses and saving you."

Ferne's brow furrowed.

"There's more. The bad news, remember? How to break this to

you … Oh, what the heck, I'm just going to come right out with it: I'm afraid they're both dead."

Now Ferne did speak. "No," she gasped. "They can't be."

"Afraid so." Pryce gave a small nod. "But if it's any consolation, this is not good news for me either. The person I answer to will not be happy."

Ferne gave him a look that said she couldn't give a shit what his superior thought. She'd lost people she cared deeply about.

"They were handed in by a teenage boy carrying a pack of tarot cards," said Pryce, tapping his lip with one finger again.

"Gavin," Ferne whispered.

"Yes, that's right. I forgot you know everyone. He might be worth pumping for information about the Book, but I really doubt we'll get anywhere with him." Pryce folded his arms. "Which again leaves you, my dear. If we can offer my boss the item he's been searching for, it might well save both our necks."

"I've told you, I don't know where it is." She sat there, a broken woman. All hope of escape or being rescued was finally gone.

Pryce bent, arms still folded. "Then I suggest you think hard about where it might possibly be. For both our sakes." He began walking towards the door. "Now, I have to attend to the arrival of the bodies … but I'll be back," he promised.

Ferne let her head drop, chin touching her chest. "Callum," she said in hushed tones that still echoed around the room. "Oh Callum, I'm so sorry I got you into this. Sorry for what I believed. But I did love you. I always will." And she realised there were more tears left in her, because Ferne began to cry again, huge sobs wracking her body.

The prophecy had been false, just a fairy tale after all.

Now there was nothing left but what ifs.

CHAPTER FORTY

The van carrying Michael Sanderson and Callum McGuire's mortal remains entered the compound first. It was directed to a side entrance, where men in uniform and caps disembarked and helped to put them on stretchers. It had been confirmed by the medical staff back at the Station House that these two individuals were indeed deceased, but a more thorough examination would be needed to ascertain whether this was actually the case. When dealing with magick users it was best not to leave anything to chance.

Sherman Pryce had ordered that the cameras be turned off in this section, blaming the temporary loss on routine maintenance being carried out on the system. He had no wish to inform Nero Stark that McGuire was dead until he could verify this for himself. Thank heavens the call had come in directly to him so he could order that no reports be filed just yet. By the time the trolleys had been wheeled into The Penitentiary, each one hand-scanned for magickal residue—with only the slightest traces registering—Pryce was there to oversee the operation.

He looked at the clipboards the officers in charge handed to him. No movement: nothing on the way here at all, not even so much as a twitch. Pryce personally unzipped each bag and felt for the men's pulses. Nothing at the wrist or the neck, and the skin was so cold. He looked down into McGuire's eyes, propping them open with thumb and forefinger. They were glassy and lifeless. There was no magick on Earth that could fake this. He needed no autopsy to tell him that these two were well and truly fucked.

Which meant he was, too.

But he ordered the procedure anyway, trailing the trolleys and talking with the men in white coats who would be performing it. When they asked if he wanted to sit in, he shook his head. His speciality was torture of the living, not the dead. There was nothing exciting about cutting into clammy, putrid flesh. Give him a nice warm victim any day of the week. There was one he would shortly be returning to, in fact, once he'd had a chance to speak to their other new guest; the boy Gavin.

"Just let me know the results, okay. But *only* me. Do you understand?"

The men in white coats, one tall, one short, nodded vigorously, then watched as Pryce removed himself from the scene.

The trolleys began to move, but then one half of the pair—the smallest—halted them a second time. He looked more closely at Michael. "You know, Phelps, there's something very familiar about this one," he told his colleague. "And just look at those scars."

"Probably happened in a fight," the other man in white said, looking down at him. "Come on, let's get this over and done with. Then we can watch some of the executions."

Shrugging, he let go of the trolley and they both followed the clanking gurneys into the autopsy room. This was where they would perform their own particular brand of magick.

The second man in white—Dr Phelps—ordered the naked bodies to be placed on two of the four autopsy tables. While they prepared their instruments, the heavily armed guards who'd come all this way with the cadavers took their positions at either end of the room.

The first doctor, Lane, held up a scalpel which wouldn't have looked out of place in Pryce's collection below ground. Then he moved towards the nearest dead body, a fair-haired ex-M-forcer who'd suddenly, without rhyme or reason, sided with the enemy and paid the ultimate price for it.

⊛

At that same point in time Superintendent Leo Wallis was arriving home. The morning's events had taken their toll on him and he'd decided to quit early. He got out of his car, holding onto the top for support, and limped up the driveway—his immaculately pressed trousers swishing as he did so. He was getting to the age when he'd need to start using a stick for that limp. Couldn't put it off much longer, not with the arthritis beginning to creep into the bones. He took his pill box out of his trouser pocket, slipping a couple of the painkillers into his mouth.

As he walked up the drive to his large house, Wallis's mind flashed back to the young man he'd been questioning earlier. How could he have known the things he did? The simple explanation was that he was Arcana, but he was more than just a magick user. In his time, Wallis had seen them perform tricks that would make your jaw drop in wonder. No, not wonder: in disgust at its wrongness. But never anything like that, never being able to see into the past. Into the future.

Wallis shook the thoughts from his head. The boy was no longer any concern of his. He'd sent him off to Sherman Pryce, so he could pick the bones out of the bugger. Literally, if the rumours about what went on at The Penitentiary were true.

Still, Wallis had taken no great delight in ripping up the kid's precious cards. But he'd pushed him just that little bit too far, was getting uncomfortably close to the truth.

"What was he, a little younger than I am? He was surrendering, wasn't he, even though you had no evidence that he was a magick user? Waiting in the alley to give himself up. You had your gun on him, were searching him—taking your time, distracted."

Wallis had certainly been distracted, a stupid rookie mistake to make.

"It took him almost two hours to die, did you know that? Two hours, Superintendent Wallis."

He rubbed his head, hard, as if that might force the voices out, erase the picture he had in there of the boy bleeding to death slowly from the gunshot wound he'd inflicted. The young fortune-teller had been right, there'd been no evidence to suggest the kid was a magick user. Wallis had just trailed him from the club before running him to ground in that alley.

"There were three of them; fucking sparkies. I think I might have winged one."

"You just take it easy Sergeant, you've been badly injured. Now let's load you up into the ambulance. You know, there'll probably be a commendation in this for you."

Evelyn had visited him in hospital every single day until he got out. She brought fruit, chocolates, magazines. She was so attentive, so loving. A love that he'd never been able to return, not even when they first got married all those years ago. It made him feel so guilty, he hadn't had the heart to tell her the truth. At least, not right away.

When he couldn't stand the fussing anymore, being told how brave he'd been, how he was Evelyn's hero, he'd blurted it out. Not all of it, naturally, but enough to ease the guilt slightly.

"For God's sake, Eve, there weren't three, just one of them. And I didn't break my leg tackling them, I slipped while I was frisking him."

She'd looked at him as if he was mad. "I don't understand."

"I made it up. I made it all up."

He thought she was going to start crying. But she didn't. He was getting a commendation and was on a fast track to running his own station house, now that he could no longer be placed on active duty. Even considering that, her reply surprised him:

"You don't tell anyone else about this, Leo, do you hear me? You're a good man and it'll ruin your career."

Then she'd straightened his collar and given him a kiss on the cheek. That night they'd made love, but it had been forced. He'd insisted on the lights being out, and pictured someone else lying there instead of her. But it hadn't worked and he'd got it over with as soon as he could, feeling sick to his stomach. He'd felt that way every time she'd touched him from that moment on. They hadn't been intimate for so long, if indeed they ever had at all, really.

Evelyn knew that part of the secret, but she had no idea about the rest of it.

Wallis reached the steps to the door and had to use the rail to get him to the top. He put his key in and turned it. He called out Evelyn's name, but there was no reply. Perhaps she was still round at one of her friends' houses, gossiping the early evening away? Putting the world to rights?

Wallis went into the living room and opened up his drinks cabinet. He poured himself a generous helping of malt whiskey and took a gulp of it straight away. It was as he was turning back to face the room, that he saw an envelope on the mantelpiece. He limped over to it, recognising Evelyn's handwriting.

Still holding the glass in one hand, he ripped open the back of the envelope and pulled out the letter.

Dear Leo,

I've been trying to kid myself for so long that things will change between us, but I know now that they never will. I know now what you've been hiding from me all these years. You see, I was doing some tidying in the basement today and I found them. All the photographs you thought you'd hidden away so expertly behind those loose bricks you were always promising to fix. I found more on your computer as well. Oh, I've known your password for some time, Leo—I'm your wife, after all—I've just never dared to use it. Until now.

Wallis's eyes scanned the rest of the lines, Evelyn's vitriol poured out onto the paper, how their marriage and their life together had been a sham, how it was never about the money or the power of his position. She loved him, she genuinely adored him, in case he hadn't noticed. It had made her wonder about that night back in the alley, just what he'd been doing. It made her wonder if she shouldn't tell someone about it.

Wallis dropped his whiskey glass and it shattered on the hearth. What in Christ's name had she been doing down in the basement? She never went down there! And on his computer, after the amount of times he'd told her that there were top secret police files stored on it. But for some reason she had, and now the cat was well and truly out of the bag.

He read the final few lines, telling him that she'd gone away for a while so she could figure things out. But he would be hearing from her very soon. The threat there was unmistakable.

"You're going to be left out in the cold when your little secret is exposed. Have you never heard the phrase about a woman scorned, Superintendent Wallis?"

Wallis collapsed into his leather armchair, clutching the letter. This was the end for him, he knew that now. How could he have been so stupid?

He stared across the room for a while, wondering just how he could get himself out of this mess. Nothing occurred to him. Even if he denied what Evelyn said about that night, she still had more than enough to bury him.

Though not if he buried himself first.

Wallis reached into his pocket again, taking out the painkillers. He'd just swallowed two outside the house, and there were plenty more left. They'd last him a good few days if he kept to the correct dosage, but instead Wallis began to put them in his mouth and crunch them like a child eating sweets.

As he munched away, he mused at how accurate the Arcana boy's prediction had been … *I wonder where he is right now, what he's going through?* Or perhaps it had been a curse in disguise? When he tore up the cards, maybe that had set these events in motion? In the end it didn't matter either way. The fortune-teller had been right, it would take him a long time to die.

As he placed pill after pill into his mouth, Superintendent Leo Wallis could see only one thing: the face of the boy he'd murdered all those years ago.

The young man Wallis had met earlier that day was in fact in one of the official interrogation rooms of The Penitentiary. They'd walked him in like any other prisoner, which shouldn't have aroused suspicion, but made sure there were no cameras working in this particular suite.

Gavin was still under heavy guard, the weapons a hair's breadth away from being raised and fired if necessary. It wouldn't be. The standard cuffs he'd been wearing had been substituted for more heavy-duty iron ones, pre-coated with amber and saltwater. When he heard the door behind him open, Gavin looked around. The guards raised their automatic rifles and trained them at his head, so he slowly faced front again.

Even without his cards, Gavin knew this would be Pryce. He'd want to ask him questions, about Arcana, about the bodies, probably about the Book as well. He'd been feeling less confident, less sure of himself since Wallis ripped the deck to pieces, but some of their power was still within him. He was no longer a boy, that was for sure. Now, he was a man.

"Hello, Gavin." That voice cut through the air like a machete. "Welcome to my humble little abode. What do you think of it?" Pryce strode round and sat opposite him across a table.

Gavin felt a shiver, but tried hard not to let Pryce see it.

"Now, you and I are going to talk sensibly, like adults. I feel as if I ought to treat you like an adult, Gavin, even though you hardly look out of short trousers." Pryce chuckled. "So, you're going to tell me the truth about what happened to Sanderson and McGuire, about why you turned them and yourself in." When Gavin didn't reply, Pryce continued: "Do you have any idea how many of your kind I've had in here, sitting where you are right now? How many I've made sing like canaries before I've finished with them?"

Not long ago, Gavin might have known. But not now. He shook his head.

"I stopped counting after the first couple of hundred," Pryce informed him. "And those that proved more stubborn, well, I have a special place I take them. A friend of yours is in there right now, your current High Priestess."

"Ferne?"

"Oh, so you have got a tongue in your head. That's good," said Pryce. "You might want to consider using it a bit more or I'll start thinking that you no longer have any use for it, and just cut it out." He mimed a scissoring action with his fingers. "I've done it before."

“I thought I might be offered leniency,” Gavin blurted out, a little too quickly.

“Naw,” returned Pryce. “Don’t buy it. You knew you were going to be banged up as soon as you set foot through the door of a station house. You’re a sparkie, son, and Arcana at that. There’s no such thing as leniency where you’re concerned.” Pryce let the words settle, then added: “Here, let me show you what I mean.”

Pryce directed his attention to the corner of the room, where a TV was positioned on an armature. He gave a nod and the set came to life, throwing back a picture of some kind of silver torpedo-shaped structure fixed to the ground. Gavin couldn’t make out what it was at first, then the scene cut to another angle a bit closer and he watched as a group of Penitentiary guards jostled a gagged and manacled male prisoner—Gavin recognised his face, but didn’t know his name—towards the torpedo. A woman in a white coat opened the door by pressing a code into a pad on its side. The gag was taken off, manacles removed, and the prisoner was shoved in. Though there was no audio, Gavin could see that the man was screaming. When the door closed behind him, he began banging on the glass front of the torpedo.

Another camera angle now, closer still, and Gavin watched as a red glowing light came on inside the machine. The prisoner looked around him, trying to figure out what was happening. Then, when the realisation dawned on him, he began thumping on the glass once more, even harder. Beads of sweat were rolling down his face as the camera angle flicked to a close-up of the glass. Something was happening to the man’s skin; it was turning the same colour as the light, bubbling and blistering, catching fire in places. There was time for one last pleading look at the camera—and the people safe outside the torpedo—before the man burst, exploding against the glass. It lingered a while before thankfully the camera angle returned to a middle distance shot where less could be seen.

“Ping,” said Pryce, laughing. “I think he might be done.” Another nod and the TV screen turned black again. “You see: no leniency, no mercy. You’re a scourge and you have to be wiped out. It really is as simple as that.”

Gavin was feeling a mixture of emotions, from panic to anger, from sadness to disdain. "Why should I tell you anything, when you've shown me what's going to happen anyway?"

"Because," Pryce answered immediately, "I can make it quick or I can make it very, very slow. In the end you might be begging me for a death like the one you've just seen, young Gavin. To be put out of your misery." As Pryce rose, Gavin sank back down in his chair.

"So," said the man with the predatory stare, "shall we begin?"

CHAPTER FORTY-ONE

The shapes were growing closer and closer, flitting about, spinning around now so fast it was difficult to make out any individual forms.

The bubble of light in which Callum and Michael were standing —their own lifeforce—had decreased even more in size. So much so that the darkness threatened to touch the tips of Callum's boots and he had to push himself up against Michael. Still unresponsive, the other man had apparently just given up and was ready to die—again. This time there would be no waking up, no being saved by Arcana. It was obvious that they'd been in here far too long. And once the darkness overwhelmed them, that would be the end of it.

As they came within inches of Callum, he found himself wondering exactly what they were. Demons? Creatures from some other galaxy? The things that live between this world and the next, or between the parallel universes Unwin had talked about? He'd find out soon enough, because in moments they would be joining their ranks.

"So, this is it," Callum said inside his own mind. "The end of everything. I wasn't anything special after all." The fact that he'd been right and Ferne, Unwin, Gavin, even the Goddess herself, had been wrong was—unsurprisingly—of little comfort to him. Right now, he would have taken the stupid prophecy over being here any day of the week. Embraced it if it meant he'd have the knowledge to fight off the darkness.

Just then, the space they were in did seem to grow lighter. It illuminated the shadows around them, at least enough for Callum to make out faces where before there had been none: only teeth that snapped periodically. A nose here, cheek there, eyes grey but now noticeable.

Below him the bubble he was standing in was suddenly widening. He looked down and saw it expand to accommodate more figures. But these were beings of light rather than dark, climbing into the circle, elbowing their way in to stand alongside Callum and Michael. On Callum's left was a face he recognised from Widow's Way: the girl Rhea, Ferne's sister, who'd taken her own life and was now in spirit form. Behind him Callum saw Rhea's partner, who'd been protected by the talisman back there and now, here, wore that same bag on his ethereal belt. Their family, too: the boy who'd been flamed at the door; his mother, who Cartwright had shot in the head; the man who'd jumped out at Callum from under the stairs, then turned into an animal.

To Callum's right was their former High Priest, Victor, hand-in-hand with his wife, Helen. They were all forming a shield around Callum and Michael, their combined energy driving back the dark. It was only now that Callum could see the creatures in the shade more clearly. The faces of human spirits not unlike their own, whose souls were anything but pure. And there, one face, one grin in particular … it was unmistakably his old partner, Gibson. Then the grin turned into a snarl, its teeth snapping, and was gone again, lost in the mix.

The bubble was widening. Callum looked over and saw Michael rousing himself. He was reaching out to Rhea, Victor and Helen. Victor shook his head. It wasn't Michael's time yet. The man pointed and a stream of brilliant illumination shot from his finger, sparks of lightning jumping from the tip. The stream widened, pushing aside the darkness to become a tunnel.

The way back home.

Victor nodded for them both to go, then smiled warmly. Callum pulled Michael, but he held fast, unwilling to leave his family. But it was too late for them, they belonged here now. Somewhere back along that blinding tunnel were Callum and Michael's bodies, and it was time for another reunion.

Knowing he had to take the initiative, Callum dragged Michael into the light—letting the shaft take them and carry them along, just as they'd been sucked this far inside the void in the first place. His companion struggled to get back into the circle, to spend just a few more seconds with his loved ones, but it was already too late. They were speeding away, as Callum and Michael were pulled back to reality, back to a world they'd left only temporarily.

Victor's path showed them the way. Now all they had to do was hold on and brace themselves.

"All right, let's begin," said Dr Lane, hovering over McGuire with the knife.

He brought down the scalpel and was about to make an incision in the man's chest when he suddenly felt some resistance. For the first time in his life, Lane's hand wasn't obeying his instructions. When he looked down at it, he realised why, though he couldn't quite process the information.

The subject's eyes were still shut tight, but its hand was now raised, fingers curled around the doctor's wrist. Lane knew that some corpses had a tendency to sit bolt upright, to moan and belch—even fart because of the gasses inside them. But this was the first time one had ever grabbed his arm. That was weird. No, worse, it was bloody surreal!

"Phelps," he called out to his colleague. But Phelps was having problems of his own. The other subject had reached out and grabbed the second doctor's coat.

Lane turned his attention back to the first corpse, which was opening its eyes. What the hell was happening?

Then he remembered. Recalled where he'd seen the other guy's face before, except it had been less grizzled then, no beard obscuring most of the face. Dr Lane remembered where he'd seen those scars before, too, because *he'd* caused some of them many years ago. Back when he'd performed the man's autopsy the first time.

Everything happened so quickly. His subject rose off the autopsy table, pulling Lane's hand—pulling the knife—up to his own throat, sliding off the table and getting behind him at the same time. The guards at the front and back of the room, like the "cadavers," were also waking up, realising that these men were clearly not as dead as they ought to be. They raised their automatic rifles almost at once.

"Hold your fire," said the fair-haired man holding Lane, "or I'll slit his throat."

From this position, as awkward as it was, Lane saw that Phelps' subject had grabbed him as well, but instead of holding the doctor to ransom, he was using him as a shield. The guards at the door opened fire on them, hitting Phelps, causing the doctor's body to dance and jerk like a marionette. The noise of the gunfire was deafening in the soundproofed room.

Whether Phelps' death was an accident or not, the man holding Lane now seemed to realise that his hostage wasn't as much of a bargaining tool as he thought. He pushed the doctor at speed towards the guards at the back of the room. Lane let out a howl as bullets nicked his arm and thigh, and he dropped to the floor, covering his head with his hands, while the guards ran at the blond corpse—aiming to put right what nature appeared to have slipped up on.

But the man wasn't about to make it easy for them. He bobbed to one side, slamming his elbow into one guard's face, knocking off his cap, then kicking out at his partner, sending the rifle clean out of his hands.

On the other side of the room, the second corpse somehow passed right through Phelps' bloodied body and then solidified to punch one guard, breaking his nose. When the remaining guard opened fire, the bearded man vanished again and the bullets hit nothing. Then he was behind the guard, reaching an arm around his throat and cutting off his air supply.

Lane's subject was now armed with the first guard's rifle, and was telling the injured guards to get down on the floor. He turned and looked at his formerly deceased companion then shouted, “Michael, that’s enough. We don’t kill if we can avoid it.”

The bearded man pulled a face before letting the guard fall to the ground, unconscious but not dead.

“Right,” said the fair-haired man, approaching Dr Lane. “Any cameras in this room?”

“T—They’ve been disabled,” Lane answered quickly, hands clutching his arm and thigh to stem the bleeding. “Commander Pryce didn’t want anyone knowing you were deceased.”

“Touching. And seeing that the walls in this place are so thick you wouldn’t be able to hear if a nuclear bomb went off, I’d say that right now nobody even knows we’re up and about again. That sound right, doc?”

Lane nodded so hard, he thought his head might fall off.

“Good.” The blond man, still naked, but less grey as more life flooded back into him, turned back to the guards on the ground. “All right, boys—strip!” They looked at each other blankly, probably because neither of them had ever been given an order by a dead man before. “You heard what I said, get your uniforms off. Right now!” Still on the floor, they began to remove their clothes. “And when that’s done, the good doctor here is going to give you all a nice injection to send you to sleep, aren’t you?”

Once more Lane nodded, fully understanding that the last person to get the needle would be himself. But he didn’t care about that. Unconsciousness was better than what had happened to Phelps. It also meant he wouldn’t have to think too hard about what had just occurred in his autopsy room, something that would probably put him off pathology for life.

He’d just seen two men rise from the dead—for one, it was the second time—and kick the crap out of four highly trained Penitentiary guards.

Yes, as far as Phelps was concerned, a little sleep right now was beginning to sound like the best idea in the world.

CHAPTER FORTY-TWO

Above The Penitentiary, clouds were gathering. To the untrained eye they looked quite normal, just fluffy wisps against the late afternoon sky. But there was a dance to be seen if you looked more closely: a tango in the heavens. Those clouds were darkening slightly, only at the tips for now, yet definitely changing colour. In the watchtowers posted around The Penitentiary, guards continued to scan the horizon. In particular the one dirt track that led to the facility. They noticed nothing out of the ordinary, nothing that warranted reporting.

But there was a storm coming.

And when it hit, nothing at The Penitentiary would ever be the same.

CHAPTER FORTY-THREE

Once all the guards and the remaining pathologist were asleep and they'd changed into the stolen uniforms, Michael chose his moment to turn on Callum. He shoved him up against the wall, breath coming in rasps.

"This is getting a bit predictable, don't you think?" said Callum.

"They were back there," Michael said through gritted teeth. "My mother and father, my sister."

Callum let his eyes drop. "Yes, I know."

"And you forced me to leave. They're dead and you made me leave them."

Looking up again, Callum replied: "Victor … your father *wanted* us to go back, he was holding the doorway open. Don't you see, Michael, he wanted you to live. He didn't want you becoming one of those things."

Michael let Callum go. "I don't know what living *is* anymore. I'm stuck between two worlds and belong in neither of them. Sometimes I think I'd be better off in that place."

"I wish I knew what to say to you," Callum offered. "What you do after all this is over is up to you. But right now we have a job to get on with. We have to find Gavin, find the kids, Ferne and—"

"When this is all over?" Michael said with a snort. "You honestly think we stand a chance against the entire Penitentiary?"

"We won't know unless we try." Callum straightened his uniform, putting a cap on his head. He picked up two M16A1 rifles and handed one to Michael. "Come on, we don't have much time before they send someone to check on us. Pryce will be waiting for a report."

"So," said Michael, snatching the gun from him, "is there a plan or are you just making this up as you go along?"

Callum grinned. "A little of both, I think." He opened the door a fraction. "Looks clear enough. Ready?"

Michael nodded.

They slipped out into the corridor, keeping their heads low, letting the caps obscure their faces. They couldn't assume that the cameras in this corridor weren't working, but it didn't matter. Nobody would be able to recognise them on an overhead monitor.

"Which way are we heading?" asked Michael, keeping his voice low. "You've been on the grand tour."

"Give me a minute, I'm trying to get my bearings. This place is a labyrinth." They walked down that corridor, passing more guards, more people in white coats carrying clipboards. When they turned the next corner and saw the glass windows on their left, Callum knew exactly where they were. Outside were the "waste disposal" units Pryce had shown them proudly. They hadn't been in use on that day, but were working overtime right now. There was a queue of gagged and manacled people waiting, all held in check by guards with rifles. The executions they'd read about in the papers had started and Pryce wasn't messing about.

"My Goddess," Michael breathed out when he looked through the window. "We have to help them."

"*Now* who wants to take on the entire Penitentiary?" Callum said. "We have to pick our moment, otherwise they'll all die."

"I know them." Michael's finger was tightening on the rifle's trigger. "They're Arcana, my friends. My *family*."

Callum rested a hand on the barrel of Michael's rifle, forcing it down. "Take it easy, you'll draw attention to us. We've got to be cleverer than that."

"You take it easy," Michael retorted. "I'm—"

"Shit!" whispered Callum, looking down along the corridor.

"What is it?"

Callum nodded and Michael saw a group of guards approaching, with one man leading them. It was Chief Inspector Cartwright. Michael ground his teeth together. "The bastard who was with my sister when she died."

"He also knows my face," Callum reminded him. "He was with me when we took the tour. What's he doing here now?"

"Probably interrogating prisoners from *The Valentine*."

That made sense. Cartwright had looked very chummy with Pryce when the mass arrests were made. He'd probably offered the inspector an opportunity to deal with some of them personally.

"I can't let him see me." Callum stood behind Michael as the group approached, keeping his head down, the rim of his cap covering his face almost entirely. Although he couldn't see Michael now, he imagined the man looking daggers at Cartwright as he went past. The footsteps receded.

"He's gone," Michael told him.

Callum looked up to see the group making their way down the corridor, probably to one of the interrogation rooms. But it was at that moment they halted, and Cartwright looked back over his shoulder. Why he did it, Callum had no idea: maybe the scene looked suspicious, maybe it was just a detective's hunch that something was out of place. Whatever the reason, the result was the same. Cartwright was looking directly at Callum McGuire.

Callum was pushing Michael behind him even before Cartwright gave out a cry of "*McGuire!*", raising his rifle milliseconds before the guards with the inspector did. Callum aimed low then pulled the trigger, hitting two of them in the shins. "Go," he called back to Michael. "Let out as many of the prisoners as you can. I'll cover you."

But Michael didn't really need cover, not with his talents. Fading away again, he was gone before he was three steps up the corridor.

Callum fired, this time drawing some back. There was nowhere to hide, just empty space in the corridor. Cartwright had obviously been allowed a gun on this visit to The Penitentiary, the same pistol which had put a bullet into that woman's head back at Widow's Way. Now it was directed at Callum, pumping out shot after lethal shot. Callum shouldered the glass at the side of him. It was reinforced; he would've expected no less if he'd been thinking straight. He risked turning his gun away from the guards for a moment and sprayed a section with bullets. It cracked, creating a spider's web effect, but still didn't shatter.

As another smattering of fire headed in his direction, Callum launched himself at the weakened glass, praying it would give in time. It did, pitching him out into the quad where the executions were taking place. The buttons were just about to be pressed to kill more Arcana when Callum crashed through. Everyone stopped what they were doing and looked across.

Picking himself up, leaving his cap where it had fallen, Callum sprayed the air above them with bullets. Arcana and Penitentiary guards ducked as one, the only difference was the former were quicker to react because they had more to lose. Prisoners broke free of their guards and went on the attack, punching and kicking as best they could. Once a couple had felled their warders, they were able to help undo the handcuffs holding them, remove gags.

"Pick up the guns, there are more guards coming," Callum called across to them. They just looked at him. This wasn't how they were about to defend themselves.

They were going to use magick.

Callum ran over, pushing aside the people in white coats, and started to release prisoners that were already in the giant microwaves—just as Cartwright reached the broken section of window. A few guards began shooting from various positions there, but one of the female Arcana prisoners had already begun spellcasting. Her mouth moved, fingers crackling as she targeted the bullets, sending their trajectory awry. They projectiles flew in any direction but at their intended targets, hitting walls, the ground, or just flying upwards.

Now his cuffs were off, another one of the prisoners threw his arm back and then hurled what looked like mud at the guards. The brown substance stuck to the barrels of the rifles, then hardened, so that when the men pulled the triggers the guns exploded in their faces.

Callum allowed himself a brief smile, then got on with releasing more of the prisoners from the torpedo-shaped death-traps.

Moments later, an alarm sounded. *That's it,* thought Callum, *the jig is up. Time to find out if we really can take on the whole Penitentiary.*

Michael saw more guards running along the corridor to answer the alarm—nine or ten at least—and decided to slow them down.

He slung the rifle over his shoulder and lay down directly in front of the sprinting men, then shifted into the real world, so that the first few guards tumbled over him. A couple more fell over them, pitching headfirst onto the ground.

Before any of the guards at the rear could shoot Michael, or even pick him out from the jumble of bodies, he'd gone again, only to appear behind two of them and bang their heads together with a satisfying clunk. Then he disappeared once more, popping up in mid-swing to give one guard an uppercut, twisting round to slam another with the butt of his rifle. He did this, vanishing and reappearing, until there were no guards left.

Then he set about opening a few cell doors.

"What in Christ's name is that?" grumbled Pryce when he heard the alarms going off. The klaxons in The Penitentiary had never sounded in all the time he'd been in charge here—which was pretty much since the first slab of concrete had been laid—except for drill practice. And there were none of those scheduled for today.

Gavin heard the alarms as well. He couldn't resist smirking.

"What the fuck are you grinning about?" Pryce asked him, but didn't get an answer. "Let's give you something to smile about, eh?" He swiped Gavin across the face with the back of his hand, a practised motion that he'd used many times, including on Ferne.

Head to the side, Gavin spat the blood out of his mouth. "You're going to come to a bad end, Commander Pryce." The words were cold and made Pryce pause. Then he marched towards the door, issuing orders, barking at guards to follow him.

Gavin let out a small laugh when he'd gone. He'd suddenly realised that he didn't need the cards to see at all. The power was inside him; had been all along. His prediction about Pryce wasn't just guesswork, it was fact—just like his prophecy about Superintendent Wallis. He'd known then really, and he knew now.

But, best of all, finally he knew how events here at The Penitentiary were going to turn out.

Gavin laughed again.

CHAPTER FORTY-FOUR

Like the rest of them, Tawny Geddes had believed her time was up.

She'd been dragged from her cell and placed in the line, several guns trained on her in case she should do something stupid. Being inside that cramped room for this long after a handful of interrogation sessions had certainly given her time to think. And the one thing she'd been thinking about had not been her impending death, but Meg and the months she'd thrown away. She'd only been trying to protect her, save the woman from harm in case Enforcement Officers traced Tawny back to her. But that had happened anyway, with them lying in wait at the supermarket.

Shouldn't have gone back there. Shouldn't have tried to warn Meg. Shouldn't have fallen in love with her in the first place, you mean.

It had never happened before. Somehow she'd dodged Cupid's arrows very effectively up till that point. Then wham! She met Meg and all that changed. Tawny could see the woman was falling for her too, that's why she had to get away. Goddess! Meg must have hated her so much.

Tawny wondered where she was, hoped she hadn't suffered the fate of most people touched—or, as they called it, *contaminated*—by magick. She hadn't seen her since the electric grid hit them at the supermarket entrance. Now here she was, about to be fried alive. Oh, she was under no illusions about what was going to happen. For one thing the "lucky" few in line had been granted front row seats of the chambers, and those who'd gone before them (thankfully none of them Meg; she wouldn't have been able to handle that).

Microwaves would heat up the molecules in Tawny's body to such an extent that she'd just pop like a bag of crisps when you squeeze it.

The sky was darkening as if it knew that this was a black, black day. Soon enough it was Tawny's turn. "Get inside!" one of the guards had ordered, poking her in the back with his rifle. Tawny had given him a vicious stare. She thought about just lifting that rifle right out of his hands and ramming it somewhere he wouldn't find it in a hurry. After all, her hands were no longer tied—make that manacled—because they couldn't allow metal in those machines. She thought about saying something, now the gag had been taken off so they could watch her scream. But there were just too many other guards waiting to put a bullet in her. What difference did it make to them, she was dead anyway. So that was that. She accepted her fate and the fact that she'd never see Meg again, never get to hold her or kiss her, tell her just how much she loved her.

"Get inside! I won't tell you again." This time the guard pushed her with the length of the rifle, causing her to stumble. Tawny picked herself up, determined to end her last few minutes with dignity. She walked into the torpedo-like machine, looking around her as the door closed with an air-tight hiss.

There were people dressed in white coats at the side, nodding as they ticked things off on their clipboards. Then one stepped up to the control pad to punch in the code, to execute the sequence ... and Tawny.

It was soundproofed in the chamber, a quiet haven from the misery out there in the lines (Tawny was trying to ignore the remains of previous "tenants"). She could make her peace with her Mistress before joining her out there somewhere in the Universe, pure energy that would never feel hunger or pain, or love. Tawny thought of Meg again and her eyes welled up with salt water, the first time she'd allowed herself to show emotion since she'd got here. The tears blurred her vision.

So much so that at first she couldn't quite make out what was happening over at the large window of The Penitentiary. Tawny wiped her eyes, trying to see exactly what was going on.

It appeared that one of the guards had suddenly gone crazy, jumping through the window and out into the open. He was spraying the air with bullets—but why? In a way that didn't matter as much as the consequence, which was that everyone fell to the ground. The prisoners in line, almost as one, began fighting the guards, taking keys, freeing themselves from their bonds.

The insane guard, the one who'd initiated this riot, was shouting something she couldn't hear. Then more guards appeared at the broken window, firing into the crowds. Their bullets didn't hit any targets, thanks to one of their kind steering them in all directions; an ability similar to her special talent, actually.

Suddenly the guard was at her chamber, forcing the people in white coats away. He was handsome, if you were into that kind of thing—blond hair revealed now that his cap was gone. He looked up at Tawny and smiled. It was comforting: oozing confidence and instilling trust. The kind of smile you'd follow into battle.

There was another hiss and the door latch sprang open. Then he was helping her out of the chamber.

"T—Thank you," said Tawny.

"Sure," said the man, who was already moving on to the next tube, freeing another member of Arcana who thought their time was up.

Tawny looked out at the state of play, her fingers beginning to crackle. They'd taken her once, when her guard was down. Never again.

She ran out, arms wide, mouthing incantations. Anything that wasn't nailed down—stones, fallen rifles, clipboards—followed in her wake. Tawny skidded to a halt, then threw her arms forward, sending the missiles hurtling at the window and the guards with tremendous speed.

The rest of the glass cracked and broke, and there was a cheer from behind her as their enemies were sent reeling backwards.

Tawny gave a satisfied nod.

That was only for starters, she thought to herself.

Nate Maxwell was in a lab, strapped to a bed, when the alarms went off.

Since his capture at the zoo, he'd been poked, prodded, injected and cut into. His ribs were bandaged where they'd been broken, a consequence of the beating he'd taken upon his arrest, but they'd given him no pain relief here. Why should they? He was only a stinking sparkie after all.

The irony wasn't lost on Nate. All his life he'd talked to animals—not controlled them as many might have thought, but made friends with them. It was his special gift from the Goddess. In the old days he would probably have been arrested and drowned for having familiars and holding unnatural council with them. He'd read about those horrible places where animals were experimented on for the good of humanity, even wondered about breaking into a couple in his time. And if he hadn't thought he might get caught, putting other Arcana at risk, then he'd probably have done it. The idea of those helpless little creatures being manhandled, exposed to all kinds of diseases, even having tissue grafted to them, broke his heart. If people could only hear what animals were thinking, saying (each having their own different language, his spellbook a key to unlocking these) there was no way they'd treat them the way that they did.

What he never, ever thought was that he'd end up in a lab just like them. As Arcana himself, he had even less rights than the animals he'd sworn to protect. The men and women in white coats flitted about, attaching instruments to him, then running electrical currents through his body, testing his pain thresholds, using the information for developing defences against future encounters with magick users.

Nate didn't resist, was in no shape to do so. He'd given everything he'd got back at the zoo and had still ended up here. He mourned the loss of his friends, many of whom had given their lives for him in vain.

The minutes dragged out into hours, then into what must surely be days. A never-ending round of assessments and trials, one of which even measured his brainwaves when he was shown pictures of animals being tortured. He tried not to give them any reaction, but it was difficult when confronted with such cruel images. They were sick bastards in this place and no mistake.

Then, out of nowhere, came the alarms. It was obvious that this wasn't a common occurrence because everyone looked up, bewildered. Something was happening, Nate knew that much for sure. Whether it was a good or bad thing, he was yet to discover.

"What's going on?" asked one of the techies.

"Not sure," replied another.

One of the women in white coats opened the door to the lab and looked out, her head swivelling first one way, then another. Nate could hear the sound of boot falls, lots of them. Guards ran past the door in groups of three or four. The woman held her arm out to flag one of them down.

He saw her asking him what was happening, but Nate's attention soon shifted lower … to the dog one of the guards had on a leash behind them both. The dog, a beautiful German Shepherd, looked up when it saw Nate on the bed.

"Hello," Nate said to it, without even having to speak. A good thing, as the gag prevented him. *"What's your name?"*

To begin with the dog didn't answer, either a consequence of its strict training or perhaps it had just never been asked its name by a human before. At least not this way.

"Come on, don't be scared. I'm Nate."

"They call me Fang … my masters."

"Hmm. What's your real name?"

Fang thought for a second or two. He'd only been conditioned to answer to his given name. *"Before I was taken away, my mother used to call me by a name. But I can't remember what it was."*

"I was taken away, too," Nate told Fang. *"By your masters. They took*

me from a place where I was free, and locked me up here. Why do you obey them?"

"Because they feed me, and they look after me."

"I bet they hit you when you do something wrong though, right?"

"Sometimes."

"They're bad people. You know that, don't you?"

Fang was quiet.

"They do bad things, and what they make you do is bad as well. If you help me, I promise to look after you properly. You'll be free to do what you want, go for walks, have as much food as you can eat. How does that sound?"

Silence again.

Nate was running out of time, the woman was finishing up her chat with the other guard.

"Please," begged Nate.

Fang looked from him to his handler, then back again. He began to pull on his lead.

"What's gotten into you?" asked the guard holding him. "Fucking mutt!"

The woman in the white coat looked over her shoulder at Nate. "Oh my God. Get that dog away from here, now."

"Wha—"

Fang jumped at his handler, who shouted for him to get down. When the man brought his hand back, Fang bit his wrist before wrestling him to the floor and scratching his face. When Fang let him go, the man ran off up the corridor. The other guard brought up his rifle, but Fang leapt at him before he could get off a shot, pushing him back against the wall and knocking him out. The female techie backed into the lab, then tried to shut the door. But Fang was too fast for her, slipping in and growling loudly. Then the dog went over to Nate, stood up on his back legs, and pulled down the gag with his teeth.

"All of you, into one corner," said Nate, now he could speak … out loud. "Or I let him loose."

The techies obeyed, cowering into one corner of the lab. Fang began pulling at the straps holding Nate down. In minutes, he was up, his gown flapping about his legs. Nate stroked the top of the dog's head.

"Thank you," he said to Fang.

"Just remember the food," the dog reminded him.

"Now," Nate said, *"could you take me to the rest of your friends? I'd like to have a word with them as well."*

Peter Finlay was dreaming.

In that dream he'd been captured, taken down by a group of M-forcers at a monorail station, then driven out to a faraway place to be drugged, tortured and left in a cell to rot. His memory was still hazy, but one thing he did understand fully was why his wife Janice had buried his real identity so deep not even *he* was aware of it during the daytime. This was exactly the kind of thing she'd been worried about, exactly the danger she'd hoped to protect him from.

Now in that dream—that nightmare—he was a broken figure of a man. Manacled hand and foot, gagged, curled up in a room that didn't even have a bed in it (and Peter did so love his bed). He felt lost, as if everything he thought he'd known had been a sham, and just when he was getting to know the real person inside—the powerful person he'd always wished he *could* be—it had been snatched away from him.

In the dream he was alone, trapped, forgotten.

But Peter Finlay knew, deep down, that it wasn't really a dream. The real nightmare was reality, and he hadn't slept at all since he'd got to The Penitentiary. It might have been something they'd given him, but he doubted it. More likely, it was just his body's way of saying: look, you're stuck here, so you'd better deal with it; no more fantasies and nice dreams for you. No escape, not even when you're asleep.

But when he saw the man appear in front of him, he had to wonder whether he really was dreaming all this, or whether he'd gone completely mad. Peter had blinked and there he was, bearded and wearing a guard's uniform. The man undid his manacles, removed the gag, then vanished.

The next thing Peter knew, the door was open. It *had* to be a dream. Why else would the door just fly back like that and there be nobody on the other side? Where were the other guards, ready to drag him off to Goddess knew where for more torment? Was it some kind of trick?

Peter decided to take a chance. He got up and walked towards the open space of the cell doorway. Tentatively, he stuck his head out. Down the corridor he saw more cell doors open, more people like him emerging from their confinement. Then he saw the bearded man again; he passed through a solid wall as if it wasn't there at all, into a cell, and then back out again. The man placed his hand on the door seal, short-circuiting it with a crackle of energy, then the door popped open.

This was no dream, Peter realised. It was a prison break.

And their numbers were growing, because for every person the bearded man released, they went on to open more cell doors. The only thing that could potentially cause a problem were the guards charging up the hallway. An alarm had started ringing, probably when the very first cell door was opened, and more would come.

"I'm awake," Peter said to himself, pinching his arm. "And I can buy them some time. Now let's see if this still works …" He mouthed the strange words, felt the energy rising inside.

Peter's feet left the ground, only a few inches at first, but then more. He flexed his arms, feeling the power—the strength—still there. Energy was crackling at his fingertips, around his eyes.

When the first of the guard's bullets bounced off his hardened skin, Peter smiled.

He was ready for them this time.

CHAPTER FORTY-FIVE

With the situation on the quad in hand, and Michael freeing as many of the prisoners as he could, Callum needed to find a way back inside The Penitentiary.

With solid walls on either side of him, and just one door that the prisoners had been brought through, which was now locked again, he opted for the windows opposite—the ones parallel to those he'd crashed through. At the moment there were no troops there, so he took his opportunity. Callum peppered the glass with bullets, then kicked at it. The windows held initially, then shattered. He made a hole big enough to climb through by smashing the rough edges with the butt of the rifle.

His luck wasn't about to hold out forever, though.

As soon as he entered the corridor, he saw guards coming towards him on both sides. "Dammit!"

Callum pointed his rifle first in one direction, then the other. But when he finally came to shoot, his gun choked; he was out of ammunition. Unfortunately for him, the guards in The Penitentiary weren't. He dived as the first blast came, both sides miraculously missing him. Callum had seconds before they dipped their rifles and aimed at the floor.

He waited for the hail of bullets that would hit him … but it never came. Callum tentatively raised his head, not knowing what to expect. But even this was beyond anything he'd seen so far during his time with Arcana. The guards on both sides were standing still, rifles raised. They didn't really have a choice, actually, because each and every one of them had been turned to stone.

Getting up, Callum stared at the human statues. It was as if Medusa had given them all a quick bat of her eyelids. However, when Callum turned he saw that it was a dark-skinned man with dread-locks who'd done this—one of the prisoners who'd been waiting in line for execution. His arms were still outspread, crackling with energy, the after-effects of such a powerful spell.

"Er … thanks," said Callum. "Are they …?"

"It's only temporary. It'll last a few hours," the man told him. "Need any help?"

"Help them," Callum said, indicating the other prisoners in the quad. "This is something I have to do alone."

Dreadlocks returned to his friends. Callum still couldn't work out which way to go: left or right. He decided to follow his instincts, so left it was.

Unarmed, he skirted past the stone guards and carried on up the corridor. They all looked the same, and he had no idea whether he was heading the right way. When he saw two guards trotting side by side, Callum hid around a corner and waited for them.

He threw out his arm, catching one across the throat—and the other he kicked squarely in the chest. Callum grabbed the first guard's gun, ignoring the man who was rolling around clutching his neck. The other was on his hands and knees so, after kicking away that man's rifle, Callum pushed him over onto his back.

"Where are the children?" he asked, shoving the barrel into his face.

"W—What?"

"You heard me." The barrel was virtually halfway up the guard's right nostril. "The children. Where do they keep them?"

The guard flung out an arm, pointing with all his fingers at once. "Up … up there on the left. The crèche."

Callum rolled the guard over and cuffed him with his own manacles. Then he followed the directions. There was only one door, so that had to be it. He tried the handle and found it locked. Next to the door was one of those hand pads he'd seen Pryce use, so Callum pointed his gun at it and fired. The electronics fizzled and popped, dying, and when he tried the handle again the door opened easily.

The room—the crèche, as the guard had called it—was fairly large, about the size of a school hall. Skirting the edges were holding bays, each with bars across them; like oversized playpens. In each bay was a child, their ages ranging from three or four upwards. Some were crying, some holding the bars and looking out at the new arrival, hoping it might be someone they knew: mothers, fathers, uncles, sisters or brothers. There had to be at least thirty or so. The children of Arcana. Callum wondered how many of them had been mistreated, how many tortured.

"They overhear things. They retain information, even if they don't know it. They're more useful than you can possibly imagine."

"My God … Goddess," said Callum.

Still focussed on the holding bays, he didn't notice anything beside him. Not until he heard someone shout: "Look out!"

Callum swung round just in time to see a burly woman in a white jumpsuit charging at him. The crèche was obviously her domain, and he was trespassing.

She ran into him, knocking the wind out of him, sending his rifle flying. The woman rammed Callum up against the bars of one cage, causing the little mite inside to cower.

Bringing her head up, she caught Callum's chin and he bashed his head against the bars. Next she aimed her foot between his legs, but he grabbed it just in time. Forcing the foot—and leg—backwards, Callum pushed her off-balance and she fell heavily.

Scrambling across the ground, she reached for Callum's rifle, which had landed near one of the bays. He ran to get there first, but was too late. The woman already had it in her hands and was sitting up, aiming it at him. Breathing heavily, she inched back on her bottom, finger tightening on the trigger.

But before she could fire, a small hand appeared behind her, nudging her arm and spoiling her aim. Another reached out and grabbed what there was of her hair and the woman yelped. Callum got to her and slapped the rifle away. Before he could do anything else, the small hands grabbed the side of the woman's head, shoved it forwards then dragged it back against the bars with a clang. The woman's eyes rolled back into her skull and she slipped down, totally unconscious.

Callum found himself staring into the eyes of the little girl from Widow's Way, the one who looked so much like her mother. There was rage in those eyes, and her face had aged years during her days in this place. She looked past him, across the room—and he realised who'd called out the warning. It was her brother, the shy little boy who'd said nothing as Callum had sat with them in the back of the van. It was time to put something right.

"I'm so sorry," said Callum. "I should never have left you both."

He checked the bay for a means of opening the bars, finding a release mechanism on the top. The girl jumped out, and Callum didn't know whether she was going to attack *him* as well. But she just wrapped her arms around his torso, burying her head in his chest. Callum stroked her hair for a moment, then said, "Honey, let's get your brother and the rest of these kids out of this place, shall we?"

They began letting the rest of the children go, Rhea's daughter acting like a surrogate mother, calming them down, drying their tears. Her brother never left her side, clutching her clothing as if he thought they were going to be separated again. It was as Callum came to the end of the row that he noticed the plastic case, the cot inside it. The third child they'd brought in from Widow's Way was still here.

Callum walked over to the baby, which was still as quiet as a mouse. It had never cried on the day they'd brought it in and wasn't about to start now. The baby looked up at him through the clear plastic and gurgled something. Callum frowned; the burbling made perfect sense to him. Though he'd never cast one in his life before, he recognised this for what it really was. A spell.

"They retain information, even if they don't know it."

"It's my book of spells ... We all have one. They're personal spells, gathered over time. Unique to each magick user ... They choose us as much as we choose them."

"You talk like they're living things,"

"In a way they are. Some say they originate from the great book that contains them all."

Living things … A living *thing … A book!*

Now it all fell into place. The spell books Ferne and the others carried helped them to work out the power inside of them, the skills, the spells individual to them, which were set down.

But what if the great book of all spells wasn't really a book at all, thought Callum. *What if the information was so powerful, so important it was never meant to be written down? What if it was hidden in the last place anyone would ever look?*

The baby gurgled again. Callum removed the plastic casing and picked up the child.

And when he looked more closely, deep into its eyes, he saw something amazing.

CHAPTER FORTY-SIX

It was at about this time that the storm hit.

The rumbles of thunder that had been masked by all the gunfire gave way to rain and lightning. If anyone had been on the hills looking across at The Penitentiary, they would have seen a magnificent display. The sky was angry, and it was taking out its fury on the building below.

Forked streaks of energy hit the look-out posts, the trucks in the compound, and the main building. Out in the quad the prisoners basked in the ozone smell and the buildup of nature's energy. The Goddess was here with them today, revitalising them, urging her people on against these tyrants.

When one strike hit the main generator, the lights of The Penitentiary flickered, then went off altogether. Inside, the alarms were silenced prematurely. There was a delay while everything was rerouted to emergency systems and the place was bathed in red from the back-up lights. Many Arcana thought it appropriate.

For them, this place had been Hell on Earth.

Now it looked like it, too.

Sherman Pryce was greeted with a scene of complete and utter chaos when he finally made it out into the corridor. Down one wing, his guards were being attacked by their own trained dogs, while along another a magick user had her hand pressed to the floor and was turning the surface into a virtual skating rink. Pryce's men were slipping and sliding about, crashing into each other and firing their rifles at the ceiling.

Pryce took out his own gun, making his way to the stairs and the lower levels, taking three of his personal guards with him. Now wasn't the time to ask how all this had happened, how things had got out of hand so quickly. There'd be an investigation later on if he had anything to do with it. For now he'd let the fight play itself out, call for help down here, and settle back to wait for the cavalry. Before descending, Pryce looked up at the camera in the corner of the corridor and wondered just how much of this debacle Nero Stark had seen.

Because he knew it would dictate just how much longer he had left to live.

The answer to that question was: Nero Stark had seen plenty.

Sitting back in his chair, he'd scrutinised events leading up to the loss of control over The Penitentiary. He'd especially found the presence of Callum McGuire intriguing—seeing as the man was supposed to be dead. If Pryce thought that his little network of spies could do anything behind Stark's back, he was wrong (and all that messing about with the cameras hadn't fooled anyone). He knew that McGuire had shown up at his old station house, along with Michael Sanderson and the boy, Gavin. Just as he knew that only one of the trio had been breathing. But the fact that he'd seen both McGuire and Sanderson in action freeing Arcana suggested that reports of their demise had been greatly exaggerated.

Stark's hand hovered over the phone to call for reinforcements, but paused when he saw Callum break into the crèche. So that had been his weakness after all, along with the whore who'd so obviously beguiled him. It was such a shame. But McGuire had made his own bed. Now he had to suffer the consequences.

He watched the fight with the nanny, then observed as Callum and the little girl freed the children. As Callum approached the cot towards the back of the crèche, Stark sat up in his chair and leaned forwards.

McGuire was removing the clear plastic top of the cot, cocking his head—staring as the baby as if hypnotised. Callum was mouthing words Stark couldn't hear or make out, not to soothe the baby, but to get things clear in his head.

"What the Devil is he …?"

Then Stark knew. It had been under their noses all this time.

Damn him for thinking too literally. That the "book" would be captured on parchment or paper like the one he kept in the glass cabinet over there. He should have known that these people never made things easy.

Nevertheless, he knew where it was now: the ultimate weapon.

One way or another Stark aimed to possess it.

CHAPTER FORTY-SEVEN

Even Ferne heard the sirens, short-lived as they were, down in her dungeon prison. She'd been mourning the death of Callum and Michael, coming so soon on the heels of Victor she thought she might actually go insane. Could you die from grief? Was that possible? *Over time maybe*, she thought, *like those old couples who only have each other then one of them passes away.*

Maybe it was just a fabrication, something to make her give up hope, give up on life? Pryce was a devious and cruel man, she wouldn't put it past him to make the whole thing up. But no, Ferne could tell it was the truth. There had been something about the way he'd spoken, that he would have preferred to get his hands on them first before they died. At least if it had been quick they would be spared her fate.

She'd give anything to see Callum alive one more time, or even Michael. As much as they fought, they had grown up together and she loved him like a brother. Oh, how much pain she must have put him through because she didn't feel the same way and now it was too late.

No. The universe had a way of granting wishes if you wanted them so badly. But even she couldn't believe it when Michael appeared in front of her. He'd walked through the wall of the torture chamber, and was standing right there, gazing in disbelief at Victor on the floor, at Ferne fixed to the chair.

She hardly dared say his name, in case he was a ghost—or even more of a ghost than usual—and would fade away if he realised it. In the end Michael spared her this by speaking himself. "Ferne? Oh little Ferne, what have they done to you?"

"M—Michael?" she croaked.

"It's me," he said coming over and bending to hug her, cradling her head against his shoulder. "I'm really here."

She cried again, tears of joy and sheer hysteria. "I can't … can't believe it. Pryce told me you were dead."

"Yes, but I've been dead before, remember?" he said, rising.

Ferne bit her lip, making it sorer still. Then she asked: "Callum?"

Michael looked at her, then nodded. "He's alive, too. Or he was the last time I saw him." She'd let out a sigh of relief, not thinking how much it would hurt Michael. But now she could see it written all over his face.

As he worked on freeing her from the chair, his eyes kept being drawn towards Victor. "I'm sorry," she told him. "He died trying to protect me."

"I already knew," Michael said. "But seeing him here, in the flesh …" He shook his head.

He'd just finished undoing the clasps when a voice said:

"What's this, a family reunion?"

It was Sherman Pryce, his pistol trained on them. There were three guards with him who all had their rifles raised. Michael's was slung over his back, but wasn't really his weapon of choice anyway. He looked at Ferne, then vanished. Pryce and his men swung their guns around in an arc, searching for him. "Come out, Michael, stop hiding … Before someone gets hurt."

Michael appeared beside one guard, brandishing a knife he'd picked up from one of Pryce's torture tables. He jammed it into the guard's shoulder, causing the man to howl. "Like this, you mean?"

Pryce turned and fired, but Michael was already gone, if only for a few seconds. When he next appeared, he had the miniature chainsaw in his hand, which he used to cut through the second guard's rifle. Michael headbutted the man, before slipping sideways out of reality once more. This left one guard and Pryce. The former was still searching with his rifle, the latter was edging sideways towards Ferne.

Michael dispatched the third guard using a whip. He snapped the rifle out of his hands, before wrapping the length of leather around the man's neck and slamming him sideways into the wall. Then he phased out again.

"Stop!" ordered Pryce, who had finally reached Ferne. He had her in a headlock with the pistol at her temple. "Stop, or I swear to God I'll kill her."

There was silence, except for the groans of the guards.

"Show yourself, Michael."

The bearded man remained hidden.

"Show yourself—now!"

"Don't do it," managed Ferne, which earned her a tightening of the headlock. She clutched at Pryce's forearm with her hands, but it did little good.

"Let her go." Michael appeared in front of Pryce, as solid as anyone else in the room. His eyes were on Ferne. "Please."

Pryce grinned. "Ah, I see. So it's the same for you as it is for McGuire? I thought you two were related? You know you really shouldn't think about your sister that way, Michael."

"Let her go," Michael repeated.

"Or what? You're in no position to bargain, freak."

"You really are sick, Pryce," Ferne murmured. "Here, let me help you with that." The hands clutching at his forearm began to glow subtly. Pryce's eyes took on a faraway gaze, a look of serenity and tranquillity that didn't fit with the rest of his face at all. His pistol hand lolled, as if the weapon was suddenly too heavy for him. Michael moved forwards, recognising a chance to get Ferne away from this psychopath. But then the glow faded. Ferne, exhausted, slumped against Pryce's body. The last dregs she had in her weren't nearly enough to heal a mind like Pryce's. He shook himself awake, the air of menace returning. When he saw Michael, Pryce quickly raised his gun.

The first shot hit him in the stomach, the second in the chest. Ferne didn't even have the energy to flinch as the pistol went off. Michael stumbled forwards a couple of steps, then touched his wounds, his hand coming away bright red. Pryce fired again, and this one dropped the bearded man. He lay on the floor of the torture chamber, blood pooling around him.

Pryce dragged Ferne up to watch. "Like father, like son," he said, aiming the gun at Michael again.

"I … Ferne, I … lo—"

Pryce fired off two more rounds, silencing Michael's dying words. "Heartwarming I'm sure. Now let's see you come back from that."

Ferne didn't want to look, but the position Pryce had her in left little option. Michael gazed upwards in death, but in a strange sort of way he seemed to be at peace now. She hadn't seen that look since they were in their teens. As Michael had said himself, he had been dead before—but Pryce was right about him not coming back this time. Ferne felt guilty again, more than sad … that she couldn't love Michael as he'd wanted her to. That she'd been able to save Callum after he'd been shot at the hospital, but not her "brother" lying there on the ground. Even if Pryce wasn't holding her, she had nothing left to give, no healing left inside her.

"If that bastard is still alive, it means your fuckbuddy must be as well," Pryce commented, finally putting two and two together. "They're the cause of all this. But …" Pryce paused, shaking Ferne. "I have a bargaining tool, now, don't I?"

With that, he dragged Ferne back to the open doorway.

CHAPTER FORTY-EIGHT

It was a strange sight.

For anyone around in the corridor, witnessing a man walking through what was practically a warzone, holding a baby in his arms and leading a troupe of children behind him, ranked amongst the most peculiar things they'd ever clap eyes on. For guards and Arcana alike, Callum's trek through The Penitentiary was enough to give them pause.

Wherever he passed, the fighting stopped—not because there were children in the firing line, as these were Arcana children when all was said and done—but because there was something about the fair-haired man they couldn't put their finger on. One or two guards did come up to him brandishing their rifles, but when they got close enough to fire, Callum simply looked at them and they forgot quite what they were doing. Either that or what they saw in his eyes made them wet themselves on the spot.

Doors flew open without anyone having to touch them, or shoot them—it was enough for Callum to be walking by. Soon, there wasn't a magick user in the place that was still held captive. And as he passed, the members of Arcana followed him, until there were dozens and dozens trailing behind. An army that had no real need to fight anymore, that had no enemy *willing* to fight them—at least not with Callum leading the way.

High above The Penitentiary, the thunder still rumbled, the lightning still struck at strategic targets. Communications were out, no mobile phones or radios would work. Guards were rounded up and placed in the cells that had once held Arcana. The small pockets of resistance soon gave up the fight.

The place belonged to them now, and no-one in their right mind was going to try and stop them.

The man with the gun rushed into the room, slamming the door behind him.

There was one prisoner in there, the guards long since gone. It was a young guy manacled to a chair, who turned around when he saw him. The man was sweating profusely, a panicked expression on his face, and he pointed his gun at the boy.

"I don't think you want to do that," said Gavin.

"Shut up. Just shut the fuck up!" Chief Inspector Cartwright replied.

"Why don't you put the gun down and let me out of this chair. You're going to do it anyway, eventually."

Cartwright kept the gun trained on the boy. "You … Your lot, you've done this. You're—"

"What? Unnatural? Abominations in the eyes of your God?"

The Chief Inspector nodded.

"You're frightened of us." It was a statement, not a question.

"Yes."

"Ever since that man did what he did to you when you were seven. He may have called himself a magician, but he didn't have any magickal powers—did he?"

Cartwright looked stunned.

"It's why you joined the M-forcers, why you killed that woman at Widow's Way."

"How did you—"

"Her name was Annie, by the way," interrupted Gavin. "Her son was the one your men set fire to at the door."

Cartwright's eyes darted around. "I …"

"Fear, it's why you're randomly firing at anything that moves out there, Chief Inspector. But you don't really believe in what you're doing, not in your heart. That's how Rhea was able to do what she did. She meant you no harm; she was just as frightened as you."

Cartwright lowered his gun.

"Believe it or not, you will come to accept us and our ways. And you'll wonder what you were ever so frightened of," Gavin said matter-of-factly. "Just as many will."

The Chief Inspector dropped his pistol on the floor with a clang. He went over and undid Gavin's clasps, freeing him from the chair.

"Thank you. Now, I think we'd better get outside, don't you?" Gavin smiled broadly. "Wouldn't want to miss out on all the excitement."

Cartwright undid the door and held it open for Gavin. As he walked through, the younger man reached into his own pocket and pulled out a set of tarot cards. They looked exactly the same as the ones that had been destroyed in Wallis's office. Not batting an eyelid, Gavin began to shuffle them.

A natural, easy motion that he'd missed so much.

When Sherman Pryce reached the top of the stairs again he found The Penitentiary a very different place.

All was quiet, all was calm. The only thing intruding upon this was the sound of the storm raging above. The light was still red, but it was enough to see by. Pulling Ferne through by her arm, the gun still to her head, he cautiously crept down the corridor.

So far, so good.

When he turned the first corner he came face to face with the new staff of the facility.

The members of Arcana, once his playthings, lives to take or save, filled the space ahead of him as far as he could see. A sea of bodies standing in his way. A light was emanating from them, an energy glow coming from their combined strength.

At the front was Callum McGuire, standing with a small child in his arms.

Pryce jammed the barrel of his pistol harder into Ferne's forehead. "So, the lunatics really have taken over the asylum, eh?" he quipped. "And you've been left holding the baby, I see."

"A very special baby," Callum said, "who showed me how blind I've been." It was now that Pryce saw the difference in this man. It was not the same person he'd shown around The Penitentiary at all. His words had authority; he carried himself a little straighter. Being dead had obviously agreed with him. "You don't seem very upset that your world has just come crashing down about your ears."

"What?" said Pryce. "This place? When Nero Stark gets wind of what's happened, he'll send more men to take it back. Now, you're going to let me go or I'll put a bullet in her pretty little brain." He jabbed the barrel again for effect. "Just like I did with the invisible man back there who tried to rescue her."

"Michael," said Callum, with a tinge of sadness.

"Correct."

"You really think I'd allow you to do that?" asked Callum. His eyebrows were sloping now, creating shadows and intensifying his stare. "After everything else you've done to her?"

Pryce laughed. "What choice do you have?"

"There's always a choice," said Callum,

"You don't scare me, McGuire. I know exactly what you are."

Callum grinned slyly. "I don't think so." He began to walk towards Pryce.

"You stay there, Arcana."

Callum ignored him.

"One more step. One more, and I'll do it. I swear!"

Callum carried on walking towards him, mouthing words, whispering.

Pryce pulled the trigger. Or at least he tried to. His brain was telling his finger what to do, but the digit wasn't obeying. Pryce frowned, tried again. Nothing. Somehow he'd completely forgotten how to shoot a gun. Pryce let Ferne go and she dropped to the floor, no strength even to hold herself up anymore.

Callum was metres away from the Commander now, so the man turned the gun on him. But he still had the same problem. No matter how hard he tried he just couldn't pull that trigger. Callum shifted the baby into the crook of his other arm, then snatched the gun from Pryce's grasp. If the man thought about attacking his foe, he didn't do anything about it. Somehow he knew it would do no good.

Tossing the gun aside, Callum got down on one knee to examine Ferne. She was incredibly weak. The torture, the healing, the emotional turmoil she'd gone through had sapped her strength almost to the point of total inertia. "My turn," said Callum, placing a hand on her stomach. It glowed, more brightly than Ferne's ever had, and Callum whispered more incantations. Pryce watched in amazement as one by one Ferne's wounds healed. The burns on her feet vanished, the bruises and cuts, needles fell out from under her fingernails—the nerve endings returning to normal—even the split on her lip healed over.

Ferne opened her eyes, blinking. "Callum?" she said. Sitting up on the floor, Pryce saw that the lash marks from the whip were also gone. She wrapped her arms around him, kissing him on the cheek. "Oh, Callum."

He stood and helped her to her feet, as she pulled her torn clothes around herself. She glared at Pryce, walking gingerly over to him on legs that wouldn't, until a few moments ago, hold her. Ferne drew back her fist and punched Pryce squarely on the chin.

He fell back, clutching his jaw.

Ferne shook her hand. "That felt sooo good," she admitted. "Okay, time to finish what I started."

She reached down for Pryce's head, and he attempted to scramble backwards out of her way. "No!" he pleaded.

"Yes. Gotcha!" Ferne placed her hands on either side of Pryce's temples, and they made the skin glow. She closed her eyes, concentrating on healing the sickness, the evil within him; her turn to speak in that strange tongue. It took a few moments, but when she was done, that peaceful yet vacant stare was fixed on Pryce's face permanently. His smiled a dopey smile, eyes not focussing, dribble pouring from the side of his mouth. He blew a raspberry.

Ferne stepped back to stand with Callum. "That's all that was left after the badness was taken away," she explained.

"A model citizen," Callum said.

Turning to him, Ferne examined Callum's features. She, too, noticed the change. "What happened to you?"

"I was reborn," he said honestly. "And I found the book."

Ferne looked puzzled. "Book? What book?"

"*The* Book."

"What? How? Where is it?"

"I'm holding it." He passed over the little one to Ferne, whose mouth was gaping. Then she started to laugh.

"Trace memories, from the very beginning. The baby told me everything."

"Told you ...?"

"Don't ask me to explain it, because I can't. But she's been waiting for me to come along for some time. The knowledge had been passed down and into her somehow, hidden, only activated and able to be transferred to a certain person. When the time was right."

"You," said Ferne.

"I think the Goddess spoke through her. Just as She must have done when the first spells were handed down."

Ferne was still gaping at him. "So you know all the spells that ever were. You have all of our powers combined?"

Callum nodded, blushing slightly.

"Then you're the most powerful being on this planet." She looked out at the Arcana who'd amassed behind Callum. "And our leader."

Callum put his arm around her. "With you ... we'll both lead, *together*, High Priestess. But Pryce was right. Nero will send more men to this place, sooner or later. If I don't face him."

"You can't," said Ferne, her voice cracking.

"One way or another, this has to end tonight," Callum told her, holding her close. "I've taken the final step, now I have to end this war once and for all."

CHAPTER FORTY-NINE

They gathered inside the doors to the compound, those who wished to see him off. Which was practically everyone, a crowd reaching down the corridor as far as the eye could see. Together with Michael, he had released them from their captivity and was now about to fight for their cause.

At the front was Ferne, holding the baby in her arms. Rhea's other children stood on either side of her. The sky was still dark and it was pouring with rain. Ferne reached out a hand and placed it on Callum's arm.

"You don't have to do this alone, take us with you. Take me."

"I can't," Callum told her, brushing her cheek with the back of his hand. "This is how it's supposed to go, Ferne. Even Unwin knew that. And I won't be alone, exactly." He looked up, knowing the Goddess —the most powerful "woman" there had ever been—was around.

"But I'm scared."

"Don't be." He smiled. "I'm coming back. We just have to have a little talk with your boss, don't we?" Callum turned to Pryce beside him, who nodded slowly, then gurgled something incoherent. "That's right, and you're going to take me to him."

Gavin broke through the ranks and joined them. "Good luck," he said, holding out his hand. It still seemed a weird adjustment to make, that Gavin should now be the group's seer. But then it was no stranger than having an ex-M-forcer as their High Priest, someone once sworn to stamp out Arcana. He shook Gavin's hand.

"You already know how this will all turn out, don't you?"

Gavin shook his head. "Not exactly. This bit's still … hazy since the cards were torn up by Wallis. I do know you will find the answers you're looking for tonight, though."

"That's reassuring," said Callum, letting go. "Well, time to leave, I suppose."

He leaned across and gave Ferne a lingering kiss. It felt for all the world like the last one they'd ever share. There were tears streaming down her face.

Callum set off into the compound, pulling Pryce alongside. He let the rain from above wash over them, gazing up at the lightning as it raked the cloudy sky. "You know," he said to Pryce, though the man was long past understanding, "in olden days they used to arrest witches for something they called 'stormbringing.' I learnt that at school in the orphanage. I think it's about time we brought a little storm Nero Stark's way."

Callum said something, then pointed at the ground with his finger, the end sparking crazily. The concrete melted where he aimed: up, down, left and right. By the time he'd finished, Callum had drawn a pentagram with a circle around it.

The symbol of Arcana.

Ferne passed the baby to a couple standing nearby, a woman named Meg and another called Tawny. They'd told her not so long ago how they'd found each other during the battle, that Meg had been released by Michael before his death, that they would never let each other go again. Conversely, Ferne felt like she was about to lose the love of her life. Again. She dashed outside, the rain washing away her tears, but at the same time making it look like she was crying a thousand more.

The pentagram around Callum and Pryce was glowing. A bolt of lightning hit all five points, causing Ferne to shield her eyes. When she opened them again, the two figures in the middle were gone. So was the storm, as if it had been sucked into the circle along with

Pryce and Callum. A couple more Arcana rushed out to help her back indoors, covering her with a blanket from one of the medical centres.

Gavin merged into the crowd again, taking the new pack of cards from his pocket. He wasn't surprised that they had come back. They were magickal cards, after all. Now they were no longer hand me downs: they were truly his, they came *from* him, the power of second sight conjuring them up.

Careful not to let anyone else see, he peeled three off the top of the deck, fanning them out so he could see them. The first was "The Magician," Callum's card. The second was "The Devil." The opponent he was about to face.

The third showed a figure of an angel encompassed by clouds, blowing a trumpet while naked figures—in their truest sense, the dead—raised their hands below.

The card's title was "Judgement."

Gavin spent a few moments studying them, then slipped the cards back into the pack. He hadn't been lying when he said he didn't know how this confrontation would end. Something was blocking his vision of Callum and Arcana's future. Perhaps there were some things even he wasn't meant to know.

What form the judgement would take when it came, Gavin had absolutely no idea.

But maybe it was better left that way.

CHAPTER FIFTY

The teleportation spell had worked brilliantly. No messing around on the monorail system, no patrol cars involved. Callum could get used to travelling like this.

Just as Ferne had used the key to *The Valentine*, Callum now used Pryce to transport him to Nero's lair—the human equivalent of a homing pigeon. For some reason, though, they ended up just outside the stone building in Chelmsford, possibly where Pryce always began his journey to see his master. Callum looked up and saw that even against the night sky, the clouds were darkening. Seconds later, there was a rumble of thunder and a crackle of lightning. The rain followed soon after.

"Come on," said Callum, pushing Pryce in front of him.

They would already have been spotted. Someone with Nero Stark's penchant for observation and security couldn't have failed to do so. But no heavily-armed guards came to greet them as they climbed the steps towards the front entrance. The doors, that usually required the visitor to buzz in, were open that night. As Callum passed through the foyer of the building, noting security booths on either side, not one person stopped him. Nobody asked for clearance, for saliva and retina checks. There was no passing through the "metal" detectors, which Callum now knew contained hidden magick sensors.

Not that it would have been much of a problem if they'd encountered resistance. The personnel in the booths pressed their fingers to their ears, receiving instructions. Callum mouthed a little spell to enable him to hear:

"They are not to be stopped, let them pass."

It wouldn't be questioned by them too much. For one thing he had Sherman Pryce with him, and for another Callum had once been an Enforcement Officer himself. But it all added to the sense that they were entering the spider's web.

And that spider was expecting them.

One man did leave the booth he was in, his white and blue uniform pristine, belt bristling with weapons. Callum tensed. Even though part of him knew he could sweep this man away with a simple flick of the wrist, there was another part, a greater part of him that still thought like a street cop.

You're the most powerful being on this planet.

He'd heard Ferne's words, but still didn't fully believe them. He might have the knowledge of how to cast every spell—and counteract them as well—but he'd never used them before. Unlike the Arcana back at The Penitentiary, who had been honing their skills for decades, he was practically a novice. Just because you have great power, that doesn't provide the confidence or experience to use it. That would only come in time, and with Ferne's help.

But the security man just pointed the way to a set of lifts at the far end of the foyer. "And you're going down," stated the man. Though he probably hadn't meant it that way, the double meaning wasn't lost on Callum.

Oh Goddess, why'd it have to be a lift? And why down, this time? Going up was bad enough, but at least there were windows when you got there. You could see the air, the sky around you. But descending into the bowels of the Earth? He'd be even more trapped down there.

For someone who's supposedly a superbeing, you're very close to losing it, he thought to himself. *Just get in and quit whining.*

Callum pressed the button and the doors opened. There was barely enough room for the two of them to fit comfortably. The reasoning being, Callum supposed, that if anyone was ever to get through the tight security they couldn't storm Stark en masse. It didn't make it any easier for Callum to step inside. Nor did the low light of the lift itself, adding to the feeling that he was getting into his own personal coffin. He searched for the spell that Ferne had used, the one that had calmed him down enough to meet Unwin in his basement, but panic was setting in, clouding his thoughts. He tried to breathe, but the lift walls just seemed like they were tumbling in on him.

Goddess, help me … Callum reached out with his mind. There was no response. Maybe he *was* alone in this place, left to face his own demons. Perhaps this was a place where She couldn't be with him? His mind flashed back to that cupboard in the orphanage, Miss Havelock slamming the door on him.

"You ask too many questions, McGuire. One day it'll get you into real trouble."

In a way she'd been right. He'd questioned the system, questioned what the M-forcers were doing to magick users, questioned himself and who he really was. It had led him, inevitably, to here.

But it had been pitch black in that cupboard, and at least there was some light in the lift. Every time it jerked or made a sound, Callum flinched. He was aware that he was being watched, the small camera in the corner whirring. It was too late to do anything about it now, no point breaking the lens with a spell, as Stark would already have seen his performance.

What if he just keeps you in here forever, never lets you out?

Callum would go insane, was the quick answer.

Just as he thought that might happen, the lift came to a stop and the doors opened. Callum pushed Pryce out, then jumped from the box himself—breaths coming in short, sharp bursts. It may have been underground, but there was space out here; lots of it, in fact. Callum found himself in an entranceway to a great hall, with bookshelves lining the walls. It was a magnificent achievement, this underground palace. There were pillars holding up an exquisitely painted ceiling, the figures classical in nature, depicting angels fighting with demons.

Their footsteps echoed around the large hall, another defence mechanism that ensured Stark would never be crept up on. If Callum had been thinking clearly he could have summoned a levitation spell, but again, what was the point when Stark was the one who'd allowed them safe passage?

The further they walked in, the more Callum saw of this place. It was larger even than backstage at *The Valentine*. There were banks and banks of monitors, all silent at the minute, throwing back news images, CCTV footage of street corners, of station houses, of The Penitentiary … still. Callum whispered something and could suddenly zoom in on one of the sets there. He saw the group gathered in his wake, Ferne still crying, the woman he'd freed from the microwave chamber holding Rhea's child.

"Information," said a voice that startled him.

Callum's eyes zoomed in on the back of the great hall, travelling past museum pieces in glass cases, all relating to witchcraft's history. There stood a man dressed in pseudo-military garb. His black boots squeaked on the wooden floor when he moved, and his baton was jammed so far under his arm it looked like it was stuck there. Much of his face was in shadow, and even as he walked further towards the pair of them, his eyes still remained dark under those thick eyebrows. Nero Stark's hair was slicked back, his moustache cropped so that it didn't extend past the corners of his lips. Everything about him smacked of money. Money and power.

"Excuse me?" asked Callum.

"Information. It's the most important thing in this world. He who has access to it, who can see everything, control and manipulate it, truly is a god. Welcome, Callum McGuire."

Callum said nothing.

"I was hoping that when we first met it would be under better circumstances. You had the potential to become the greatest of all the M-forcers, you know." Nero's boots squeaked again as he drew closer. "Ahh, where did it all go wrong?"

"It went wrong when I saw how you all operate, how you treat people."

"Treat people? The scourge you have chosen to side with *aren't* people. They kill innocent bystanders, Callum, or had you conveniently forgotten about that in your rush to save them? People like them killed your parents."

"I hadn't forgotten," said Callum.

"Then why? Why help them? Why *free* them?"

"Because they're people … and because they would never have done the things you claim."

"You know them that well, do you," sneered Nero, "after only a few days?"

"I know them well enough. I know they're fighting for their survival because you've made it impossible for them to live normal lives and—"

"Normal!" Nero's bellow was part laugh, part exasperation. "How could any of them ever live *normal* lives, practising the religion they do? Having the abilities they possess?"

"They were never given the chance!" shouted Callum. "You demonised them, making people hate and fear them."

"No, you're wrong." Nero took a few steps forward again. "They did that to themselves, going right back to the days of my forerunner, Matthew Hopkins. Even further than that, in fact. With their actions they proved themselves tainted by evil, in league with the unnatural order."

"They're men, women and children. Human beings, just like you or I."

Stark raised an eyebrow, but the eye it sheltered still remained covered. "Not like you. Not now. You've chosen another path. And after everything that was done for you."

Callum frowned. "Done for me?"

"You were special, Callum … still are. Anyone could see that. From your early days at the orphanage I took an interest in you. You showed promise, potential. Up until recently you hadn't done anything but make me proud."

What was this? Was Callum expected to believe that Nero Stark, a man he'd never even met before today, was really some kind of father figure, guiding him from behind the scenes? Bullshit!

"How do you think you got such a good education, were given individual attention?"

"The kind of attention I got, I wouldn't wish on my worst enemy," said Callum.

"Nothing wrong with discipline." Nero took his baton—which apparently wasn't stuck there—and smashed it against his leg. "I thought you'd learned that lesson, which is why you progressed through the ranks in London so swiftly. You kept your head down, didn't buck the system."

"There was nothing *to* buck. I was catching dangerous criminals."

"As an M-forcer you were meant to catch much more dangerous fare than muggers and rapists," Stark reminded him. "That's why the transfer was green-lit. But you started to ask questions again, started to let others influence you. In retrospect it *was* a mistake to send you to Widow's Way so soon, Pryce was right about that. You let your personal feelings for those children influence you, not to mention your feelings for that worthless sow." He pointed with his baton at the screen where Ferne sat crying. "If we'd had any idea she was one of them ..."

"You say one more word about Ferne and I'll—"

"What?" Stark said with a laugh. "Kill me? Prove that you're just like them, an animal?"

"Arcana don't kill," Callum informed him. "I've seen it for myself. They'll defend themselves, but not even when provoked will they take a life if they can help it. It's not their way."

"Yet they have done. Repeatedly," Stark pointed out. "How do you explain that?"

"I can't," said Callum, "yet. But I'm starting to have my suspicions. You say to control information is everything. How about controlling events as well? Manipulating reality so that it's slanted in your favour. You'd stand to lose all this if it was ever shown that Arcana are peaceful, wouldn't you?"

Stark was the one who stayed silent now.

"I saw the way Pryce worked on the prisoners' minds inside The Penitentiary. It wouldn't be too much of a stretch of the imagination that he might then send them out there to commit these terrorist acts. On your orders, obviously."

"That's quite an accusation," said Stark, coming even further into the light. "A pity there's no evidence to back it up with."

"Oh, I don't know," said Callum. "I'd lay odds if I was to trawl through some of the footage you've compiled from those cameras I might find one or two juicy pieces of 'information.' I am … or *was* a policeman myself, as you reminded me."

Stark smiled: it was a thousand times more chilling than Gibson's or Pryce's. "I doubt very much whether you'll have the opportunity to do that, Callum." He tapped the glass case he was standing next to. It contained a weathered book with yellowing pages. "You know what this is, I take it?"

"A copy of the *Malleus Maleficarum*. My old teacher used to have one a bit like it."

"I hardly think so. You see, this is the original, Callum. The very first edition. It's extremely rare. But then," he tapped his temple with his finger, "so is what you're carrying inside of that head of yours. You have no idea how long I've been searching for *that*."

The corner of Callum's mouth raised a little. "Which is exactly the reason it wasn't written down."

"To think, we had it in our possession all along. But then, if we'd known, it wouldn't have given us a chance to have our little … chat." Stark scratched his cheek, a signal he'd prepared earlier, and Callum was suddenly aware of someone behind him. He turned, seeing not one, but two cloaked figures. Cloaked in more ways than one. They'd somehow been masking their presence in the room the whole time. Before he could do anything, the one nearest Callum pulled back his hood, revealing a smooth scalp, and locked onto him with those piercing eyes of his. Callum couldn't move, a suggestion that this man had planted in his mind—even more powerful than the magick Callum had used on the guards and Pryce at The Penitentiary.

The second cloaked figure approached, pulling down his hood.

"Members of the Cerebral Order of Monks," Stark explained, joining the group, "groomed by The New Church of Benediction. They've trained their whole lives so they can rip your mind apart in seconds, leave you thinking you're a tadpole if they so desire. Pryce used to be really afraid of them." He looked his second-in-command up and down, and the man returned the gaze with one that made him appear half-asleep. "Of course, he had more to worry about from your lady friend than these people. Arcana might not kill, but sometimes the mess they leave behind is much, much worse. Put him out of his misery," Stark ordered the second Cerebral.

The bald man placed a hand on Pryce's forehead and fixed him with an intense stare. Pryce's eyes rolled back into his skull, then he fell sideways to the floor, his mind completely wiped.

Callum tried to move again, struggling to overcome the silent commands.

"My advice is, don't fight it. When I have the Book, when they've finished transferring it to me, I'll let you go. Or what there is left of you," Stark promised. Then, leaning in closely, he whispered, "Did you ever wonder why Miss Havelock use to shut you in that cupboard so much, even when you hadn't really done anything?"

Callum clenched his teeth, trying to break the hold this Cerebral had.

"It was on my orders. A little failsafe in case anything went wrong, in case you *did* choose the wrong side. As I said, you were always special, and we could never be truly sure which way the wind would blow."

So Stark had known about his weakness even before stepping into the lift. Had engineered it so he would have the upper hand in any conflict, just like he'd manipulated so many things.

The second Cerebral, the one who'd put Pryce out of his misery, approached Callum. He felt his head prickling, scalp crawling. The man was penetrating his mind, breaking down defences like they were made of paper. He'd be amazed if these people hadn't had something to do with that brainwashing he'd spoken about, forcing magick users to do horrific things against their will; quite possibly the only ones even capable.

Suddenly Callum was back in the dark again. He reached out and felt the "walls" just inches away, on all sides. He was no longer in the hall with Stark and the two robed figures, he was somewhere else. Not in the cupboard at the orphanage, not in the crawlspace at *The Valentine*, but somewhere he'd never been before. This was his one, big fear.

He was trapped in a total void, with no way in and no way out. The others at least had doors, exits, a means of escape. This place didn't, because it was inside his own mind.

The Cerebrals had discovered the secret place he kept locked away in his head, the place he dared not even contemplate visiting. They were keeping him here so they could rummage around the rest of his psyche, pick out the Book and give it to Stark. He had to get out of here, stop them before it was too late. If he didn't then he would no longer be the saviour of Arcana.

He would be its destroyer.

Callum banged on the walls, punching them with his fists, kicking out. He tried to think of a spell that might work, but nothing came to him; that part of his consciousness was shut off.

Goddess, if you're out there, I could really use some help right about now.

He waited, but again there was nothing. Not even a sign.

How am I supposed to fight them when they have me trapped? When they know my deepest fears?

"To be unafraid of something," a tinkling voice said that sounded so very far away, *"you need only fear it no more."*

Great, thought Callum, *that helps a lot.* But oddly it did. The very fact that the Goddess had spoken to him was a comfort, just as it had been when she brought light to the cupboard, to the crawlspace.

Callum concentrated on the walls. *It's* my *mind, and I'm keeping* myself *trapped in here just as much as the Cerebrals are. All I have to do is not be afraid anymore, not fear.*

He reached out and touched the blackness again. Unlike before, there was a rubbery feel to it. The barriers were no longer as solid as they once were. Callum stretched a wall taut, raking it with his fingernails.

It began to tear.

Now he could see it was possible, Callum ripped a gap in the black, collapsing the confines he'd found himself in, letting the light flood into the darkness. He climbed out across the pink-blue landscape of his mind.

He saw the two cloaked figures, rooting around, searching the storage compartments of his brain, filing-cabinets which they'd opened and were ransacking for the memories and recollections.

"Hey," shouted Callum, "didn't anyone ever tell you it's rude to enter somebody's head uninvited?"

The two cloaked men looked at each other, both trying to work out how he'd escaped the prison they'd placed him in—with a little help from his own irrational fears. Callum ran at them, ducking when the first Cerebral swung his staff. Bringing up the flat of his palm, he smacked the Cerebral in the face, spinning around to kick the other.

They were totally unprepared for the attack, and not trained in unarmed combat like Callum was. Both went down easily. He grabbed them by the backs of their necks.

"Okay fellas, let's see if we can't cut a little deal. There are a few things I'd quite like to know about your employer."

Unlike Callum, Nero Stark was expecting the intrusion into his mind. In fact he was waiting for it. How else were the Cerebrals expected to transfer the contents of the Book across to him from McGuire?

What he wasn't expecting was for them to start searching his mind as well. Memories, events, hidden information.

Beginning with throwing that hag Elizabeth Clarke in prison, having her strip-searched and the finding of a third teat about her person. Back then, torture was illegal, but he saw her starve and go without sleep for three consecutive nights, until on the fourth she confessed to her witchcraft and subsequently to having carnal relations with the horned one for the last six or seven years. Along with her cohorts, she was tried and executed on this very land.

And from there, obtaining his commission from Parliament—through nefarious means—building up his team of assistants, which included "witch-picker" Jack Stearne and Mary Philips, charging up to £25 to cleanse a town. But it wasn't really about money, was it. It had been an obsession: to rid the towns, rid the country of magick users, using any methods he could lay his hands on. The pricking technique, for instance, utilising a knife with a retractable blade to leave the "devil's mark" on those he suspected of having the power. Or "swimming," dunking people in the river to see if they would sink or swim, to see if the witch would reject the water of baptism.

Some questioned whether the commission from Parliament existed at all, and that bastard clergyman John Gaule persisted in trying to discredit him, to turn the public tide against him. But he ventured on, and thanks to some friends in very high places, managed to avoid the fate that *should* have befallen him: that of being accused of witchcraft himself.

It had been necessary. Know thine enemy, that had been one of his first teachings. To catch a witch, you had to understand them. Sadly, his experimentation with magick had led him down a path most witches would never tread, to parley with creatures they themselves were accused of contacting. It warped and twisted him, bending his sanity and his will. The lines between good and evil blurred, but the only thing that mattered was the eradication of the magick users as a species. That, and to possess the Book.

In exchange they extended his years beyond that of any mortal man, returning again and again when everyone he knew was dead, pretending to be his own relative to carry on the good fight against the biggest threat to mankind the world had ever known. In time, he would shut himself away, make sure that none but a few would ever see his face in case the connection was made. But his empire had grown to such a degree by then, his followers making the rules on his say-so alone, that it didn't matter anymore whether he was a man or simply a myth.

Of course, periodically the population needed a reminder of why he and his troops were necessary. A jolt to show them just how dangerous magick users could be. It was no worse than what they'd done with the "pricking," a simple exacerbation of the inevitable. Groups were already being formed to "protest" against their treatment by the government, by the M-forcers, so it was a simple matter to turn them into enemies of the state. Yes, sometimes it had been a case of brainwashing and just sending those people out again with a different agenda, other times he'd trained up men and women personally to use magick in a destructive way, or simply blackmailed those who were only just getting started but showed great potential. Whatever the case, the results were the same: destruction in the name of the magick users, and the public would be right behind the cause—in spite of the many misjudgements the Enforcement Officers made when arresting suspects. The establishment had executed just as many ordinary citizens to stop them squawking about unfair treatment and torture as it had actual magick users. But, again, it was necessary to maintain control and power.

He'd known about the legends for a long time, naturally. The half-baked prophecies that magick users told their children at bedtime. A tale of an ordinary man whom the Goddess—damn her eyes!—would choose to free her people from slavery. Of the High Priestess he'd fall in love with, and his quest for the Book containing all spells. It was up there with *Cinderella* and *Sleeping Beauty*.

Yet, like all fairy stories, there was usually a grain of truth to them so he hadn't dismissed it entirely out of hand. Who'd have thought his own actions would have led to the discovery of the Chosen Child? That sending those "Arcana" to blow up that restaurant would have left a certain boy without his parents. It was meant to be, fate if you will, that Callum McGuire had dropped right into his lap. His masters had pointed the lad out, told Stark to keep a watchful eye on him as he grew. Perhaps they could plant the seeds of loyalty early on, so that when—if—the day ever came when he would infiltrate Arcana and discover the Book, he would simply hand it over to Pryce or Stark without a murmur, happily betraying those who thought him to be their friend or, indeed, liberator.

It hadn't worked out quite that way, though, had it? That streak of morality they'd tried to weed out of him just refused to lay down and die. Yes, Stark had done his best, set doubt in his mind by orchestrating more Arcana attacks—which had the added benefit of making sure the public hated all magick users without question—but in the end he'd chosen to side with them anyway. To side with that bitch, the Goddess.

Nevertheless, events had still brought him here on this night, with the Book, and soon it would be in his possession. Soon he would wipe out every single magick user in the country, in the world.

All except one. Him.

So why weren't the spells and counter spells being implanted in his mind by the Cerebrals? Why were they delving around in things that didn't concern them, dredging up all this stuff while his own defences were down?

Because Callum McGuire had forced them to, that's why.

Stark broke off the contact, the mental equivalent of chopping off the Cerebrals' hands after he'd caught them raiding a till. He sent them reeling back to their new master, though how much of the information they'd raided was in his possession Nero Stark had no way of knowing.

Inside the hall, the Cerebrals fell to the floor, their own minds burnt out by what they had seen. Which left Callum McGuire and his enemy facing each other. One look from the former told Stark that he knew everything about him now.

"My parents," said Callum, gnashing his teeth.

Stark didn't miss a beat. "Casualties of war."

"A *misguided* war. All those innocent people, dead, just so you could fuel your warped crusade. And the worst part is, you've become the very thing you supposedly set out to destroy."

"Nonsense," said Stark.

"You made a pact with evil, Hopkins—"

"I don't go by that name anymore," Stark corrected. "Haven't for a long time."

Callum pointed at him. "You're blind, your hatred has made you crazy."

Stark wasn't taking any notice. "All I care about is the Book. When I have that, the rest won't matter anymore."

"And how are you going to get it? You fried your pet Cerebrals."

Stark smiled again. "You think I need them to extract it? They were to save you unnecessary pain, boy. Now I'll have to do things the hard way."

Callum's fists crackled with energy—and for the first time it felt good, it felt natural. "You're welcome to try."

Stark ran at him, brandishing his baton. He got about three paces before Callum mouthed an incantation and hit him with a blast of pure energy that pitched him halfway across the room. Stark hit the first of his museum cabinets, shattering the glass and sending its contents spilling out onto the floor: the original *Malleus Maleficarum.*

Stark picked himself up, brushing shards of glass from his clothes. "I see," was all he said.

Using another spell, Callum lifted himself up off the ground and floated towards Stark, tossing an energy ball as he went. It exploded to Stark's right, setting *The Hammer of the Witches* alight, and tossing him up into the air to land awkwardly on the glass cabinet containing a witch's broom.

Callum set himself down and picked Stark up by the scruff of the neck. He screamed at the man, a cry that carried him off on a shock-wave of sound to hit the back of the hall at speed. Stark slumped, head lolling when he hit the ground. He didn't move.

That can't be it, thought Callum. *It can't be as easy as that.* He approached the still figure, bending to check if Stark was breathing. As he did so, Stark grabbed hold of Callum, standing at the same time. He swung him round and around with a strength that belied his size, then launched him towards the bookcases. Callum raked along them, knocking dozens of old hardbacks off the shelves, before dropping to the ground himself. He sat up, shaking his head.

You had to ask, didn't you?

Stark was striding across the hall like a man possessed. He took a run up and kicked Callum in the side, sending him sprawling across the floor. Callum rolled over and pointed at the air above Stark, finger spitting lighting, and the man looked up to find several huge rocks falling on him. He was buried beneath the boulders, obviously crushed.

But as Callum got to his feet, there was movement beneath the rocks. Then they seemed to explode as Stark shrugged them off, sending them flying every which way. "You'll have to do better than a few parlour tricks and flashy special effects," Stark informed him.

Callum thought fast, running through the many thousands of spells now at his disposal. *Ah, okay. Try this on for size!* He mouthed a few words and sent a crackle of electricity Stark's way.

At first nothing happened and Callum wondered whether he'd used the chant correctly, but then Stark's skin began to wrinkle and crack. His hair receded, turning grey, then white—as did his moustache—and his body began to stoop, as if he didn't have the energy to remain upright. The nails on his fingers grew rapidly, curling underneath his palms.

Stark crumpled, years being added that he'd dodged before. His eyes were sunken in his head, which was itself turning skeletal. Stark reached out with bony arms, the flesh falling off. Then the thing that had been Nero Stark collapsed into a pile of clothes: the remains ancient and worn.

Callum looked on in disgust, that such a thing had been kept alive all these years by the forces of evil. Stark had no right to call anyone unnatural; it was the irony of this General's reign. And all in the name of "God." He turned his back on what was left of Stark, eager to get away from this place, to get back to Ferne and the others.

He heard the sound of guffawing behind him.

Callum spun round and found Stark standing there as he had been before the spell, untouched, unaged. "When are you going to learn, you *can't* kill me! They won't let you."

"Who?" said Callum, exasperated. "Who has given you powers like this, Stark?"

"You want to meet them?" Stark thought about it for a moment. "That can definitely be arranged." The General closed his eyes, his turn to mouth incantations, but there were none that Callum understood. These weren't from the Book inside his head, had nothing to do with the white magick Arcana and the majority of users practised.

Stark twitched, then his skin seemed to ripple. It was darkening in colour, accompanied by a glistening wetness, like he was sweating oil. The blackness oozed out of him, from every pore and orifice: especially the mouth, nose, ears and eyes … as if he was crying tears in negative. The dark matter whirled into a shape above and behind Stark, solidifying but transient at the same time. Then it opened its eyes: thousands of them, large and small, which flicked this way and that, connected by patches of slimy sinew. Veins ran criss-cross between the orbs, thick and dark purple, like worms. The eyes themselves were a multitude of colours: blues, greens, browns, even reds. Various shades that kept changing.

This was Stark's god, if a thing made up of multiples could be called by a singular name. An all-seeing creature that belonged in the shadows. It looked so out of place in this world that it was only able to show bits of itself. If Stark was Callum's opposite number, then this was the Goddess'. As hideous to behold as she was beautiful, as full of blackness as she was of light. Destroyer of things where she was the creator.

Stark stared at him, his eyes still glistening with the residue of those black tears. "I'm under their protection: the Multiplicity," he said to Callum. "So you see, it doesn't matter what you do to me, I'm going to win. And you …" His smile was terrifying. "You, Callum McGuire, are going to lose … *everything*."

CHAPTER FIFTY-ONE

Callum backed up a few paces.

If what he'd seen in the past week or so had caused him to doubt his sanity, if what had happened to him that very day had been impossible to believe, then the scene in front of him was out of this world … quite literally. The creature protecting Stark was writhing around, impatient. It wanted what was inside Callum's head, just as much as Stark did. In fact it was only using him to get to it, hungry for its power. This had never been about destroying magick users, it had been about so much more. The stakes so much higher.

"And so it ends," said Stark eventually. "How sad." He raised his hands, crackles of black energy, of dark light, dancing at his fingertips. Suddenly, he let loose with a blast of his own, just as powerful as Callum's first volley.

It struck the younger man and flung him across to the entrance of the hall. Callum's body smoked from the attack, every muscle aching. He wasn't ready for this. He'd been expecting to fight a man, not a god. And even with all of his powers, all of the spells he could muster, as Stark had pointed out, there was no way Callum could ever defeat him. The sound of laughter came again, the triumphant cackle of a victor waiting to collect his spoils.

Stark's boots clacked and squeaked on the floor as he strode towards Callum, hands raised to deliver another blow. The obsidian energy flowed from his hands, but this time it was met by its equal. Callum was amazed to find that even in his weakened state he was letting loose his own power. Except it was being doubled, tripled, pushing back the darkness. Callum was aware of someone behind him, arms across his shoulders, then under them, lifting him effortlessly to his feet. Her presence gave him strength.

"Goddess?"

"It is I the Multiplicity wishes to eradicate, it has done for centuries," a tinkling voice whispered in Callum's ear, *"but you are of me, and I am of you. We are connected; woman and man, greater than the sum of our parts. And just as this feeble-minded pawn is protected, so are you, Callum McGuire."*

They stood there, Callum and Stark, with their own deities at their respective shoulders. The intensity of the magick increased, black hitting white and sparking where it touched. Hardly any ground was given by either side. The black light would inch closer to Callum, but then the white energy would push back and edge closer to Stark. The two men were the instruments of cosmic forces, each determined to win over the other. It was an incredible battle. And though they could not see it buried deep within this building, the storm was raging again high above, thunder rolling, lightning clashing.

The buildup intensified to such an extent that where the charges met, the energy exploded with a *boom* and propelled both Callum and Stark backwards in opposite directions.

Stark was up first, standing taller than he had moments before. In fact, as Callum watched, the man grew larger still. He was filling out, the Multiplicity seeping back into him and causing him to expand. But he was also changing shape, his clothes ripping as his muscles bulged, his shoulders uneven, his torso lengthening. His boots were shredded as his feet broke out, claws lengthening as he stomped back towards Callum. The Multiplicity was coaxing growth, Stark becoming something monstrous, not just on the inside, but outwardly too. His mouth elongated, horns appearing on top of his head.

It towered above the crouching Callum, and when it opened its mouth, the Stark-creature belched out a jet of flame in his direction.

Callum held up his hands and quickly produced a crackling barrier, a shield to protect him from the blast. *Gibson was so wrong,* Callum thought, *that's the dragon standing right there. The head of the M-forcers. But I'm no St George.* "I … I can't hold him back for long. How do I stop him?" he asked The Goddess.

The musical voice came again: *"Stark is the Multiplicity's link to this world, just as you and the other Arcana are to me. Sever the link and the creature will be banished. But I cannot do this for you."*

Sever the … " All right, Stark," Callum shouted from behind his shield, "you heard the lady. Your friends have overstayed their welcome." Closing his eyes, he searched his mind for the one spell he never thought he'd have to use. Callum vanished, slipping sideways into the other plane. He ran towards the Stark-beast, knowing full well that it couldn't see him.

Shouldn't *be able* to see him … yet its many eyes followed his progress. The Stark-creature reached out with a clawed hand, pawing at Callum. He ducked the swipe, returning to the real world once more, then ran at Stark.

"Buckle up," he said through gritted teeth. Callum dived at the monster, wrapping his arms as far around him as he could. He blinked again, disconnecting himself from his own body, and dragged Stark's spirit kicking and screaming deep into that other plane along with him.

CHAPTER FIFTY-TWO

Callum simply allowed the slipstream to take them. Stark, returned to his normal shape, reaching out for the dead flesh he was rapidly leaving behind, had no option but to go with the flow. His spirit was cut off from the Multiplicity here—just as Callum was separated from The Goddess—and the man was petrified. Lost, beyond the Earth, in a place between worlds.

Suddenly they were there, deep inside the darkness. Just like before, they were attracted to anything bright—like their lifeforce—and apparently wanted to devour it whole. In the glow Callum saw brief flashes of faces. He couldn't see Gibson this time, but did recognise Wallis, transformed, teeth snapping, feeding on the luminescence. And a new arrival, Pryce, even more animalistic than he had been in life.

Stark was struggling to be free, wrestling with Callum as the darkness folded in on them. But this time Callum wasn't scared. He had friends here. Appearing not far away were the ghosts of Arcana members, like Victor and Rhea … and now Michael, finally reunited with his family. The latter nodded at him, as they all formed a protective shield, Michael taking great pleasure in keeping Pryce at bay. He pointed the way back and Callum mouthed his thanks—then set off, leaving Stark behind. He knew that soon his fellow Arcana would ascend to another realm entirely, that they'd only hung on here to help him. Even now, their light was fading, stranding Stark with the insane souls that were anything but his friends. The man opened his mouth to scream when he saw his fate, the snapping of teeth all around him, but no sound could be heard in that place.

By this time Callum was already on the path back home again, rocketing forwards and zeroing in on his body.

He woke with a jolt on the floor of the hall, still holding on to Stark's corpse. In the real world it had also regressed to its normal state. The link with the Multiplicity had been broken; with no soul to manipulate the creature had retreated to whatever darkness it had come from. Stark's body was just a shell, as lifeless as Callum's and Michael's had been when they were stranded back in limbo.

Callum rose to his feet and looked around him. The place was a mess: books scattered around on the floor, smashed cabinets, cracked pillars, the painting on the ceiling scorched. He walked past the bodies of the two Cerebrals and Pryce, a smoking ruin of a book catching his eye. The very first *Malleus Maleficarum*, *Hammer of the Witches*. He toed the charred pages, sending ash into the air.

It was over. Stark was defeated.

Callum was still aware of a presence in the room, and he turned to see the shimmering form of the Goddess in all her glory. It was a magnificent sight, a humbling sight.

"The battle is far from over," she warned him in that tinkling voice of hers. *"I have many enemies. If Stark was infected by this evil, then how many more?"*

"You're saying that he might not have been the only one?" Callum asked.

"It is up to you to redress the balance, my child. Only you can bridge the gap between the normals and the magick users, for you have been both in your time."

Callum looked to the bank of monitors. He might be able to prove that Stark had been responsible for the terrorist attacks, but who would believe him? And who would ever believe what Stark really was?

"In time," The Goddess said to him, *"in time. You have the power*

now, even though you are only just beginning to understand what that means. Use it wisely, Callum McGuire. Use it wisely."

The Goddess floated towards him and kissed him on the forehead. Then, before he could say anything else, She'd gone. It didn't matter; Callum knew he would see Her again.

He thought about the worlds Unwin had mentioned, where magick users and ordinary people lived side by side. Where they were even thought of as heroes rather than feared. Perhaps now, without Stark, that situation might develop here as well.

As The Goddess had said, only time would tell.

But right now he had work to do.

CHAPTER FIFTY-THREE

They were strange times after the death of General Nero Stark.

In spite of Callum jacking into Stark's system—bypassing the codes with a little help from a spell or two—and sending out evidence of Stark's involvement in the attacks, very little of this came to light. All the networks focussed on was the "murder" of the two key figures in the MLED ranks by a former officer, one of their own who'd gone rogue. Everything else was covered up quite capably, and the state funerals of both Stark and Pryce were televised one Saturday afternoon.

Whether the bodies inside those coffins being lowered into the ground belonged to them was another matter entirely.

Witnesses at M-forcer headquarters told their superiors that they'd seen the suspect, Callum McGuire, entering in the company of Pryce, and at General Stark's request, but never saw him leave again.

"I remember it quite distinctly," said the guard who'd shown them to the lift, "because it was just before that terrible freak storm."

The fact that there had been two robed figures present when the dead men were discovered was also glossed over pretty swiftly, probably because representatives of the New Church of Benediction took over temporary control of the M-forcer division. At the same time

The King—who was enjoying his new-found power—made an announcement that several key laws might well have to be reviewed and quite possibly revoked. There were calls from certain quarters for Parliament to be resurrected to debate about all this. The truth may not have come out about Arcana, but without Stark controlling everything the cracks in the system were definitely beginning to show.

No one came to The Penitentiary because no-one except Stark or Pryce actually knew for certain where it was. Those drivers who'd made runs to the place were all still being held captive but, like the rest, were released after being subjected to a forgetfulness spell. Even if troops had stormed the place, they wouldn't have got very far. Arcana members kept a watchful eye from the towers, and the security systems were restored to work in *their* favour now.

The waste disposal units were dismantled, the torture chamber below gutted, and the implements destroyed. Cells were expanded, transformed into liveable rooms, while dining areas were made of the canteen—which had enough food stocks and water to last years under siege—and the crèche turned into a proper nursery. It would do as a bolt hole for the time being, a place they could lay low until it was time to return to the cities. It seemed fitting in a way, for this place of captivity and death to be transformed into one of hope and security.

Arcana held their own funeral ceremonies for the dead, including Victor and Michael, and their bodies were buried out in the fields so that they would be at peace with nature and the Goddess.

When he returned, Callum never spoke about what had happened in the underground palace or the battle with Stark; only the barest details about who he'd been, and who had really been responsible for the terrorist attacks. Ferne didn't push for any more, she'd just hugged him more tightly than ever, kissing him all over his face.

"Thank the Goddess you're all right," she said.

"You can say that again." Callum held her, returning her kisses. They'd made love again twice that night, finding a quiet corner of The Penitentiary. Afterwards, as they lay in each other's arms, Ferne told him about her plans to adopt Rhea's children. She was hesitant at first, not knowing if he would be pleased or angry, but the smile on his face soon put her at ease.

"Ferne, I think that's a wonderful idea." In the months to come, he'd find her telling them new fairy stories, tales that might one day become prophecies for the future. Just like their story.

Then she'd asked him the question she'd been dying to broach since he got back. "So, where do we go from here? You have all those gifts, Callum, all that power. You could travel to different worlds, back and forth through time if you want, put an end to Stark's reign before it even began."

Callum kissed her on the mouth before saying, "For now, all I want to do is be here, with you. What happens afterwards … Well, even I have no idea about that."

EPILOGUE

One person did, however.

Gavin sat downstairs in the former torture chamber, table in front of him. He peeled off cards from the tarot deck and placed them face down, then proceeded to turn them over one by one. The distant future was still a bit vague, but he could make out this much. Some of it was good, some of it was very, very bad. Some of the events he was being told about might spell the end for of them all.

The end for Arcana.

But for now at least there would be peace. For now they could rest.

He heard a noise behind him, but when he turned there was nothing there. Gavin could have sworn he heard Master Unwin's soft chuckle, but it might just have been his imagination.

Then again, it might have been so much more.

ABOUT THE AUTHOR

Paul Kane is the award-winning, bestselling author and editor of over eighty books—including the Arrowhead trilogy (gathered together in the sellout *Hooded Man* omnibus, revolving around a post-apocalyptic version of Robin Hood), *The Butterfly Man and Other Stories*, *Hellbound Hearts*, *The Mammoth Book of Body Horror* and *Pain Cages* (an Amazon #1 bestseller). His non-fiction books include *The Hellraiser Films and Their Legacy* and *Voices in the Dark*, and his genre journalism has appeared in the likes of *SFX*, *Rue Morgue* and *DeathRay*. He has been a Guest at Alt.Fiction five times, was a Guest at the first SFX Weekender, at Thought Bubble in 2011, Derbyshire Literary Festival and Off the Shelf in 2012, Monster Mash and Event Horizon in 2013, Edge-Lit in 2014, HorrorCon, HorrorFest and Grimm Up North in 2015, The Dublin Ghost Story Festival and Sledge-Lit in 2016, plus IMATS Olympia and Celluloid Screams in 2017, as well as being a panelist at FantasyCon and the World Fantasy Convention, and a fiction judge at the Sci-Fi London festival. A former British Fantasy Society Special Publications Editor, he is currently serving as co-chair for the UK chapter of The Horror Writers Association. His work has been optioned and adapted for the big and small screen, including for US network primetime television, and his audio work includes the full cast drama adaptation of *The Hellbound Heart* for

Bafflegab, starring Tom Meeten (*The Ghoul*), Neve McIntosh (*Doctor Who*) and Alice Lowe (*Prevenge*), and the *Robin of Sherwood* adventure *The Red Lord* for Spiteful Puppet/ITV narrated by Ian Ogilvy (*Return of the Saint*). Paul's latest novels are *Lunar* (set to be turned into a feature film), the Y.A. story *The Rainbow Man* (as P.B. Kane), the sequels to *RED—Blood RED* & *Deep RED*—the award-winning hit *Sherlock Holmes & the Servants of Hell* and *Before* (a recent Amazon Top 5 dark fantasy bestseller). He lives in Derbyshire, UK, with his wife Marie O'Regan and his family. Find out more at his site www.shadow-writer.co.uk which has featured Guest Writers such as Stephen King, Neil Gaiman, Charlaine Harris, Robert Kirkman, Dean Koontz, and Guillermo del Toro.

IF YOU LIKED ...

IF YOU LIKED ARCANA, YOU MIGHT ALSO ENJOY:

Griffin's Feathers
by J.T. Evans

Elements of Mind
by Walter H. Hunt

Clockwork Lives
by Kevin J Anderson

OTHER WORDFIRE PRESS TITLES

Our list of other WordFire Press authors and titles is always growing.
To find out more and to see our selection of titles, visit us at:
wordfirepress.com

Lightning Source UK Ltd.
Milton Keynes UK
UKHW041034290519
343302UK00002BA/22/P

9 781614 759805